the ASSASSIN BRIDE

ANASTASIS BLYTHE

the ASSASSIN BRIDE

THE ASSASSIN BRIDE

www.AnastasisBlythe.com

Hardcover ISBN: 978-1-960606-06-8

Jacket Cover design by Saint Jupiter.
Laminate Cover and Interior Design by Dragonpen Designs.

FOR ANNE ELISABETH

A few sentences are a criminal lack of space to express my gratitude for you. So, suffice it to say: Thanks for being such a dear friend and the best author mom in the whole world. And if I don't stop there, we'll end up with another book no one asked for.

CHAPTER 1

THE NIGHT BEFORE a job, I always have strange dreams.

Sometimes, they're nightmares about an arcing blade and my baba's unflinching gaze. Other times I'm a child, running and running and running, but no matter where I hide, or how fast I try to escape, my pursuer always catches me. The worst nights are the ones where my pursuer comes into the light, throws back her hood, and I see a pair of ice-cold brown eyes set in a dark, hardened face. A face of chiseled edges, spattered in red. *My face.* Except matured, set atop a tall form wreathed in severe black and holding a knife in each hand. In those dreams, she crouches down before me in a dark corner, and I stare back, barely recognizing her through my pleading sobs.

But nothing can stop her knife from plunging deep into my heart.

Tonight, however, I have a new dream. One that is the strangest of all.

I stand before a throne of polished beryl in a grand hall awash in a fiery red glow. Rubies hang suspended from the ceiling like sparkling shards of rain. Their reflections glitter in the glass-like surface of the floor. Stone lions flank the throne, guarding the steps up to the dais.

More than the dazzle around me, however, is the pull I feel toward that throne. Seated upon it, silhouetted in crimson, is the tall shape of an obsidian shadow. Like a man standing before the sun, its light stealing his features.

He sits with his legs wide, knees against the armrests. One hand hangs loosely off the side, reflected in the mirror floors. The other twirls a crown around a long index finger, an enormous ruby in its center flashing with each rotation. One wrong move, and the crown would go flying to the ground. His head is tilted slightly, his posture almost casual. As if he is so powerful he has no need to sit straight.

I cannot make out even the faintest trace of his face.

When he speaks, his voice has the thunderous force of a waterfall.

"Nadira al-Risya," he says. And then—he chuckles. It rolls out from him like stones grinding, one upon one another. He flicks his crown, then catches it in his fist. "Will you not bow to your Neverseen King?"

I'm not sure what to feel, whether fear or thrill, whether dread or awe. But does it matter?

After all, it's only a dream.

So I don't bend. I don't bow. I keep my legs firm, planted wide, as I level my gaze at the shadow and lift my chin.

He chuckles again. Twirls the crown on his finger—and lets it fly off. It crashes to the ground between us, the sound echoing off the ceiling, the archways along the wall. The dripping jewels shudder on their cords. The crown rolls and rattles until it comes to rest at my feet, its huge ruby sparkling up at me like an unblinking eye.

And then suddenly, the shadow is before me.

I flinch and my eyes widen, but I manage to hold my ground. My heart picks up its rhythm, and my hands itch for the weight of a blade. But I won't betray the terror pooling in my stomach by reacting.

The shadow is warm. I feel it as he comes closer. His chuckle grates all the way down my spine. "They call you the Mourner, in your world."

This time, I don't flinch. But I'm braced like a tightly coiled spring. Now would be a good time to wake up.

He draws even nearer, so close that I can almost feel his breath on my face.

And then—a finger. A finger wreathed in darkness catches beneath my chin. A gasp slices between my teeth, and I jerk away from that touch. Yet even so, I lift my eyes to where his must be.

"Yes," he says, and I'm not sure if he is addressing me or himself. "You will be perfect."

Then my dream fades into dawn, its strange echoes and visions swept away by the foreboding knowledge of what awaits me tonight.

Death.

"Wretched sultan's beard," I growl. It's the only indulgence I will give my frustration. The rest of it I try to lock deep inside myself with full, expanding breaths through my nose. Either that, or die. And I'm not dying. Not on a stupid job like this. I've planned this out painstakingly, thinking through everything that could go wrong. I've considered every variable, managed every risk.

Except one.

Her name is Eshe bint-Kinid.

I cannot mitigate the risk associated with her. Nor can I plan for it. All I can do is expect it. Right now, hiding in darkness that smells of feed, excrement, and leather tack, I stare through the opening of the stable doors at the sliver of a milky moon hovering above the dome of what I know to be the ceiling of the mansion's library. The floor plans I've been studying flash before my mind's eye.

In these moments waiting for Eshe, I have a sudden, sharp urge. One that involves turning around, slipping through the door on the other side of the stables, and *running.* As far and fast as I can. Maybe this time, I could get away.

A hand clamps down on my shoulder.

Panic floods my senses. I whirl toward the shadows, my knife driving at my assailant. It plunges straight into a bale of hay. Right above a ducking form that wears a familiar grin.

"Just checking your reflexes, Nadira," Eshe says, teeth shining white against the darkness of the stables. She hops upright as I pull my knife free from the hay and glare at her. "Nothing like a nice thrill on a fine night!"

I don't like thrills. And I hate surprises.

I sag, my breath nearly whistling through my teeth as I suck it inward. Without a sound, I sheathe my knife. I flex my hand, as if that would stop it from trembling.

What was I thinking, even considering escape? I know Jabir, and though I might not know *how*, he has tracked down every escape mere hours—sometimes, mere minutes—after they were attempted. No matter how carefully crafted my attempts, they never got results. Never mind the impulsive ones. If I didn't know better, I'd think he had somehow gotten ahold of magic to bind me to his side.

My only option, now and ever, is to be what Jabir raised me to be.

I'm sorry, Baba.

I tip my head up, enough that I can meet the jewel-like glitter of Eshe's eyes beneath her hood. As much as I want to be angry, to rebuke her for being late, all I can do is smile weakly. I hold out my fist to her, and she grins in response, bumping it with her own.

"Are you ready for some priceless artifact stealing?" she whispers a little too loudly for my comfort, stretching and nearly giving me a heart attack when she goes to crack her knuckles. She catches herself at the last second, opting to yawn instead and arching her back like she's a purring cat begging for scraps.

"Unfortunately, I won't be stealing any priceless artifacts," I say. "You'll have to do that part on your own."

"Right, right, because *you* are doing the important part of this mission."

That's the nice way to put it, I suppose. Makes it sound like it's the more desirable of our jobs, when it will only add to my catalog of nightmares. I shake my head softly, then shoot Eshe a sidelong glance. "You remember the plan, right?"

"Plans, plans, plans," she says.

That cavalier tone of hers is going to be the death of me.

"No stunts this time," I say firmly, fixing my features into their sternest arrangement. "Follow the plan, and no one will know what happened until the morning."

"But where's the fun in that?" She flashes another grin. One that makes dread drop like lead into my stomach.

"*Please* follow the plan."

"If something goes wrong, you know I'll find a way out. I take pride in my quick thinking and improvisation."

"I have nightmares about your improvisation," I say dryly.

She tosses me a lazy smile, fist-bumps me again, and whispers, "We've got this." Then she saunters out of the cover of the stables. Her robes swish silently around her, and from the folds of her cloak she pulls a length of rope. Then she vanishes into the shadows of the mansion.

My smile vanishes with her.

I shake my head, watching her leave. If she wasn't so good at her job, I'd refuse to work with her. Sometimes I think our friendship would be smoother if we didn't work together. But if we didn't, I'd never see her. Not with Jabir's leash around my neck.

Besides, we can pull this job off tonight. I know we can.

My blood pressure should be the only casualty.

I pull the folds of my cloak tighter around myself, brush a hand swiftly over the knives buckled at the hip of my sirwal, the two holstered on my biceps; wriggle my ankle to feel the one in my boot, then *the* knife I have strapped to my side.

I can delay no longer. No matter how much I might wish to.

The moment my feet are in motion, my brain finds its focus like a hunter prowling the night. Except, sometimes I'm not sure if I am the hunter. The rush of wind against creaky shutters and polished pillars, the grit of sand in the air, and the faint scent of spices drifting from the nearby bazaar are a welcome distraction for my racing heart. I focus on my movements, on silence. On becoming one with shadow.

There's a window on the first floor, near the shockingly huge washroom. No one will be there at this hour, and it is far away from the wing where the baby is sleeping—but reasonably close to the library, where I know my target is half-asleep at his desk.

Finding the window and slipping past the guards takes less than a minute. I glance over my shoulder, just once, before I take hold of the sill and hoist myself up.

It's locked.

I anticipated this. With my exposed back begging for a knife, I slip my tools from my sleeve. It's the work of a heartbeat to ease the hinges off the shutter. I'm sweating so much that I wonder in amusement if that alone might work to prevent any squeaks. But no, just a few drops of oil from my pouch and the shutters come off soundlessly.

I remove my slippers as I enter, exchanging them for a special pair before my feet hit the ground. They're stitched leather, soft and worn, practically molded to my feet by now. They don't make noise on any surface, and I keep them so clean that they would never leave a trace.

Carefully, I set the loose shutter back on the sill, and only the faintest crack of moonlight betrays that it isn't completely closed. I'd set it back on its hinges if I didn't need to get back out in *hopefully* less than a quarter of an hour.

I crouch in front of the windowsill, staying in the darkness, as I begin to count.

One. Two. Three.

It forces my erratic breathing to steady.

I don't like creating plans that depend on precise timing, but alas, it couldn't be helped. I needed to give Eshe enough time to do her job, while leaving as little time as possible between the completion of mine and our escape.

Every moment inside a target's house, even one as grand as this one, is a risk. The longer we're here, the more likely we are to be caught.

The washroom around me is laden with fresh laundry, which reeks of lye soap and too much cloying perfume. Large wooden tubs line one wall, empty of the steaming water they usually hold. I dodge through lines strung with imported silk, my tallness lending me no favors. I don my gloves as I go, flexing fingers inside the camel leather.

Four. Five. Six.

Suddenly, I'm confronted by a tiny pair of cloth shoes hanging in front of my face. It's next to downy-soft swaddles and cleaned nappies.

I stop counting. I swallow a salty mouthful of bile.

Then I'm moving again, counting my lost second, and grinding my teeth as I softly pry open the door and slip into the servants' hallways.

Now is *not* the time to think about what I'm about to do. Certainly even less of a time to *feel*, to mourn that a child will have no memory of his father because of me. All I have space for is the plan. Making sure it is executed flawlessly, making sure Eshe doesn't get herself caught.

I certainly have no room for regret or wistful wonderings of how the twists and turns of my life could have landed me literally *anywhere* else in this entire world than here. No time to entertain the notion of stiffening my spine, spinning myself around, and attempting a harebrained escape.

Ten. Eleven. Twelve.

When I reach the kitchen, I find yet another reason to clench my fists and swallow hard. There are voices, but no hum of dishwashing or silver polishing. I move silently through shadows until I can peek around through the crack in the door.

A bearded man holds a cup of tea, grinning and chatting next to an unmade tray of refreshments. Biting back a curse, I slide away from the kitchen.

The steward hasn't been up with his master's tea. That's not the issue though—I'd been hoping he hadn't been up yet. Then I could have pulled out the draw-stringed pouch from my sleeve and sprinkled in enough poison to kill my target in an instant. My knife would never leave its sheath, and blood wouldn't be spilled. The issue is that the steward hasn't even made up the tray to take, and he looks in no hurry to do so.

I can't wait around hoping he will. After all, in my planning for this job, I *knew* the steward greatly varied the time he brought up his master's late-night tea, and I also knew it had something to do with the rosy-cheeked cook.

I knew this might happen. I knew I could find myself in this position.

Which is why I planned for it. It just wasn't my preferred plan. Blood never is.

Twenty. Twenty-one. Twenty-two.

I must be extra careful, because now I have confirmed another variable: the risk of *when* the steward will bring up his master's tea. There are certainly some very, *very* inopportune moments he could choose to do so.

I bite my lip and taste copper.

Then I'm slinking through the darkness, dodging the light cast by flickering sconces and the rare shuffling of feet. No one except a sparse handful of servants should be awake; those remaining in case their sleepless master requires their service.

I wonder if the lord of this house has taken inspiration from the Neverseen King, who is said to rule our land during the night and vanish during the day like a phantom. Unseen. Unknown. I'm not fanciful enough to believe such legends. No, I know it's all a ruse.

Anything to instill healthy fear and mystery into a monarchy that is crumbling before our eyes. After all, I've learned that there are two advantages one may have in a fight: being strong and being perceived as strong. Sometimes the latter is even better than the first.

A mysterious sultan might have been more enthralling to previous generations, what with his supposed stealing of human brides every hundred years, but now people are starting to question things—as they should. Ever since our neighboring kingdoms started taxing our incense exports and undercutting supply prices for trade, our economy has been hamstrung. Fairy tales don't feed hungry bellies.

Sometimes I wonder if we'll have a revolution.

Thirty-three. Thirty-four. Thirty-five.

I'm not sure what makes me suddenly pause. A tickling down my spine, or a sense of unease. Slowly, I twist my head, one hand reaching up to my hood, the other going to my dagger.

The hallway I stand in is empty, save me and the shadows.

So why do I feel like someone is watching me?

Licking my dry lips, I hurry onward. I take a servant staircase to the upper floors, losing a whole minute to the painstaking climb. My lips are cracked from too much licking when I finally reach the top floor.

No one should be on this floor. Except . . .

A dark figure struggles down the hallway, wind from the open window ruffling her hair and cloak. Rope hangs out the window, and I wince. Before I address my friend, I cross the distance to the window and, with one terrifying glance down to see if anyone had spotted the rope, I wind the length of it around my arm until there's no sign of entry. It's tightly woven *jurbah* rope, very thin and strong—I always keep some on my person—but it doesn't matter how thin the rope is. It can still give us away. I hook the bundle over my shoulder.

Then I'm at Eshe's side, glaring at her.

"I didn't think this lock would give me so much grief," she whispers, arching a brow.

"Anyone could have seen the rope," I growl. "And then this would have been over before it'd even begun!"

She grins wickedly. "But no one *did* see it."

"You don't know that!"

"What are you even doing here? I don't remember part of the plan involving you coming to check my work."

"The plans changed because the steward can't shut his mouth and stop yapping with the cook. I can't move too quickly now. If he goes up while I'm—"

"Then you can just fling yourself out of the window and all will be fine."

"That window is not an escape route, not with the streets lighting up that side of the mansion."

"Pfft. You'd be fine."

"It is too risky, and not just for my sake. If the steward discovers my completed job before you've gotten yourself away, the guards will be up here in an instant. And what if you're inside the vault then, with the door unlocked from the outside? There's no escape."

She presses a hand to her heart, pausing her lock picking long enough to shoot me a wounded look. "You have no faith in me."

"If you mean I have no faith in your ability to slip through solid walls and fly, then yes. How much time do you need me to delay?"

She rolls her eyes and shrugs. "No need to delay. Just get your job done. It's just this last pin. It's set, but the cylinder isn't turning, so it just needs a little more fiddling . . ."

Eshe doesn't understand logistics and planning and risk mitigation. But she does, however, understand me. Even while her deft fingers work the lock of the vault, she eyes me in the darkness. "You're stalling."

"I'm timing things carefully," I reply stiffly.

"Stalling."

"Being *smart.*"

"Stalling."

"And if I am?" I demand. "He has a *baby*, Eshe." The words are slightly choked. Hastily, I swallow back the emotion.

Eshe's face grows unusually serious, her brow firming and jaw tensing. "No one said we were heroes, Nadira. But comfort yourself that it's not personal, that you didn't choose this target. Sands, Jabir probably doesn't even know the name of the person who did. This lord runs the city guard and is a staunch supporter of the Neverseen King—of course he has enemies. And if it makes you feel better, only a scumbag could run the city guard and allow them to do . . . what they do."

A memory flashes before me of the night Eshe and I met, of the one kill I don't regret.

Her words aren't comforting at all. At one point in my life, that excuse was the only thing that kept me sane. Now, however, I see it for what it truly is.

A lie.

The lock clicks beneath Eshe's fingers. "Ah ha!" she says triumphantly, too loudly.

I wince as I hand off the rope, then whirl in a flurry of dark cloak back toward the stairs. "Remember the rendezvous point."

There's no delaying the inevitable any longer.

My fingers wrap around *the* knife, Separator.

CHAPTER 2

I'M OUTSIDE THE library much too quickly. The steward may bring the lord his tea any minute, so I have no time to waste, no time even to attempt a poisoning instead of using my knife. Everything could still go wrong at this point, but the deed will only take a split second. And if I can't make it out of the room before it's discovered, I've planned several potential hiding places.

Now that it's time for my job, I start counting again in my head.

One, two, three.

I oil the hinges and latch before I even attempt to open the door. I focus my mind on my actions, on the curved, gold-plated handle, the carved frame, the faint whiff of lilac and candle wax.

Four, five—

The door creaks when I open it.

My heart flies to my throat. If I hadn't frozen so completely in the shadow of the doorway, I'd have stared flabbergasted at those hinges. They weren't supposed to make a sound. For a split second, I consider the possibility of magic, of the lord hiring a spellcaster to make a warning bell of this door, but immediately I brush it away. There are better ways of accomplishing that feat. Besides, am I so unwilling to shoulder the blame that I'd foist it off on something as rare as a spellcaster?

No, I'm not being careful enough. I've allowed myself to be rattled. I'm losing my sense of control over this job, which is *never* supposed to happen.

Briefly, I cast a look behind me. No matter how I search the darkness, there's not a sign of another human being. Why am I so off-kilter tonight? I've learned not to doubt my intuition, so why is my intuition saying that there is another person in this hallway with me when there clearly isn't?

Six, seven, eight.

A wave of dizziness forces me to pause. I don't want to move. I want to stay here; wait until I'm discovered, arrested, killed. Wait until I've sabotaged my own plan and there's no hope that this job will get accomplished.

It's a foolish hope. Utterly ridiculous to entertain the notion.

I need to pull myself together. My mind flits back to what I used to recite to myself, only a few years ago, when I was fifteen and sent on jobs like this. *I'm a killer. I don't care about my victims.*

It didn't take me long to realize that, for some lies, it doesn't matter how often I say them. I can't keep my gut from reacting, from immediately insisting on the truth.

So, I developed my rules and techniques for assassination. Jabir may be able to force me to kill, but he can't tell me *how* to kill. And I know for a fact that of all the assassins here in Risya, capital city of Arbasa, I give the swiftest, most painless death.

It is my way.

My first rule of assassination is that it must be dignified. My victim is dead; there is no need to humiliate him too. Second, it must be swift. I do not kill with average weapons or random poisons from the bazaar. I kill with my knife, Separator, and with kizmiba extract. Third, they must not be afraid. I refuse to suffocate; there is far too much panic and pain involved. My goal is never to torment, and never to allow for the spiking of a heart rate. Far worse than death itself is the fear of death. But worst of all—the fear of the breath just before death. That moment you realize the end has come, and now you must lose everything you've spent your life gaining.

I spare my victims that fear. That moment. And though I never try to reason away the blood on my hands, sometimes I think to myself that the death I deal my victims is far better than any natural causes awaiting them.

Eleven. Twelve.

I can't close the door without making a sound, so I leave it open and slink through the bookshelves toward the back of the library, where I know Lord Kishon manages his estate at this late hour.

"Steward? Is that you?" a sleepy, gravelly voice calls into the stillness.

I bite back a curse. He heard the door. And he won't hear my footsteps or the clatter of porcelain on a tray.

Thirteen.

There's no choice left if I'm to spare him his fear.

I break into a silent run and rip my knife from its sheath. Since I'm still hidden by bookshelves, the lord doesn't see the blade catching the light. In less than a second, I'm behind him, his face in his hands as he stares between parted fingers at the accounts before him. He looks nearly asleep, his graying beard trailing on the desk as if it's taking every bit of strength to keep his eyes open.

"Perfect timing on the tea," he says groggily.

I swallow. *Fourteen.*

The entire world goes sticky with warmth before my eyes.

And then I'm sitting cross-legged on my bed. My toe catches in a hole on the patchwork quilt. I blow a lock of dark hair out of my face, using the back of my wrist to shove a particularly stubborn strand away. My hands move rhythmically, counting the strokes as I sharpen my knives.

Fifteen, sixteen.

By now, my hands know exactly what to do. I don't need to think or feel. I merely exist, listening dully to the *shing* of my blades.

Seventeen.

"Master! I've come with your tea!"

The blackness clears, and I am no longer blind. Candlelight flickers on the desk, just like it had been mere seconds ago, but now blood pools around its base, seeping into parchments and dried ink, staining wood and the robes of the corpse.

Eighteen, nineteen, twenty.

I wipe my blade on my own garments, never on the garments of my victims. Numbly, my fingers move of their own accord, and I feel like I'm slogging through syrup as I watch myself sheathe my blade and withdraw a note from my cloak to prop against the candle.

I'm oddly calm, even though my brain can't think. If Eshe asked me my name right now, I couldn't answer. It's like *I* am the corpse. That's my blood dripping onto the floor. Over in a flash, without even a blink of fear or realization that the end had come.

Twenty-one.

My limbs are moving, and I'm climbing the nearby bookshelves and laying myself flat atop them in the second it takes for the steward to round the corner and drop his tray in a shattering of boiling tea and porcelain.

When a scream pierces the air, I almost think it's mine. I wish it were. I hear scuffling footsteps, frantic panting, and I close my eyes as I hear him pick up the note. His voice is gravelly as he reads it aloud:

"*I am sorry.*"

A dead silence follows. My own words, written on that note, echo up into the dome of the library roof.

Then, "Murad! Guards! Lord Kishon has been murdered! The Mourner has struck!"

I close my eyes, keep myself from rubbing my hands together, wishing I had a bowl of water to wash them. But I'm wearing gloves, a hood that covers my face. Hardly an inch of flesh is exposed anywhere on my body—there's no blood on my skin.

Armor clanks as the clamor of guards grows to a crescendo. I stay atop my bookshelf, wanting to believe I'm too numb to care if they find me; when in truth, the numbness is wearing off, and I can barely contain my own gasps of terror.

No one said we were heroes.

No, indeed.

Thirty, thirty-one, thirty-two.

Eventually, I'll have to get up, leave my hiding place and slink away. My heart shudders in my chest, despite my contingency plan. I know the risks and the pieces at play, but this was definitely my least favorite outcome.

Above the din, above the shouting and clattering armor, I hear a new pair of footsteps run into the room, and I try to force away the flashing visions of dozens of faces, long enough to think clearly, to note the moment I can escape.

"The vault!" comes a panting gasp. "Someone's broken into it!"

"What?"

The faces finally vanish, and I'm staring up at a domed ceiling with shadows dancing across gold-trimmed plaster. Everything inside me narrows to those voices below me, and the fog dissipates into clarity.

No.

They shouldn't know already that Eshe broke into the vault. They shouldn't . . . They should be smart enough to send someone there first, to ensure it is still intact, and then potentially paranoid enough to search its locked depths, but they shouldn't already know something was missing.

Unless . . .

What did I *tell* her? I'm up in a flash, crouching on top of the bookshelf and looking out at the guards crawling below.

"He's very warm. The killer might still be nearby."

"We found her upstairs by the vault!" someone shouted. "We found the killer!"

Adrenaline surges frantically through my body. Keeping track of every pair of guards searching the room, I move swiftly from one shelf to the next like a creeping spider that now *actually* wants to murder someone.

Eshe.

I told her! I told her exactly what to do if this happened, if she ran out of time. If she'd followed the plan, she wouldn't have gotten caught.

But now . . .

Now I must enact my final contingency, which involves a dizzying number of uncertain variables. At least they're less likely to discover me if they believe Eshe to be the murderer.

I perch atop the shelf closest to the door, keeping my body low, and try to listen over the commotion to what might be waiting for me in the hallway, since I've already eliminated the window as an escape route.

Though I'm beginning to wonder if a few streetlights might be preferred to a hallway of guards. *Risk, risk, risk.* Everywhere I turn, I see a thousand different ways I could get caught, and then my life will be over. Sometimes I wish it would be. But then I remember the sight of criminals impaled on stakes, mounted on the city walls, and I'm so sick I'm afraid I might vomit and doom myself right there.

Jabir had scoffed at my insistence that one of my contingency plans involve a rescue, should worst come to worst. I allowed the tiniest voice in my head to say, *"I told you so."*

Eshe might know me better than anyone else, but I also knew her better than anyone else.

Where Eshe is, trouble follows.

Why didn't she go to the hiding place I'd told her? The shadows of the roof by that window would have concealed her—I'd made sure of it when scouting.

Thirty-nine. Forty.

I drop to the floor soundlessly, my neck and back prickling. I whip my head around, glancing toward the deepest shadows of the library, but no one has spotted me yet.

I slip out of the door, dodge beneath the shadows of a decorative long table, and fold myself tiny as another guard hurries past. The moment he's gone, I start moving, heading in the direction I know *not* to go.

Jabir's scratchy, grating voice rings in my head, telling me that I'm only going back for the artifact. I clench my jaw and give my head a quick shake. Just like Jabir can't tell me how to kill someone, he can't make me not plan and enact a rescue for my friend.

I move in the shadows, and my breath catches every time a guard steps close, every time I fear I've been spotted. But though I might have lost my cool the moment I stepped into that washroom, my muscles know what to do. I let instinct guide me, the specifics of the plan for Eshe's rescue running through my brain.

My heartbeat pounds faster than the counting. Nearly twice as fast.

Forty-four, forty-five.

How did everything manage to go so wretchedly?

Typically, I hide in the deepest, darkest shadows. But tonight, something about the very darkest corners in this low-ceilinged servants' hallway makes my skin crawl.

A hand clamps hard around mine.

I'd scream if I hadn't had that knee-jerk reaction beaten out of me by Jabir. Instead, I'm wrenching blades from my bicep sheaths, and plunging them toward my attacker.

"You look like you've seen a ghost," a chipper voice replies, easily dodging my knife.

My legs turn to water at the sound of her voice, and I nearly collapse. "Eshe?" I gasp, glancing back over my shoulder to ensure we're still alone. "Sultan's beard! Didn't they catch you?"

A flash of white teeth, and then we're all but running together, silently, with me leading back toward the washroom. It should still be as safe an exit as before, though I suppose we won't be sure until we get there.

"They *did* catch me," she says around pants. "Or, at least, they *thought* they caught me. You didn't actually believe I'd be unable to get myself out?"

"I heard them say they'd caught you!"

"Just because you freeze when things go wrong doesn't mean I do," she replies.

"Did you get it?"

"Pfft. Of course!"

We reach the washroom, and I refuse to let myself search out that tiny pair of cloth shoes. I won't think about it. I *won't*. Instead, we barrel toward the window, and I slip back into my outdoor shoes as we swing out. In less time than it takes to spit out a date pit, the shutter is back on its hinges and we're escaping into the night.

Sixty.

I stop counting.

"That's a lot of shouting," Eshe says, glancing back at the dozens of torches held in the hands of more guards as they pore over the grounds. She fishes something out of her cloak and holds up a golden egg. Rubies and emeralds stud its surface, with a fat, glittering diamond at its middle. It's smaller than my fist. "Pretty, isn't it?" She grins.

I raise an eyebrow, purse my lips, and then we're disappearing into the dark city like ink into sand, taking the path through the bazaar.

I still feel like eyes are following me.

CHAPTER 3

THE BAZAAR ISN'T as abandoned as one might think this deep into the night. Most of the stalls are closed, but that doesn't stop city guards from patrolling, drunkards from creating scenes, and dirty urchins from begging. Eshe has a small bag of dried fish on her hip, and as we progress deeper into the city, she tosses tiny chunks to the feral cats that rub against her ankles.

"You shouldn't feed them," I say. "They're pests."

"They're sweet peas."

"You're making the overpopulation worse."

"Yes, I will single-handedly make the population of cats in Risya explode by giving one bite of fish to half a dozen cats."

I roll my eyes but stop arguing with her. Only a minute later, she pulls out the last strip of dried fish, and, instead of breaking it and feeding it to the boney orange tabby at her heels, tosses it to a little boy leaning against the wall of an alley. A little girl sleeps with her head in his lap.

It hardly lands in his hands before three more children appear from nowhere and begin wrestling for it until it's nothing but crumbs and the sleeping girl is awake and crying.

Eshe's brow darkens. She turns away, her pouch empty. We are several streets beyond the scene before she speaks. "It's gotten worse. We rarely were desperate enough that we destroyed food like that."

"You had a good leader who didn't tolerate that, and who made sure everything was shared," I reply. "Most of these urchins don't have a gang to protect them. They're just fighting to survive."

"It's not just the gangs, Nadira. *All* of it is worse. Jabir has you locked up so often you don't see much of it. Food prices keep going up. Just today I saw a sack of dates going for a copper fal. It's insanity."

It is rare that Eshe gives vent to these sentiments. We each have enough to focus on ensuring our own survival that there isn't much time for us to pity the orphans and stray cats. Perhaps it is the weight of a bejeweled egg in her pocket that makes her speak now. She could feed all the urchins in this quarter of the city for weeks if she didn't owe the egg to Jabir, who will deliver it to whoever hired us.

"I'm still wondering where the money goes from my assassinations," I say dryly. "If my rations were any indication, I'd think cutthroats could be hired for five or six fals apiece."

"And Jabir doesn't drink?"

"I wish he would." Then maybe I could take advantage of his inebriated state.

Eshe let out a humorless burst of laughter. "Since he doesn't live much finer than you, that leaves only one option: he's eating the money. Perhaps gold and silver soothe his digestion. Is he still angry about the Neverseen King?"

"Still?" I scoff darkly. As we turn down an abandoned alleyway, one that leads to our destination, my stomach sinks a little lower. My legs become heavier, my shoulders slouching. "He's been furious with our sultan for as long as I can remember. He likes to rant about the export taxes, as though our sultan's preference for hiding during the day is to blame for other kingdom's decisions. Sands, he'd blame the Neverseen King for the weather."

The instant the words are out, I regret them. I toss a covert glance around us, trying to ensure someone isn't watching us or listening. Jabir has his own mysterious ways of learning each of my treacherous words and actions.

It's not as if I have any reason to defend the Neverseen King, beyond wanting to defy Jabir.

Eshe seems to have the same thoughts, for she immediately launches into a stream of consciousness. "Speaking of the weather, is it just me or has it been especially hot these last few days? Maybe that's part of the reason dates are so expensive—"

"Definitely not," I interject.

"—and actually, did I tell you why I was at the bazaar in the first place? Kolb's little sister has been so sick this past fortnight. The poor boy is getting desperate, and you know they have nothing. I took on an extra job to earn enough coin to get them a few things. She needs medicine, though. I cannot afford that and wouldn't have the slightest notion what type to get her anyway."

At the mention of Kolb and his sister, my chest tightens. "I haven't seen Kolb in weeks. I was hoping they were alright. Apparently not."

"The little girl will pull through. She's tough, and Kolb takes such good care of her."

I very much hope so, as much for Kolb's sake as for the girl.

We reach my least favorite street in all of Risya. Dust and sand coat the uneven cobblestone, and in the darkness a single lantern shines from a rickety pole. Illuminating a heavy, scratched wooden door.

I'm not the only one who slows my steps just a fraction. Eshe tosses such a bright grin my way, it's obvious that it is overcompensating for her own fear. "Well, this has been fun! I suppose I won't see you again for another four months, now will I? Maybe if we're lucky, it'll only be two or three months this time."

Lucky.

“We’ll have to see,” is all I can manage around the lump in my throat. Then, because I’m afraid of what I might do the longer I delay, I step up to the door and knock. It’s a coded knock. Eshe steps up and knocks her own code on the door. The lantern rocks slightly, sending light and darkness skittering like rodents around the narrow street.

Nothing.

I frown. Jabir should be—

Hurried footsteps coming up the alleyway make me spin around and lay my hands on the hilts of my hidden blades. Eshe and I move by instinct to the shadows, each of us finding a different small spot to melt into.

A cloaked figure appears in the lantern light, his tread unmistakably furious.

Dread sinks into me like a stone.

He has been out. That is never a good sign.

He reaches the door, unlocks it with shocking disregard for keeping silent. Then, without a single glance my way, he growls, “Come inside, Nadira.”

He’s always had a sixth sense for where I am. I slide out from behind a fallen stack of crates without a sound.

“Give it to me, bint-Kinid,” he demands with little patience, holding out his hand toward Eshe’s hiding spot.

She materializes and slinks forward, a linen pouch in her fist. “Payment first.”

“I’m only paying you half.”

“Half?” Eshe demands, immediately retracting the egg.

“I’m not negotiating with you when it’s *your* fault, *your* carelessness, that has the city guard combing all of Risya for you two. No one was supposed to know until dawn. Hand the artifact over, bint-Kinid.”

Iron enters Eshe’s gaze, her mouth setting in a stubborn line. But then she looks past Jabir to me as I step over the threshold of my prison. She knows I’ll pay for whatever fight she puts up. Without a word, she throws the egg at Jabir's face with unnecessary force. He catches it easily and tosses her another sack in return—one that is pitifully light as it flies through the air.

Eshe shoots me a look of mingled fury and concern. She wears her emotions so plainly that sometimes it shocks me.

Then the door is shut, and I have no choice but to walk further down the claustrophobic hallway if I want any distance between me and the man who now tosses his cloak to the floor and stomps toward me.

I turn my back on him and try to ignore the prickling down my spine as I march into my room and brace myself for another multi-month imprisonment. It shouldn't matter at this point: the sight of the gloomy room with only a single flickering candle to light the space. Behind me, Jabir loudly fiddles with a lantern before storming after me.

I don't care that he's angry, I tell myself in the privacy of my own thoughts, and quickly take refuge behind the bowl of water and small brazier I set on the floor before I left. I sit cross-legged and blow on the coals, bringing them back to life just as Jabir fills the doorway. Which, unfortunately, is only a pace from where I sit due to the smallness of the room.

"What a *mess*!" he all but shouts into my face. His beard shakes with the force of his voice, catching droplets of foamy spittle that would have otherwise landed on me.

I ignore him, sprinkling incense over the coals and breathing in its sharp, earthy aroma. Unfortunately, though my work earns Jabir a fortune, he doesn't allow me to choose my own incense. Instead, he gives me what I'm certain is the cheapest thing at the bazaar, and instead of smelling sweet, it's *almost* repugnant. As though it's mostly dirt, with only the barest hint of saffron and myrrh.

"Look at me!" he growls.

When I ignore him still further, he reaches out and snatches my jaw, the tiny spikes in his gloves piercing my skin. My blood drips over the leather, but I'm used to this pain. I can bear the feeling that he's about to puncture bone and yank my jawbone right out of my face.

I lift my eyes to his, unflinching. There's a curl of satisfaction in my stomach when his small, beady gaze shifts just barely away from making contact with mine, like he's fixated on my eyelashes instead of my pupils.

"We succeeded," I say at last.

"You failed!"

"The lord is dead, and the artifact retrieved."

He scoffs, loosening his grip and stepping away to pace the length of my small room. He bumps into my cot, his heel twisting into the faded, threadbare rug. His boot makes a familiar *clang* whenever he steps on the drain in my room. Because my room isn't really a room—it's more like a cell, with high walls and a narrow grate just below the ceiling instead of a window. There's nothing but my cot, ground space for laying out my floor plans, a small chest for my spare changes of clothes, my incense, and the tools I use for my knife care.

"And the *entire* city knows about it already!"

I glare at him, barely keeping my eyebrow from arching.

"I've told you once, and I will keep telling you," Jabir seethes. "Do a good job and you won't end up like your parents. But this job would make my mother and her mother roll in their graves! And mountains of Ildrid, stop burning that incense! Your prayers make my eyes water."

I say nothing, staring at the door and wishing he would take his watery eyes and remove them from the premises. The cuts on my jaw sting, but I ignore the pain, which is easier than ignoring the slide of blood down my neck.

Jabir lets out a long-suffering sigh and shakes his head briskly. "It is done. I will be lenient this once, but I expect a more careful plan for this next job. Here are the blueprints. I expect you to start on it first thing in the morning. We've only got a month for this one."

I don't even look at the rolled parchments he hands me before I say, "Only a month? I need more time than that!"

"You'll do it."

I hold my breath as I unroll the parchment, hoping against hope that it's a simple layout. It is most definitely *not*. My mouth angles down with my brows as I peel back the top layer to reveal two more sheets of parchment. "Three floors? And that's not including—is this a six-story *tower*? I need more time. I can't—" I cut myself off abruptly, frowning even harder. Then I look up at Jabir's beady gaze and thick beard. "Where's the rest of it? This isn't the full building."

It is made to *appear* a full building, with walls sketched where there definitely aren't any. Now that I've realized it, the whole thing looks absolutely ridiculous. A building of this size—with a tower? Where is the rest of the wall? There must be more towers. And this hallway ends suddenly, even though there are no passageways that branch off it or rooms to justify it.

Jabir sniffs, his nostrils flaring slightly. "The rest of the plans are coming. They are still in progress."

"I can finish them," I say, latching onto the hope of being allowed to scout and forgetting for the moment that he tried to *fool* me with this.

"No, I will bring them to you."

Frustration burns in my lungs. "I cannot work with incomplete plans—especially on this timeline. You must give me more time."

Jabir's sudden outburst slaps me in the face. "I must give you *nothing* of the sort! You will come up with a plan. You have a month. When the rest of the floor plan is ready, I will give it to you. Until then, find a way to get in and out without getting caught. I want a plan for night, and a plan for daylight."

My jaw drops open in shock. It's shock that loosens my tongue further, despite his crackling temper. "A *daylight* assassination?"

"I didn't say it was an assassination. All you need to know for now is that the client just wants a plan for entry and exit. And—"

"Without any of the servant patterns? The guard rotations?" I flip through the parchments with increasing horror. "And you won't let me scout it? Jabir, I cannot—"

I shut my mouth and don't let myself dodge when he backhands me across the face. I stay where I am, not moving, just breathing through my nose as the sting blooms across my cheek and slowly ebbs.

We're both well aware that I can easily avoid his fist.

We're both also well aware that it would be so much worse for me if I did.

"You'll do it," is all Jabir says in the silence that follows his blow.

I don't reply.

"Oh, and you will not be working with bint-Kinid anymore."

The words hit me harder than any slap. Ice fills my belly.

"You work better on your own," Jabir continues. "Her carelessness makes you careless. Our clients don't pay for sloppy work, and after tonight they might find another assassin who can cause less of a scene."

I wish they would. My limbs are cold as I try to process this revelation, this realization that I'll likely never see Eshe again. Never have her beam of sunlight shining on my face again.

Anger flares hotter than grief, but I know better than to fight Jabir over this. It's a miracle I've been allowed to work with her this long. Why couldn't she have just *followed the plan* tonight? If things had gone smoothly, Jabir wouldn't be in this foul mood. He would leave me alone to my incense and prayers, and he wouldn't have taken her from me.

He gives another of his long-suffering sighs, the one that makes it sound like he's being so patient with me, the unruly child. "Get some sleep. I want you working on this first thing tomorrow. Now, up and give me a goodnight kiss."

With my cheek throbbing, I stand obediently but slowly, cross the distance between us, and meet his gaze. I'm very tall for a woman, but Jabir still has at least five inches on me. I stand on my toes and press a kiss to his bearded cheek. I pull back, meeting those hateful eyes with the force of my own.

He doesn't shrink from me, and I don't from him.

"Goodnight," he says and shuts the door behind him.

The familiar click of a key in the lock rings through the air, and heavy footsteps tread away. Boards creak under his boots, and I wait until the last bit of sound fades to nothing. Then I take a deep breath, survey my cell-room, and kneel before my incense and bowl of water again, disregarding the horrible floor plans for the moment.

I take my black towel and slowly wipe away the blood from my face, knowing the little cuts will stop bleeding soon enough. They will heal, but leave scars to join my collection. I think that's why Jabir keeps the spikes on his gloves—not because of the pain, not because he can wield his power over me, but because they leave a mark.

A reminder that I am not, and never will be, my own.

Finished with my wounds, I remove my gloves, tugging on each finger carefully as I ease them off. Smooth, bronze skin glistens in the candlelight, but all I can see is red. I swallow and, with one deep, fortifying breath, I plunge them into the water.

The wetness seems to crawl up my arms, slide down my spine. I shudder, but I force myself to continue washing. I keep my eyes wide open, to prove to myself that it's just water I'm touching, but my vision clouds, and for a second, I'm sitting in the midst of a graveyard with unburied corpses strewn beside me, lying in their own blood.

I blink, and I'm back in my room, smelling the incense and washing my hands with water. Once my hands are dry, my attention trails back to the floor plans. What is this building that Jabir wouldn't let me scout—and wouldn't want me to even know *which* building it is? Why did he try to fool me by giving me these partial plans? I study them as if they have an answer, but even though the arrangement of passageways, staircases, rooms, windows and doors sink into my memory, I'm no closer to understanding Jabir than I was before.

Finally, I set the plans aside and continue my ritual. My mouth moves, and the names flow off my tongue with the ease of a well-oiled hinge swinging back and forth.

"Seyyid, Urwah, Yakub—"

"Back already?"

The voice wrenches me from the darkness, and I nearly knock over my bag of incense in my haste to turn around.

It's Kolb. He winces as he wiggles his way out of the drain in my room, and I watch as his tall, slender body seems to keep coming and coming, until he's finally squatting beside it, head tilted and mouth spread in a stupid grin. His hair is a rat's nest of much-too-long curls that frame a boyishly handsome face. He's older than me, but a stranger would easily take him for younger. His clothes are torn and patched, hanging off his frame like a pet monkey's might after it had escaped into the wild.

Part of me wants to crumple into tears at the sight of his familiar face after so long. I didn't want to confess to Eshe how much I'd worried about him, how many nights I'd lain awake hoping he would rescue me from my nightmares with his sweet smile.

"Already?" I say in a casual tone that belies my own relief at seeing him. I remove my cloak and arrange my gloves and special shoes beside them. Separator follows, and Kolb watches as I unstrap all my weapons and lay them out for cleaning and sharpening.

"Well," he replies, standing and turning toward the wall with the grate window. With a leap, he swings his way up like a chimpanzee to the grate. "I heard it was quite exciting tonight. Yet you're back on time. Early, even."

"You ought to remind Jabir of that for me."

"I'm not reminding Jabir of *anything.*"

Kolb hooks his ankles around the bars on the window and slowly lowers himself backwards, so he hangs upside down, hands crossed beneath his head, looking yet again uncannily ape-like. Albeit extra boney and lanky.

I can't help my smile. His response is another grin, and then a series of quick movements I can't follow. In a flash, he twists, loosens his ankles, and flips back down to the ground. Then he's got an arm around my waist, his other hand pulling back my hood so it can tangle in my hair. He pulls me into a kiss and I don't stop him, even though everything inside me tells me what a horrible person I am to murder one minute, and then accept comfort for it the next.

Kolb pulls back, his face serious for a rare moment. "Sometimes, I wish . . ."

"Don't wish," I say, smiling ruefully. Then I tilt my head, letting my smile twist into a frown. "Eshe told me about your sister. Is she alright?" He seems shockingly chipper for someone who Eshe had described as *desperate*.

"You don't know?" Kolb asks, grabbing hold of my shoulders as a grin breaks across his face. We're almost exactly the same height. "Jabir took her in and told me he'd get her proper medicine and care. Oh Nadira, I was so worried for her. Now I could fly!"

I blink at him, not comprehending. "Jabir?"

"I'm beginning to think I've judged him too harshly these years. It's hard not to, when he keeps you here like a prisoner and . . . are those cuts fresh?" He winces at my jaw, and I'm only glad he doesn't notice the swelling of my cheek. "Anyway, contrary to what evidence might suggest, I think it's possible he has a heart."

"What did he ask for in return?" I ask warily. Kolb may fancy Jabir to have a heart, but I've known for years that is utterly impossible.

"He just asked me to run a few errands for him when he needed them. Oh, come now! You look as though I've sold my soul to the devil. They're *errands*, Nadira. I would give so much more for my sister's life."

My unease doesn't leave me, but I manage to say a placating, "I hope she gets better soon."

"Me too." He sighs, glancing at my incense and the bowl of water. "I suppose I ought to let you finish your rituals and get some sleep. You look . . ."

I purse my lips, waiting for him to finish that sentence. Daring him with my glare.

His mouth splits into a slow, sheepish grin in response. ". . . Ravishing."

I roll my eyes.

He hesitates, then hauls me in for another kiss. Part of me breaks at that bit of physical contact, at the disbelief that anyone would *want* to kiss me after what I've done tonight. I tighten my lips, signaling the kiss is over, and Kolb pulls back. He salutes me, flashes another grin, and begins the arduous and painful-to-watch process of squeezing back into the drain to get out. I'm not sure how much longer Jabir will allow him to "sneak" in to see me. For all I know, this is the last time I'll ever see my only other friend again.

The moment he's gone, I feel a shift in the air.

My breath whistles through my teeth as I turn, looking over my shoulder like the paranoid girl I am, and though the room is as empty as always, the hair on my neck rises. Apparently, I'm still rattled enough to imagine nonexistent threats.

I've dealt so much death that I can't free myself from the sense that mine is next, and there's nothing I can do to stop it. The only question is: shall I die a slow, agonizing death, or will I be dispatched how I dispatch my victims—too fast for thought? Will I even realize the end has come before it's over? Do I *want* to realize it? Or do I wish that the grave would swallow me whole before I have a chance to be afraid?

I climb into bed, the smell of incense somehow stronger and yet more muted than it was a moment before. I swallow, gripping the covers, and the silence unnerves me so much I nearly wrench back the blankets and lurch to my feet. Instead, I slip my fingers under my head cushion, feel the solid comfort of a knife hilt, and I force myself to breathe, to count, to recite. "Murtadi, Shawar, Tibon."

The air grows thicker, thicker, my panic mounting. My denial, my insistence of my own paranoia vanishes in an instant.

I know without a doubt that I'm not alone.

I lick my lips but force myself to keep whispering names. My awareness sharpens, and each breath becomes so painful I fear my own knife is shoved between my ribs.

As my mouth keeps moving, my voice soft and lilting in the dark, my mind is reeling, trying to think of every enemy I've accumulated, trying to guess if this is some trick of Jabir's, or if one of my two friends have betrayed me. After all, I didn't think it was possible for anyone to break into my room except for Kolb, and that's only because Jabir allows it for whatever evil purposes he's devised.

How can silence feel so empty and yet so full?

Then—a whisper of sound. Of movement. Coming toward me.

CHAPTER 4

THE MOMENT I fly through the room, knife raised, I half expect to meet with nothing but air—proof that I am merely inventing threats of death in my dark imagination.

But a hand wraps around my wrist. A real hand. A large, strong one.

I shouldn't have disarmed myself before bed. I reach for the knives at my biceps, only to be met with skin and cloth. I gasp, blood roaring in my mind, but I bring up my leg to land a blow to my assailant's knee.

The pressure on my wrist and the bulky presence behind me vanishes. It didn't let go—it simply . . . *vanished.* I whirl, but there's nothing there.

Is there . . . *magic* in this room?

I'm crouched in the dark, eyes peeled for any sign of my attacker, but I can't even guess where he has gone before my feet are knocked out from under me. I roll before I hit the ground, and I'm almost certain I hear the plunk of a knife into the floor where I'd been only seconds ago.

ANASTASIS BLYTHE

Someone is trying to kill me.

The thought shoots a bolt of terror down my spine. I shove it away, noticing that I've rolled into a crouch beside my knives. I grab one in each hand, and then I'm moving again as the black bulk coalesces beside me.

I can't always be on the defensive now, can I? Not if I'm to have any hope of surviving. Even my reluctance to shed more blood tonight isn't enough to keep my blade from flying through the air, straight at the unseen figure before me.

There's a sharp grunt of surprise, but my knife hits the wall, not a person. He's dodged it somehow.

Suddenly, wind rushes around me, and then a body hits me, my wrists snatched and pinned as my back hits the floor. No matter how my eyes strain in the gloom, I can make nothing out of the face above me.

I console myself that both his arms are occupied by pinning mine. He's unlikely to stab me through my pounding heart.

A low, dark voice fills my senses.

"You are better trained than I anticipated. Delightful."

I frown, wriggling my wrists to distract him as I tuck my knees to my chest and prepare to kick against his face. "Who sent you?"

There's a bark of surprised laughter above me. "*Sent*? Surely you don't think anyone *sent* me! What a notion." He chuckles, and the sound is like a knife down my back, leaving beads of blood in its wake.

I kick.

The bottoms of my unshod feet meet with a hard, partially bare chest. I nearly let out a sound of disgusted shock at the contact of flesh on flesh, and when I try to dislodge him, he's like a boulder above me.

Unmovable and impassive.

I sag in his grip. Not because I'm out of ideas, but because I want him to believe I am. I glare at the darkness above me. "Who are you?" I ask, proud of how my voice doesn't shake.

"*Who* am *I*? You cannot be serious." There's a pause. Then, in a softer, lilting version of his darkened voice, he asks, "*Are* you serious?"

"I do not know whom I've had the pleasure of being assaulted by tonight."

Another snort. Then I grow warmer, as if he's leaning closer.

"I am . . ." he says, pitching his voice lower, ". . . your worst nightmare."

Now it's my turn to snort and raise an eyebrow. "I *seriously* doubt it."

He doesn't say anything, and I almost have the impression of a head, canted to one side. I strike. I kick hard, this time lower than my first blow, intent on causing real pain.

The presence above me dissipates into nothing yet again. I don't even look as I stab my knife behind me, hear another grunt of surprise but my blade slices through nothing. I growl, moving more by instinct than rational thought as I whirl, dodge an unseen blow, and land several of my own. My frustration mounts as none of them connect. Somehow, he is evading me, and I can't help my disbelief. No human should be able to move so quickly. I've never been *not* able to kill something.

The weight of helplessness that settles over me is almost as alarming as the haunting feeling of blood on my hands.

Then, to my shock, I'm slammed face-first into the wall. I gasp, barely turning my head to the side in time to not break my nose. He pins my hands again, leaning his weight heavily into mine. My chest heaves against cold plaster.

Again, however, his hands are occupied with mine. I'm not sure how he intends to kill me, but if he moves quickly enough, he can release one of my wrists, snatch a knife, and stab me.

My breath comes hard and fast. "What do you want?"

"You, of course." As if it's obvious.

"I'm not for sale. Jabir wouldn't—"

"*Sale*?" There's a confusing sound behind me, and I'm not sure if it's amusement or shock, or perhaps a strange combination of the two. "I don't *buy* people."

"Just kill them?"

"And kidnap them," he replies promptly, as though we're discussing this over a cup of qahwa and not between gritted teeth.

"Is that what you have come to do, then? Steal me away from my slaver?"

I feel him shrugging, and I nearly shake my head in bewilderment.

"You are a slave?" he asks, instead of answering a simple yes or no.

I grind my teeth. "Of sorts."

"Then you're better off coming with me anyway."

"Am I?" I choke on a burst of terrified laughter. "I don't even know who you are. Better the devil you know, right?"

"Wrong. How is it a risk to come with the devil you don't know—yours truly, to be clear—when the current situation is so . . ." He makes a sound of disgust. ". . . Wretched?"

He might as well have stabbed me through the heart. I choke on a sob, my muscles straining against him. But I manage to swallow my tears firmly, and say, "False dichotomy. An unknown risk is always worse because you cannot prepare for it."

A silence follows my words, and I think there's surprise in the air between us.

"Then we must agree to disagree," he says.

I duck, butting my head backwards as hard as I can. I hit—nothing. Yet, even before my body finishes moving, he's pinned me again. I nearly whimper in frustration, in disbelief, that someone could overpower me without even getting injured in the process.

It's almost as if he's moving faster than humanly possible to avoid my blows. My life could end in the fraction of a second, any moment now, and I haven't—

"This might be too personal of a question to ask right now," the voice continues with a lilting edge of curiosity and maybe something else . . . something almost *angry*. "But why is there a fresh corpse in the other room?"

This question surprises me enough that my next attempted strike loses some of its gusto. "What?"

"You were unaware of it, I assume?"

Fresh corpse. Jabir wouldn't have hurt Kolb or Eshe, would he? He wouldn't—

Kolb's sister.

My eyes widen. The realization hits deeper than I expect, even though I've never met the girl. I stop fighting just for a moment, panting hard against the wall. "Was it a child? How did she die?"

If Jabir killed her . . .

"I didn't find any wounds on her. It seemed like illness."

Those words send fire ripping through my limbs. I throw my body back against his, meeting a wall of unyielding flesh, and stab as fast as I can at his side. He dodges to one side, but I stab there too. The pressure behind me vanishes in an instant.

Jabir took in Kolb's sister on the promise of getting her medicine, only to let her die and not tell my friend. I funnel my rage into a new attack against my shadowy assailant and don't stop even when he has me against the wall once more.

"I still cannot believe you don't know who I am."

My world freezes. My jaw drops open, so far open I'm sure it's in danger of landing on the floor. Realization floods my blood as my stomach fills with ice.

"You . . ." My voice trails off, and my throat feels like it has a frog wedged in its narrow space. I stare disbelieving up at the shadow, the face that leans close enough to mine that his warmth caresses me.

That might even be a glimmer of eyes, of teeth in the darkness surrounding us.

"Ah. So you *do* finally know who I am. I was beginning to give up all hope. Humans, the most forgetful race that ever breathed. But though you might have recognized me now, don't think my feelings still aren't hurt. They are, in fact, *quite* wounded."

I don't have enough mental energy to filter out the genuine from the sarcastic in those comments. Instead, my entire awareness seems to narrow on what I'm now sure are a pair of glittering eyes.

They are startlingly near my own.

"You are . . ."

"Out with it! We haven't got all night!"

If I was being smart, I'd delay. I'd surprise him again, give myself more time to think, to plan, to hope that Jabir will come to my rescue. The last thought nearly makes me choke out a hysterical laugh.

But I'm not being smart. My brain is like melted emaa, swirling around the cavernous space of my skull. I can't think. I can't plan. I can't even hope.

All I can do is breath: "You are the Neverseen King."

There is a distinct sense of satisfaction in the darkness before my face. Then, he says, his voice low and rich, "A pleasure to *finally,* properly make your acquaintance, Nadira al-Risya. I'm afraid our introduction was vastly overdue. I'm utterly delighted. And unbearably charmed."

Then he lets go of one wrist, and I nearly panic. He can kill me now. He *will* kill me now. I twist, fighting harder, but suddenly his grip turns to iron, and I am no more able to escape than I am to see the face of the monster before me. He's much stronger than he seemed a moment ago, and with sickening dread I realize he has been *letting* me strike at him.

Why is my sultan here, in my room, letting me fight him?

A more chilling question occurs to me in those final moments: *how does he know my name?*

It's not the razor-sharp edge of a knife that touches my face, however, but a hand. An enormous, warm hand lands to cup my face, and I gasp, its calluses catching on my upper lip. There's muttering in the dark beyond that hand, beyond the fingers pressing against my forehead, my cheekbone, the thumb that rests on the scars along my jaw.

"Rest," he says.

The world falls away.

CHAPTER 5

LIGHTNING BOLTS THROUGH my skin. Sensations flood me—warmth, movement, sweat. A spasm rips through my body. My limbs flail wildly. I reach, catch hold of something solid, and let out a gasping protest.

"Calm, you feisty kitten," rumbles a low voice against my ear. "You're supposed to still be asleep."

That voice, that unsettling closeness—my head is against a warm chest. I'm being carried, held in strong arms. My fists clench around fabric—clothing. Everything is addled, murky and fogged.

"What is happening?" My words slur and trip over one another.

"I'm rescuing you, of course. To be my bride."

Every hundred years. Panic cuts through the fog, and instinct takes over. I reach for a knife, only for my hand to close around emptiness. My panic flares brighter. I struggle, and only succeed in making his arms tighten around me. I'm blinded, and I don't know if the world is just dark, if my eyes are closed, or if it's some spell he has cast on me that renders everything blacker than night.

"Don't act quite so repulsed, my dear. You'll hurt my feelings."

His feelings? In a burst of clarity and rage, I shift upward. And somehow, I find the strength to reach and drive my fist straight toward his throat. I hit hard, hard enough to cause damage to him—and my knuckles.

He stops moving.

I freeze, caught between surprise that my blow actually landed this time, and sudden terror that I have just poked a stick at a monster who will set talon and fang into me and devour me whole.

"That was . . . probably called for," he says, not even a hint of choking or pain in his voice.

Then I go whooshing through the air, finding myself clinging frantically to my assailant as my head spins, and I land on something soft. *A bed.* My panic redoubles until I'm practically clawing with my fingernails at anything within reach.

"I'm not y-your—" I can't finish the sentence because I can't draw a deep breath.

"Easy, easy there." His voice has grown softer, gentler. I jerk and shudder as a broad hand lands on the curve of my shoulder and a thumb presses into the hollow of my throat. "Breathe."

Immediately, my airways open, my ribs loosen, and I drag in a deep breath. My hands fist in soft blankets as the warmth of his hand retracts. It's so dark I cannot catch even the barest sight of that movement.

"Nadira," he whispers.

I tense, ready to bolt.

"Though there are many things to fear in this House I've brought you to, I can assure you of this: you need not fear harm from my hand. I can also assure you that I do not bring you here because of my kingly whims, though I'd prefer that was the reason. You're here because your people need you. Your people and . . . many—*many* others."

Did his voice just break?

I don't have time to wonder. His hand is over my face again, and my awareness slips into nothingness.

My bleary eyes flash open, and I'm suddenly wide awake. I lurch upward, sweat streaming down my back, making my clothes cling to my skin. There's a large canopy bed over me, mahogany brocade curtains falling like heavy tapestries all around me. I'm sitting in downy sheets, a goose feather cushion beneath my head and heavy quilts pinning my limbs to the soft mattress. It's like lying in a cloud, but far heavier.

A pained cry wrenches from my throat, and I fly out of bed, my hand going instinctively under my head cushion to find my knife, but it's gone. Oh no. *Oh no.* Where am I? What is—what am I wearing? I'm in a nightgown. *Akhh*, why am I in a nightgown? I never undress like this for bed. I never—

I rip the canopy aside, and sunlight hits my eyes hard. I wince, stumbling, and knock straight into a large wardrobe. My legs are like noodles, and I reach out to grab the bedpost to keep from falling. I cling to its solidity as the world around me tilts, and I fear I will fall through the air, right out the window. My chest heaves against cold wood.

Rug tassels catch between my bare toes, and it only makes my heart pound more. *Where am I?*

Not home. Not in my cell-room.

New, new, *new.* Everything from the curving dark wood of the four-poster bed, the gold leaf trimmed vanity, the carved legs of the curling table at the foot of the bed with an ornate porcelain pitcher and washbasin, is entirely new. It's sumptuous, a chamber fit for a queen.

A queen.

I turn and catch a glimpse of myself in the copper mirror above the vanity, staring back with wide, hollow eyes that don't seem to belong to me. I'm looking at a stranger, one whose mouth is open and panting, bronze skin glistening with sweat across her brow, black hair matted and twisted into a wild mess, the dotting of pale scars across her jaw.

The Neverseen King. He kidnapped me last night. Was it last night? Foggy memories of his arms holding me, those choking fingers of helplessness wrapping around my throat as I tried to fight him, as I failed over and over again, return to my mind like an avalanche. I feel his hand, large as my head, covering my face and telling me to sleep.

A spell.

Suddenly, a new fear enters my mind as I glance down at the unfamiliar nightgown. It is a lovely shade of turquoise, soft and breezy to accommodate the heat, and yet it reaches from my throat to my toes, covering me completely. I swallow. I must find out who changed me last night, and if it was my sultan, I will personally ensure Separator finds its prompt way into his heart. I do not care if murdering a king starts a war—he should have thought twice about kidnapping an assassin for his bride.

Fragments of a vague memory cross my mind. A voice, deep and dark. *Your people need you.* And, softer: *You need not fear harm from my hand.*

The door opens. I whirl.

"Rise and shine! Isn't it just a lovely day, my lady? Couldn't have asked for better weather for what's ahead of you today. Sunny without a shred of cloud to be seen, but just the loveliest breeze!"

In a second, I'm across the room. I have no knives at my disposal, but that isn't a true hindrance. Not to me. My hands close around a neck, and I use all my weight and leverage to fling the body against the wall, my fingers digging in perilously close to a pressure point.

"Where am I?" I demand.

Suddenly, my vision clears, and the gasping face before me is the soft face of a woman, the gentle lines around her eyes betraying the slightest bit of aging, her plain tunic and cream-colored sirwal revealing her status. My own eyes widen, and I loosen my hold.

The woman crumples to the ground, heaving breaths in and out, pressing a hand against her chest. A fallen tray is at her feet. At first I blanch, thinking the red liquid seeping into the rugs is blood, but then I realize it's only tea, and the broken porcelain beside it is the tea pot and cup this . . . *maid* was bringing me.

I take a step back, and I'm not sure who is breathing harder, me or the woman.

"Sorry, sorry! I'm so sorry!" I gasp, croaking out of my too-tight throat. I swallow. "Where am I?"

I *must* know. Or else my heart will burst from the sheer panic flooding my veins. I don't know this place. I don't know its layout, or how to get *out*. I don't know anything. It's all new. And I have no plan. *No plan.* I *must—*

"The palace of the Neverseen King," the woman manages, her fingers trailing along the marks I've left.

She's not at fault. I know she's not, but I can't think straight, not while my mind is spinning. I cling tighter to the bedpost. "Why am I here?"

"The Neverseen King brought you here."

I swallow again. At the sound of footsteps, my attention darts to the open door. My eyes fly wide, and then I'm ignoring my vertigo and run-stumbling my way around the bed to the other side, looking for some hiding place.

"Nadira al-Risya." The voice is clipped, edged in polite snobbery. When I don't answer, it repeats. "Nadira al-Risya."

I think of five different ways to kill the man calling my name. I glance desperately at the window, wondering if guards will cut me down should I dare throw myself out of it.

Drawing a deep breath, I force myself to stop cowering like a beaten animal and stand, straightening my spine as everything inside me blanches.

It's the first time I've stood before a stranger in years, without the shadows to hide me. My heart trembles inside my chest, my lungs heaving. But I won't bow beneath the weight of my fear. I will stand straight. I will face what is before me.

No matter that I still wear nothing but this nightgown.

A man stands in my doorway. He is of average height, with cheeks that sag below his jaw slightly, bags under his eyes, and gray eyebrows set above sunken sockets. He's standing even straighter than I, but it's not fear fortifying his spine. It's the confidence of a military captain with the rugged edges of one who has stood before danger and prevailed.

"I am the Emin, Steward of the Neverseen King, and overseer of this House," he says.

He *has* stood before danger. If my fragmented memories of last night are to be believed.

"You are Nadira al-Risya, are you not? The Mourner?"

There's no pride in the upward tilt of my chin. I hate that title. I never would have chosen it for myself. Wouldn't have chosen any title, for that matter.

"Very well," says the steward briskly. He waves the terrified maid out of the room, and she scrambles to obey. "Leave the tray," he says, hardly glancing at the shards mingling with staining tea and a few date cakes. His eyes return to mine, heavy and unflinching, but also mildly assessing. They rove over me from head to toe, as though analyzing my every strength and weakness. "You've successfully almost butchered one of my servants, so I suppose you should do quite nicely. Come, take your breakfast." He waves his hand at the mess on the floor.

I don't move.

"At the height of the hour, we will convene in the Golden Hall to discuss the rules."

"Rules?" I ask.

"For the competition."

My stomach bottoms out. I barely have the strength to croak, "What competition?"

"The competition for the Neverseen King's bride, of course."

CHAPTER 6

AM I TO believe now that aside from being a kidnapped bride, I am not the *only* kidnapped bride? Does he intend to make a harem of stolen women? Surely not, right? The steward said *bride*, singular.

My mind is spinning too rapidly for rational thought. *The Neverseen King. A bride. Competition.*

What sort of competition? Why am *I* here? I'm not the wife sort. Much less the wife of a sultan. I'm a coldblooded killer. I take lives without hesitation. I am ruthless. Terrible.

Wretched.

A bead of sweat trails down my arm, wet and tickling. Even after the door closes, and I'm left alone in this room once more to dress, my heart won't slow. It keeps raging like a monster intent on breaking free from its cage.

A plan.

If I'm here without a plan, then I must devise one. I spare a thought for how much better Eshe would do in a situation like this. She would thrive in a palace of darkness and mystery, laughing in the face of the Neverseen King who dared abduct her. She would be the sunshine streaming through my window. And she would find a way to escape.

I can't keep losing my cool. I must approach this rationally. Carefully. Systematically. I must live up to the reputation Jabir has created for me. Breaking out of a palace shouldn't be too difficult, so long as I learn the layout, watches, and servant patterns. Until then, I need only to survive.

Once I escape, where will I go?

The thought brings the thunderous roar of my blood to a sudden stop that sweeps down my spine like ice. No, I wouldn't go back to Jabir. Of *course* I wouldn't go back to Jabir.

I would . . . I would go . . .

Does it matter where I go? Won't Jabir find me like he always does? Will he not find me now, here in the Neverseen King's palace?

Best to worry about that later. Right now, I need to focus on surviving. This starts with finding something to wear besides this bright nightgown. The wardrobe has a few changes of clothes, all muted shades of brown and black. Hastily, I pull on a loose linen tunic and sirwal, wrap my wild hair in a scarf and tie a sash around my waist. There is a pair of new leather sandals—so new, the leather hasn't been broken in yet. I pull them on, but they do nothing to dispel the strange bareness I feel without my knives.

Finally dressed, I stare down at the tea leaves and crumbled cakes strewn across the floor. I press a hand to my hollow stomach, glad for its sudden revolt at the thought of eating.

I need to confirm that my food isn't poisoned before I give in to the temptation to satiate my hunger.

The thought stops me short. Poisoned? Why would a sultan poison his potential bride? Doesn't he have use for me? I grit my teeth and turn away, striding across the room to the one large window. It never hurts to be careful until I understand what is happening.

I place my hands on the stone ledge and lean out, the warmth shivering up into my cold fingers.

Before me is a courtyard. A fountain burbles in the middle, with chirping birds flapping on the edge of the basin and splashing water over their feathers. Palm trees arch beneath the bright sun, casting shadow over the bursts of pink and white flowers blooming on low shrubs. Framing the courtyard are buildings supported by marble pillars with dozens upon dozens of doorways and open windows, brightly colored curtains wafting in the gentle morning wind. Domed towers rise above the rest of the buildings, and beyond the wall surrounding the complex, is the far stretch of the bustling city of Risya.

It's beautiful. It's serene.

Too serene. Though the sun has risen, and the world is awake, no matter how far I crane out of my window I do not find a single servant or guard.

Unseen guards are far worse than seen ones.

I swallow, ducking my head back into my room. This is going to be more difficult than I'd hoped. But it should be—after all, if a sultan kidnapped an assassin, he'd better be prepared for the consequences.

I am considering options for scaling the wall when footsteps tread in the hallway behind me. I whirl, gaze darting around the room wildly for a place to hide.

No. I'm not hiding. I will face what's coming. No matter how my knees knock together.

If only I *knew* what was coming. Then I could be stronger.

The door opens, and it's a guard this time. Only one. He seems normal in every way; a trimmed beard, dark eyes, an armored breastplate, a sheathed jambiya at his hip. Perhaps a little on the short side, but I can tell he's strong. He is just the sort of guard I'd imagine at a palace. So why is he the only one I've seen so far?

He says nothing, only beckons me to follow.

I could take him down. If I had my knives, certainly. But even without, I think I can manage it. Is my sultan that dimwitted as to send me a guard I can overpower and escape?

Somehow, I think not.

I don't know what his Glorious Exaltation is planning, and until then, I cannot be rash. I will follow through the motions, appear to be a docile little bride with dreams of my sultan. I'll submit, and then when he lets his guard down and I know what mysteries shroud this strange bridal competition, I'll strike.

And my Neverseen King will rue the day he dared to kidnap the Mourner.

The moment I step outside of my room after the guard, I stop.

A cobalt rug unfurls before me, matching the tapestries hanging on the hallway between doors like mine. Sconces frame each doorway, lit despite the morning light that is coming from—

I crane my neck, and above me stretches a ceiling of glass. The sky shines blue above it, cloudless and vibrant. My neck begins to ache as I stand there. I don't mean for my mouth to fall open, especially in front of my guard, and I mean even less to allow for the soft beginnings of *wonder* into my soul.

I'm a prisoner. Not a tourist. Glass ceilings notwithstanding.

But it isn't the innocuous appearance of the hallway or the expanse of sky and sun above that makes me pause. It is a slow prickling of the hairs on the back of my neck. It ripples in waves down my spine, pooling around my tingling toes. I fight to draw a deep breath into my too-tight lungs.

When I turn around, no one is there. Only unending silence and a hall that seems to reach so far east it'll wrap all the way around to the west.

Something spills out beneath one of the doors, seven down from mine, on the opposite side of the hallway. It looks like dirt. I force myself to turn away, to shove down the bubbling panic in my breast.

New.

I realize with alarm that I've never been in a building where I did not know the layout by heart. I shake the thought away, clinging to the crumbling bits of my sanity. My only choice is to *learn* the layout. I note every doorway we pass, adding it to my mental floor plan like I'm sketching it myself. Some of the doors are cracked, and I strain to catch a glimpse of what is concealed.

In the first room, I think I see the gleam of a golden harp. The sultan has a taste for music, perhaps? The next, I'm sure I hear a sound like a gurgling stream. An indoor fountain? Like the one I saw in the courtyard?

I nearly freeze at the next door.

Vines crawl through punctured wood, climbing down the doorframe, and curling around the handle, tendrils digging into the keyhole such that I doubt it can be unlocked. Or locked, rather?

They're real vines.

Is this some kind of freakish décor trend that I'm unaware of? It is only confirming my conviction to never involve oneself with royalty.

I am so occupied with noting everything I can about what we've passed that I nearly fall down the pair of stairs we descend, and then I almost run straight into an enormous pair of double doors. They stretch so high above me that they disappear into the shadow of rafters. The glass ceiling is long gone, and it's too dark despite how daylight streams in from a nearby open window. I close my sagging jaw just in time for the cold sweat to return.

A pillow appears before my face, and I stare blankly at the items atop it until my mind quickens with sudden relief. I dismiss my mental layout in a flash. *My knives.* I cannot describe the comfort I feel as I strap each one in place, feeling less bare and exposed now.

I look up, and my focus narrows in on those two doors being dragged open by straining servants, at the narrow crevice before me widening—

Into a hall of solid gold.

The floor is gold, the pillars gold, the fire flickering from a glittering, gold-cut chandelier casting the room in an array of gold . . . and shadows. Distantly, my mind registers eleven women standing at attention, their dress as different from one another as they are themselves, some garbed in black and others in lighter, brighter colors. I'm vaguely aware of the steward at the front of the room. They're all looking at me, presumably the last potential bride.

But my focus isn't on them.

Instead, my eyes are drawn as if of their own accord to a shadow deeper than the rest along the far wall. The sultan is there. I know he is.

Our Neverseen King.

Am I wrong to believe I see a flash of white teeth in that impenetrable darkness? Is that a twisted version of a grin? Has he noted my notice of him? Is he pleased that I have spotted him in a room full of seemingly oblivious women?

Only then do I turn my attention to them. There's a familiar figure among them. My chest immediately clenches so tightly I can't breathe, as my eyes lock with equally surprised ones.

Eshe.

Eshe, who I was never to see again.

My *friend*.

"Please take your place," says the steward.

And turn my back on the Neverseen King? I don't want to. Everything inside me balks at the idea of presenting my captor with that much of my vulnerability. But then again, he apparently wants a bride, not a bloodbath. He has had ample opportunity to murder me so far, but hasn't.

I walk to take my place, one determined footstep after another. My vision clouds, but a fierce, determined blink clears it. Though my exposed flesh tingles, I firmly turn my back to my captor and suck in a deep breath.

I'm standing next to Eshe. She reaches out, takes my hand in hers. I squeeze back, grateful almost to tears for this scrap of familiarity. It's followed by another burst of panic, one wondering how on *earth* she ended up here too.

"You're pale," she whispers.

"Didn't have time to eat."

"You refused to eat."

"The sultan is behind us."

Her eyes go wide, and a battle ensues in those dark irises. She wants to look. Thankfully, she has the sense to not.

The young woman on the other side of Eshe is tall. Taller than either of us, she peers down at me suspiciously over the edge of a coarse cloak that shields half her face. I regard her mildly in return, and then try to see what I can make of anyone else in the line.

The next girl has eyes as wide as wheels on a cart in the bazaar. She looks younger than the rest in line, but that might just be her small frame, rounded face, and wild mop of curls. She breathes hard—almost frantically.

It's the last young woman that draws my attention next. She wears harsh black that only makes her pupils seem even more like endless voids. It's not her clothes that make ice fill my gut, but the way she studies me with an unveiled murderous rage. Startled, I barely manage to keep myself from stumbling back a step. Who *is* this girl? Does she look at everyone this way?

Apparently she does, because when my attention is demanded at the front of the room, the force of her hatred redirects to Emin.

"Welcome," says the steward, clasping his hands behind his back and looking at each of us in turn. "The Neverseen King welcomes you all cordially."

I cannot be the only one fighting a snort.

"He would like to thank each of you for participating in this competition for his hand in marriage. Your sacrifices to be here are not overlooked."

It's a good thing I've learned to regulate my features, because if I hadn't, my jaw would have hit the floor in incredulity.

"The Neverseen King doesn't care to thank us in person?" says a crisp, clear voice next to me. *Eshe.* My stomach tumbles over itself.

Please stop talking, I want to beg.

Of course, she doesn't.

"During the competition, the Neverseen King will dine privately with each of you. I will leave it to his honored discretion what he chooses to discuss," replies the steward with a polite smile that doubles as a warning.

My skin crawls with the presence at my back. I don't turn around.

The steward continues, his voice deep and rhythmic. "The Neverseen King is hosting a series of competitions of varying types to determine your competency as a potential bride."

Will these competitions involve debating tariffs and trade routes? Mixing swaths of fabric for décor? Pairing jewelry with gowns, seeing who dances the most elegantly? Reciting poetry or singing ballads?

Because I will fail all of those, and I won't even have to do it on purpose.

"Whoever wins the competition will have the honor of wedding the Neverseen King and becoming Queen of Arbasa."

Some of the women in the line perk up at that. I'm not sure how they've fared so far at these turns of events, but I don't doubt that some of them find their circumstances suddenly much more favorable. After all, who doesn't want to be a queen?

Me. I don't.

My heart plummets when Eshe tilts her head, as though reconsidering her original notions. Of course *she* would love to be a queen, though I'm not entirely sure what part of it sounds appealing to her. Outfitting the palace in drapes that suit her liking? Wearing a crown upon her lovely head? Bending the knee to none but her sultan? Being *free*?

Something inside my chest stutters at the last thought. I quickly quash it with all my willpower. Being the Neverseen King's queen will be a slavery even deeper than the one I've borne most of my life. It doesn't matter how many jewels he may string around his bride's neck; one twist of his wrist on those strings of pearls and gold-encrusted emeralds, and she dies.

While I know little enough of my sultan, I know he's powerful. Somehow, he's got magic at his disposal, and if I've learned anything from my years with Jabir, it's that the more powerful the master, the less hope for the slave.

"You will remain here in the House through the duration of the competition," continues the steward. House—not palace? Interesting. "There are two rules that you must abide by."

I wait, my breath snagged between my teeth.

"The first rule is to never, under *any* circumstance, at *no* time"—The steward emphasizes these words carefully, and my throat tightens into a thick knot I doubt will ever come undone—"open your doors after nightfall."

Because the sultan prowls these hallways at night? And he doesn't wish to be seen while he rules our kingdom? Or for another reason? That is another mystery I must unravel if I'm to have any hope of escape.

"Second, the House requests that you place soiled clothes in the designated baskets instead of leaving them on the floor—it bothers the House. And please, no manhandling the servants." This is stated with a pointed glance at me.

"You didn't," Eshe hisses at me under her breath.

I don't deign to answer that.

"As for the matter of the first competition . . ." The steward glances once more toward the shadows behind me, a glance so brief I almost miss it. "It will begin in about . . . nine seconds. May the stars shine bright upon your path."

With that, he tucks his chin to his chest, turns, and sprints for the back wall.

"What?" the tall girl demands furiously. Two more race after the steward, but aren't fast enough to slip through the wall panel that is apparently a secret exit. It slams shut behind the steward.

Nine, eight, seven—

Counting is like breathing to me. I turn just in time to see another girl run to the main entrance, feel for handles, and then throw herself against the doors. They don't budge. It's almost like there never were doors there, and it's been golden paneling this entire time. Trapping us.

Six, five, four—

Instinct flares in my chest, and I whip out my knives, whirling in place as the girls around me begin running, scattering across the hall, gold shimmering on colored and dull fabric alike.

The round-faced girl with the curly hair stands in the middle of the room, shaking. She looks so small standing there—a personification of how I feel in this moment. I don't know what's coming. I don't know what is about to hit us. I don't know where to be in the room. The eyes that I meet across the room are as clueless as mine, shading in various degrees of anger and panic that echo my own. I don't know—

"Nadira!" Eshe is at my side, her brow set and eyes flashing. "Back to back?"

I meet her gaze, and I cling to her calmness in a world that is falling to pieces around me. I nod, and set my back to hers. I may not have a plan, may have the utter inability to *make* a plan, but I know I have a friend guarding my back.

Together, we can face this madness.

Against my will, my attention swivels to the dark corner of shadow. My sultan has stayed to watch this competition.

"What's your name?" Eshe calls to the terrified girl.

"Hulla," she gasps.

"Come stand with us!"

She breaks into a run, nearly crashing into me and Eshe. She shivers against us, but to her credit, she pulls a thin jambiya from her belt and stands with her shoulders touching ours.

Three, two, one—

Silence falls across the room. I haven't been the only one counting. All twelve of us are silent. I fix my gaze on that darkness, and a chill races down my spine, like he's staring back at me. It's so quiet in the room I'm certain my heaving breaths are the loudest sound.

Then a deafening *rip* erupts around us. I twist to look over my shoulder, over Eshe's shoulder, nearly wetting myself as I watch the air split apart.

A wave of shrieking blue pours into the room.

CHAPTER 7

MY MIND DOESN'T want to comprehend what I see. I'm facing a large circle, one as high and wide as I am tall, suspended a few feet above the golden floor. The edges are sizzling and snapping like lightning, bright white with sparks of blue, and looking into it is like peering through a window into another world.

An entirely different world.

A world bathed in midnight with three moons hanging in the sky above a field of green that's moving—wait, not a field. A body of . . . water?

No, that rippling green sludge is definitely not water. And through this window of sorts, *things* are scrambling over the bottom edge and dropping to the floor, shrieking like a thousand birds.

These *things* are blue. Small—they don't even reach my knees. And though they look like a waterfall gushing over a cliff, they disperse into individual beings. Beings that have oversized fangs reaching past their fat lips, curling almost under their chins and jutting up to their eyes, which are yellow and cat-like beneath sagging, hairless brows. Their bodies are a deep, inky blue from head to . . . talon? The leathery folds of their skin almost look black against the lighter blue of their protruding bellies.

It takes me so long to even realize what's happening that Eshe has to scream, "Fight!" before my limbs begin moving. And then there's one right in front of me, snarling and wielding something like a tiny sledgehammer. He brings it down hard, apparently intent on smashing my toes. I leap out of the way, almost blinded by the dazzle of blue swinging from the chandelier above us, almost deafened by the screeching of dozens upon dozens—hundreds?—of these *creatures*.

"Goblins!" someone cries.

Goblins don't exist. And yet one just launched itself straight at my face.

My knife is up in a second, so sharp that I barely feel resistance as the creature embeds itself on my blade. His shriek dies into nothing, and inky blackness spills over my hand, my arm, my garments.

My vision starts to go black. I see the flicker of firelight, feel the tatters of a patched blanket beneath bare feet tucked beneath my hips. In my hand is a pumice stone, and I'm dragging my knife across it—

"Stay with me," says Eshe sharply, grabbing my arm and dragging me backward toward the wall.

Right to where the shadows lurk, watching.

Watching—and doing *nothing!*

Screams are hitting the ceiling, inky blood mingling with red blood on a glittering floor, the shadows and sparkles flaring from the swinging chandelier. Hot droplets of candle wax fly, hitting the skin of my bloodstained wrist. The sultan moves aside, enough for Eshe and I to press against the wall—and then for Hulla to squeeze in too. Neither of them see him. They don't know he's right beside them as Eshe turns to me.

"Think of something," she gasps, and I see, for possibly the first time ever, something akin to panic in her eyes. "Or we will all die."

"I can't think like this!"

I can't *exist* like this. I'm helpless, my knives no weapons for the kind of mass killing that needs to happen here—with more bodies pouring over the edge of the window, falling onto their bellies, and then leaping into the fray with snapping jaws and shrieking calls.

"You *have* to," says Eshe.

Then she lets go of my arm and hurls herself back into the tumult with nothing but a single knife. She has never kept as many weapons on her person as I. She hadn't needed to—she is a thief, not an assassin. Not a killer.

But here she is, killing. And here I am, a killer, unable to move.

Hulla seems suddenly torn between staying with me and following Eshe. Her blade shakes uncontrollably, but she plunges after my friend, hacking as she goes.

Invisible eyes weigh on me, measuring each of my shallow, frantic breaths. I can't think as two more blue bodies launch themselves at me, and all I can do is let my knives fly, cling to my instinctive reaction to protect my own life.

What about the lives of the other young women in this room? What about the screams of the ones hiding in the corners mingling with the ones boldly confronting our enemies? The tall one I'd stood near wields two long scimitars, slicing and dicing blue limbs from blue bodies, letting black spatter the hood over her face. Someone shouts at her for aid—calling her Fathuna.

A pained cry goes up. My head swivels by instinct, and I instantly regret it. Red blood gushes from an open wound, a girl falling to her knees, and my vision clouds yet again.

No, no, no—I need to think. I can't disassociate now. I must fight the goblins attacking me behind and before, sledgehammers bashing. I must think of a way to get this all to stop.

I turn away from the wounded girl, but out of the corner of my eye, I see Eshe leaping over bodies and nearly slipping in blood to get to her side. I try to survey the room even as I'm fighting, spinning and thrusting and dodging in a dance I've known all my life. I try to let my muscles take over, to give my brain the space to *think*, to plan. But all I can think is: *Don't die! Don't die! Don't die!*

Until one other thought cuts through the cacophony around me.

What kind of sultan stands to the side and watches women fight for their lives, never stepping in to lend a hand? What kind of sultan demands a bloody competition of his potential brides?

Clearly an absolutely wretched one.

Suddenly it's my anger fueling my strikes, it's anger behind the knife I throw to the complete opposite end of the hall, stabbing a goblin straight through his heart just before he pounds Eshe's leg as she bends over the fallen girl.

It's anger that makes me turn to the window. To the thing that must be some sort of portal. We'll never win this battle unless we close it, unless the barrage of blue bodies stops long enough to kill the rest.

I don't know magic. I don't know how to close a portal. But I bet my life someone in this room does.

My unsteady feet stumble over blue bodies, my hands stained almost black, and I fight my way to where my sultan lurks in the shadows. It's the one corner that is not sprayed with goblin blood.

"How do I close it?" I demand, unable to stop fighting long enough to glance his way. "Tell me now!"

There's a pause that could only be for a split second, but it feels like an eternity. I kill three goblins in the span it takes for his deep voice to rumble, "Blood."

A goblin leaps—impossibly high for one so small, and catches me around the neck. My balance is thrown as he swings onto my back, sharp nails digging into my throat. He shrieks in my ear, a noise that sounds alarmingly like the cry one makes when throwing all their strength into a blow.

He's going to bash my brains out.

I tuck my chin into my chest and hurl myself into a somersault, landing on claws and talons, and my shoulder hits a hammer. I bite back my cry of pain and stab backward, and it's the sudden *"Yeep!"* that tells me I've hit my mark. I can't even distinguish the flow of blood anymore.

I stand in a literal blood bath. One that covers the floor so thoroughly that not an inch of polished gold is visible. I fight my way toward that portal, every step the effort of a hundred horses against the torrent of blades and fangs and blue.

Eshe is suddenly beside me, her face smeared with black. I've never seen her look so serious in my entire life. Neither have I seen her boundless energy reducing so quickly, her single knife striking much too slowly.

"Blood!" I call to her. "We need to close the portal with blood!"

One of the other girls is only a few steps away. She's much shorter than I, wearing a set of robes that, beneath the blood, were once fine. She turns her head, hearing me. Then she begins shouting, the strength of her voice belying her small frame and hunched shoulders.

"Close the portal with blood!"

Then we're racing toward the sides of the portal, unable to approach the front because of the incessant stream of bodies. I realize belatedly that I didn't ask *how* to close the portal with blood, whether there was some sort of *something* we had to do. But we are too far away from the sultan now.

Eshe bends down, scoops up a handful of liquid and splashes it straight onto the white and sapphire glittering edges of the portal. It shudders in response. A surprised goblin cry goes up.

More of the young women fight toward us, scooping and tossing blood onto the portal. It shakes and shudders, and I know I need to bend down and help. Submerge my hands. I need to do it.

I *can* do it. I can. I will. I start to reach down. Everything inside me revolts.

But then more goblins launch themselves at me, at Eshe, at the others coming to help. I don't stay my blades. They need someone to watch their backs—they don't need more cupped palms. They need me to keep them alive long enough to shut down the portal.

So I fight. And I tell myself that I'm not a coward for fighting.

The cacophony only gets louder and louder, a sharp sizzling cutting through their cries. I barely am in time to look up as the entire portal shudders, and then snaps shut like an enormous eyelid. It slices straight through the goblins.

It's the work of a minute for the twelve of us to dispatch the rest—no, eleven. There's only eleven of us. I spin, casting about in the sapphire ruins below a broken, glittering chandelier, but I see no sign of the fallen girl. Is she . . . buried?

I press a hand to my stomach, then bend over and dry heave. My entire body is shaking, shaking so hard I can barely stand. I don't even want to look at the other young women, the ones I have saved, who have saved me. My reflection stares back at me in black.

It was only then that I realize the sultan is gone too.

I'm drenched. From head to toe. My hands are covered, my blades dripping.

Dark spots erupt across my vision. I barely hear a familiar voice call out, "Nadira!" and I have just one moment to ensure that Hulla's shaking form is still standing before I stumble, fall—into darkness.

CHAPTER 8

I'M WET. NOT just in wet clothes, but completely submerged, my chin barely above the water. I thrash, my limbs hitting something solid. Trapped—I'm trapped.

I'm drowning.

"Quit with the flailing and gasping. You're being dramatic enough to put me to shame."

My eyes fly open. I'm—not drowning. I'm being gripped under the armpit by a strong hand, held submerged in liquid, and above me arcs a glass ceiling and a clear blue sky.

I start to look down.

Something catches my chin, tilts it so far backward that I'm staring up at the sky again. And a smirking face.

"Eshe!" I gasp.

"Don't look down," she says. "The water is a little . . . ahem, murky."

My eyes widen, my head instinctively fighting her hold to look.

"Now what did I just tell you? Quit being disobedient. You're welcome to scrub yourself though. I'd prefer to decline that responsibility if it's all the same to you."

"How do I scrub myself without looking?" I ask dully.

She arches her brow. "Make a plan, if you must."

Then she thrusts a fat, slippery bar of soap that smells like lemon and jasmine into my hands, along with a brush, and lets go of me. I find my limbs are willing to move again, and I settle my toes on what feels like mosaic tiling. It's hard to see without looking down at the water, but I can tell enough from where I'm hugging the ledge to know that I'm in a gigantic, recessed bathtub of sorts. A pool. One large enough to bathe an entire army of women.

My thoughts stutter.

"What happened?" I demand, working quickly to bathe, reassuring myself with every breath that I'm *not* standing in blood. Water. *Water.* "What—"

Eshe tugs on a lovely midnight-blue sirwal and matching tunic that I've never seen before, her long wet hair falling over her shoulders and dripping onto the floor. She gets that look on her face, a wry look that means something dryly sarcastic is about to pass her lips.

"Well, we were kidnapped, brought to the palace of the Neverseen King, told we were his prospective brides, and then chaos ensued and we fought an army of tiny vicious blue things. And we closed what seemed to be a portal to another world. Oh, and you passed out."

"What happened to that girl? The one who died?"

"She's gone."

"Oh," I say, a rock sinking into my gut.

"No, not *that* gone—that is, I don't know if she's dead. I was trying to help her, but I had to keep fighting, and when I turned my back for more than a few seconds, she was gone. Just . . . vanished. I didn't see her among the other women who bathed. No one knows what happened to her."

I shiver, blinking rapidly as I lather my arms, scrubbing beneath my fingernails. I'm just about to open my mouth to ask a question when Eshe interrupts me, straightening to her full height and lacing up the gold-threaded ties of her tunic.

"So. How does it feel to be a prospective bride? Quite thrilling, isn't it? One of twelve, chosen out of all Arbasa."

"I love thrills," I say.

Eshe laughs. I marvel at how unshakeable she is. But then I remember the look I'd seen on her face in the Golden Hall. No matter how collected her composure, she can break just like me.

"We need to get out of here," I say, lowering my voice to a whisper.

"And lose the opportunity to earn a bridegroom? I don't think so."

"Be serious."

She snorts softly, rolling her eyes and crossing her arms over her chest. She stares down at me, at the soap that keeps slipping out of my grasp. "Why do they want us to keep from leaving our rooms after dark?"

I'm glad she caught the ominous tone of that command too. "Probably because they don't want us escaping."

A grin splits her face. "Want to test it?"

"Not until we're certain it's safe. Clearly this palace houses more mysteries than I originally thought. If that truly was a portal that opened to another world in the hall today, then we need to be careful."

The understatement of the century.

Strange how not even a full day ago, I was going over my plans to assassinate a city lord, and now I'm talking about portals and other worlds. Stranger still how normal the words feel on my tongue.

"I don't think I can wait three months for you to develop a perfect escape plan. By then, we'll be skewered or married!"

She's right. I bite my lip. Hard. "I suppose we have no choice but to start scouting. Immediately. You'll have to help me, because I can't scout this whole palace *and* make a plan before we're dead or married."

"Of course!" she chirps. "It'll be like old times!"

"Old times . . . as in, yesterday?"

"Yesterday is old!"

I hoist myself up out of the pool, take the towel Eshe throws straight at my face, and dry myself. I didn't know how tense I'd gotten until my limbs nearly melt with relief as every last drop is wiped from my skin. I could fall to the ground right here and sleep for days.

I didn't die. Eshe didn't die.

A bundle of cloth hits me in the face yet again. I catch it and shoot my friend a glare before looking down at what she's given me. It's an ankle-length qamis and sash, complete with delicate-but-functional sandals. Now that I am less panicked than I was when I first dressed this morning, I can notice that they're vastly finer than anything I've ever worn before. Interestingly, these garments are notably more conservative in both cut and color than Eshe's. It's almost like whoever set them out for us knows Eshe prefers a little flash of drama, and I am drawn more to function and practicality over beauty. Yet even the gentle brown of my garments is its own sort of elegant, glossy with gold-threaded embroidery. Subtle, but tasteful.

"The sultan wants us competing in style, apparently," she says. "Speaking of which, we're to have another competition tomorrow. You might want to think of a plan for that. Until then—farewell! I'm off to scout!"

She doesn't give me a chance to call after her. Doesn't give me a chance to display the weakness and panic suddenly bubbling up inside my chest at the thought of being alone in this strange place. The door shuts behind her, thudding softly and encasing me in silence.

I dress quickly, but no amount of movement can ease the shuddering of my lungs. I'm breathing too fast—I need to calm down. I'm a stars-cursed assassin, for the sultan's sake! I strap on my knives, noting Eshe must have cleaned them.

But the mental coaxing that used to work on my stubborn body doesn't seem to work anymore. I'm not at home in my horrid cell-room.

I'm not on a job, or planning for one, studying floor plans and guard patterns for hours on end.

I'm in a bathing chamber after slaughtering strange creatures in a bid for the hand of a sultan I've never seen. No, nothing that has helped me control the simmering fear beneath my self-restraint in the past is helping now. Nothing is familiar.

Nothing is safe.

Nothing, except Eshe, and she just left me.

Something bumps my foot. I leap aside, a gasp clogging in my throat as my heart nearly flies straight through the glass ceiling above me.

There, on the polished and painted tile floor, is a vine.

It's sapling green with little leaves bursting from its sides, mingled with buds that have just the faintest sweep of yellow peeking out. It is poking out from behind the dressing screen, which is situated near a paneled wall and a shuttered window.

It definitely wasn't there before.

I stare at it, and it's as frozen as I am. Did I bump it? Maybe it *was* there, and I just was too caught up in trying to calm my pounding heart that I didn't notice I had moved toward it.

I'm sure it wasn't there.

My senses go on high alert, my breathing calming by habit. I almost start counting. I stare down the plant. And then—it twitches.

"Ah ha!" I cry, whipping out a knife and brandishing it at the vine.

A high-pitched *squee* erupts from the vine as it rears back, lifting its curling tail like the head of a snake. I take an aggressive step toward it, shoving my blade in its . . . face? The vine reacts, coiling back in on itself. But it doesn't back down completely.

"Are you magic?" I demand. "Are you poisonous?"

The vine tilts its curled end to one side, leaves shaking . . . irritably?

I try not to let my voice color with sarcasm too much. "Am I offending your vine-ness?"

The vine does something that, on a human, I would have taken to be a huff. It rises a little higher, then sags, as though exhaling.

I frown.

The vine drops to the ground. I startle, brandishing my knife lower. It doesn't respond, though, only twists like it's rolling over, rustles its leaves, and to my shock, bursts open its buds into yellow flowers the size of my hand, with a soft pink center and pistils of dark magenta. The sound it makes is rather like a burble, though quiet and high-pitched. I raise my brow.

"Seems fair to assume, after this morning, that you are magic," I say slowly, and startle at the growling of my belly. No wonder I feel so weak. That's another problem I have to solve. I clap a hand on my stomach, not missing how the vine's curl seems to twist toward it. As if it heard the sound. "If you're magic, then I can't trust you."

It whines so sharply I wince and almost cover my ears.

"Can you blame me?" I ask. "You could choke me when I turn around. Who knows what other kinds of devious tricks you could play upon me? So don't mope like I've deeply wounded you."

The blossoms fold back into buds, leaves rustling loudly. Then, faster than I can react—which is very, very fast—the vine darts out. My hand is moving with the knife, ready to slice.

But the vine merely bumps into my leg. Then again. Like the cats in the city who rub on Eshe.

I stumble back a step, flash my blade, and growl, "No. Don't do that. Stay away from me."

The answer I receive is the vine drawing back, lifting its curl up almost to eye level, and then letting out a soft keening. It's like the magic plant is guilting me for being skeptical that it isn't another of my sultan's gruesome competitions.

"None of that," I say sharply. "Now you listen to me. I'm going to leave, and if you try anything when my back is turned, I'm going to slice you to bits. Understand?"

Its leaves shrivel slightly, twisting inward, but its curl nods. *Nods.*

I can't help either the shiver of premonition along my spine, nor the gut-twisting sensation of guilt in the pit of my stomach. The vine seems harmless enough. But it can move quickly, and I dare not trust anything in this palace.

Slowly, step by step, I begin to back out of the bathing chamber, holding my knife in front of me. I keep my attention locked on that sapling green, *daring* it to test me. To prove that I'm right, and it can't be trusted.

It doesn't move. Not even when I turn my back and slip out the door.

I can't deny my relief. Nor the thickening of guilt that I'd been too harsh when it hasn't tried to hurt me. But I'd be a fool to let my guard down here. Whatever sentience the vine might have, surely it can understand that.

I blink, wondering how I ended up threatening a vine and then being worried about its feelings. This is ridiculous. I need to get out of here.

The doors close behind me, and I find myself standing in a long corridor. Despite the fact that it must be high noon, judging by the sun, and that there are at least ten other young women somewhere around the palace and servants enough to maintain this place, there's not a sound.

It's silent as death.

CHAPTER 9

SOMETHING ABOUT THESE hallways seems endless. I have the sense that, no matter how long I walk in a single direction, I'll never arrive at a wall. It's just hallway and more hallway and more hallway. My toes tingle the further I walk.

I curse my stupid knack for falling unconscious at the most inopportune times. If I'd been awake, I'd know exactly where this chamber is in relation to my room and the Golden Hall. As it stands, I'm utterly clueless.

But I won't panic.

No, I'm scouting. Everything that is to be familiar must first be unfamiliar, and I must learn to operate without detailed floor plans. I will make my own detailed layouts, just like I've often done before. The next time I stumble across a servant, I will ask them for parchment and writing supplies. Unless that is too risky? Will they report me to the sultan? Will he have me killed?

I set my jaw and force my steps into a regular rhythm. The tap of my heels on stone makes me look down and realize this hallway is different from the one my room was in. There's no rug here. I'm not sure if I'm alarmed or somehow placated, knowing these hallways *do* indeed have an ending point.

From my view outside my window this morning, it didn't look like the palace had no bounds. I find a small servant staircase and hurry down to ground level.

Either the architecture is very clever, or magic is involved. I suspect both.

Most of the doors I walk past are closed, normal doors, rather like the one of my own room. But the further I walk, the more frequently I come across strange doors. One has heavy chains strung from frame to frame, as though a single lock isn't enough to keep people out.

Or *in*.

I shiver and move on. The next door looks normal at first glance, until I come close enough to see writing carved into the door itself. Heart thumping in my ears, I step closer, my hand reaching out of its own accord to brush an unfamiliar character. It's not a language I know.

The characters pulse with light in response to my touch.

I yank my hand away with a gasp. The light fades, and the characters seem to sink deeper into the wood than before.

I don't like this place, I almost murmur to myself. But I must be careful what I say in a magical palace. This silence is too quiet, and I have the notion that if I utter the softest word, it will ring against stone all the way up to the crystal sky above me.

Where are the other women? Surely I'm not the only one scouting this place. I couldn't study each of them as carefully as I had wanted to, but only one had been overwhelmed by the goblins. The rest had stood their ground. Even Hulla fought well.

My competitors are worthy. I hope one of them wins and distracts the sultan long enough for me to make my escape.

The door ahead is wide open.

My steps slow as I approach, the outward swinging door blocking any glimpse I have of the room within. Silently, I draw one of the knives at my belt, holding its hilt close to my chest, ready to stab in an instant.

A sound whispers out of that door. It's the first noise I've heard since I left the bathing chamber. It's like a sigh, of wind or paper. A gentle rustling, one that sends my senses prickling and my focus sharpening.

I reach the door, and with a quick glance behind me to ensure no one is trailing my back, I inhale silently. Then I lean around the door and peer into the room.

There's no glass ceiling here.

Books.

It's a large room. One with a domed ceiling that narrows into a small opening at the center, through which pours a meager amount of sunlight for the thousands of books that are piled inside the room. I can't catch my breath as my eyes trail from the mountain of open books on the floor, a draft fluttering pages softly, up the walls lined with stuffed shelves, to the makeshift staircase of books leading up to a massive tome in the center. It's bigger than me without question, and I imagine it would take my entire body to turn those heavy pages.

I'm being watched.

I turn, fingers flexing along the hilt of my knife as I step out of the doorway. I don't touch the door as I move away from the room, disconcerted to have my back to it. All is normal and bright in the hallway, but I *know* this feeling. I know who is here.

"You need not hide, Sultani," I say.

My voice rings in the stillness. Slowly, every last dreg of sound ebbs away into nothing, and silence permeates again. It's so long that, if I doubted my intuition, I'd think that I was alone.

I'm not sure where he is, only that he's here. My eyes can't quite land on a shadow deep enough to hide my mysterious sovereign.

"I am the Neverseen King," a low voice responds from . . . somewhere.

My breath hitches, and even though my eyes dart all around the hallway, I am still as clueless as before about where he is.

If I don't know where he is, he can kill me.

No, I won't think like that. Those thoughts only land me in darkness. I must think clearly. Mustn't make myself more vulnerable than I already am.

"Do not call me Sultan," he says, and his voice is like wind. Everywhere. Nowhere. "It is too . . ."

I wait.

He says nothing more.

A thousand accusations, and even more questions, flood my mind at once. I should have planned what to ask if I happened upon him! I should have thought through this. But of all the things swirling in my mind, there's one question that leaps to my lips, and I'm speaking before I realize.

"I thought you vanished during the day."

There's a snort. "Do you *see* me, little assassin?"

Little assassin. How condescending! "I can hear you," I say. "Typically, when one vanishes, their voice vanishes too."

There's an amused sort of silence that follows. Then, quite suddenly, I'm warm. My mind flashes back to last night, in the dark, when I felt the solid closeness of my sultan—ahem, *Neverseen King.* When he placed his large hand over my face and closed my eyes.

My heart quickens, my teeth clenching. I'm not surprised when his voice is suddenly very, very near my ear. But every inch of muscle in my body is strained with tension. With the need to flee, the will to stay.

"*Typical,* what a wretched word! I am not *typical,* now am I? And neither are you, Nadira al-Risya."

My name on his lips, whispered so near, sends a shiver down my spine. I swallow, trying not to gasp. Trying not to betray myself.

"Why am I here?" I ask.

A chuckle sounds in the air, growing quieter as it shifts away from me. His warmth retreats. So my sultan becomes invisible during the day. No wonder our market trade is crumbling to pieces. If a king can't manage to stay corporeal long enough to rule, then I suppose one can't blame the economy for suffering.

The legends are true, I realize. The rumors of my Neverseen King. They aren't a ruse. Aren't just fear tactics. And if they aren't just legends, then what else isn't a legend? What other secrets does our sultan hide?

"You are here because I want you here," he says.

"That's not an answer."

"Isn't it?" There's that wry amusement again.

I think he's coming closer again. Can I stab him if he's invisible? Might be worth a shot. Except that if I miss, I'll have shown him my hand. I cannot risk it just yet.

"You are here, Mourner, because I find myself in want of a bride."

"Then why are there eleven"—I stop myself, swallow thickly—"*ten* other women here?"

I can feel his grin. It shimmers in the air, unseen, but no less real.

"Can a king not have his selection from which to choose?"

"Can a woman be courted by a sultan and not fear for her life?"

It seems like a reasonable question to me. But he doesn't answer. There's a long silence. Then, very softly, his voice reaches out to me across the empty space. Tugs at my heart like there's a string fastened to it.

"Do you fear death, little assassin?"

My eyes shutter closed. I draw a deep breath in through my nose, my chest expanding. Then, slowly, I release it through parted lips. I open my eyes.

He stands before me.

I can only make out the edges of his form, barely visible in the sunlight. He's nothing but an impression. But one that I can catch the slightest glimpse of—one that *he* has chosen to reveal to me.

He's tall. Much taller than any man I've ever seen, and though I am tall myself, I am dwarfed by this glimmering perception of him.

Something inside me lurches. I tell myself it's fear, and it certainly might be. But if I'm honest . . . it's not *only* fear. What else, I'm not certain of.

"We all must die," says the Neverseen King. "It is better to make peace with it before it happens."

Something bursts like a laugh from my mouth. I smile, and it's as cold as the sun above is warm. "Have you made peace with death, my sul—Neverseen King?"

A dark chuckle. "I certainly should have, now shouldn't I? Bringing vipers into my House. Do you intend to bite me, little assassin? Strike when I'm least expecting it?" His wry laughter is mocking, and I remember what it was like to stab at him and have my blades kiss air.

"Who changed me into that nightgown?" I blurt.

"My servants, of course. Do you think I have time to attend to such tedious tasks as dressing all my potential brides for sleep?"

"You had time to kidnap us all."

There's that rumbling chuckle again. Apparently my modesty and I are vastly amusing. But I know enough about fighting to know that one never wins only on the defensive. I lift my chin, high enough to where my eyes pierce where his must be.

"Are you cursed?" I ask.

The silence is abrupt. Startled. The shadowy outline of his form vanishes, and now it truly is fear and only fear that rushes through my veins. Have I stepped too far? Crossed some boundary? Will he strike me dead?

My chest is too tight to breathe. I hate my weakness. I hate myself.

Finally—a dry snort. "You think I'm cursed because I'm invisible? Do you truly think this is against my will? I shall try not to take your lack of confidence in my power to be offensive. But sometimes, I simply cannot *help* but be offended!"

"I mean no offense," I say woodenly.

My tone only makes him laugh more. "Aye, aye, you don't!" There's another snort, and then a contemplative silence.

Warmth again. I bite my lip and stiffen.

"It's a good thing I don't have a heart," he murmurs, "because if I did, I have a suspicion that you would break it."

Then, he's gone. His voice, his warmth, his wry chuckles—it's like he was never there at all. I gasp in a deep breath, barely keeping a hold on my knife so it doesn't clatter to the ground and dull its tip. I spare a backwards glance at the strange room with the open door. Except it's not open anymore; it's fastened shut, with paper stuffed into the keyhole.

CHAPTER 10

THE FULL FORCE of my idiocy hits me in the face as I make myself continue down the hallway. I could have asked him dozens upon dozens of useful questions, but instead I wasted my chance, and now he's gone.

What I *really* want to do is find my room, curl up in a ball, and freak out for a solid hour or two—and eat.

But that won't get me out of here, and it won't answer my questions—the questions I failed to ask my sultan while he was with me. Why didn't I ask why he hadn't helped that girl who'd fallen in the Golden Hall? Was she dead? Why had she disappeared? Why didn't he kidnap a foreign princess for his bride, or why doesn't he just make a harem out of us twelve instead of making us compete? I could have demanded to know why he needs a bride who can survive an avalanche of blue goblins. I could have asked about this palace, that impertinent vine in the bathing chamber, his invisibility, the portal, the strange book room.

The instructions to never leave our rooms after dark. The mysterious silence that seems to reign heavier than my sultan over these walls.

My heart won't stop pounding, and I refuse to look at the doors I'm passing. For a split second, I wonder if perhaps I *don't* want to know the answers to my questions.

I haven't sheathed my knife. I'm not sure I ever will again. It remains clutched tightly in my fist as I march down the hallways, wishing I dared to break into a run. But that would feel too much like fleeing at a time when I'm supposed to be the hunter, the one uncovering the mysteries and scouting the layout of the palace.

What did his last comment mean? Was it a terrible attempt at wooing? I don't think he'd stoop to wooing when his inclination thus far seems to be brute force.

Suddenly, there's a break in the hallway of doors. I swallow back a strangled choke of relief to find myself approaching a sprawling polished oak banister to my left, one that matches its twin on the far side of a massive staircase that curves outward when it hits the ground. My gaze drags up those stairs, dizzy at their number, until it twists, and I realize I'm staring up at a spiral staircase. The underside of them blocks their destination from my view. Should I climb it?

My spine shivers in response. It takes far more strength than it should for me to reach out my hand toward the carved, smoothed edge of that banister.

It's warm.

Because of the sunlight, of course. Everything is warm. Why should I expect it to be cool to the touch? Gritting my teeth, I take a step closer, sliding my fingers up the railing.

The banister shudders.

That's the only way I can describe it. It's almost imperceptible, more of a mental notion than a physical experience, but I just can't help but *know* this piece of wood just responded to my touch.

I swallow hard and nearly yank my hand away. Instead, though anxiety shoots through my veins like fire, telling me to *not* touch,

I slip my finger just under the lip of the banister and trail it upward a few inches.

Wood creaks in a groan, and not just the wood beneath my hand, but all around me. This time, I can't keep my hand still. I draw it back, heart pounding, but my fingers stay poised in the air between my chest and the banister. My grip on my knife in the other hand grows slicker.

Then, to my utter shock, the banister *moves*. Defies the stiff, unforgiving wood of its make, and bends with a creak into my hand. Warm wood presses against my skin, nudging me with that lip.

Spots flare in my vision. Oh stars above, why must I be a fainter? Why can't I be literally anything else—a crier, a screamer, a yeller? This is so inconducive to what I need to accomplish!

I draw in a deep breath, fighting the urge to jerk away from the fixture that is currently doing something uncannily like a nuzzle against the back of my hand. I must be practical, reasonable about this. Must stop being surprised when things are magical.

This is normal, I tell myself. Wood that appears to like being pet. Completely rational. Something resembling a laugh catches on a sob in my throat. Am I getting hysterical? Losing my mind? Maybe this is just some wretched dream that I've conjured up after my job last night.

Carefully, I take my knuckle and rub it along the lip of the banister. Wood groans in response, and then I'm quite literally scratching it. Fingernails and all. The wood is too smooth to splinter into my nail beds, yet with the way the staircase creaks, apparently it feels very, very good.

I'm laughing before I know it, tears dribbling out of the corners of my eyes as I put both hands to work, finding the best spots that elicit the loudest creaks and groans. It's like when Eshe would scratch under the chin of a tomcat, its eyes closing in rapturous delight, and I realize half-hysterically that I'm making a pet out of a staircase.

When I finally pull away, there's an audible popping sound. The leaning of the banister toward me tells me I wasn't wrong in suspecting that popping was a disapproving whine of sorts.

"I can't pet you all day," I say sternly. And nearly choke on another bubble of laughter. "But I'm sure I'll be back later."

The railing sinks a bare half-inch.

"None of that sulking! A body can only handle so much guilting, all right? Be glad I petted you instead of being sad it must end. Now straighten up and behave yourself or I won't come back."

It straightens to its full height immediately. I let out a sigh, stare at it stupidly, and then reach out and give one last pat. A draft blows in my face, coming from the upper windings of the staircase. Like it's sighing in response.

I turn my back on the banister, trying to shove away the feeling that I've let it down somehow, and face where the staircase opened into. My lips part in surprise.

A pair of wide, arch-like doors open into the glittering sunshine, straight into the flagstone courtyard I'd seen from my window. Blinding rays gleam on the water gurgling out of the marble fountain, lush trees and shrubbery framing behind the perimeter of long stone benches.

I cannot help the ache in my heart at the flash of beauty, the suddenness of my relief. My mental floor plan earns a few more notations, and my knees go wobbly. I'm not lost.

I'm not alone, either.

Perched on the edge of the fountain in robes of soft pink, a gold-edged veil covering her hair and spilling down her back, with golden bangles lining her wrists and her feet shod in woven sandals, is one of the young women from the Golden Hall. She trails her fingers in the water of the fountain, leaning over the edge and smiling serenely into what might be a reflection of her face, or the little shreds of clouds gathering in the otherwise clear sky.

I never would have guessed she was fighting goblins a mere few hours ago. She's lovely, even from this distance, and there's an elegant refinement to her movement, testifying to her high birth and education.

She seems every inch the bride-to-be of a sultan. The beautiful trophy for a powerful ruler. I swallow, fidget slightly, and can't help my self-conscious glance down at my much more practical and dark robes. I'd never wear such a light color as the rosebud pink she wears—bloodstains wouldn't come out.

Why do I feel suddenly so out of place? I've felt out of place since the moment I woke up this morning, but this is a different feeling. That was a sense of waking up in a whole new, strange world that I didn't understand. This is the sense of being in a world I *do* understand, but definitely don't belong in.

A slave in the presence of a lady.

I have the startling and painful urge to bow. But I don't.

The girl looks up, seems to startle when she sees me. She lifts a dripping finger from the fountain and smiles sweetly, one hand reaching up to draw the bejeweled edge of her veil out of her face.

"Who are you, lurking in the shadows there? Come! It's so dull here by myself," she calls in a voice as sweet as her appearance.

My gut twists. I regret not petting the banister longer. Seeing no other choice besides acting suspicious or joining her, I make my limbs work, slip my knife into my sheath, and step between the doors. It's immediately hotter, the fountain louder, and the green of the shrubbery brighter. I try to betray as little about myself as possible as I approach the pink girl and sit on the bench closest to where she rests on the lip of the fountain's basin.

She smiles. I realize she asked me a question. For a split second, I consider giving her a false name. If Eshe weren't here and doubtlessly bound to let my real name slip, I would have done it.

But Eshe is here, so disaster must be expected.

"I am Nadira," I say with a small returning smile of my own. "And you?"

"Dabria. Dabria bint-Abaas."

Bint-Abaas. I barely manage to control my flinch. A lord's daughter indeed, of a man whose eldest brother I assassinated but two years ago. This courtyard is suddenly much, much too bright and hot.

"A pleasure to make your acquaintance," I say, glad the fat whale of my tongue decides to cooperate.

"Likewise! I was beginning to give up hope of ever seeing another human face in all the long stretch of today. What a fortunate thing to find you."

Not fortunate. Terribly unfortunate.

She shifts her gaze back to the fountain, and I take the opportunity to study her hand as she swirls it in the water. I believe those are calluses. A hand that has held weapons. I wish I'd had more time to study all the contestants earlier today before the first competition. I didn't have the mental capacity to watch how the other young women fought, and now I very much wish I had.

"What do you make of this place?" she asks me, lifting her head toward the palm trees surrounding us, then the stone archway I've just come through, the windows looking out at us.

I turn a few different responses over in my head, wrestling with how much to reveal of my own thoughts and scouting, and how much I dare dodge her question. "There appears to be magic," I say at last.

She chuckles. "My baba always said our kingdom was special because we were ruled by a sultan of legend, one that sowed our soil with magic and breathed it upon our sea. He told me this when I was a child, and I believe it was something his father told him, and his father before that." She turns toward me now, a slow smile playing on her dainty features. "Do you think the sultan my great-grandfather spoke of might still rule today?"

A muscle tics sharply in my jaw. I meet her gaze as unease stabs through my lungs. Both from her words, and the way she speaks them. As though we are sitting beneath a brightly colored pavilion drinking qahwa, sipping its bitter blackness until our insides are as hot as our skin beneath the sun. As though we are discussing our sisters' arrangements for marriage, or a particularly insistent seller in the stalls of a bazaar.

"I do not know," is all I say. Do I want to know? I'm beginning to doubt that.

"Who do you think the Neverseen King will call for a private supper tonight?"

Her question sends a jolt of surprise through me, and I'm beginning to get the suspicion that she's doing it on purpose. Trying to get a reaction out of me. It makes me even more uncomfortable than I already am.

I feel dull and stupid saying yet again, "I do not know." But how could I? She doesn't know either. I suppose we shall find out at some point this afternoon or evening. Another bout of apprehension rolls through me. What if it's me? What if the Neverseen King beckons me to join him? What if I haven't prepared my questions?

I need to leave this conversation.

Yet something inside me shifts, and something like a flash of boldness rushes through my blood, making me lean forward just a hair and ask carefully, "Do you want it to be you?"

Dabria laughs. A light tinkling, pretty sort of laugh. Her eyes spark when they meet mine, glittering almost as brightly as the gold she wears. "I would love to have the honor of dining with my king."

"Even if he must remain unseen?"

Her smile widens, and she tosses the edge of her veil over her shoulder. "Why, that only adds to the mystery, Nadira. Haven't you thought of what it would be like to be the one person in all Arbasa to discover the face of our Neverseen King?"

My heart responds before I do, skipping over itself. "Perhaps he hides his face because he is ugly."

She chuckles. It's a sound I'm growing more and more uncomfortable with. "I take it that *you* should prefer not to dine with him tonight?"

Do I? Something warm stirs in my gut. Perhaps I *am* curious. Or rather, it would give me an opportunity to ask more questions and get the answers I need to escape. But the sun is beginning to decline overhead, and the emptiness of my stomach combined with the heat isn't helping me think clearly. What if he poisons the woman he brings to dinner tonight? What if I'm unprepared? What if I'm too hungry to think straight?

"I'd rather not be the first," I say honestly. Probably too honestly. I need to learn conversation skills—that's Eshe's strength, not mine. As it happens, one doesn't need to talk much when they're slicing open a jugular.

She laughs again, and I fail to understand why she keeps laughing. We're prisoners here. We were almost overwhelmed by hundreds of tiny blue monsters with strange hammers and the ability to jump unusually high. Dabria gives no sign of being bothered by any of this, and it makes me wonder what sort of father she was raised by. What sort of man would dress his daughter in silks and put a blade in her hand?

I wonder if she loved the uncle I killed. I wonder why someone wanted him dead.

The thought makes me blink rapidly. I ought to move to the shade. Instead, I cross my arm over my torso, trying to subtly put pressure on my hollow stomach. Sands, I need food. I'll starve before I find an escape.

Dabria flicks her wrist and lets water droplets fly. She twists toward me, revealing that her clothes have been designed to leave a few inches of toned abdomen exposed. The thought of wearing such vulnerable clothing nearly makes me dizzy again.

"Tell me about yourself," she says.

I blanch. Talk? About myself? To her? What—what in all the forbidden deserts am I supposed to tell her about me? *"Well, I've been a slave ever since my parents were killed in front of me, my slaver raised me to be an assassin, and now I go around killing people like your uncle."*

I lick my lips, avoid the urge to bite them, and manage what I hope is a convincing shrug. "I am but a commoner."

"A commoner who wields a blade? A commoner whom the Neverseen King is considering for his bride?" She gives me a knowing smile, as if we're sharing a private joke, as if she's urging me that we're friends and I can tell her anything. "What did you say your surname was?"

I didn't. "Al-Risya," I say. My stomach growls.

Dabria pretends she didn't hear the loud rumble, even though there is no way she didn't. "Hmm. Nadira Al-Risya. I cannot say I've heard your name in my family's circles, no."

I try to disguise my sigh of relief as an exhale. Then Jabir was correct—the identity of the Mourner is, indeed, unknown. When I glance at Dabria again, however, her fingers trailing in the water, I'm suddenly unsure.

I let out a deep breath and stand, offering the politest smile I can, and say, "A pleasure, Lady Dabria."

I again resist the urge to bow—after all, aren't we equals here? But my back prickles as I turn away from her and stride toward a different door than the one I exited, one that I hope will take me to my room.

If I don't melt or faint on the way there.

When I finally return to my room, there's a fresh tray resting on the table in the sitting chamber. It's made of silver, laden with polished utensils and bowls with intricately designed lids featuring a boar and hyena growling at each other. I step over hesitantly, clamping a hand down on my growling stomach as the smell of cardamon and roasted meat waft into my nostrils. My mouth waters so suddenly it's painful. I tighten my lips to keep from drooling.

Dare I partake?

There's a note. Crisp parchment lies folded on the tray, warm yellow against cool metal. Hesitantly, I reach out and pluck up the note.

"My lovely, darling, and very hungry Nadira," it begins. I blink, startled, and almost turn around for a sign that Eshe has been here, playing some fool joke on me. But no, it's not written in her hand. I skim the rest of the note quickly.

"Have no fear, I can assure your fragile nerves that the food is not poisoned. If I wanted you dead, Mourner, I'd have killed you already, as I imagine you've probably reasoned. Yet something tells me you're still skeptical, so I thought it necessary to assuage you of your fears before you starve yourself into uselessness. Besides, you should know that I'd never stoop to something as banal as poison. So for heaven's sake, eat."

It's signed with a flourish.

Your Neverseen King.

CHAPTER 11

I'M NOT SURE if I'm relieved or terrified when a servant comes announcing dinner. Desperate is probably a more apt description of what I feel—utter desperation for physical nourishment despite the meal I ate a few hours ago, and desperation knowing that I'm walking into yet another unknown.

The only way I can somewhat rationalize away my worry is by telling myself that I will be able to scout through more sections of the palace I haven't seen before. Hopefully Eshe will be there. I can face whatever danger a meal might present if Eshe is there.

The servant who escorts me is different from the poor one that I nearly strangled this morning. She makes no mention of whether I am to dine with the sultan tonight or not. She wears a bright smile across her face, walks with a bounce in her step, and doesn't even flinch when we pass a locked door spattered with what looks like blood.

Maybe this truly is a dream. How else can she be so at ease here?

Is *she* magic too?

If I don't stop the endless caravan of my thoughts, I'm going to sweat straight through my robes. Or I'll plant my foot, spin around, and march back to my room. As if it's some sort of haven—have I gone mad?

But I need to eat, so I cannot keep working myself up into a fluster.

"Where is dinner?" My voice rings in the stillness. I fight a cringe.

The servant turns a bright smile up at me. She's so short she barely reaches my chin. Though she walks at the side of an assassin who has an abundance of knives strapped to her, she doesn't seem at all uneasy. But then, what is a simple assassin girl compared to the Neverseen King?

"In the Emerald Hall," she chirps.

"Not in the Ruby Hall?" I deadpan before I can stop myself. Then I'm kicking myself for my idiotic sense of humor. Only Eshe would find it funny.

"The Ruby Hall is typically only used for receiving foreign dignitaries," the girl says without blinking. "So, no."

"Has the Neverseen King mentioned who he is to dine with tonight?"

She casts a smug look up at me. "*That* is to be revealed."

It still might be me. Still might be Eshe. I draw in a deep breath, then set my face forward, resisting the urge to glance to my left through the open windows and wafting crimson curtains out into the courtyard. The orange embers of a dying sun cast lengthening shadows around us. There will be little time between the completion of dinner and nightfall.

Do not leave your rooms after nightfall.

"Here we are!" says the servant girl, and beckons grandly to a pair of gold and emerald-studded doors. Guards in black grip the twisted gold handles with gauntlets, and at my approach they open the doors.

I am immediately overcome.

The hall is, to be short, aptly named. It glitters from the cut of a thousand—or more—emeralds, hanging from the chandelier, set into the smoothed and reflective paving stones, dangling like diamonds from the ceiling. The walls are painted the same rich, jewel-green, trimmed in ornate gold filigree. Three arches of gold-threaded emerald agate are recessed into the far wall, opposite the stretch of a long table with a deep, dark green tablecloth, chairs with backs of gold, and place settings of faceted crystal.

My first instinct is to gape, to tilt back my head and stare at the way the candlelight catches upon the refracting stones hung suspended above the guests seated below it. My second instinct is to run. I might have done just that if Eshe hadn't called out, "There you are!"

I drag my eyes down from the ceiling to the figure leaning, elbow on the elegant table, out to look at me, a roguish grin on her face. "I saved you a seat!" she says, ignoring the looks the other young women shoot her way.

Those looks—which *I* cannot ignore—are what keep me from smiling back at my friend. As my shoes pad softly across the polished floor, I scan across the women seated at the table. *Ten.* I am the eleventh. No one is missing besides the fallen girl from the Golden Hall.

My heart pounds even faster as I slide carefully into the chair beside Eshe, and opt to not place my arms on the engraved golden armrests. It feels grand enough to be a throne, and yet here I am, sitting in it.

Eshe, of course, sits smack in the middle of the women. Which means I'm now sitting in the middle of them as well, and the potency of their hawk-like gazes burns into me.

Sitting on my left is a narrow-boned, slightly hunched girl. Her hands are clasped tightly in her lap, as if she's unsure what to do with them. Her clothes are of fine make, but are shockingly simple in contrast to Dabria's lavender silks and silver edging across the table. I can only see her profile, but she seems lovely enough. A full mouth, with a sharp nose and long lashes that fan her cheek as she looks down.

"We were just getting to know each other," says Eshe brightly. "That is Safya next to you. Then Fathuna is across from us."

I look up from Safya to follow Eshe's gesture. I find myself meeting a pair of rather hostile eyes, set in a square-jawed face. This is the tall girl I noticed from the Golden Hall. *Fathuna.*

"And you are?" asks Fathuna coldly. Her narrowed eyes trail up and down what is visible of me above the tabletop.

"That's sweet Nadira," says Dabria with a cheerful smile. "I met her in the gardens earlier this afternoon."

My hackles rise. Sweet, am I?

"What happened to your face?" asks Fathuna, running her finger along her flawless jaw, indicating the scars on mine.

"Chicken fight, years ago," Eshe says promptly with a sad shake of her head. "I don't know what it is about Nadira and chickens, but she's always loved them, despite what vicious creatures they can be."

Slave, or blindly devoted to—and horribly inept around—chickens? I think I prefer the chickens.

Fathuna curls her upper lip skeptically. She opens her mouth, and I'm certain she's about to ask what *really* happened. Eshe will, of course, deadpan that that *was* what happened.

I might be more skilled with a blade than Eshe, but I know I'll be served up on a platter for this banquet without her. The only expression I can allow on my face, however, is one of mild disinterest. Definitely not fear or intimidation.

Eshe interrupts before Fathuna can keep asking about my scars. "Nadira, you remember Hulla here next to me. She's—oh, deep breaths, darling. We're only here for a lovely meal, is all!"

I peer around Eshe's turned frame and catch a glimpse of the round-faced girl with her bounty of curls sitting on the other side of my friend, pale and almost hyperventilating. My lips tighten, something in my chest hollowing out.

I know how you feel, I want to whisper. I wish I was next to her, even to be able to reach out a hand beneath the tabletop so no one could see and clasp her hand in mine. To help her know that she's not alone, that we're in this frightening experience together.

"Deep breaths, that's right," coos Eshe gently, rubbing Hulla's back and tucking curls behind her ear. She glances up at the nine pairs of eyes on her, flashes a grin, and says lightly, "I'd say we're doing pretty well as a group in light of our collective kidnapping! What do you say, Raha?"

Raha is the young woman who gave me a death glare in the Golden Hall. She wears all black and stares at Eshe with irises so dark they swallow up her pupils, saying nothing. Those eyes shift to mine, nearly slicing me in half with the look of one who kills often and has never once been bothered by it.

Dabria gives a light, tinkling laugh beside her, her manner and brightly colored garments a sharp contrast. She's easily the loveliest person in the room.

My eyes drift to my crystal goblet and plate, faceted to catch the glimmering beauty of the emerald chandelier. I swallow thickly, wishing I was still in my room.

The doors open.

Everyone sits up straighter, except Dabria, whose back was already primly erect. I crane my neck, angling to get a better view of the steward marching through those majestic doors. He doesn't tilt his head back to survey the gemstone ceiling. Not even the faintest trace of appreciation crosses his face at the sight of the hall. He stops at the head of the table, regarding each of us coolly.

"For his private dinner, the Neverseen King requests the presence of—"

Something threads down my spine, pooling in my gut with an uncomfortable tingling. I'm not sure what I'm hoping for.

"—Itr," says the steward.

There's a collective *whoosh* of released air, soft and almost inaudible, but I don't miss it. Whether it's from relief or disappointment, however, I'm not sure any of us know.

The girl in question, Itr, stands. Her hands tremble. She hides them in the folds of her robes, smiling bravely with a firm set of her shoulders. "I-it would b-be my honor," she stutters.

The steward bows, beckons, and Itr follows. Dabria looks after her with a small smile tilting up the side of her mouth. Fathuna looks angry, though I'm not sure why.

The doors close without a sound, swallowing up Itr.

"If she has better food with the Neverseen King, I'm going to riot," says Eshe.

Fathuna gives a pathetic excuse of a smile, her nose twitching.

"We can ask Itr about it when she comes back," says Dabria diplomatically.

"*If* she comes back," says a girl I haven't met yet. Her face is twisted in a dark sort of pout, one that makes me wonder if she often says morbid things.

Eshe's laugh rings out across emerald and crystal. Dabria hides a smile as she takes a sip of her wine, slim fingers elegantly gripping the goblet stem. I try not to frown as I glance from the girl back to Dabria, and then finally to Eshe, who I realize still has her arm around the hyperventilating Hulla. Eshe's face is a mask of mirth, but beneath it, her eyes shoot daggers at the nameless girl.

"Mahja," says Eshe, still chuckling, "what a cheerless sense of humor you have! I'd bet my two hands that Itr will return to us safe and sound, and probably much fatter than before if her supper looks anything like ours. Come, let us eat!"

"Besides, we ought not to speak ill of our sovereign," comes a voice from the far end of the table. When I glance, I find a pair of large green-and-gold-flecked eyes and a straight-toothed smile that I cannot read.

"That's Gaya," whispers Eshe to me. "Next to her is Kanza."

It's Kanza who says almost reverently, "I'm sure there's no need to speak ill, for there can be no doubt that the Neverseen King has a good reason for this."

I hope my face is still blank and that I'm not betraying anything of myself. In fact, I rather hope I can disappear in this crowd and be forgotten. Hearing these names, I'm beginning to wonder if perhaps Dabria isn't the only one with a relation that I've assassinated.

"A good reason," says Raha darkly, so quietly I almost miss the scoffing note beneath her tone. She picks up her knife, spears it straight into a hunk of meat on a platter, and brings it to her plate.

I look away before she glances up and finds me watching. Eshe exchanges barbs with Fathuna, all while she keeps a comforting hand on Hulla and manages to have the brightest smile at the table.

As everyone begins to eat, I force myself to take a portion from the dishes, my stomach suddenly feeling very full from the meal the Neverseen King provided for me. But if I don't eat, I'll draw attention to myself, and to blame my lack of appetite on the circumstances is to offer information I don't want to give my competitors—even if they all received meals, too. So I eat, slowly, carefully, and try to study as much about the other women as I dare.

But my mind drifts. I wonder if Eshe is right, if Itr will have a lovely time with our sultan, or if there's more at play here. I wonder what they will discuss, if they even discuss anything at all. I wonder if she will return hale and whole.

I think back to the note he'd left me with the meal. I hadn't been able to bear leaving him with the last word, and apparently I was emboldened after a full meal. I'd taken the paper he'd left, scavenged my room until I found ink and quill, and wrote on the verso:

One could never accuse you of stooping to poison when a flood of goblins awaits your bidding. Thank you for the food. It was delicious, and so far I am not dead.

–A less hungry captive

I cannot be sure if the note I left for him on the tray will find its way to him, but I figured it was worth a try.

As the dinner progresses, the light in the room shifts, and the shadows lengthen. I didn't see windows when I first arrived, but I can't crane my neck around and look now without drawing attention.

Instead, I watch those shadows and force myself to keep eating, trying to pay attention to the chatter around me.

Evening is swiftly approaching, bringing with it my first night in the Neverseen King's palace.

Never leave your rooms after dark.

I swallow my bite thickly. It lands like a rock in my stomach.

The hall's doors swing open suddenly, and Hulla jolts sharply. She's not the only one, either. My own heart leaps, but I'm surprised when the hunched girl next to me, Safya, doesn't flinch a single muscle.

It's the steward who marches through those doors, head tipped back and a blank expression on his face. All has gone silent when he speaks.

"The Neverseen King bids you return to your chambers, as night approaches. He also bids you a good evening."

The walk back to my rooms is even quieter than the first, for the birds have gone silent, and the only sound is the rush of wind through the portico as I'm escorted by a different servant girl. The wind tangles in my hair, kissing my face as I walk, and the sun turns a fiery orange on the horizon. When I pass the courtyard, I realize with a start that the fountain has stopped, leaving an eerie silence in its wake.

We pass the banister I came across earlier. It makes no sound, no movement. A tiny part of my brain wonders if I invented the way it creaked beneath my hand, the way it bent toward me. On impulse, I reach out and touch the smoothed wood.

Nothing.

It's even colder than before, without the faintest acknowledgment. I purse my lips, pull my hand away, and follow behind my escort.

Only once I'm in my room with the door shut and locked can I breathe again. I stand at the closed door, my eyes trailing over the darkened room, the canopy bed, the curtains wafting through the window. And then my eyes land on the table where the tray of food had been waiting earlier. It's empty.

Save for a slip of parchment.

Eyes widening, I hurry across the room and snatch it off the tray, my heart's rhythm kicking up several notches. But it's dark, and I can hardly make out the characters. Blinking and widening my eyes against the night, I head to the window. The last rays of sun are slipping away rapidly, but it's enough. I lean against the stone and tilt the paper toward the sparse light and read the missive.

I hate goblins. They chew through magic like mice through clothes.

CHAPTER 12

I BLINK, FROWN, and reread the message. This is it? This is all he wrote? He hates goblins because they chew through magic? What does that even mean? I go back to the table, flip the note over and scrawl an even simpler message than his: *Why?*

The sun vanishes, and my world is plunged into night.

Slowly, I lift my head. When I set down my quill, the metal nib makes a louder clack on the wood than I expect. It echoes in the silence, but only for a moment. The wind picks up, stronger, whistling through the opening of my window, sending even the heavy canopy of my bed swaying. It catches tendrils of my hair, drives them into my face. The frantic pace of my breathing is swallowed up in wind and night. My chest heaves as I glance around my empty room, my lips parting. I lick them, swallow.

Tucking my feet beneath me, I carefully stand and turn toward the door.

Never leave your rooms after dark.

I move silently, trying to ignore the howling wind, the way it catches up the note I've written, and prowl toward the door. In a flash, I have a knife in each hand as I stare at the handle. I swallow again.

If I was brave, I'd open this door. I'd be willing to risk my life to discover what secrets my sultan keeps from me, from all Arbasa. If I were Eshe, I'd already be out in the darkened hallway beyond my room. She might be scouting even now as I hesitate.

I grit my teeth. I don't want to act like a coward, but I also cannot afford to be rash or foolish. I ought to gather more information before I blithely disregard such ominous instructions, spoken so sternly.

But I don't feel wise and self-controlled when I sheathe my knives and march toward my bed, not even bothering to undress. When I slip beneath the quilted covers, my hand fisted around the hilt of one of my knives, and my mouth begins moving by habit, I feel like a coward.

"Murtadi, Shawar, Tibon," I begin to whisper.

An ear-splitting scream slices through the air.

I sit bolt upright, nearly choking on my own gasp. That scream—a woman's scream—echoes through my mind, or perhaps I'm hearing it echo through the hallways, dancing off the glass ceiling and locked doors.

I throw the covers back, swing my feet to the floor, and slip off my bed, ducking into a crouch. My blood pounds furiously through my veins, the erratic pulse louder in my ears than the howling wind, than even the silence left behind after that scream.

My hands are slick with sweat around the hilts of my knives, and more sweat drips from my hairline down my temple. *Deep breaths,* I tell myself. Now is not the time for panic.

That scream came from one of the other contestants—or someone else, like a servant. Or perhaps it's another monster like the goblins the Neverseen King released earlier.

Never open your doors after dark.

My breath comes faster and faster as I slink into the shadows wreathing my room, approaching my door cautiously. I'd bet almost anything right now that the scream came from one of the contestants sneaking out of her room, which is even more terrifying when I remember how the women hadn't screamed when we'd been faced with a bloody onslaught today.

So what is making someone scream now?

Air shudders out of my lungs as I reach my door. I squeeze my eyes shut, gritting my teeth.

Is it Eshe?

A sob from nowhere bubbles up in my throat. I swallow it down fiercely, then leap to my feet, my heart pounding, and grab the handle of my door. Whatever Eshe is facing in the palace of the Neverseen King, I won't let her face it alone. No matter how my bones quiver in their sockets, I'm *not* leaving Eshe.

My fingers flex on the knob, and then with a determined huff, I twist it, start to pull it open—

Something slams against the door above the knob, shutting it.

I gasp, jolt. Every sense floods with alarm. Then my vision focuses enough for me to see the shadowy outline of a huge hand forcing the door closed. Slowly, breath rapidly sweeping in and out of my parted lips, I twist. My fist still grips the knob, but my gaze travels up from the fist against the door, up the impression of a large wrist, a forearm, all the way to the shoulder of a darkened presence.

My awareness sparks with recognition, even though he is nothing but night beside me, tall and looming. For a long minute, I freeze, bracing myself for what, I cannot know. A blow?

But he doesn't strike me. He stays still, and I think his eyes are studying me.

"Eshe—" I blurt, gasping, breaking the silence.

"Do not open this door." His voice is much darker, much colder than I've heard, lacking every ounce of dry sarcasm.

"But someone screamed—Eshe, she's in trouble!"

"If you take one step outside this door, you will die, and there will be nothing I can do to save you."

My eyes widen, my mouth falling open. My crudely propped up courage crumbles in an instant, but even so my grip on the handle tightens. "I can't—"

He leans forward so suddenly I flinch, and for a second I think I can see the flash of two eyes. But it's his warmth that I feel strongest. Then I hear his voice, low and rumbling, saying as though between gritted teeth, "Do. Not. Open. This. Door."

The wind howls, sweeping into my room, whipping around the curtains of my bed, sending my hair flying into my face, my mouth. It seems to give a last cry, blowing so hard I squeeze my eyes shut, tighten my grip on the knob of the door.

Then all is quiet. Deathly still.

The fragrant perfume of roses is suddenly, inexplicably, nearly overwhelming. I open my eyes.

Moonlight shines through my open window, illuminating what was almost pitch black just minutes ago. My room is silent, and the wind is gone. My curtains hang so still they could be made of iron instead of fabric.

The Neverseen King is gone.

A deep breath shudders into my lungs. My hand is still clutching the knob. A choice is yet before me. I must make it in the ringing emptiness after that horrifying scream, the wind, and my sultan's deep as night voice.

If I open this door, I will die. Unless he's lying to me, which is always possible. But no matter how I try to convince myself he's lying, I believe his words. I believe I will die if I leave. Why, or how, I do not know.

Does this mean . . . does this mean that if Eshe has already left her room, that she is beyond saving? Does this mean . . .?

The risk-to-reward ratio for this situation is wildly imbalanced. The way the odds seem to me, opening this door is foolhardy at best, suicide at worst.

But if that was Eshe's scream . . .

I let out a groan, one that's half sob, and sheathe my knives. I release the knob, lean against the door, and slide to the floor until I hit it with a thud. Then I draw my knees to my chest, wrap my arms around them, and fit my eye sockets to my kneecaps. And try to swallow my tears.

I'm trembling, tasting salt on my lips.

"Just because you freeze when things go wrong doesn't mean I do," she'd told me during last night's job. Sitting here—does it mean I'm trusting her to take care of herself, or does it mean I'm the stars-cursed coward I feel like?

"Eshe," I choke, "if you die, I'm going to kill you."

I clench my hands into fists so tight my nails nearly pierce my palms. I leap to my feet in a sudden burst of fury, and the wind picks up. I let it swirl around me, breathing it into my lungs.

Then I'm running toward my window, ripping one of my knives out of its sheath. I jump onto the sill, not losing my balance as my toes grip the edge of cool stone. I whirl around, away from the world outside my window, and fling my knife with all my strength at my door.

One, two, three.

I throw them in quick succession, in a straight line down the middle of the door. They *plink* satisfyingly into the wood.

Four, five, six.

I hop off my ledge, landing in a crouch, and then straighten to my full height. My shadow reaches out before me, dark and slim, outlined in moonlight. I lift my chin, swallowing the last remnant of my tears as I stare at my knives, perfectly spaced down the center of the door. I probably shouldn't have thrown them into the door—it'll take more work to sharpen them again. But it is enough. Enough for me, in this moment, to not feel utterly helpless.

I may be captive in an unfamiliar world. I may be alone, save Eshe—and I may not even have her anymore. I may be facing a deadly bridal competition with rivals I don't know.

But I am not helpless here. Disadvantaged in about every way possible, certainly. But I am not helpless. I *won't* be helpless.

I won't break.

The next morning, a servant enters like the day before. I'm already awake and dressed in the fresh set of clothes left for me, tailored perfectly for my height and build, styled to be unassuming and simple. I'm awake because I barely slept—listening for another scream, for something that would tell me Eshe was still alive. Instead, I heard howling wind that wasn't quite loud enough to drown out the strange creaking and whistling noises. Once or twice, I thought I'd heard something like a yell, and another time there was definitely a distant crash.

Thrice, I'd thrown aside the covers, approached my door, and stared at it. And thrice, I'd eventually returned to my bed. But finally, dawn came at long last, and with it my dizzying terror to discover what had happened last night—*who* had screamed.

If Eshe had gone scouting last night . . . if she hadn't survived the night . . . I didn't want to think about it. I had anyway, and not even the familiar rhythm of sharpening my knives could soothe my shaking hands. This morning I feel wretched from the lack of sleep, bloated and sluggish, but I don't care.

I'm ready and waiting when the knock comes, and the door opens.

"Good morning!" chirps the maid with a broad smile. Her arms are full of a pewter tray laden with what must be my breakfast.

It takes every ounce of self-control to not fly across the room, grab the poor girl, and demand answers. Instead, my hands clenched around the gilded arms of the chair I'm forcing myself to sit in, I ask breathlessly, "What happened last night?"

With a clatter of dishes, she sets the tray on the table, tweaks the arrangement of the dishes, and glances up at me with another smile. The sun shines brightly in her dark eyes. "Oh, just the usual. Would you like some qahwa? It's freshly brewed!"

"One of the competitors left her room last night, didn't she?" I say, unable to even *think* about qahwa or breakfast or anything until I know if Eshe is safe.

"Oh yes, one of them did. A shame. She was warned not to." She sighs deeply and shakes her head. "And now she's lost."

"Lost?" I sit up straighter. My nails are almost being pried off their beds with how hard I'm gripping the chair arms. I'm just a hair's breadth from racing out my door, screaming Eshe's name, and trying to find where her room is in this labyrinth of a palace. Instead, I force myself to sit rigidly still. "What do you mean, lost?"

At this, the servant girl finally meets my gaze, the chipper light gone from her eyes as she says plainly, "She's dead. She opened her door during the night, so of course she is dead. Now come eat your breakfast. It's not much, because of your competition in a couple hours. But the Neverseen King was concerned you might not have enough to eat, so he bid me bring you this."

"Who?" I demand.

"The Neverseen King?"

"No, who is dead? Who left her rooms?"

The girl shrugs as she pours a cup for me. Fragrant steam wafts from the spout, the rich liquid so strong it's almost black. "I don't know who."

My lungs close, my panic escalating so rapidly I can't catch a breath. I can't think a coherent thought, even as the maid's brow wrinkles and she says something, offering me the cup she's poured. I can't think of anything except that there's no way it *wasn't* Eshe who left her rooms.

Eshe is dead. I haven't stopped it. I couldn't have stopped it—but *could* I have if I was braver? I cannot—absolutely *cannot*—lose her. It's my fault that she left. It's my—

Everything darkens around me suddenly. But I can't think of it. I need air, air, *air*. But my lungs are throttled by some unseen force.

Until something warm presses against my throat at the same moment that a hand cups over my forehead.

"Breathe," comes the low command.

And I can. I can finally breathe. I draw in a deep lungful, sagging backward in my chair. My panic eases away, my heart rate lowering to a steadier rhythm.

That's when I have the wherewithal to process what is happening, whose fingers are pressed to the hollow of my throat and on my forehead, who is standing behind the chair I'm all but collapsed in. The darkness that filled the room wasn't a curtain being drawn over the window, but the entrance of the Neverseen King.

The maid is nowhere to be seen.

My relief over simply being able to draw air into my body again is short-lived. My sweat-slicked hands clench the chair arms once more, my blood starting to pound in my veins. My sultan doesn't remove his hands, and this time I can sense the effects of magic, of some spell he's asserting on me to calm me down. It is like the rocking tide of cold waves against my body, lulling but forceful.

While I'm glad I can breathe, I don't *want* to be calmed into a puppet. I need to know if Eshe is dead. I jerk away from his touch, scramble out of the chair, and whirl to face him.

The darkness recedes the moment I look, until I'm standing in my sunny room once more. But I feel him, can *almost* see the towering height of my sultan against the wall, nigh invisible in the shadow of my fluttering curtains.

"Is Eshe alive?" I demand. "You must tell me. I cannot bear another second of not knowing."

"Yes."

My gaze shoots up to where I think his must be. "She's alive?"

"Yes."

My knees give out.

I fall back into the chair, not caring that he is still behind me. My head sinks into my hands, every muscle in my body from head to toe quivering with relief. "She's alive," I say, not quite believing the words.

I'm almost able to swallow back all my tears, but a couple slip free, run down my cheek, and drip from my chin to the rug. I feel my sultan watching me, but I cannot care. I cannot be bothered to ask him any of my questions and make use of this time that I have with him before the second competition. If I were smarter, I'd ask what the next competition was.

But I'm too relieved that I haven't lost Eshe to care about anything else.

There's a shift in the air the moment he leaves. Bird song floats through my window. The sun shines brighter. I let out a breath, then drag my hand away from my face and stare at the tray the maid left for me.

I sit bolt upright. There's something on that tray that wasn't there when she first brought it in. A folded piece of yellow paper. My eyes widen with realization, darting around the room even though I know it's empty. I lean forward, pluck up the note, and read it.

Your request lacks clarity. Fortunately for you, the answer to either question—why I hate goblins and why they chew through magic—is the same. Goblins are insatiable and stupid. Also, have some faith in your friend. She has more sense than you give her credit for.

Something about the note further eases the knot inside my chest. I hesitate over my reply for some time, nibbling on tangy za'atar spread across manakish as much as my unsteady stomach allows. The sesame seeds keep getting stuck in my teeth as I think. I use the side of my thumbnail to dig them out, except for one stubborn one I resort to using my smallest knife to remove.

Finally, I write.

Who left her room last night? And why didn't you stop her like you stopped me?

And then I wait. Staring at the parchment on the tray. Hoping for any answer as the hours trickle by until footsteps come down the hallway toward my door. I rise to my feet, check my knives by habit, and run my hands down the front of my vest, smoothing it. A deep breath gusts out of me.

The same guard from yesterday opens my door. Beckons me to follow. It's time for the second competition.

When I glance back at the tray, my note has disappeared.

CHAPTER 13

MY HEART IS in my throat as I'm escorted through the palace toward the second competition. Everything is as it was yesterday. No blood spattered on the wall. No sign of struggle. The birds have returned to the fountain, which burbles and flows as if it had never stopped.

It should ease my nerves. Instead, it only serves to worry me more.

Who is gone? Will it be elegant Dabria? Tall and rude Fathuna? Hunched and unimposing Safya? Will it be Raha and her death glare? Itr, who dined with the sultan last night?

I'm surprised when the route we take is familiar to me. I keep expecting us to veer off course, to take a left at the hallway convergence instead of a right. But we continue exactly as we did last night.

My brow bunches when we stand yet again before the doors of the Emerald Hall. The unflinching guards do not even glance at me as they reach, grasp the polished handles, and swing open both doors.

The hall glitters even more in the sunshine. I'm still not sure where the light is coming from, but it dazzles my eye nonetheless. I'd have thought that seeing the beauty of gemstones embedded in the floor and gold-threaded agate archways against the far wall would have numbed me to its effect a second time. But no. I have the urge to crane my neck and take it all in again, just as I wanted to last night.

I don't.

Because, apparently as is routine, I'm the last one to come. Nine other women are seated before another banquet spread, and my eye catches on an elaborate arrangement of cut pineapple in the center of the table.

Nine women. There are two empty chairs at this table now besides my chair next to Eshe. One for the girl who fell in the first competition, and the one who left her room last night. Will all of us still be here tonight?

My eyes find Eshe's immediately, and the sight of her lovely face, the smile showcasing her crooked front teeth, is so relieving I almost stop in the doorway instead of continuing to my seat.

The Neverseen King did not lie to me. Eshe lives.

But someone else is gone.

I look over the women, registering their names in my brain. *Eshe. Fathuna. Dabria. Itr. Raha. Safya. Gaya. Kanza. Mahja.* Who is missing? Who have I forgotten?

That's when I realize that Eshe's smile isn't her typical flashing grin, but a front. I've never seen such a forced smile on her face. She must be rattled by the disappearance. That revelation is followed by another: I've never seen Eshe scared.

Never in my life.

The name of the last girl, the one I overlooked, hits me with the force of a desert storm.

Hulla.

Hulla, the girl who was hyperventilating at dinner last night. The one Eshe comforted. The girl I pitied. She must have panicked and tried to flee last night.

I am sick as I take my seat. Eshe grabs my hand beneath the table. I squeeze it hard.

We're in this together, I want to say. Whatever this second competition, whatever things we face, we can do it together.

I don't want to look at any of the women sitting beside and across from me. And then I don't have to, because the steward enters only a second later. Emin holds himself regally as always, and I marvel at how unfazed he can be by any of this while I'm barely keeping down the snack from earlier this morning.

"The second competition will commence in a moment," he says.

With those words, the tentative control I had over myself nearly snaps. My own breathing increases, my heart threatening to gallop away from me. I don't want to kill again. I don't know why we're sitting at a table. I don't know *anything.*

Will I be the next Hulla? What if this is my last—

Eshe squeezes my hand. I exhale, shut my eyes for a split second. *Together.* Eshe has my back. She'll be strong for me. But that means I must be strong for her, too.

"Listen carefully, because the rules will only be given once. One of you has been given the task of killing someone at this table."

Oh sands, no. My insides drop like a stone to the ground.

"The woman charged thus has been granted two accomplices, whom she knows and who know her. If the killer succeeds and kills one of the women seated at this table, she and her accomplices will be acknowledged as the winners. If, however, the killer is identified before she succeeds, then the one who identified her is the winner."

Eshe's hand has gone clammy in mine. I lace my fingers in hers, firming our grip. I breathe deeply into my nose, telling myself over and over again that we can survive this. This is what I'm trained in.

Does the fact that I was issued no prior instructions mean that I am neither killer nor accomplice? Am I relieved by this?

"The prize for winning is dining with the Neverseen King tonight. The competition begins now," says the steward, and gestures at the meal spread before us. "You may begin eating."

Across from Eshe, Fathuna bangs her knife down on the tabletop. "Are you saying we're supposed to eat knowing that someone is trying to kill us? What if it's poisoned?"

I blink. Is this why the Neverseen King sent me food earlier—because he knew I wouldn't eat? Did he send food to everyone, or just to me?

"You are to eat, yes," says the steward. "Prior to the arrival of the first contestant, all the food was tested for poison by the order of the Neverseen King. Everything was safe for consumption. Now, please begin."

With that, he turns and leaves the hall. But, subtle as it may be, I don't miss when someone else enters—someone who hangs by the shadows at the apse of the hall.

The Neverseen King has arrived to watch the second competition.

"Who was here first?" demands Fathuna. "When I arrived, Dabria, Raha, Eshe, and Kanza were here."

"I didn't poison anything!" says Kanza quickly, eyes wide and glancing around her. She is seated between Fathuna's scowl and Raha's black-eyed glare.

I scan the table seating arrangement quickly, trying to watch everything at once while not appearing too alert. The opposite side of the table, from left to right, is seated thus: Mahja, Dabria, Fathuna, Kanza, and Raha. My side of the table, from left to right, is Gaya, myself, Eshe, Itr, and Safya.

"That's exactly what someone would say who had poisoned something," says Fathuna, swiveling her suspicious scowl to Kanza, whose eyes widened even more.

"When I arrived," says Dabria, reaching out and lifting her steaming cup of qahwa, swirling it before taking a bold sip, "Eshe and Raha were here."

All eyes turn to Eshe and Raha. Except mine. I'm trying to see where everyone's hands are so I can monitor them. Itr's, Mahja's, and

Raha's hands are below the table, while Dabria always keeps both in plain view. I half-wonder if that is on purpose. The rest have one hand visible, and one below the table.

Mine are below the table, I realize. Because I'm still holding Eshe's hand. I risk a split-second glance down at our hands and see a knot of white knuckles.

"I was here first," says Eshe after swallowing.

"Did you poison the food?" demands Fathuna, her butter knife gripped in her fist on the table.

All eyes focus on Eshe.

"I thought you were too nice," says Mahja dryly from the far end of the table.

I bite my tongue sharply to keep from snapping something and drawing all attention to me. But Eshe, despite how tightly she clenches my hand, says with shocking calm, "I didn't poison anything."

"If you were here the whole time, then did you see anything suspicious?" asks Fathuna.

Eshe shakes her head.

"You're a-asking a-a lot of q-questions," stutters Itr. "M-maybe you're just t-trying to distract us."

"Stop trying to turn this on me. I'm neither the killer nor the accomplice. No one talked to me beforehand," says Fathuna with a scowl. "You dined with the Neverseen King last night. Have you told anyone how it was? Or are you going to keep us in the dark?"

"I-I-I will t-tell you!" Itr cries in apparent frustration. "B-but we're t-trying not to get k-killed!"

"Stop stressing her out," Kanza shoots at Fathuna with a glare. "She told me about it. She said he was very nice—just like I *told* you he would be! He didn't hurt her. And the food was very good, apparently."

A sudden loud scraping to my left sends instinct flooding my veins. I release Eshe's hand, block my side with my forearm, and whip a knife out of my sheath.

Gasps go up around the table, and I think it's Kanza who lets out a half-scream.

But my eyes lock on Gaya's gold-and-green eyes next to me as she flies to her feet, backing away from the table. My knife remains poised in the air, and then I process what happened.

Gaya wasn't coming to attack me. She was shoving back her chair and getting up. I let a sigh of relief escape me, and then I sheathe my knife.

I turn to find eight pairs of eyes fixed on me.

"You're the killer," gasps Kanza.

"Nadira isn't the killer," says Dabria. She's wearing bright turquoise robes today, with a gold circlet across her forehead and pearls in her hair. She reaches forward, helps herself to a plate of stuffed figs, and doesn't brace herself when she takes a bite. "She reacted in self-defense because she was startled. She's not the killer."

I'm not sure if I'm grateful or wary.

Fathuna frowns, watching her eat. "You say that so confidently, and you're eating the food that might be poisoned. You know who the killer is, don't you?"

Dabria chuckles and dabs her mouth with her napkin. She lifts her gaze, meets mine. "No. I don't know."

"She's definitely an accomplice," says Mahja. "If not the killer."

I'm almost inclined to agree with her.

Dabria only smiles. "Then you'd better watch your back. Cheers." She clinks her own cup of qahwa on Mahja's, which sits on the table untouched.

"Why are you still standing?" Fathuna asks Gaya, who hasn't returned to her seat, but stands a few paces away, arms crossed over her chest.

"Because I don't trust any of you."

"Or you're trying to signal to one of your accomplices," says Fathuna.

Eshe has been extraordinarily quiet, I realize suddenly. I glance at her, find her face deathly pale. Dread plunges into my gut. Is Eshe the killer? Or an accomplice? Is that why her hand is trembling?

Oh stars above.

"It's not me," says Gaya.

"Whoever it is had better make a move, because I'm getting bored, and we don't have all day." Dabria clinks her glass on Fathuna's this time, tossing another sparkling smile her way.

It's an effort not to flinch at every movement.

Fathuna's brow pinches, and though my eyes are scanning every which way, I note how she glances at Eshe, Safya, then Raha. "Safya," she says, drumming her nails on the table, "I don't think you've spoken a single word since you got here."

Safya stares at her empty plate, but slowly lifts her attention to Fathuna. "Do you want me to speak to comfort your nerves?"

I barely keep my brows from rising. Fathuna, on the other hand, draws back, clearly affronted.

"I'm trying to figure out who is trying to kill one of us," says Fathuna. "Which is why—"

"Is it because you want the Neverseen King's attention for yourself?" asks Kanza. "You're trying to find out who it is so that you can dine with him."

"I'm trying not to *die*."

Raha, who has also been quiet, snorts. When we all turn to her, she's smiling faintly. And then she reaches forward with her knife, spears a piece of meat, and brings it to her plate. She begins eating without even a sniff for poison.

Gaya is still standing a ways off, arms folded across her chest. "Someone toss me a bite," she says.

It's Mahja who picks up a slice of pomegranate from one of the plates before us and throws it to Gaya. She catches it in one palm, then opens her fingers to inspect its ruby pearls of fruit. She brings it to her nose, sniffs it, and then tosses it to the ground.

"Poison?" asks Kanza, her voice suddenly high-pitched.

"Not that I could tell," says Gaya.

"Then why'd you throw it away?" asks Fathuna.

"For the same reason I'm not sitting at the table. I don't trust any of you. Especially not one who would give me food." This is said with a pointed glance at Mahja.

Eshe still isn't saying anything. She's one of them, then. Surely she isn't thinking about killing me?

No. I won't think like that. I won't think so little of my friend.

Your friend has more sense than you give her credit for.

In my bid to carefully watch everything at the table, I've forgotten about the Neverseen King. How he studies our every move. I feel the prickling of his eyes on me even now.

If I thought the last competition was brutal, this one is far worse. What sort of sultan would ask this of his potential brides? To kill each other?

Raha slices a piece of her meat with vicious intensity and uses her teeth to bite the chunk off the tip of her knife. Kanza, sitting next to her, stiffens and tries to scoot over—only to glance and find she didn't want to be any closer to Fathuna either. I can't help but pity her position. I sit at the safest position on the table, with a friend on one side and Gaya having vacated the chair next to me.

Then Raha speaks, and the sound of her rough voice chills me to the bone. "I don't care if I was given the assignment of killing or not. If one of you is the Mourner, your days are numbered."

My thoughts stutter to a complete halt. I barely remember to maintain my blank expression before I reveal the sudden terror pooling in my gut.

But Mahja almost chokes on laughter. "The *Mourner*? *Here?* Is this how you start every conversation with a new group of people?"

Kanza looks like she wants to give an uneasy laugh, but wouldn't dare while sitting right next to Raha.

Apparently this subject sharpens Eshe's mind enough for her to interject: "But isn't the Mourner a man?"

Dabria plops a grape into her mouth, chews, swallows, and then says, "Actually, I have it on good authority that the Mourner is a woman. One of the city's lords—Lord Kishon, who runs the city guard for the Neverseen King—was assassinated the night we were brought here. And it was a *woman* the guards almost apprehended for execution. So if the Mourner is a woman, it's quite probable that she would be here."

Eshe. She's talking about Eshe, not me. I doubt anything Dabria could have said would have horrified me more. I squeeze Eshe's hand before she opens her mouth one more time to insist that isn't possible for some incriminating reason.

My efforts are in vain.

"But isn't—" Eshe begins.

"Getting slo—" says Mahja at the same time.

They both stop. Glance at each other. And Eshe nods too quickly at Mahja. "You first."

"I was just going to say the Mourner must be getting sloppy," Mahja finishes. "How many years has it been? A decade nearly? Not once has he—or *she*—been seen."

Quiet falls around the table. I want to melt into my chair and die. All I can hope is that Dabria doesn't know anything about the so-called Mourner's appearance. If she was told the woman was short, as Eshe is, that effectively eliminates me as a target and places the bull's eye on my friend.

My friend, who cannot get a proper grip on her demeanor today.

"What were you going to say?" Fathuna asks Eshe, narrowing her brows.

Raha's gaze flicks up from her food, and pauses mid-chew to hear my friend's answer.

This is bad.

"The same thing," Eshe says with a laugh that nearly makes me wince. "I would just be surprised if it was *actually* the Mourner who was caught. How do we know it wasn't an accomplice?"

Death by being impaled on a spike would be infinitely preferred to this.

"So between the Mourner, Raha, the killer, and her two accomplices, you're telling me that there are potentially *five* people at this table who would murder me?" Fathuna asks, smacking her knife back down to the table and getting up from her chair. "Oh *sands* no."

That's when it happens.

It's so slight, so subtle, I *almost* miss it.

More women have been braving the food on the table, reaching forward and hesitantly eating. Fathuna stands a pace back from her chair like Gaya, arms crossed, while the rest of us say nothing. Eshe draws a deep breath beside me and wraps her fingers around her cup of qahwa.

At the same time, Itr reaches for the tower of pineapple and takes several slices back to her plate. The sleight of hand was so practiced, so proficient, I didn't even see it happen. I would have missed it, except for the one little bubble appears in Eshe's qahwa just before she brings it to her lips.

Fast as a snake's strike, my hand darts out. I grab Eshe's wrist and slam it down to the table. Qahwa sloshes over the rim, splattering my hand with heat and staining the white tablecloth silty brown.

Eshe gasps, along with everyone else at the table. She looks at me, at my grip on her, but I'm not looking at her. I'm looking at Itr.

"You poisoned Eshe's drink," I say.

Kanza lets out a piteous whimper and sets down her own drink that she was about to sip. Raha beside her just keeps eating. Fathuna's face is a mix of horror and triumph.

"The killer is Itr!" Fathuna cries, putting more distance between herself and the table.

Itr pales and shakes her head vigorously. "I d-didn't d-do it! I p-promise! I'm n-not the k-k-killer! Nadira is a-accusing m-me to take b-blame off herself!"

Eyes swivel to me, sudden doubt written across their faces. Dabria has only lifted one brow and keeps eating.

"I saw you," I say to Itr. "You poisoned Eshe's goblet while you reached for the pineapple."

"I'm n-not the k-killer!"

"You're the killer or one of the accomp—"

Something flashes. A flash I know well. I grab Eshe's arm, yank her toward me as I whip out my own knife.

But the knife doesn't come for Eshe. It all happens so fast I can't breathe, can't think, can't react. All I can do, along with everyone else at the table, is stare at Itr's shocked, frozen face.

And at the knife protruding from between her shoulder blades.

She falls forward onto the table. Dead. Next to her, Safya stands, her frame not quite so hunched and narrow as I thought before. She places a hand on Itr's back and yanks the knife out. The flowing blood makes dark spots dance across my vision.

"She's right," says Safya. There's not a scrap of emotion on her pretty, blank face. "She wasn't the killer."

Then she turns and marches straight toward the shadow along the far wall. My jaw drops open. She is aware of him too? Like I am?

"What's over there?" asks Gaya.

Kanza is weeping softly across from Itr's body, her hands covering her face. I'm so sick I don't think I can stand. But I watch as Safya boldly approaches the darkest part of the room, shoulders back.

"I shall see Your Highness at dinner tonight, then?" she asks.

To the apparent shock of everyone at the table except for me, the deep voice of our Neverseen King rings out across the hall. "Indeed, I shall see you tonight, Safya bint-Rashid."

Even Dabria's lips are parted. This confirms it then; no one can sense his presence. No one knew he was here the whole time. Except me.

And Safya.

CHAPTER 14

ESHE AND I quickly make our way back to my room. She has this shell-shocked look about her, mouth open and eyes wide, unfocused. At least she follows me without protest, and I don't need to take her hand. I'd rather not let the other women see how close we are. Some of it is unavoidable, but if I'd thought we needed to tread carefully before, I know how imperative it is now after watching Safya take out Itr without a hint of remorse. And then there is Raha, who wants me dead but might find evidence leading to Eshe.

Once the door is closed and locked behind us, I turn and face my friend.

She goes straight for the window, plants her elbows on the sill, and stares emptily down to the sunny courtyard.

"Were you the other accomplice?" I ask carefully, keeping my voice quiet in the case of eavesdroppers.

She shakes her head, lets it drop.

I head to her side only to freeze halfway there, my eyes suddenly glued to the scrap of parchment pinned beneath a golden paperweight that looks like a small egg. The sultan wrote back already? About why he didn't stop Hulla from leaving her rooms last night?

Eshe doesn't glance back when I lean over the table and pick up the parchment with two fingers to keep from loudly crinkling it.

Oh the ash I taste in my mouth admitting this to you! In fact, why am I admitting this to you? I shouldn't. You clearly find my mysteriousness intriguing. I ought to play that up more. But alas, I've started this note so I might as well finish it and answer your question.
Why didn't I stop Hulla from leaving her room like I stopped you? A good question indeed. The answer is very simple. As lightning quick as my reflexes are, despite the power I have at my fingertips, despite even my devilishly good looks that you wouldn't be aware of, there are some things that happen too fast for even me to stop.

I stare down at the message, at the elegant hand. I can almost hear his voice speaking the words, the puff of dry arrogance underscoring his comments about his power and looks. But am I wrong to imagine the unexpected sincerity, and perhaps even regret, beneath his last few words?

I don't think I'm wrong to believe *"some things"* might involve more than just Hulla's demise. What I need to know, more than ever, is why we're here. This isn't just about finding a worthy bride, that's for certain.

This is a test.

My sultan needs something. Something beyond a pretty face and the ability to carry offspring. Something beyond even noble blood.

I need to find out what it is.

I look up to find that Eshe hasn't moved. Silently, I set the note back down on the table and cross the remaining distance between us. I step to her side, facing her, and cross my arms over my chest as I lean against the window frame.

When I glance at her face, the dullness of her expression has given way to a furrowed brow, watery eyes, and a severe frown. Her fists are clenched against the stone sill. I stay silent, not hurrying her. She'll talk when she's ready.

It's not long before she bursts, "I didn't think we'd actually be killing each *other*!"

I glance self-consciously at the door, hoping her voice hasn't carried through. But I keep my paranoid observations to myself and say instead, "I didn't either."

"How am I supposed to trust them now? How can we be a team against the Neverseen King if we don't—"

"You don't trust them, Eshe," I say firmly. "Not even a little bit. Assume all those women will stab you in the back if given half the chance."

For the first time since we left the Emerald Hall, Eshe looks up at me, anger and tears warring together in her jewel-like gaze. "This is your life, isn't it? Waiting to get stabbed in the back?"

I blink, and quickly look away, shoving down the sudden emotion bubbling up inside me, threatening to spill out. "Don't trust them. That's how we navigate this situation. You can't trust anyone here except me." My attention is drawn against my will to the note on the table. I say with even more resolution, "No one except me."

She drops her face into her hands and groans. "*Nadira*—I was going to leave my room last night to scout. I was lacing up my boots when Hulla screamed. And . . . then I was too scared. I didn't leave. I didn't try to save her. Nadira, I could have saved her—"

"No, you couldn't have."

"Yes, I could have! Or at least I could have—"

"—died with her? Eshe, if you'd left your room, you would have died. There was nothing you could have done to save Hulla." Have I become the Neverseen King? Why am I repeating everything he said to me? Why am I justifying her fear as quickly as I justified mine?

Eshe meets my gaze. Hopelessness flashes in those dark depths, unshed tears catching the morning light—how is it not even noon yet? She closes her eyes, presses the back of her hand to her mouth, and a sob shakes her frame. *Oh Eshe.* The confidence, the cavalier jokes, the unflagging fearlessness is utterly swept away. By guilt. By fear.

I know how deep those lines can be scored upon the soul. I don't want Eshe bearing the burden I do, of dozens of lives ended at my hand because I was too helpless to free myself from Jabir, to fight back, to escape.

A flash of fragmented memories assaults me, of a dreadful moment with Kolb when we were trying to escape, and we ran straight into Jabir, of being wrenched out of Baba's arms, of standing there, frozen, unable to run or fight as my parents were taken from me, of nights breaking into houses and spilling blood before dawn stained the sky.

I reach out, clasp her hand. She grips mine back like her life depends on it. That's when the full torrent releases, and she leans on me as she cries and cries and cries. I stroke her arm up and down, softly.

And in those moments, I find my thoughts straying to earlier this morning. To the memory of someone else easing my own panic. Someone being there with me while I cried.

The Neverseen King . . . who will dine with Safya tonight.

I shake myself mentally and focus my attention back on my friend. Once her tears have run their course, I squeeze her hand and whisper, "We're in this together."

She nods her head, dashes away her tears, and draws in a shaky breath. "But what if one of us dies? What if you hadn't caught the poison in my drink today?"

If I let myself think about that, I will spiral completely out of control and lose the tenuous hold I have on my composure. So I merely assure her briskly, "We will watch each other's backs. Just like we've always done. Don't forget that I'm the Mourner, and you're the best thief in the capital. We are not without resources and skills here."

"Why aren't you panicking?" she asks.

"Because you are," I say with a rueful little smirk. "We can't both panic at once, now can we?"

The haunted gleam in her eyes slowly ebbs away, and a tiny bit of that sparkle returns.

"So you're saying—"

"No," I say, lowering my eyebrows. "Whatever you're about to say I'm saying, I am definitely not saying it."

At that, she actually grins. It's a wet-faced grin, but the sight of it uncoils the tension in my shoulders. "You're saying that the trick this whole time to keeping you conscious in terrible situations is that *I* need to have a crisis? To think I could have had so many more crises and they would have actually benefitted you!"

I glare at her.

"The next time I see you struggling to hold it together, I'll just let myself nearly get stabbed and—"

"No!" I snap, jabbing a finger into her face. "You flirt with death enough as it is. I do *not* need you doing it on purpose."

She only grins mischievously at me, and I sigh, wiping a hand down my face. She knows I cannot be angry at her. Not now, at least. I turn and walk away from the window, heading toward the vanity to ensure I don't look a fright after that competition.

It feels like a crime to think it, but I am so glad Eshe is here with me.

I'm so glad that two nights ago wasn't the last time I ever saw her.

My attention snags on the note, and for a second I consider hiding it. But I don't want to look suspicious, and I don't have anything to hide from Eshe, right?

As if my thoughts beckoned her, Eshe swoops across the room, eyebrows raised, and plucks the note off the table.

"What is this?" She opens it, eyes darting right to left as she reads. They grow wider with each pass. "Is this from the sultan? He leaves you notes?"

I turn toward the mirror to hide my flush and busy myself fussing over my hair, even though I care very, very little about it. "He doesn't leave you notes?" is all I can think of to ask in response.

"Um . . . no," says Eshe as if it's the most obvious answer.

"He sent me food yesterday with a note telling me it wasn't poisoned, and I took the opportunity to write him back and ask him questions. Thus far he's answered everything."

"What kind of food? I need to know if it was nicer than what he sent me."

I glance at her, a hairpin between my teeth as I continue fussing. So I *wasn't* the only one to receive food. "It was some kind of roast with sides."

"That's disappointing. I got the same thing, but no note. What kind of preferential treatment is this correspondence, and how do I get it? Are you his favorite?"

My flush deepens. I return to my hair and hope my shrug is nonchalant. "He knew I wouldn't eat it without his assurance that it wasn't poisoned." How do I tell her I've seen him several times now? That he's visited me in this very chamber?

"Pffft! Always concerned about poison. It *is* better to starve than be poisoned," Eshe says sarcastically. When I open my mouth to argue, she only continues. "You'd better watch out. He apparently thinks you like him too. Intriguing mysteriousness, ha! He certainly thinks highly of himself."

I change the subject. "We need to do more scouting today, and I need paper and ink to start my floor plan for planning our escape. Do you think you can find some for me?"

She raises her right hand in the air, then presses it over her heart. "I, Eshe bint-Kinid, do hereby solemnly swear to thieve some paper and—"

"No vowing, Eshe. Just get the materials, please."

She lifts an eyebrow, drops her hand, and puffs out a breath of irritation. "I Am Making a Plan Nadira is back, and she's no fun."

I pause, glance at her sidelong, and then say slyly, "Want to see something fun? Something I discovered yesterday?"

She perks up. "Yes! What did you find?"

I smile and motion for her to follow me as I make my way toward the door of my rooms. Her face is flushed and puffy, but she's otherwise looking like her regular self. It's a profound relief.

"What is it?" she whispers when we're out in the hallway.

"A banister," I say in response. "You'll love it."

Eshe is eyeing me suspiciously when we arrive a few minutes later at the banister that opens out into the courtyard. She arches her neck as she stares up at the spiral staircase.

"What's up there?"

"Don't know, though I assume it leads at least in part to the floor with our rooms," I say, and step closer to the banister. My hand is suddenly clammy, and my heart beats oddly fast. Am I nervous? Of course not. It's just a banister. But what if it doesn't behave like it did yesterday? What if it's cold like it was last night? I don't want to babble like a crazy person to my friend about how *yesterday* it had moved into my touch and purred like a cat.

Shoving aside my trepidation, I gently lay a hand on the polished wood. It's warm, but motionless. I can't help but wonder if it's hesitant because I've brought a friend. I refuse to glance back at her, and instead take one finger and slide it up the lip under the railing.

The wood squeaks. Eshe jumps. I laugh.

I scratch it gently, earning more creaking groans. "Didn't I tell you I'd come back? And look, I brought a friend. You'll love her."

Eshe is staring at me like I've lost my mind, eyes wide and darting back and forth between me and the banister. "What . . .?"

I can't help but smile. "It's magic, Eshe."

If our roles had been reversed, I'm not sure Eshe could have convinced me to touch something obviously magical on purpose, no matter her assurances of its safety. Eshe, however, hardly hesitates before reaching out her hand.

A gusty draft blows down the staircase as she begins scratching the banister and ruffles her hair. She startles, tenses, so I say, "That means it likes you."

Her large eyes swivel to mine, and I know without a single word the thoughts flying through her mind. The wonder, the confusion, the uncertainty. *How did we end up here?* she wants to ask. *Is this real? What else do we not know about our kingdom and our sultan? Why is there magic everywhere?*

We're going to find out, I tell her with my eyes.

But instead of being frightened, Eshe responds with enthusiasm. She sets to scratching the banister with gusto, talking to it like it's a beloved pet. "Look at you, such a good banister. Yes, yes, you are! Does that feel good? Oh, yes it does!"

And then—we're not alone.

I whip my head toward the staircase, lift my eyes to the curve of the spiral, and though I can see nothing with my naked eye, it's like my imagination fills out the image of a tall form marching down the steps toward us, a cloak billowing behind him.

I pull my hand away from the banister. It goes stiff beneath Eshe's fingers, and she glances up with a knotted brow, only to catch sight of my face, and follow my gaze into the emptiness of the staircase.

She flinches when his voice rings out across the narrow space between us.

"What are you doing to my House?" the Neverseen King demands.

Neither of us respond.

"Attend your duty, House of mine," he barks at the staircase, "or I will sand down your finish."

Though it doesn't move, and though I no longer touch it, I can feel the banister stiffening. And almost . . . *quivering.* It's just a banister, but heat spikes in my lungs. How could he be so harsh? And why does the sultan make sanding the banister sound like such a heartless punishment?

Eshe levels her shoulders at our invisible sultan, tightening her grip on the railing. *Oh no.* She's going to stand up to the Neverseen King on behalf of his furniture. Stars above, what is life?

Swiftly, I reach out to the banister, hiding the movement with my sleeves, and press two fingers to the wood. At the touch, I feel it trembling, which doubtlessly is what Eshe feels too.

Easy, I say in my mind to the House, imagining sending out shooting bursts of calm and reassurance through my fingers. *He won't sand you. I'll make sure of it.*

Immediately, the quivering stops. The wood warms against my fingers, and there's no denying the sense of peace and trust that seeps into my skin.

The Neverseen King's attention whips to me so sharply it's like his gaze is a knife slicing into me. I barely withhold my gasp.

"What did you just do?"

Eshe seems to know he means me, because she turns to look at me, eyes wide.

"Nothing," I say. I don't move my hand from the railing.

I have the distinct sense of him climbing down two steps toward me, leaning forward as he demands in a voice that is both angry and yet edged in something almost eager, "No, you *did* do something. What did you do? Why has my House stopped trembling at my voice?"

Eshe is talking before I have a chance to stop her. "Maybe it's because Nadira was kind to it while you're just a big, invisible bully!" Those words come out more petulant than I think she intended.

Silence falls like bricks.

It's heavy, so heavy, I fear I will drown in the dread of it. The three of us—Eshe, me, and the banister—hold stone-still. Awaiting death, it feels like.

For a split second, I'm not standing before a magic-wielding sultan, but before a vengeful Jabir. I still remember that moment, still feel the plunge of terror like a weight in the ocean, of crawling out of that drain with Kolb and finding myself at the feet of my slaver. At his mercy.

A thousand other memories flood after the first.

I cannot bring myself to move. Even if a knife came plunging toward me, I don't think I could dodge it. My feet have grown roots into the stair I stand upon.

Warmth flows into my fingertips, from wood straight into my soul.

Easy, something tells me. It's not a voice, but a feeling. A feeling that sounds like my words caught in a web and distorted to resemble the groan of wood, the creak of a door, the swish of drapes. *He won't sand you. I'll make sure of it.*

It's like one of those macaws in the bazaar that mimics words of the shoppers.

He won't sand me? I send the impression of those words back into wood.

The reply is almost instantaneous: *He won't sand you. I'll make sure of it.*

The Neverseen King's attention returns to me, away from Eshe. I meet his invisible gaze, this time without flinching, and the memory of Jabir slips away until I can breathe again. But he turns back to Eshe, and I almost see swimming shadow as he steps closer to her, down to the step above her. She stares straight through his chest, not seeming to have any idea of where he is.

"Is that any way to speak to your king?" he asks with lethal calm.

Eshe startles so hard she stumbles down one step, almost bumping into me. Yet, in typical Eshe fashion, once her initial fright is past, she lifts her chin and glares as only she can, straight into the sultan's face. Sweat like ice slicks down my spine.

He won't sand you. I'll make sure of it, whispers the House to me.

I don't want him to sand Eshe either, I manage in response.

Easy. Easy, easy, easy! Eeeeeasyy.

Perhaps I should expand the House's vocabulary at a less stressful moment.

As suddenly as he appeared, the Neverseen King steps away from Eshe. My held breath whistles between my teeth as I release it, my shoulders relaxing. Eshe still glares into nothing.

"You are dismissed," says the sultan.

Eshe's head whips to the new place he stands. Frustration mounts between her eyebrows, marked in furrows and a scowling mouth. If

I don't take this opportunity to drag her away, she'll spout something about how irritating it is to have a conversation with someone she can't keep track of.

I don't want him to sand Eshe, says the House.

As oddly loathe as I am to do so, I let go of the banister, grab Eshe's elbow, and make to drag her off. We need to scout anyway, I tell myself. She needs to find drawing supplies for me. There are things we need to do besides anger our monarch and pet banisters.

"Not you, little assassin."

Eshe and I freeze as one. Then, before I can stop her, she bursts out, "If you get one of us, you get both of us."

I simultaneously admire the boldness while also dreaming of stuffing her foot and all her other appendages into her mouth. *"Eshe,"* I whisper urgently.

"Run along, thief."

Eshe casts me a look that is equal parts frantic and determined. Her hand squeezes around mine, and I shake it off quickly before the sultan sees more of our weakness than he already has.

"Listen to the Neverseen King." My tone is not cold but clipped enough to give her the message. To tell her to leave me and not worry. But she has that stubborn set to her face. That face that means she's resigning herself to death if it means staying by my side. So I draw a deep breath and snap, "Now."

Her palms clench into fists. For a long moment, she only stares at me. Challenging me. But at last, to my relief, she turns and marches down the hallway. I don't doubt that she's cursing the sultan under her breath with every step.

Firming my resolve in my heart and bundling up the tentative shreds of my courage, I lift my gaze to my sultan's.

"Come with me," he says, and turns with a sweep of invisible cloak to march up the steps.

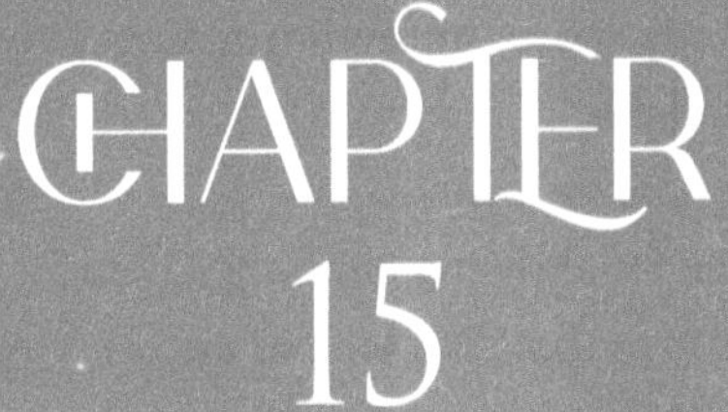

CHAPTER 15

AS I FOLLOW the shadow of the Neverseen King up the stairs, he seems to sink deeper into invisibility until I lose my imagined projection of him altogether and am forced to rely completely on my intuition that he's still ahead of me.

I can't bring myself to touch the banister again.

So I walk alone, moving one foot to the next stair, and the next, trying to ignore the clamminess of my hands, and the way darkness spots across my vision with each step. At this point, I don't believe he will kill me. Not outside one of his heartless competitions. But that doesn't make me any less afraid of him, and it doesn't ease the tightness in my chest. The sense that I am a lamb walking mindlessly to the slaughter.

By habit, I begin counting, despite trying not to. *One, two, three, four, five, six.*

His deep voice cuts through the silence, and it sounds like he keeps his back to me. "I cannot help but notice how your heart has not stopped racing since the competition. Especially since Itr was killed."

He can sense that?

I lift my black-spotted vision from my feet to the curve of the seemingly empty staircase before me. "I cannot help but notice that you didn't stop her from being killed."

A foolish thing to say. My hand goes instinctively to the hilt of a knife at my belt, and my fingers flex about that comforting weight. As if it would be any more protection against the Neverseen King than it was against Jabir.

Fifteen, sixteen, seventeen.

"You resent me for allowing her to be killed."

I don't dare affirm that. My lack of answer stretches out into a reply of its own.

"I couldn't have stopped that blade any more than you could have," he says quietly.

"Why not? You move faster than lightning." *And you clearly have stores of magic at the tips of your fingers.* A mystery for another day, if I cannot escape soon enough.

"Because I wasn't expecting it either."

I find that hard to believe. He must be hiding something. Some other reason he wouldn't intervene.

The sultan continues, filling my silence. "Safya is more skilled even than you."

I feel the weight of his invisible gaze, like he's looking back at me and measuring my reaction to his words. But I won't let my face betray me. I stare ahead coldly, even though my gut does a strange series of leaps and dips. His statement was both praise and criticism—that I am *one of* the most skilled women here, but I am not *the* most skilled woman. I withhold my tongue, not wanting to give him anything that would betray my thoughts.

I've lost track of my counting. Good. Maybe my brain will stop it now.

Except it doesn't. It starts again.

One, two, three.

"And Safya is ruthless to her core," he continues. "Unlike you."

A dry scoff escapes me. Does he know how many people I've killed? While other girls veiled their faces and wedded their father's choice, I've been scaling walls, slipping poison into goblets, slicing Separator across the throats of fathers, husbands, uncles, sons, merchants, councilmen.

"Will Safya serve your purposes as a bride?" I ask.

"She would."

"Then select her. Let Eshe and I go."

"You do not ask whether you would also serve my purposes?"

"I don't want to serve your purposes."

There's a snort. Then the sultan's frame suddenly coalesces into dark shadow three steps ahead of me, and my eyes have something almost physical to look at. His hand rests on the banister—which is stiff and unmoving—and he twists to look back at me.

He wants me to look him in the eye. That's why he's made himself partially visible.

My heart races faster with every breath. I consider not meeting that gaze, looking over his shoulder or perhaps staring blankly at his chest. Or my own toes.

But avoiding his gaze makes me feel weak. Weaker than I felt avoiding Jabir's gaze as a child. So I do what I learned to do with Jabir—I match that gaze. I won't flinch. I *won't*. I won't let him know I'm terrified of him. I want him to remember that I have taken lives. Blood stains my hands. There is a knife at my hip, one that I know how to wield with deadly precision, and I am not afraid to use it.

Defiant compliance was how I survived this long as Jabir's slave. I may obey, but I will never submit.

I stare into my sultan's unseen gaze, and I don't flinch one muscle.

He's the one who looks away first. Triumph thrills in my belly.

"You do not know what my purposes are." He resumes his climb, and his form slowly ebbs away into invisibility again. "From what I've surmised of your character thus far, I'd rather think you'd prefer my purposes to mindlessly killing innocents, no?"

With three of the twelve women he brought here against their will already dead, I'm not sure how his purposes don't involve killing innocents. But he won't bait me that easily. "Better the devil you know," I say as I follow him. The staircase seems to go on and on, spiraling around and around forever. Will it ever end?

He rounds on me so suddenly, becoming partially visible again, that I step down a step, my neck craning as I stare up at him. My heart leaps with fear, a gasp catching in my throat.

"You've said that before. But do you truly believe that? *Is* the one you know better? Will you opt for a wretched existence because it is safe—or familiar, rather?"

I stare at him, frozen.

Something warm comes near my face. A hand. He reaches out a hand toward my face, and its heat blooms beneath my chin, hovering beside my cheek. But at the last second, he draws it back.

I am not sure I will ever breathe again.

When he speaks, his voice is low, and desperately earnest. "Cast your lot with me, Nadira, and I think you will find the gamble is worth the potential reward."

I realize with a sudden spike of terror that he isn't choosing me. He's asking *me* to choose *him*. What is this reward he speaks of? Riches? Honor? The so-called freedom of being the queen of a fragmenting kingdom? He wants me to cast my lot with him, to bet on him. Against what? Or whom?

I've never liked games or gambles. I've never been a good sport either—and I know that. Games are no fun because sometimes you lose, and most of the time it's not even your fault. It's dumb luck. I'm not willing to bet anything on luck. I'm pragmatic. A good weigher of risk and reward.

This, unfortunately, is a terrible ratio of risk to reward.

And I don't even want the reward.

I lift my chin. "Do you really think you can kidnap an assassin and expect her to willfully bind herself to her kidnapper?"

He gives me no response. He merely turns and keeps climbing the stairs.

I hesitate, not quite able to make my feet move to follow. Shivers race down my spine, through my arms, until my hand is quaking. I place it on the railing and lean into it.

Warmth surges into me. *I won't let him sand you,* comes the garbled voice of the House into my fingers, flooding like pleasantly warm water through my skin and into my awareness.

"Don't believe a word it says," comes the sultan's annoyed huff from further up the stairs.

Can he tell what the House is saying to me? Or is he just aware of the communication? I grip the railing tighter. I catch the inside of my cheek between my teeth and clench my jaw hard until it's painful, and I taste blood.

Then I plant my feet. "If you want me to follow you, you have to tell me where you are taking me."

The railing gives a slight creak, as if it were warning me not to challenge the sultan. But I keep my chin lifted, my gaze unbreaking. Only I know how sweat slides from my armpits down my ribs like a wet, tickling finger.

Finally, I hear his voice. It's deceptively calm.

"You make demands of your Neverseen King?" he asks.

That voice. That voice, which communicates such a tight rein on the force of his power and persona, is more cutting than the sharpest edge of anger. *Sands,* I'm terrified of him. But I'm also angry. I'm angry, confused, frustrated, and I feel like a cornered animal.

A cornered animal may cower, but it also bites.

I contemplate bowing my head and feigning submission, following after him as I plot his demise. I consider turning around and marching back down the steps. If he wants to show me something, he'll have to drag me there.

But I don't want to be dragged against my will.

"You cannot play with a viper and expect not to be bitten," I say instead. After all, wasn't that his description of me and the other women—vipers? Perhaps if I use his words, he won't realize . . .

Realize *what*? How much he scares me?

Surely he knows that already.

"Then shall I soothe you with honeyed words and the hypnotizing tunes of a flute?" he says, coming down the steps he'd mounted until he stands onto two above me, staring down at me from his towering height. His voice is steeped in bitterness, almost cutting. "Do you *want* me to woo you, Mourner?"

I draw back sharply. "N-no! Didn't I just tell you to take Safya as your bride and leave me be? You clearly admire her so much."

Something in my voice seems to make him pause. He tilts the outline of his head to one side, and I swallow, suddenly feeling the weight of his acute study.

"You have surmised by now that I have a particular need for a bride, one that does not involve . . . the more tender variety of sentiments. I do not need your trust, as it were, or your positive opinion of me. What I need is a mutually beneficial agreement, and it's one that I need you to want. I will not debase you by attempting to manipulate your emotions by flattery or courting. I want a level-headed commitment from you, to stand at my side and fight with me."

"Fight?" I croak. "What are you fighting?"

He doesn't answer. Another secret, apparently.

"You do not need my trust," I say carefully. I swallow and draw a deep breath before I continue. "You do not need my trust, and yet you ask for it."

"I do not."

"You ask me to follow you," I snap, hurling my words at him in a burst of anger as I clench my fingers tighter around the railing.

I won't let him sand you. I won't let him sand you, whispers the House to me.

The Neverseen King ignores the House, and instead shoots back, anger lacing his voice, "That was not a request for your trust. That was a command from your sovereign to obey."

Just because I don't want honeyed words and flute playing does *not* mean I want poison and barbs. I'm not a child to be ordered about, though I withhold those words lest I sound like one.

A split second later, I have a knife unsheathed in each hand as I take one determined step up until I'm only one below my sultan, and I'm practically arching my neck to stare up at him. I hope he can see the fire burning in my gut through the glare I fix on him.

He doesn't flinch away as I slide one knife up to his ribs and fit the blade of the other one against his throat. He's only partially corporeal, so I doubt I could kill him, his unnatural speed notwithstanding, but I hope he feels my threat as sure as I feel the closeness of his warmth.

"If you want my commitment to stand at your side and fight," I say, pitching my voice low, "then you cannot treat me like your slave. Force your will upon me, Neverseen King, and you may temporarily gain my compliance. But know that if you do, I will defy you to the ends of the world."

I finish my speech, still glaring up at him, my heart racing. It's only the racing adrenaline in my blood that keeps my hands from trembling.

I wait for his response, my breaths shallow and rapid. My pulse is the loudest thing in my ears.

He sighs. It stirs my hair. Then he turns, loses all but the faintest outline of his form, and marches up the stairs.

I stand as though frozen, my two blades poised in midair.

"Very well," he says, and his voice is dry again. "Then follow me if it so pleases you, Nadira al-Risya."

What? He's given up on forcing me? Just like that?

"Where are you wanting to take me?" I ask warily, lowering my blades but not sheathing them.

I can almost make out his palm clenching into a fist on the railing above me. Cold sweat breaks out on my brow, but I hold my ground.

"If you want to know, then follow me. You wish not to be ordered about, which means that if we are to interact, then there must be some semblance of trust between us. So I will not order you to follow me. In exchange, you will trust my leading."

"I don't have to trust you to follow you."

There's another sigh. Then his low, muttered voice drifts to me, and I'm not sure if he intended for me to hear.

"Oh yes, you do."

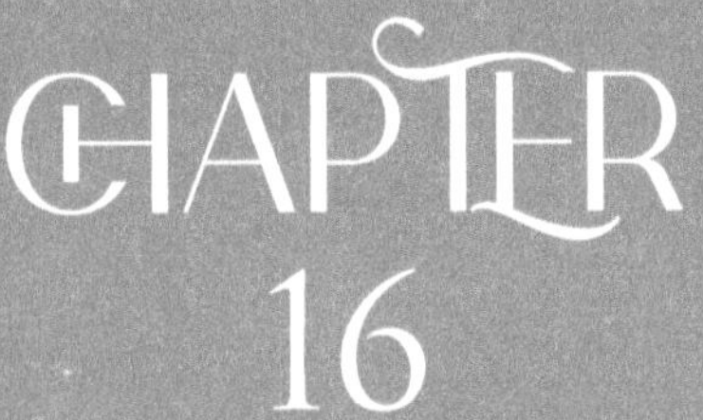

CHAPTER 16

EACH STEP IS a war between my instinct for self-preservation and my curiosity. I *want* to turn around and march down the stairs, never letting go of my knives for a single second. I *want* to keep scouting the layout of the palace, to begin constructing a plan of escape.

But apparently as much as I want those things, I also want to know where the legendary Neverseen King is taking me.

What if it's a trap?

This was part of his plan—to make me so curious I couldn't resist, and then lure me to my death.

I hate him.

Yet my feet keep taking one step after another. They don't stop, not until we've reached a new floor, then another. I stay several steps below the Neverseen King's shadow, my palms sweaty around the hilt of my knives. At least this is still productive, right? I am seeing parts of the palace I haven't seen before.

When I reach the top of the staircase, all is quiet. Neither of us, invisible sultan nor assassin, make a single sound. I refuse to be the one to break the silence. I stay with my hand on the banister, taking this little trickle of comfort from the half-sentient House.

Then the sound of a door handle turning cuts through the air like a blade slicing through flesh; a sound of wood, stone, metal. I barely keep from flinching.

The door swings wide, and I half expect a monster to leap out of the opening and tackle me down the staircase.

Nothing happens.

In front of me is a wall. I had expected to stare down another long hallway, as this palace seems to have them at every turn. But when I mount one more stair hesitantly and peer around the corner, I realize this door does open into a hallway; we just happen to be facing it perpendicularly.

The shadow before me turns, manages to beckon me forward in a way that I can neither see nor hear, yet still understand. I swallow the lump in my throat. I've come this far. There's no use turning back now. No, I need to know what he intends to show me. I need to take advantage of every opportunity to discover any scrap of information that might reveal something about what my sultan hides from me, from my fellow competitors—from all Arbasa.

I need to know if I have any hope of escape.

Gripping my knives tighter in my fists, I follow the sultan up one last creaky step until I stand in the hallway. It stretches out before me, a red carpet unfurling to the far end. I tilt my chin to the side as I take in the rather severe décor of this part of the palace. The stone walls are bare, save for a single row of unlit sconces on either side. The lighting is dim, as though the only light comes from a distant window or two. I had really thought that after seeing the grand and glorious Golden Hall and Emerald Hall, that this would be . . . *more*, somehow. That every inch of this palace would be magical and regal.

But what am I to say? It's not my palace. This isn't my place to have expectations.

I take one more deep breath, as though building up an army of inhalations will somehow prepare me for what is ahead. The Neverseen King regards me wordlessly.

Am I to trust him?

No, I'll never trust him. No matter what he says, I cannot and will not trust him.

"Will you still not tell me where you are taking me?" I ask.

I've almost lost where he is. He's somewhere to my right, but I cannot quite place him. Then his voice rumbles low and deep, and strangely soft. I'm not sure what is causing that underscoring current.

Every muscle in my body tenses for what he has to say.

"Mourner," he says, "I wish to show you a room. Do you remember the room you found yesterday? The room with the open door, full of books?"

I nod silently, not willing to give him any other assent.

"I wish to show you another room."

"Another room?" I ask, baffled. "What does this room have, if not books? Your collection of assorted teacups?"

He gives a wry chuckle, but there isn't as much humor in it as I thought there should be. As though he hides a secret from me. As though I should be nervous about it.

Well, I am.

He walks ahead of me, darkening into deeper shadow so I can better see where he is. I refuse to walk beside him, because—well, I'm too afraid of him. But I can walk behind him.

Walking behind him gives me the opportunity to wonder if I could stab him right now and not face any consequences.

We reach a door. It's strangely . . . plain. Nothing like the magical, strange doors I found on the floor below. It's something completely different—simple wood, decidedly lacking all elegant embellishments or architecture. No fancy keylocks or decorative hinges.

A key seems to come out of nowhere, like he's pulled it from some invisible pocket. I watch as that key moves forward in the air. I can just make out the shadow of an enormous hand. A hand that's bigger than my face.

I'm struck again with the realization of just how *other* he is. And then, before I can stop myself, I blurt, "You're not a human, are you?"

The key freezes in the lock.

He doesn't answer for a long moment, and it's so deathly quiet that my skin crawls and I want to rake my nails across my chest, my arms, my neck. I feel as though I will take one step and fall into the space between us—and promptly sink into the silence.

If he was a human in possession of great magic, he'd have said so by now. But this hesitation, this distinct lack of a response, hollows out my stomach and confirms one of my insistent, niggling fears.

All I can do is wait for his answer. I don't know why my very soul is hanging as though by a thread to *know*, to have him say the words himself. But it is.

"Did you think I was human?" he asks finally.

My own answer surprises me. "No. I didn't."

That is the truth of it. From the first moment that I sensed his presence back in my cell-room, I knew he wasn't human. He was something else. Something that terrified me. Something that was made of dreams and nightmares, starlit skies and expansive oceans. Something that was far, far beyond me.

Something very *other*.

"You're a djinn," I say.

The key clicks in the lock, slides out, and returns to be swallowed by the invisible pocket. But the shadow of that great hand stays on the doorknob.

His voice, which has been low and serious for so much of our conversation today, is suddenly light. A chuckle bursts from him, and not a wry sort of chuckle. A truly amused one. One that catches me completely off-guard. I take a step back.

I can almost feel the grin that he swivels my way.

"You think that I am a djinn? A genie in a bottle, one that grants three wishes? You think I'm a character in a child's fairytale? You think mothers tell stories of me to their misbehaving brood to make them heed their instructions?" He laughs, deep and warm and yet so wholly terrifying that I take another step back from him.

"Are you not?" I demand. "If you're not a djinn, then what are you?"

He acts as if my guess is utterly absurd when it's the only thing that makes sense in the situation. He is a being of magic, and unless he is some earthbound demon or a god's illegitimate son, I don't know what else he could be besides a djinn.

"Do you really wish to know?" There's a lilt in his voice that makes me pause.

Do I really want to know? Do I want to know the truth of this Neverseen King, who wishes for me to take a place at his side?

Do I want to know *what* he truly is?

His hand turns on the doorknob. I watch it turn, my heart climbing higher and higher in my chest, so high that I fear it will fly straight out of my throat and beat in the air between us.

"Tell me," I say.

"Very well," he says, "I will tell you what I am. *If* you come into this room with me."

A choice. My choice.

I realize quite suddenly that I have never had so many choices set before me in my life than I have here, in this palace. All my life, Jabir decided what I ate, what I wore, what incense I could burn, where my next job was going to be. He decided everything for me.

But now the Neverseen King keeps placing these decisions before me.

I'd be lying if I said I don't thrill at the power of choice. Quick on the heels of that thrill, however, is a sharp burst of wariness. He's doing this to make me trust him, isn't he? He's enticing me with freedom even as he keeps me bound.

Why?

In terms of immediate self-preservation, walking through that door would be the dumbest thing I've ever done. It's a risky gamble. One that I want to walk away from, but just cannot *quite* make myself do yet.

Maybe I don't hate danger as much as I've always thought I did. Maybe I simply hate being forced into it. Maybe, when the choice is set before me, there's a part of me that does want to know what is beyond the world of safety and comfort. Maybe that's why I haven't fled him already.

Because he promises something else—something more. *I don't want something else or something more,* I tell myself. *I want escape. Freedom.*

If I'm going to decline his offer to enter that room, then I want all the information so I can decline him properly, rather than impulsively.

"What's in the room?" I ask, lifting my chin.

"Where's the fun in telling you?" the Neverseen King replies, a smirk in his voice.

"This isn't about fun. This is me trying to figure out if you're going to have me killed the moment I walk in that room."

"If you won't trust me, you should trust my need of you."

"Don't the eight other women here speak to my being disposable? How could I trust your need of me?"

He sighs, and the latch clicks as if he's leaning against the door. His gaze burns into me, traveling over every inch of my face. Perhaps he's using magic to sift through my mind, read my thoughts. I don't move a muscle.

"Let me extend an olive branch to you," he says at last. His tone has an oddly *honest* timbre to it.

I say nothing, waiting.

"The first girl didn't die."

I blink. My heart kicks up its rhythm several paces. A beat of sweat slides down my temple. My voice comes out scratchy and wary as I ask, "What do you mean?"

I saw her fall in the Golden Hall. If I close my eyes, I can see all that sapphire blood flowing, drenching me, spattering on golden walls. I blink fiercely against the memory, against the burst of black spots that always come at the most inopportune moments.

"I pulled her from the throng before she was killed. She was returned to her home, injuries healed, with no memory of her time here in this House."

I stagger a step toward the wall and reach out a hand to steady myself. My skin meets with the unforgiving ice of stone. My lungs clench, squeeze, my heart picking up its pounding rhythm. Why does this information strike me so? I should be relieved, should breathe a sigh, smile and move on.

But it doesn't make me relieved.

It drowns me.

"Nadira?" His deep voice cuts through the blackness closing in on my vision. "Nadira? Can you hear me?"

I can hear him. I just cannot breathe enough to respond. Because I'm trapped. I realize now, more fully now than I've understood since the moment I arrived, what my fate is to be.

I will die in these competitions. Or, if by some miracle, the Neverseen King manages to intervene and spare my life—unlike with Itr today—he will return me to Jabir. Back to killing for his greed. To taking lives I have no business nor desire to take.

Back to being a slave.

My only other option is to win this competition.

Or escape, if I can manage it. If I dare attempt it after Hulla's death last night.

One large, warm hand lands gently on my back, between my shoulder blades. I flinch, but my world is so caught up in that one frantic thought—*I cannot breathe*—that I do nothing to push him away.

Then his thumb is pressed to the hollow of my throat, and he mumbles something under his breath. The relief is so strong a sob catches in my throat.

"Don't send me back to him," I gasp, letting my head drop forward against the wall. His warmth seeps into the skin of my back while the cold of the stone chills straight through to my skull. Even though I can breathe, the urgency of my words doesn't abate. "Please don't send me back."

Energy pulses from the shadow beside me, formless but strong. I don't know if it's magic or emotion, or a strange combination of the two.

"On the graves of my fathers, I swear I will not send you back to that *gravbak.*" The last word, spoken in a tongue I don't recognize, is spat out with more indignation than I expect. Viciousness underscores the low spoken vow.

"Y-you won't?" I stutter. "Then where will you put me, should I fail but survive one of your tests?"

"Wherever you like."

He's still touching me, his hand resting between my shoulder blades. That touch seems to blaze hotter every second it lingers. I swallow, then twist so he's forced to let go or take my arm instead. He draws away immediately.

"Jabir will find me," I say. Somehow the bitterness of those words bolsters my composure. Being angry is better than being afraid. "You cannot put me anywhere that he won't find me."

"That," he says, "is categorically false. If you believe that, then you grossly underestimate me."

"If you dismiss the possibility, then you've grossly underestimated him," I shoot back, drawing up stiffly, away from the wall.

His shadow deepens. Darkens.

"If he comes within a thirty-foot radius of you, I will drive tiny needles into every one of his pores until he dies. And then I will remove his extremities, starting with his fingers and toes, continuing until he's nothing but a torso."

It's a deeply unsettling threat.

The shock of it hits me first, then a shiver of fear. But on its heels is something unexpected: *thrill.*

I cannot help the dark chuckle that bursts from my throat. I smile up at the Neverseen King. Does he pull back from me slightly? "You'd do that for me? How sweet."

He growls, and the sound isn't human at all. I get the impression of him turning away from me, sweeping his invisible cloak around him. In . . . *irritation.* Have I flustered the Neverseen King? It's so ridiculous a thought that another chuckle escapes me, this one brighter than the one before.

"Who knew you were so protective of your prospective brides," I say smoothly, pressing to see if I'm right. "Or is it just me?"

And Safya. The thought hits me like an unwelcome pile of bricks. I shove it away. None of the other women matter right now. What matters is getting information.

"Enough of this nonsense," he growls. His hand is back on the door handle. "I don't have all day to waste with you. I am a king, you remember. My hands are full between this kingdom, this competition, this House, and *especially*—" He cuts himself off abruptly.

My gaze sharpens on him. What did he almost let slip?

He clears his throat. "Come with me into the room or don't. Your choice."

Perhaps it was his promise not to return me to Jabir. Or his threat to dismember him if he dared approach me.

Or maybe it was because I finally found something, tiny as it is. He has another responsibility. *That* is what he wants us for. That's what he wants *me* for. I'm certain of it.

"Very well," I say, and sheathe my blades just long enough to wipe the sweat from my hands before drawing them again. "Open the door."

CHAPTER 17

THE NEVERSEEN KING'S hand turns the knob and pushes the door open. I brace myself, half expecting smoke to billow out or something else terrifying and magical.

Instead, the room seems mostly empty. The dull light from the hallway bleeds into the dark space, illuminating just enough for me to make out where the walls are. I take one step closer, leaning to get a clearer view.

It *is* empty.

I glance suspiciously at the sultan, who watches me keenly.

"You first," I say.

"I thought ladies went first," he replies, and there's a flash like grinning teeth in his shadow.

I snort. "We both know I'm not a lady. You first, Sultani, or I won't go."

There's an impression of a mocking bow, and then he sweeps past me. Air rushes past me as he moves, and the scent of desert roses drifts into my nostrils. I narrow my eyes and grip my knives tighter.

"Well?" comes his deep voice from the darkness.

I've hesitated and delayed long enough. Any longer and I'll prove myself an irredeemable coward.

I follow him into the dim room.

I don't realize where he is until the door shuts behind me. I whirl in the sudden darkness, my heart leaping to my throat, raising my knives in defense.

"I'm not going to hurt you," he says quickly.

I don't believe you, I think, but do not say it aloud. I stay where I am, unmoving, in a guarded crouch.

"There is a door in this room," he continues. "I want to see if you can find it."

"You're standing in front of it," I growl.

Even in the darkness, I haven't lost my awareness of him, and don't miss when he shakes his head.

"There is another door."

"You want me to find a different door? Not the one we came through?"

"Yes."

Slowly, I unwind from my crouch, rising to my full height. It's so dark I can hardly see anything except a little crack of light from beneath the door. That crack is broken by what must be two black ankles—the Neverseen King as he blocks the exit. Does he intend to trap me in here until I find the other door? This other escape, presumably?

"This wasn't part of our deal," I say. "I said I would come into this room if you would tell me what you were. I did not say I would agree to be trapped in here."

"I said I wanted to show you something. I'm showing you something."

"It sounds like you want me to show *you* something."

A frustrated growl bursts from the darkness by the door. "By the mountains of Ildrid," he says, and it startles me to hear one of Jabir's curses on his lips. "Would you just . . . *work* with me for a minute?" He waves a hand at me vaguely. "I promise my intent is not for your harm, in any form."

I stumble back. Just one step. Then I grit my teeth, clench my fingers tighter around the hilts of my knives, and reclaim that step—and take another. "Does my caution vex you? I used to trust and see how well it turned out for me. Not all of us have the luxury of living in a palace, being attended to by servants for our every need, never having to bow the knee to another. Not all of us—"

The shift in the air is sudden, terrible, almost palpable.

"Do not presume to know *anything* about me or my life," the Neverseen King snaps, taking two steps toward me until he's just close enough that if he reached out, he could strike me. Each of his next words are spat out.

"Because you know *nothing* about me. I know you have no reason to trust me or my words, Nadira al-Risya, but I ask for a small measure of it nonetheless." He sighs, whether frustrated or exhausted, I cannot tell. His voice softens, pauses, almost like he is considering coming closer to me, but he doesn't. "I wish to show you something beautiful. Something I think you will like."

I blink. His words don't quite compute in my brain. "Why?"

"Because you've seen some of the horror of magic already. I want you to see some of its beauty."

Magic.

"Why?" I demand. I cannot help my questions, my hesitancy, my unwillingness to dive into something unknown. If those things bother him, he ought to let me go. Ought to free me.

But Jabir will catch you.

I shudder involuntarily.

"Because magic will become important for any bride of mine," he says.

"You want to see how well I acclimate to it?" I ask, my tone dry as parchment.

For a split second, I see a flash—a pair of eyes. Too bright, too sharp. The voice of the Neverseen King follows, low and equally dry as mine.

"You've already proved your acclimation to it."

I frown, unable to deny that I know what he means. All I can come up with to say is, "Is it due to this that I owe your special attentions?"

"You're not the only one to have acclimated," he replies, almost defensively, as though denying he has given me any special attention. Perhaps he hasn't. "Three others also have, remarkably well."

"Safya," I say, unable to keep the bitterness out of my voice.

"Safya," he agrees, "Dabria also has. And after the banister, apparently Eshe too."

Stillness lands thick and heavy between us. Perhaps he is waiting for me to say something. Perhaps I am waiting for him to continue.

Whatever the case, I feel a sudden *something.* An upwelling of fierce emotion I don't recognize. It's not jealousy, that I'm sure of. It's something . . . something else . . .

I want to beat Safya.

The realization makes my lips part slightly and my eyelids buzz—though that might just be because of the dark.

I want to beat her. I want to prove that betrayal isn't the only way to win. And I want to show Dabria that even slaves can have dignity.

Eshe, however, I want to protect.

I never want to be made to feel small ever again. Not by Jabir, not by Safya, not by Dabria. I never want to feel too powerless to protect my friend.

Perhaps the Neverseen King is key.

I'll just have to discover his weaknesses. Everyone has them. And once I have those, then he cannot overpower me.

I flip my grip on my knives with a twirl and sheathe them at my waist. "Very well," I say briskly. "I'll find your door. But if you prove false in your promises, I swear on the grave of my baba that I will make you regret it until your dying day."

"I would expect nothing else from the Mourner," he replies archly.

Immediately, I set to work. I drop into a crouch, running my fingers along the unfinished, splintering baseboards of the room, taking care never to fully turn my back to the sultan. There's no other door like the entrance, but I didn't expect there to be. After all, where would the challenge be in that? I move swiftly, touching the wall, brushing the lumps and bumps of dried plaster.

Nothing.

My next pass of the room, I stomp all over the wood floor, listening for hollows or anything else suspicious. I withdraw a knife to pry up a loose board and find nothing. It's almost impossible to see, but I think the Neverseen King is leaning against the door, arms crossed, while he watches me. I ignore him, but I'm forever aware of him, of his every move.

Once I've been through the room again, I stop. Tilting my head back, I stare up at the pitch-black ceiling. It's too dark to tell how high it is, but my intuition tells me not very. A room just *feels* different with a low ceiling rather than a high one.

My hand goes to the length of thin *jurbah* rope and pronged anchor I keep on my person. But I force myself to let my hand drop, flexing my fingers as I do. There's nothing to anchor the rope on. It's useless.

Setting my mouth into a determined line, I turn around and back up against one of the far walls. My heart picks up the pace, and I wish there were more light in here. But the scrap of it from under the door is enough to tell me where the opposite wall is, so I don't run smack into it.

I sprint across the small space, palms clenched into fists. At the last second, I jump against the wall, planting my toes on the plaster and boosting myself up higher, reaching with my fingers.

They hit the ceiling.

There's nothing to grab hold of, so gravity pulls me back to the floor. I stand, huffing slightly as I stare at the wall, much too aware of the Neverseen King's gaze.

There could be a door in the ceiling, but it would be very difficult to find—much less get through in the dark with no proper tools. Perhaps that is the challenge he's set for me.

My intuition tells me he didn't bring me here to watch me attempt to defy physics or pry up every floorboard. I've already felt along the wall for anything that might serve as a lever or button to activate a turn mechanism.

Magic will become important for any bride of mine.

I suddenly feel foolish. Of course the door isn't an *actual* door. It's magic. He wants me to find a magical door. My eyelids flutter shut for a brief breath of frustration. Then they're open again, and I'm staring at the Neverseen King's shadow. That tall, imposing shadow I saw in my dreams.

My mind returns unbidden to the Golden Hall, the flood of sapphire blood and limbs, that border of lightning around that strange portal.

A door.

"Oh no, I'm not doing this," I say.

I think he grins in response to that.

"If you think you can kill me as easily as telling me to open a portal that is going to be full of things that want to kill me, you're wrong." I march toward the door he stands in front of. "Move aside and let me out."

"I promise it won't kill you," he replies, not budging.

"Yes, indeed, I'm sure."

"Bargain with me then."

Something about that tone, those words, makes my blood run cold. "Bargain?"

"Your thief friend's exemption from tomorrow's competition, in exchange for you finishing this task I've set before you."

"What?" I blurt, unable to help myself.

"Finding the door will not result in your harm," he says, "but to prove it, I'll exempt Eshe bint-Kinid from tomorrow's competition. As long as she follows the rules of the House and doesn't open her door after dark, and so long as she doesn't put herself in a position to be harmed by one of the other women, she will be safe for the next day."

Put herself in a position—as if it would be Eshe's fault if one of the women murdered her. I glare at him, ready to spout off that we have no bargain. But I stop myself just in time.

What if I *can* spare her whatever awaits us tomorrow? And if I make the bargain, I'll find a direct way to test the weight of the Neverseen King's word. If I agree, and he doesn't exempt her, it will prove once and for all that he cannot be trusted, and his word is as good as the wild hyena's. If he *does* honor it, then I will have spared my friend.

"Deal," I say.

Something sparks in the air between us, something sharp and searing. I jolt back, snatching my wrist to my chest as the tender inner skin burns.

"What—" I start to demand.

"We made a bargain," comes the low voice of the sultan. "Magic binds us now to fulfill our word."

The burning wears off in my wrist. I draw my hand away from my chest and turn it over. There, softly glowing in a shade of violet with pinpricks of gold, is a design tattooed on my inner wrist.

It's a wilted rose with a thorn-studded stem.

I yelp and jerk away—as if I can run from my own appendage. "What—what did you—"

"I have one too."

I look up, clamping my palm down over my glowing skin. There, in the darkness before me, is another glow. Coming slowly toward me, as though he's reaching out his hand. My eyes widen when it's but a foot from my face, and I see the violet and gold glow of his wilted rose. It barely illuminates the skin surrounding it, but it's enough that for the first time, I see a scrap of his flesh and three pronounced veins running through his wrist. It's proof that he's more than a shadow.

I'm breathing much too hard.

"Part of the design will disappear when one of us has fulfilled our side of the bargain. The rest of it will disappear when it is completed."

"So I have to find the door to make my obligation vanish?" I ask. My voice comes out too breathy and uncertain. I hate that he's found yet another way to unnerve me. But even as I'm put off balance, my mind is working, spinning, reeling. As terrifying as this magic is, I think I can use this in my favor.

"Yes. Once you find the door, your obligation will vanish. Once the third competition passes, and I exempt your thief from participation, mine will vanish too."

I draw a deep breath. "Well, then. I suppose I ought to open this door." This *portal.*

My heart is hammering, my gut churning with uncertainty as I draw my knife. I know what I need to do. Or, at least, I *think* I know.

I take my knife and very, very carefully, nick my lip. I won't hurt my hands, not unless I want to limit my ability to defend myself. So I make my lip bleed, taste copper in my mouth, and catch several drops on the tip of my blade.

Those fat beads on my blade reflect the scant light. I stare at them for a few minutes, not sure how I'm to go about this. Then I give a tiny shrug, drop into a crouch, and tilt my knife.

My blood falls like glittering rubies to the floor.

CHAPTER 18

NOTHING HAPPENS FOR a long moment.

Then a spark catches. I scuttle back a few steps, my eyes widening. Apparently, I hadn't believed anything would happen. Yet something is indeed happening. That spark grows, glowing like a single star in this darkness.

I feel the Neverseen King's gaze on me. And yet I cannot seem to close my gaping mouth. I keep backing up until my heel hits a wall. There I stand, watching that star expand before my very eyes, growing from a pinprick to the size of my hand, then my face, and bigger still. Its light reaches into the room, illuminating the plank floors and the bare whitewashed walls.

It reveals everything except the corner where my sultan stands. The light burns my irises until tears leak out of my eyes, and I'm forced to cover my face. It's going to swallow us whole—I'm sure of it. And I'm on the opposite side of the room from the door. A thrill of panic races down my spine to my toes.

Then a dot of blue appears in the center of the star. I watch between my parted fingers as it widens, splitting the middle of the star into . . . a thousand more stars.

Into a midnight sky.

I won't ever breathe again.

There's a rustle of silk as the Neverseen King takes a step toward me, then another, and despite the blinding light surrounding us, I can make out the subtle glow of his rose tattoo on his wrist, reaching out for me.

I draw back to the wall.

"Nadira," he says gently.

I don't think anyone has ever said my name so carefully, so gently. It makes my hands find the hilt of my knives, and a snarl bare my teeth. He stands a few paces away, near the apex of the shimmering portal that is not unlike the one in the Golden Hall. That glowing tattoo reaches out to me.

Waiting.

"What?" I demand.

"Come see," he says. "If you want to."

"I don't want to," I snap back.

And yet . . . my foot takes a step. I don't want to come close to him. But my neck cranes as I try to get a better glimpse of this *thing* he brought me to see. I glance over at the Neverseen King again, at the tattoo that is the only visible sign of him . . . and realize with a jolt that his tattoo has changed.

The thorny stem has vanished, leaving behind just the wilted rose on his wrist, glowing softly. I flip my own wrist over, and my heart stutters to see the same lonesome blossom on my skin, its petals on the cusp of falling. The thorns are gone.

"Your part of the bargain is fulfilled," he says. "You found the door. So our markings changed."

"What if I hadn't been able to find the door?" I ask.

"Then your part of the tattoo wouldn't have vanished, and I wouldn't have been accountable for my side of the bargain."

My mind cannot keep up with the implications of this, how it will all spell out. One thing that I'm becoming more and more certain of, is the fact that I can use this to my advantage. If his word is bound by magic when we make a bargain, then I don't *have* to trust him. I can simply bargain with him.

This will change everything between us.

I lick my lips, then take another step forward. "Very well. Show me this magic."

His hand remains outstretched toward me. I hesitate, glancing between him, the door, and the strange glowing portal before me. He doesn't intend to take me inside, does he? My chest tightens. Perhaps I should bargain with him for my safety.

Safya would take his hand.

The thought is wholly unbidden, and it makes my jaw clench. It also makes me let go of my knife hilt and reach out toward him with my sweat-slicked hand.

The moment my fingers brush his, lightning shoots up through my arm. I flinch but force myself not to draw back. It's just a hand. He has promised not to hurt me, and he's given me the power of bargains. I can do this.

My heart racing, I slide my hand into his. It envelopes mine in a shock of warmth and calluses. I've felt this hand before. Yet it is an entirely different sensation when his fingers close around mine, encasing them in the heat and roughness of his skin. It's a hand that is accustomed to weapons—not something I would have expected of our Neverseen King, who has not led our people into war for well over a hundred years.

A hundred years. Three words I might drown in.

He draws me to his side, slowly, carefully. I react by squeezing his hand tighter and slipping my finger onto that tattoo on his wrist.

I catch the faintest impression of surprise in the air between us. But I'm not holding on to him—I'm checking his pulse.

It's racing even faster than mine.

This makes me blink twice and frown. Why would his heart be beating so quickly? Does he intend to harm me? Is he—

"Don't be afraid," he says. Without realizing it, I'd begun withdrawing, but his voice stops me.

I'm not afraid, I want to spit. *I'm angry, and I hate you, and I want you to leave me and Eshe alone.* But I hold my tongue.

"Look," he whispers, pulling me back to his side.

I force myself not to resist. Force myself not to think about his hand in mine, how close he is, with all his tallness and . . . and . . . *shadowiness.* Then I lift my eyes.

And I find myself staring into a sea of stars. Except it looks more like an *explosion* of stars, of color, of . . . clouds? It's like I'm *in* the sky, realizing how much vaster it truly is. From the ground, staring up at the stars, the sky is black with tiny dots of winking lights. But *this* . . . I had never known how bright and colorful the night was beyond what I could see. The stars are like paint splatters of white and blue and orange, all different sizes. There are clouds the shade of rose and violet, climbing and mingling with those splatters.

It's magnificent.

"It's called a *nebula,"* says the sultan beside me, his voice sounding close like he ducks his head toward mine. "And there are a countless number of them, each different. Each beautiful in its own way."

I manage to shut my sagging jaw and draw in a sniffling breath. Is my cheek wet? Why would my cheek be wet? Hastily, I reach up with my left hand and rub my face. "It's a door," I say, my voice shaky. I swallow and clear my throat, trying again. "It's a door. Does that mean you step out into . . . this . . . *nebula?"*

He shakes his head. My traitorous eyes suddenly wish I could see his face and read what he thinks beyond the vague impressions of movement I get from him.

"There's no air out there," he says. "We'd die."

"Would we fall?"

"No. We'd float."

I frown, then shoot him a glare.

"I'm not lying," he says, and I think he might be grinning. His hand tightens on mine, and I have the sudden urge to pull it away.

"Can't you just use magic to breathe?" I ask and give in to the impulse to pull my hand out of his. He doesn't resist, letting me go.

"Magic cannot solve all problems."

I frown at him again, but he doesn't say anything this time. Instead, he steps forward, leaving me against the wall, and approaches the sparkling, white-rimmed portal. For a terrifying moment, I think he's about to walk into it.

He doesn't. He starts murmuring something so quietly I cannot discern the words. Even if I could, I'm not sure I would be able to understand them. Perhaps magic has a different language than Arbasa.

He's a black silhouette against the shining starlight. He's almost as tall as the portal, with a long cloak hanging from his broad shoulders. I'm surprised to find that, when the light casts him in stark relief, he wears a hood covering his head. He lifts his arms wide, as if to embrace the world beyond him.

I stare, transfixed, waiting for something terrible to happen. Waiting for the white starlight to start crackling, perhaps burning him, or for him to fall straight into the portal and drift away into a world I don't understand.

He grabs the edges of the portal. Which doesn't seem possible, but at this point, I'm operating under the assumption that literally anything is possible.

As he speaks, he *pulls*. He steps one of his legs back, as though bracing with effort. His arms flex as he bows his head, still speaking under his breath, and beneath his grip, the portal starts to shrink. My eyes widen. He grunts, throwing his full weight into what he does.

But he said in the Golden Hall that blood was the way to close that portal. My blood opened it. So why doesn't he use his blood?

I watch as he forces the portal into the size of a head cushion, then catches it between his hands like a ball of fire and keeps shoving down on it. The smaller it gets, the dimmer its light becomes, and the more the edges crackle, as if it's trying and failing to resist.

Then it's the size of my fist. I scurry to the side to see what happens next, since his back is to me. He holds it in his palms now, and I watch with wide eyes as he crushes it between his hands, the light snuffed out.

I only know he opens his hand when I catch the glow of his wrist tattoo, and the faintest diamond of light hovering in his palm.

He tilts his fingers, and lets that spark fall to the ground. A small blade appears in his hand, and he slices across his thumb, presses its bleeding pad to the floor.

The spark is swallowed up in darkness.

I scurry out of the dark room before the Neverseen King can say anything to me. My mind is spinning, reeling, and I'm suddenly aware of how desperately hungry I am. Was it just this morning that we had the second competition, that Safya murdered Itr?

I need to get back to my own room. Think, plan. Sort through what I've learned today. Perhaps Eshe will have found me supplies, and I can start on my floor plan of the palace.

The last thing I want to do is run into any of the women. I don't want to answer questions, I don't want to be polite, and I don't want to be murdered. By Raha or anyone else.

He shuts the door behind us. I don't turn around.

It's foolish, really, to turn my back on the Neverseen King, who has just demonstrated some strange magic. Magic that I don't understand. I don't trust him, but at the same time, part of me knows he won't stab me in the back. At least, not *yet*.

I ought to say something to him. Some deferential pleasantries that show I am a loyal subject who knows her place.

Instead, I flee.

I don't give him a chance to call out to me. My hand still tingles from his touch, and no amount of clenching and unclenching will make it stop. I need to get away from him so I can clear my head.

Making a beeline for the door in this bare hallway that led to the spiral staircase, it hits me only now how odd it is that such a grand staircase leads to such an unadorned part of the palace. I shove the thought away; there are vastly more important mysteries to work out first.

I reach out, grab the brass doorknob, and swing the door open.

I'm immediately face to face with Mahja. Her nose is only a hand's breadth away from mine.

I leap backward, my heart nearly flying out of my throat. No sound escapes me except the tiniest gasp. I've drawn two knives in a flash.

Instinctively, my gaze rakes over her for any sign of weapons, but she seems unarmed. Her hands are empty, listless at her side. That is when I take in the rest of her. Her swaying form, her twitching fingers, her skin that has drained of all its color. Her eyes that stare wide and unfocused.

Something's wrong with her.

"Mahja?" comes the Neverseen King's voice from behind me. His footsteps are heavy, quick, as he reaches my side.

Just in time to watch the girl fall forward.

I jump back. Black spots erupt across my vision. My breathing comes hard and fast.

The Neverseen King catches Mahja before she hits the floor. It is a strange contrast, the girl's paleness and solidity against his dark coalescing shadow. There is a sweep of cloak as he lifts her up into his arms.

"Emin!" he thunders so loudly I flinch. His voice is nothing like it was when he said my name and told me not to be afraid. "Emin! Mahja, can you hear my voice? *Emin!*"

I stand frozen against the hall's wall, my breath shallow, my heart barely beating. The Neverseen King's voice, loud and powerful enough to shatter glass, goes on shouting, but all I can hear is the panic in his voice. True panic. Panic I know too well. The kind of panic that is contagious.

Someone is running up the stairs. The steward's face comes into view, with his ramrod straight back and his drooping cheeks. His face is set in hard lines, a contrast to the frantic notes of the sultan's voice.

What is happening? What is happening? What is happening?

I cannot stop that one question from repeating in a vicious cycle through my mind, like an echo through an empty cavern. It's a question that will hollow me out, make me shrink into a ball on the ground and hug my knees to my chest, rocking until it's all over.

"Get all the women to their rooms immediately," commands the Neverseen King to the steward. "Get meals sent to them and tell the servants to shelter. Don't let anyone out tonight, House!"

A draft rushing through the hallway, ruffling my hair, is the House's immediate response.

I cannot move.

"I can take her," says the steward, reaching out for Mahja.

"No," snarls the sultan, pulling her closer. "It might not be too late to save her. Just get the rest safe before they fall ill too."

He cares about her. The realization startles me.

Then his head swivels, and the power of his pulsing, frantic energy fixes on me. "Go with him. Do not leave your rooms until I send someone saying it's safe."

I don't move. I stay against the wall as if I'm a new hallway fixture, grown into the floor. A breathing statue. The steward is at my side in an instant, grabbing hold of my elbow. I snarl like a wild animal, ready to stab him to pieces. But he knocks aside one of my knives and pushes me into motion, stronger than I anticipated. Once I'm moving, however, I don't fight him. I flee, past the Neverseen King, past Mahja's collapsed form in his shadow arms, down the stairs, gasping, angry at how slow I am, how tall this staircase is. With a growl, I leap on top of the banister and slide the rest of the way to the bottom, almost falling several times from the curvature.

I slide off the banister, land on my feet, and break into a run.

Eshe. Eshe. Eshe.

"Nadira?"

Her voice makes me spin around, panting. She's standing just inside the open doorway to the courtyard, the light breeze and sunshine catching the dark strands of her hair, twirling them around her raised eyebrows and puckered lips. Her sirwal hangs differently on her frame than it did earlier, like it's weighted down. She's found me supplies, then.

"What's the matter?" she asks.

"I don't know!" I cry in return.

I reach her side in a flash, grab hold of her sleeve, and drag her after me as I start running again.

"You can't drag me without telling me what's going on!"

I ignore her, hurrying faster. "Stars, Eshe, why are you so slow?"

She chooses that very moment to trip and stumble. I catch her upper arm and drag her back to her feet. It's good that I'm taller and stronger than her; we hardly slow for a second before we're off again. I drag her up the servants' staircase I've used before—though I suspect the large stairway would get us there too—onto the second floor where our rooms are.

"Nadiiiira," she whines, panting. "I need answers!"

"You need to run faster!"

"Answers!"

"Faster!"

"Answers!" she shrieks as I fling open my door, practically toss Eshe inside, and shove it closed. With a flick of my wrist, I throw the bolt.

And then I stop. Breathe. Turn around.

Eshe is gaping at me, her eyebrows a tangled mess of furrows and confusion and alarm. "What is going on?" she demands, her voice low and serious.

I step away from the door, my hands running over each of my knives by habit, checking to ensure they're all in place. "Something's wrong," I say, keeping my voice equally low. I grab my leather-bound set of things for my knife care—the Neverseen King had apparently brought it from my room—and set it on the bed. I climb atop it, cross my legs, and pull out my *halah* stone. I take my smallest knife from my shin sheath beneath the layers of the fabric of my sirwal, and begin swiping the blade against stone.

My hands fall into the familiar strokes. *One, two, three.* My heart calms, my breathing evens, and my body sinks into the one scrap of safety it finds. It allows my racing thoughts to clear enough for me to address Eshe, who stands scowling at me with her arms crossed over her chest.

"Mahja is sick," I say. "The sultan and I found her."

Six, seven, eight.

"How unfortunate," says Eshe with an unexpected amount of sarcasm. "One less treacherous knife to worry about."

"The sultan panicked when he saw her."

"She's a favorite too, eh? How does it feel to be lumped in with *her*?" Eshe's tone makes it clear what she thinks of Mahja. This surprises me, because excluding city guards, Eshe thinks well of people to a fault. Perhaps she feels betrayed by Safya and now doesn't know what to think about the rest of the women.

"He demanded that we all stay locked in our rooms until someone comes to get us."

"Oh, so now he's using paranoia to get us to submit to him?"

"Eshe."

My hand moves faster. *Twelve, thirteen, fourteen, fifteen, sixteen.*

"What?" she snaps, glowering at me. "Don't *Eshe* me."

"I think something *is* wrong. And I think that because I've finally figured out what is going on at this palace."

She blinks, and the scowl is gone in a flash, replaced by wide, eager eyes. "What? What did you discover?"

My hand stops, my blade hovering over the stone. I lift my gaze from the silver-threaded embroidery on my sirwal contrasted against the bronze skin of my ankles. I meet Eshe's eyes.

It feels preposterous to say, but after the *nebula,* the goblins in the Golden Hall, and those dozens upon dozens of strange, magical doors I've seen all over the palace, it's the one thing that makes sense.

"This," I say slowly, carefully, "is a palace of portals."

CHAPTER 19

"A PALACE OF portals," says Eshe, her raised eyebrows clearly indicating exactly what she thinks of this idea. "Well cut my legs off and call me short."

"I don't have to cut your legs off to call you short," I reply without thinking, drawing my blade faster across the stone in my hand. "If there's someone who wouldn't be short without their legs cut off, it's me."

I glance up. Eshe looks at me in surprise, then throws back her head and chortles.

"Anyway," I say, blinking, as if that will get my scattered thoughts to focus. Bit by bit, I tell her my theory, about the magic filling this palace, about the things the Neverseen King said to me.

Eshe manages to only spout off a few sassy comments throughout my discourse. At one point, she tries to take one of my knives and start cleaning the blade. I take it back. The last time I let her do that, she dented the blade and no matter how many hours I spent trying to fix it, it was never quite the same.

Since she cannot sit still, I set her on the task of preparing the parchment and sketching tools she managed to pilfer.

"It makes sense," I say, "based on everything that I've seen so far of this palace. Two days, and I've already seen two portals in two rooms. It's not a logical leap to assume the many strange doors all over this place lead to more portals."

"And how does knowing this help us escape?"

"Because if we know what the sultan is hiding from us, what he wants from us, and so forth—if we understand *him*—it'll be easier to escape."

"I thought we just had to understand the layout of the palace and the guard patterns."

I shake my head, not even bothering to give an answer to that. This would be why I always made the plans for our heists, and not her. "Every unknown is a risk," is all I reply. "The more things known, the less risk, and therefore the higher the likelihood of succeeding."

Finished with my knives, I slide off the bed and crouch beside Eshe before the low table as she uses her sandals and mine as paperweights. I take up the bit of charcoal she nabbed and begin my rough sketch on the top layer. Eshe helps me, telling me about parts of the palace she has explored that I haven't seen yet. I go back and forth from my window, leaning out and trying to see beyond the courtyard to the arrangement of buildings around us to get a better idea of the exterior arrangement of the palace. I'm not convinced the layout of the palace isn't magical, and I don't dismiss the possibility that the inside doesn't quite fit what it looks like on the outside.

We work for hours. During those hours, no tray of food is delivered. It's sundown when we're forced to give up from the lack of light. I'm starving, but it's a feeling I'm rather accustomed to these days. The thought of food makes me a little queasy anyway.

Eshe is flung over the back of my settee like a quilt, her hair trailing on the ground, her backside in the air, while she whines that it is only with the settee's back digging into her stomach that she's able to tolerate being so famished.

I sigh, frown at my sketch of the palace, at the vast unknown parts that neither of us have visited. Tomorrow, if all is resolved with Mahja, we'll have to explore those. As it is, much of the area around the courtyard is fully sketched and scouted. I need only to draw it more precisely on the final version.

I glance through the different sheets of parchment, looking through what we have so far.

And then I pause. Something about these floor plans strike me as strange. I can't quite put my finger on it.

I sit up straighter.

This tower that Eshe and I have marked but haven't explored . . . Eshe estimated it to be six stories. My attention sharpens like a blade. The rest of this section—it's just like the incomplete floor plans Jabir gave me.

Coincidence?

I'm a little terrified to think of what it would mean if it *wasn't* a coincidence.

It would mean that one of Jabir's clients was trying to get into the palace. At least that would explain why Jabir hadn't given me complete plans and why he'd refused to let me scout. He didn't want me knowing that his client was aiming for the palace.

With an unsteady breath, I roll up the parchments, fasten them with a bit of twine, and shuffle the rest of the supplies into the best hiding place I can find—on top of my bed's canopy. This involves more shimmying up unsteady bedposts than I prefer, which convinces me no one else will want to do it either.

It's almost dusk before the air quickens, and I sit up straight, my gaze shooting toward the door. Eshe, oblivious, keeps moaning from her undignified position on the settee while she braids her hair upside down.

The Neverseen King doesn't open the door, but rather appears inside of it, invisible save for the large silver tray he holds in his hands. My mouth opens, my heart picking up its rhythm, and I stand, about to ask what is going on, if everything is alright. But apparently everything isn't alright, considering that he's the one delivering our food.

He sets the tray on the table before the settee, seems to hesitate slightly at the sight of Eshe's arrangement on the furniture, and only a second later, he vanishes.

Without a word.

I stare dumbfounded at the steaming tray. My stomach roils.

Why do I feel snubbed that he didn't address me? Didn't give me a chance to speak to him?

No. I give myself a firm shake. I'm letting his attentions go to my head. I'm believing that I'm somehow deserving of them, and that is much too dangerous of a notion for me to espouse, even unintentionally.

Resolving myself, I make my way over to the tray and find quite a large dish of what seems to be stew after I remove the filigree lid. Alongside it is a stack of flatbread, a side of hummus topped with roasted pine nuts and some kind of green swirl. There's also a dish of sweet, shredded coconut lokum and two baklava pastries filled with pistachios.

"It smells delicious," moans Eshe.

"Want a lokum?" I ask.

"You're cruel, you know that? Asking questions like that to a starving woman."

"I'm an assassin, Eshe. Cruel is my middle name. Stop hanging upside down and come eat. The food will get cold."

Eshe chokes on a surprised laugh and slides off the back of the couch. "Cruel is your middle name? Truly? *That* is what you decided to say? Nadira Cruel al-Risya. I've got to admit, it has a nice ring—oh, there *is* food! Sands, why didn't you say so? I'm starving!"

I sigh, but can't help smiling just a little bit as I ladle a dish of stew for her. The Neverseen King must have known she was in my room, because he's brought enough for both of us—which is saying something, since Eshe eats a *lot*.

I eat my bowl of stew, dipping my flatbread in it, while Eshe downs all the lokum and both the baklava first—dessert for two—and then slathers almost the entire dish of hummus on one flatbread and eats that. Only then does she take yet another piece of flatbread and use it to eat the stew I've given her. She finishes everything in the pot, and I let her.

"You won't be competing in the competition tomorrow," I say, breaking the silence.

Eshe looks up, and I can barely make out her face as the sun slips behind the horizon, plunging our world into night. This was the one thing I hadn't told her earlier, but I'm telling her now, and watch as her brow furrows deeper.

"Why?" she asks.

I guzzle down one of the two glasses of goat's milk on the tray and wipe my sleeve across my mouth. "The sultan bargained with me."

She starts nodding, still frowning and looking a little crazed. "Um . . . makes perfect sense."

A loud groan rips through the air. Eshe's gaze whips to mine, and I stop breathing. It came from outside our room. It sounded like creaking wood, but it could be anything. We stare at each other, listening, waiting.

Then there's a distant yell. We probably wouldn't have heard it if we weren't being so quiet, if the fountain hadn't stopped gurgling and the outside world gone quiet in the wake of the sunset.

We wait for several long minutes but hear nothing else. I chew the inside of my lip, then get to my feet and pace to the window. The world is blanketed in night, and I have a sudden thought.

The sultan dismissed the servants for the day. Does that mean . . .?

Is it possible that his guards are no longer on duty?

My hand goes to the *jurbah* rope on the inside of my waistband. My heart quickens, my mind reeling. This might just be the most daring thing I've ever considered doing.

"Aren't you going to sleep?" calls Eshe from the settee. "Out of the goodness of my heart, I'll even let you have the floor."

"I wish I had a candle," I say.

"Candle? Why didn't you say so? I snatched one earlier. Along with fire."

I can't help closing my eyes and smiling as I shake my head. "Of course you did. What else did you find?"

Before I know it, she's reaching into her clothes and pulling out two tall, thin wax candles—without their holders, unfortunately—a fire box, a leather-wrapped sewing kit complete with both straight and rounded bone needles, an iron skin scraper, a roll of bandages, a silver dinner knife, and a knot of string. They come out of all sorts of places from her person.

She's good at what she does. She always had deft fingers. If she hadn't been so upset by Hulla's death, she would never have missed when Itr poisoned her glass.

I'm so relieved she's not competing tomorrow.

As I watch Eshe bring out all these trinkets, I catch sight of a peeking white bandage near her elbow. I tilt my head to the side as she quickly draws her sleeve lower, flashing me a grin as she shows off the string she pilfered. My gaze goes past the string to her sleeve. I wouldn't have noticed it before, and it's especially hard to see in the dark, but now I see a tight line of mending. I swallow and grit my teeth.

"Who hurt you?" I ask.

Eshe just rolls her eyes, sits on the ground cross-legged, and picks up the fire box. She slides it open, takes out the tinder, a small wooden rod, and a slab of limestone with a hole drilled in it. She inserts the rod in the hole, lines up the tinder to catch the spark, and begins rubbing her hands together around the wood rapidly. Eventually the spark lights the tinder, and she lifts it to the wick of one of the candles.

The light is sparse and flickering, just illuminating our faces and Eshe's haul on the ground between our laps. She flashes me a quick grin and hands over the candle. I take it, but don't move.

"Who hurt you?" I ask again.

She waves a hand, and the shadow of it leaps upon the bed behind her. "Oh, it's nothing. Fathuna and I just got in a little scrape."

I sit up straighter. "When? How? What did she—"

She's still shaking her head, trying to tell me to drop it, probably because she's embarrassed that she managed to get hurt. After all, she's a thief, not an assassin. She's not as well-trained in combat as I am.

"She was just prowling here and there with Gaya and Kanza. They saw me poking around, and Fathuna demanded to know what I was doing, why was I ignoring them and what was wrong with me at the competition." She mimics Fathuna's voice, tossing it a pitch higher. "Gaya said something about how she wanted to make sure I wasn't doing anything that would *harm the Neverseen King*. Nonsense like that. They were just trying to intimidate me and make sure I know they're on top of the pecking order."

"They're not," I say.

Eshe snorts. "I probably shouldn't have slipped Fathuna's bracelet off and then dangled it in front of her face. I was wearing Gaya's sash though, before she realized I'd taken it. I didn't take anything off Kanza, because she was telling the other two to stop being mean."

I want to laugh and cover my face at once.

"You ask for too much trouble."

She grins at that. It's a grin I think I might do anything to protect. It was gone this morning, and I never want that to happen again.

"So that's what the bandage is about." Eshe shrugs. "Fathuna just nicked me with her knife. Payback for the bracelet and the *attitude*."

"Do I need to look at this nick?"

"Nope!"

"Do I need to go show Fathuna and her crew what happens when people hurt my friends?"

Eshe laughs, grabbing hold of her knees and rocking back. I believe her assurance that Fathuna didn't nick her badly, which is good. Good for Eshe, for me, and *definitely* good for Fathuna.

"You'd win," she says, still laughing. "You'd win against everyone here."

I don't answer because I'm not so sure. I'm very intimidated by Safya, more than a little terrified Raha will discover my identity, and I do not want to be guilty of underestimating Dabria. She seems the type of person who takes advantage of the fact that she doesn't look like she could wield a weapon. There's also the Neverseen King's comment about her adjusting quickly to magic. Her voice drifts into my mind, light with her sweet, tinkling laughter.

"Haven't you thought of what it would be like, to be the one person in all Arbasa to discover the face of our Neverseen King?"

The back of my neck feels strangely warm.

I don't want to underestimate any of them. They're all risks I don't fully understand, people whose personalities and interests and motivations I don't know.

"If you are not hurt," I say, climbing to my feet and taking the candle she's lit, "then let's explore."

Her eyes widen. "You want to leave this room? What about sleeping? I'm exhausted! And besides, what if something eats us? What about the sultan's warning to never leave our rooms?"

"About that warning," I say, walking toward the window and peering out at the night-blanketed world. "Has anything struck you as odd about the way he and the steward always issue that warning?"

"Um . . . no?"

"Up until this afternoon, when he was panicking, they always said the same thing." Something had itched in my mind about that warning, especially since the sultan's specific warning this time had changed. Not intentionally, I think. *Accidentally*.

Eshe looks at me blankly. "Not to leave our rooms?"

"That's what we heard, but that wasn't what he explicitly said."

Now she's glaring at me. "Stop teasing me and just *tell* me, stars above!"

I smile—a slow, devious smile. "He said not to unlock our doors."

"I fail to see the point," Eshe grumbles, but the moment the words are out, her eyes widen. "The *doors*."

My smile widens. I tap the sill I stand beside. "He didn't say we couldn't leave through the window."

Even the sparse candlelight illuminates how pale Eshe has gone. "But what about Hulla?"

"She opened her door. That's what the maid said this morning."

Eshe rubs a hand up and down her arm. "I don't know, Nadira."

I step away from the window, my tight shoulders dropping a little lower than before. Even my daring friend thinks this idea is too risky. Am I being blinded by my own desperation to be free? Have I latched onto an idea that is questionable at best, downright dangerous at worst?

Still, I cannot shake the feeling that the sultan was being intentionally specific about ordering us never to unlock our doors.

The only respite from the suffocating darkness are the twin flames dancing atop the candles we hold. They cast freakish shadows that, combined with the occasional groan of wind and wood, make my arm hairs stand tall.

I drop onto the settee, staring at what I can make of a painting on the far wall to avoid looking at my friend. "Maybe we should just sleep then."

"We should scout the grounds tomorrow," Eshe says, probably to make me feel better. "We'll get out of here soon. Preferably before Raha tries to murder us."

I huff a silent, mirthless chuckle as my eyes trail over the unremarkable fresco of a desert with sprinklings of acacia trees and a silhouette of a camel caravan on the ridge of a dry wadi. The gold filigree frame is pretty, though. "Watch your back when you're scouting. Don't let any of them get too close to you."

"The only one I'd consider trusting is Kanza. She seems to be sweet spirited."

"Safya seemed timid," I growl. "Don't trust any of them."

"Yes, Mother."

I sit upright. Eshe startles. "Does something about that frame look odd to you?"

She frowns, then follows my gaze and squints at what is visible of the painting on the wall. "About the frame? Of the fresco?"

I step closer, lift my candle, and slide my fingers along the golden filigree. There, so subtle it's almost impossible to feel, is a hairline crack.

"Hold my candle," I say, handing it back without waiting for a response. Once both my hands are free, I take a footstool, set it before the painting, and stand atop it. I run my nails along that crack up the sides—the painting is so large I barely have any arm span left to spare—until I find what I'm looking for.

A tiny latch.

It clicks when I flip it. The hairline crack parts just enough for me to slip in my fingernails and *pull.*

The top layer of canvas and frame comes off smoothly, lightweight and clearly custom made for what is hung on the wall beneath it. I carefully lower it to the floor. Behind me, Eshe gives a soft intake of breath. I look up at what the desert fresco was hiding.

I am stunned.

It's the portrait of a beautiful woman.

CHAPTER 20

MY EYES MEET blue ones, for the first time in my life. They're set in a lovely pale face with rosy cheeks, long blonde lashes, and a laughing mouth framed by golden ringlets. The woman has dimples, and inexplicably the artist has somehow managed to use them to draw out the sparkle in her eyes.

Blue eyes are beautiful.

"This is a new level of low," says Eshe dryly. "Hanging pictures of another woman in a potential bride's chambers. Does this woo you? Because it certainly doesn't woo me."

Do not presume to know anything about me or my life. Because you know nothing *about me.*

That's what the Neverseen King had said.

A bride every hundred years.

"It was hidden," I say absently.

"Inexcusable."

Eshe keeps prattling, but I tune her out as I study the portrait of the beautiful woman who doubtlessly was the Neverseen King's wife once upon a time. Why has my heart dropped? Why do I feel like a ship without wind in its sails?

What is *wrong* with me?

"We need to get out of here." I turn around too quickly and almost knock into Eshe's candles. She jumps back to prevent the crash, but only a second later I feel her gaze on my face. Reading too much.

I fix my features into as blank of a mask as I can manage, and dodge around the settee and low table to the window. I yank my rope out of my belt, affix it to its anchor with a quick knot, and try to ignore how my pulse has begun pounding.

"Don't you dare risk it," Eshe demands. I ignore her.

Escape.

What does that even mean anymore? If I leave, will Jabir hunt me down? Don't I have a better chance at freedom surviving this competition? Clearly, winning it is out of the question. The woman in the portrait is dead. I don't want to be another fresco on a wall. But *surviving* it . . .

I shove away those thoughts. Obviously this place is even more dangerous for me than working for Jabir. I need to stop overthinking things. For once in my life, I need to throw caution to the wind. I need to run, run, run and never look back.

"I will kill you if you go through that window," Eshe threatens.

We'll be killed if we stay here.

I've anchored the rope, and I'm about to toss it over the edge of my windowsill when I look out into the silent, flagstone courtyard with its dead fountain and silver-leafed foliage . . . and see something move.

A silent gasp lodges in my throat. I duck behind the wall, taking refuge in the darkness beyond the glow of moonlight.

"What did you see?" Eshe hisses. "Is it going to eat us?"

"Someone is climbing the wall," I hiss back, heart thumping and mind spinning. "Coming this way. Quick—hide!"

Eshe's eyes go wide in the candlelight, but it only takes her a second before she snuffs both wicks with a twist of her fingers and ducks into the darkness. I unsheathe two knives and slip behind the curtain, just on the edge so I am nearly invisible, but have a clear view of the window and anyone who might enter. I draw my scarf up to cover my nose and mouth.

And then I wait.

One, two, three.

A faint scuff sounds from outside the window. Whoever is climbing is very, very quiet—but not completely silent. More scuffs pepper the silence, and once there's a soft gasp and a pebble falling to the ground.

Louder.

He's getting closer.

Ten, eleven, twelve, thirteen.

What is this? Another fool competition of the Neverseen King? Some trick he's pulling out of his sleeve after scaring the daylights out of me with his reaction to Mahja?

Seventeen, eighteen, nineteen.

Hands grasp the sill. My breathing stops. I dare not move.

Wild curls, turned silver from the moonlight, come into view. It's a man who hoists himself up, forearms straining, until he drops into a crouch on my floor. He's tall, but a cloak obscures his other features.

I take one step closer, knife upraised.

Twenty-two, twenty-three.

Then, to my shock, his hands go up as though in surrender. A familiar voice whispers through the air between us, though he is turned away from me.

"I know you're there, Nadira. Don't kill me."

My knife freezes. Shock pulses in one wave after another through my blood, rendering my tongue useless for several long seconds until I can finally manage a croaking, "Kolb?"

He turns at the sound of my voice. Moonlight illuminates half of his familiar, boyish face, and half of a ridiculous, crooked grin as our eyes lock.

"What are you *doing* here?" I gasp.

He crosses the distance between us, dodges around my knife, and pulls me into a completely unexpected embrace. I stiffen, my fist clenching around the hilt of my blade. Tears prick the corners of my eyes.

I'm thunderstruck.

Kolb came for me.

We have been friends for years, sometimes kissing, and had tried to escape together that one fateful time, but I'd never thought his feelings for me went this deep. We'd been solaces for each other in the midst of terrible lives, but this . . . This is devotion. How did he even find me? To track me down like this, to face the wrath of the Neverseen King, to brave the danger of this palace—for me?

I lower my knife, sag into his arms with a half sob.

"Are you alright?" he asks.

I'm wonderful. "I'm alright."

"Good," he says, flashes me another of his grins—and ducks his head to kiss me.

Moved as I am, I haven't forgotten Eshe, who is definitely watching. I step out of his arms quickly, barely dodging his kiss, and begin scratching my shoulder even though it doesn't itch.

My face is hot. "How did you find me? Are you here to help us escape? I've been trying to form a plan for days, but—"

"Actually," he says, shuffling his feet and rubbing his neck, "I'm here to tell you to win the competition."

My world of warmth and sunshine, of promises and love and devotion, evaporates into dust. I shake my head. "What?"

"You need to win this, Nadira, and I know you can."

I'm still shaking my head, as if that will help me make heads or tails of this nonsense. My voice comes out far too small. "How do you even know about the competition? And you want me to marry the Neverseen King?"

He only nods.

I look away from him, swallowing heavily. The moon outside enraptures my gaze until my thoughts consume me so deeply that I'm not seeing it at all.

I'm a fool. I knew Kolb didn't love me. But at the first, *tiniest* indication that he did, I let myself believe it. I let my vision cloud; I doubted my intuition. I let myself *hope*.

How wrong I was, to believe for even a second that someone besides Eshe was devoted to me! It's this flaw of mine that has already been making me think foolish thoughts about the Neverseen King, and now it's rearing its ugly head with even more ridiculous thoughts about Kolb.

I won't be blinded. I won't be a fool.

I hate this weakness.

But I won't be weak anymore. Enough is enough. I won't play the fool with Kolb for another instant. I take one step back from him, putting distance between myself, sheathe my knife, and cross my arms over my chest.

"How did you find me?" I demand.

He doesn't meet my eye, glancing down at his bare feet. How he managed to scale the wall without a rope is beyond me, but that's always been Kolb.

"Jabir found you," he says.

I sink two inches into the floor. "What?"

"He knows you're here."

"How?"

"I don't know!" he throws up his hands in frustration and starts pacing. He could never sit still for more than thirty seconds. "But he knows you're here in the palace, that you're competing for the hand of the Neverseen King."

I give a rueful snort. *He always finds me.* Apparently my insistence to the sultan that he shouldn't underestimate Jabir was fair. That's another thing I'm a fool for—believing for even a second that I could get away from Jabir. "I suppose he sent you because he wants me back?"

Maybe Kolb suggesting I win is actually his way of trying to protect me from Jabir. Maybe—

"He sent me to tell you to win."

Apparently I still haven't learned my lesson. I grit my teeth. "Why?"

At this, Kolb walks past me and plops down cross-legged on the settee. "Our people are fed up, Nadira. The incense tariffs have gone up, and with Idamea's port city soon to finish, they'll capture much of the spice trade from us. Prices keep going up. People are starving. Our sultan never shows his face, isn't trying to repair our trade relationship with other kingdoms—he isn't doing *anything* to help us. This is our chance. Our chance to infiltrate his domain so we can overthrow him and choose a new sultan."

"Watch your seditious tongue. These walls have ears."

At that, he clamps his mouth shut and looks around the darkness warily. He's lucky I can sense that the Neverseen King isn't here, but he doesn't need to know that.

"So you want me to get married," I say.

He nods vigorously. I try to stop my gut from sinking.

"You can learn his weaknesses, his secrets," he says, lowering his voice until I can only barely discern what he is saying.

"You want me to win the competition, marry the Neverseen King, and then betray him," I say slowly. I choose not to articulate what I'm thinking: *And Jabir wants to continue using me as his pawn.*

Kolb nods.

My next words are foolishly bitter, but I have to speak them anyway. "Do you intend to keep crawling through windows and drains to kiss me?"

He ducks his head. So he's not *completely* shameless. "I've been doing it this long," he says at last with a sad shrug. "But this opportunity is too good to pass up. I *know* you can win."

"I don't want to win. I want to get out of here."

"You cannot leave! Not when you could change everything for us, for our people. Don't you see that you, Nadira, are our salvation?"

I don't deign to respond to that. He should know better than to believe those words. As long as Jabir has his hold on me, I cannot save anything.

"Does everyone know about the competition?" I ask instead.

He shakes his head. "No one knows. It's a secret."

But *somehow,* Jabir knows. Unease prickles down my spine.

"How did you get in?"

"Oh! That was the easy part. This apparently breaks down djinn magic, so I was able to get in." He fishes in the pockets of his tattered clothes and pulls out—

—a golden egg studded with rubies, emeralds, and one large diamond.

My focus narrows to the small but priceless treasure in his dirty palm. My voice drops to a lethal octave. "Where did you get that?"

His gaze sharpens at my tone. "You've seen it before. Has Jabir made you use it too?"

Jabir. Jabir. Jabir.

There's something obvious here that I'm not understanding. Something my blindsided brain is not comprehending. Why hasn't Jabir given the artifact to whoever ordered it stolen?

Was Jabir the one who wanted the egg in the first place?

"It breaks down magic?" I ask, watching the moonlight catch on the refractive surface of its jewels.

"It works much better than you'd think. When Jabir said the first errand he wanted me to do was to break into the palace to speak to you, I thought I was dead. Everyone knows you don't just sneak into the Neverseen King's palace. I was terrified you were right to be nervous about the deal I made with Jabir. I don't want my sister to be left alone without anyone to take care of her once she gets better. But no, I didn't have any trouble getting in. I'm glad for it."

Nausea hits my gut at the mention of his sister. His *dead* sister.

He doesn't know.

I should tell him. He needs to disentangle himself from Jabir and run as far away as he can. But my throat closes, my stomach roiling, and I can do nothing but stand here.

Kolb unfolds his long legs and gets up off the settee. Numbly, I think I'll have to clean off the dirt he leaves behind to keep his visit from being discovered. "I have to go," he says, coming toward me as though for another hug. Or perhaps a kiss.

I clench my jaw and tighten my arms across my chest. "Then go."

"I wouldn't ask you to do something if I didn't think it was for the best," he says softly, stopping before me, but not touching me. I nod once, but between what feels like his betrayal and the knowledge I cannot bring myself to share, I refuse to soften toward him. He looks like he wishes to reach out to me. *Please don't. Please don't. Please don't.*

He turns, and in a flurry of tattered cloak, drops himself out of the window, swallowed up by night and that eerie silence.

"What was that?" Eshe whispers from beneath the bed. Sand and stars, why did she pick the worst hiding spot in the entire room?

A nightmare, I want to snap back. In three paces, I've crossed the distance to the window. The stone ledge is cool beneath my fingers as I lean out and find the gangly shadow slipping through the courtyard.

He knows how to get out of here without getting killed.

Resolve hardens in my breast as I grit my teeth. I grab the rope that I left pooled on the floor, wind the end around my hand, and hop onto the window ledge. "Be right back," I say to Eshe.

"Nadira!"

I pull my hood low and start scaling the wall. My heart pounds the entire way down.

CHAPTER 21

MY FEET TINGLE when I land on the flagstone pathway. My thoughts are like the chaos of color amid the bursting of clouds and stars in the nebula portal, except they're not at all beautiful like the world the Neverseen King had shown me. They're a twisted mass of wretched self-loathing, confusion, and the realization that, as much as I despise gambles, I must choose who to throw my lot in with.

Each step hugging the shadows and chasing after Kolb is a step that makes the Neverseen King's offer sound better and better. With him, I have protection from Jabir. If I escape my sultan's palace, I will be on my own against my slaver—and if he found me here, then I'm not sure I can run far enough to be free of him. *Ever.*

I'd consider assassinating him if I hadn't already tried that years ago. Several times, actually. It worked about as well as running from him did.

Each step—*I'll never be free of him.* Each breath—*the Neverseen King will protect me from him. If I let him.*

But who will protect me from the Neverseen King?

What about Eshe?

Those are problems for another day. I've made two decisions for tonight. First, I'm going to find out how Kolb got in and out of this palace—the artifact only helps with magic, not with armed guards. Second, I'm not going to escape just yet.

On the other side of the courtyard is an arch leading to a covered promenade with a mosaic floor and decorative columns every few paces. Kolb is moving so fast I can barely keep up with him while still trying to be careful and keep track of my whereabouts. He navigates through more walkways, ducking into doorways and sometimes even windows as he scurries like a monkey through a jungle. I lose him a few times, but never for long.

Suddenly, we're at the gates.

There are no guards that I can see. It's another courtyard, framed on the east and west by palace walls, three arches to the south leading to the rest of the palace complex, and the gates to the north. Flagstone paves the area, save for along the walls where palm trees and hibiscus bushes grow. I slip behind one of the palm trees, discover that the walls have half-circle recessions every few feet, and hide in one of those as Kolb walks boldly up to the gate.

Is he going to scale the wall? Is some guard going to jump out of hiding and cut him down? The thought makes my fingers flex around the hilt of a knife in my belt. I may be mad at him and feel guilty about his sister, but that doesn't mean I want him dead.

To my bewilderment and shock, Kolb walks directly to the gate, opens it, and vanishes through it. It closes silently behind him.

I want to throw up my hands and give a huff. I don't, of course, but I gape. Is the gate unguarded just tonight, or is it like this every night? Could I have just walked out all this time?

Can I walk out? Right now?

Butterflies erupt in my stomach. Is freedom but a few steps away?

I'm not leaving tonight. I've already decided that. Not until I know how to handle Jabir. But what if I *can* leave? What if I can get Eshe out tonight? She isn't a slave, after all, just a street-smart orphan who has made her way by thieving. She has no Jabir to run from.

I brave one step out of the wall's recess. Then another, and another. My mouth has gone dry. I cast about each way but see no sign of a living thing. A stifled laugh in my throat, I move faster. Toward *freedom.*

I'm not leaving tonight . . . but maybe a few steps outside the gate wouldn't hurt, right? All I want is a taste—one moment, when I can believe that I'm free. With a hand pressed to my chest, I take one more step. I'm halfway there.

Something like rope wraps around my ankle.

It all happens so fast.

I choke on air. There's no time to breathe before my leg is yanked out from beneath me so fast I barely catch myself with my palms on the ground before my face smashes into flagstone. I try to roll to my back and sit up, but before I can, the rope around my ankle yanks hard, dragging me backward. The fabric of my sirwal rips loudly.

To my horror, whatever has caught my ankle snatches the other one, binding them together. It yanks, not backward, but *up.*

No, no, no!

Before I know it, I'm strung upside down from my ankles, dangling in midair. I'm too stunned to make any exclamation. I'm too stunned to hardly think a single cohesive thought. The night around me darkens at the edges of my vision.

Then my instincts kicks in, and I'm fighting. I whip a knife out and flex my core hard, pulling my torso up so I can catch hold of my ankle bindings. It's harder than it should be—apparently I've grown lax in my exercises. But in all fairness, when I plan heists and assassinations, I don't allow for situations where I could possibly end up strung from the ceiling like a butchered lamb.

I try to slice through the bindings holding me—and realize with a jolt that it's not rope holding me.

Vines.

"Squeee!" says the vine as my knife plunges toward it.

Another living rope whips out and catches my wrist at the last second. It grabs my left wrist as I reach for another knife, holding all my limbs. Panic flares hot and desperate in my blood. My torso and back tingle with vulnerability. Then, to my shock, the vine actually tries to pry my fingers off the knife I'm holding.

"You may *not* take my knife!" I snap, wriggling and twisting and yanking desperately to free myself. My scarf falls out of my hair, landing on the ground beneath me. It's too far for me to reach because of how high this *stupid* vine has me hung. My tunic rides up, exposing a few inches of my torso.

I knew not to trust this vine! It's going to take my blade from me and run it through my stomach. *A horrible way to die.* I gasp as I struggle, but it's to no avail.

"Put her down, you worthless vegetable."

"Prrrr?" says the vine, freezing.

The sultan is here? My blood runs cold. I was so occupied with the vine that I didn't feel his approach. But now I'm so *desperately* vulnerable. It's getting harder and harder to breathe. The vine starts making a chorus of noises that sound like protests, and I hope they're loud enough to hide the whimper that slips from my lips.

"Yes, I am aware she was trying to leave," snaps the Neverseen King, "but I have given you an order, Bahd-a. Put her down this instant."

I fall so suddenly I barely catch myself and roll before I break my neck. My knife blade gets dented in the process—badly enough that I might not be able to fix it. *Wretched vine.* I scramble hurriedly to my feet, only to discover that the vine still holds onto my left ankle.

"He said—" I start.

"Let. Her. Go." The Neverseen King's voice drops in both pitch and volume. Lethally calm.

The vine releases me with a burbling protest, unwinding its tendrils and slinking like a snake into the hibiscus bushes. If I were alone, I'd press a hand to my chest and drag in a few gasping breaths. But I've shown enough weakness to my sultan tonight as it is. I scoop up my hair scarf and stand tall, sheathing my knife, and stare wordlessly into the space beneath a palm tree where the starlight doesn't penetrate. I won't be the one to break the silence. I won't explain myself. I'll give him nothing.

The darkness takes a step toward me. Every movement that brings him closer is like a tide in the ocean, breaking against my ankles, then my knees, my thighs, my waist, until I must decide it's too deep and make my retreat.

But I don't want him to know I'm afraid of drowning.

A hand made of night reaches out. My whole body flinches when warm fingers grasp my jaw, tilt my face up toward the sky—toward him. But he's made of shadow, and I cannot find the gleam of his eyes among the stars above me. My heart thunders in my chest, and I hate that he knows it. I hate that it's ice washing down my spine instead of fire burning in my gut.

I want to be angry, but my hands won't stop shaking. What will he do to me?

He tilts my face to one side, and his thumb runs gently across the length of my jaw down to my chin. *Along my scars.* My stomach somersaults. Another gasp catches in my throat.

"Who did this?"

"What?" I'm breathing much too hard. I'm waiting, bracing myself, for the sharp pierce of spikes to drive into my jaw. Jabir made me look at him like this—often—and it always *hurt*. But though the skin of the Neverseen King's fingers is rough, his touch is gentle. For now.

I continue bracing for the moment the pain will begin.

"Nadira, who did this to you?"

His words, more urgent than before, cut through phantom pain and the fog of my mind. I frown. Haven't I told him the name of my slaver before? Why does he ask as if he does not know?

"J-Jabir," I manage, swallowing and lowering my gaze.

He speaks his next words gently, but nothing can soften the way they fall heavy like stones. "Then why do you run back to him like a dog to its vomit?"

My eyes shoot upward, and for the span of a firefly's flickering light, I'm certain our gazes meet. I wrench free of his grip and stumble back two steps.

"I wasn't going back to him," I snap. "I would never."

"You wouldn't? Then where are you going, little assassin? Back to that *boy* who steals kisses but cannot give you anything in return?"

My eyes widen, my skin going hot. Did the sultan listen to our conversation after all?

"Haven't you told me yourself that Jabir will hunt you down? Don't you realize that so long as you stay within the walls of this palace, you are under my protection, and he cannot harm you?"

I know, I know, I know—I know I know I know—

I want to tear my hair out. I want to rip or break something, because then maybe I'll feel less horribly trapped. Maybe then I won't feel helpless. Since when does an assassin need protection? Since when does she find it in her kidnapper?

I say the only thing I can think of: "I wasn't leaving."

It's eerily silent. If I left through those gates, would I be assaulted by the bustle of city? Or has the sound of death stretched across all the kingdom too?

Does he believe me?

His question breaks the silence. "Who was that boy and where did he get magic?"

"Magic?" I blurt, then shake my head. "He doesn't have magic." It was just an artifact that counteracts magic . . . or is that magic too? I'm suddenly unsure.

"He entered my palace."

"Because the gates were unguarded," I say, afraid of what might happen to Kolb if I reveal the truth of how he entered the palace.

A quiet scoff bursts from the darkness a step away. "Unguarded? You think I'd leave my gate to be secured by mortal hands?"

I chew the inside of my lip, suddenly uncertain and confused. "So the gate isn't open for just anyone to walk through."

"Correct."

"So I cannot walk through it."

"If I said you could, would you?"

Traces of amusement mix with something *else* in his voice. I cannot tell if he is giving me some riddle, teasing me, or testing me. I clear my throat and stand straighter.

"You were afraid of something today," I say. "But you seem at ease now."

"How cunningly observant you are."

"I do not wish to be mocked."

"I am not mocking you."

"Yes, you are," I snap back, indignant.

He sighs and crosses his arms. At least, I *think* he crosses them. "Mocking you is not my intention. Rather, I do not feel like being questioned, and since I am king, I can deflect your questions however I like. I'm much more in the mood to question you, since you are the reason for this security breach tonight."

He closes the distance between us. I step backward, avoiding him. He advances again. I swallow, determined to not continue my retreat. There's a flash of teeth like he's giving a rueful grin at my dilemma—stay still and let him come close or keep backing away and show my fear.

"He was in your room. Tell me his name, Nadira. Tell me why he came to visit you. Tell me how he got his magic."

He asks the questions as if he has all the time in the world. As if his earlier panic today had never happened. I level a glare at him. "No."

"Nadira."

I glare more fiercely. He cannot say my name like that and expect me to repent. If he wants to get Kolb's name out of me, he's going to have to force me.

Why do you protect Kolb? a small voice in my head wants to know. *He doesn't want to protect you. He doesn't care about you. No one does, except Eshe, and she cares about everyone. Kolb would give you up in a heartbeat. He already has.*

"I'm not telling you."

So you will remain loyal to him without his loyalty in return? Pathetic.

"He visited you the night I brought you here," says the Neverseen King.

"If you know that, how is it possible you do not know his name?" I demand.

"Did I say I didn't know his name?"

"You asked for it." The moment the words leave my mouth, realization dawns. I shut my eyes against the sudden onslaught of that voice in my head, insisting over and over: *Fool, fool, fool. You are a fool, Nadira.*

It was a test. He knows Kolb's name. He wanted to see if I would lie to him. He was—*is*—testing how much he can trust me. I'm failing that test quite spectacularly.

"I don't think you have any idea what kind of danger we're in," says the Neverseen King, dropping his voice lower and coming yet another step closer. My breath comes faster, hitches when his hand takes hold of my elbow. We're so close, so *close,* and the air between us is made of lies and riddles and secrets. He tilts his head down toward mine, and for one wild moment, the warmth emanating from him makes me wonder if he has ever thought of kissing me. "Mourner, do you realize that we all could have been dead by dawn? If I hadn't been able to—"

"To close a portal?" I ask, lifting my chin as I stare up at him.

I swear he blinks twice at my words. Then he smiles, and it makes the air between us shimmer like light twinkling on dewdrops. But like the dew, that smile vanishes in a moment.

"Bargain with me," he says, voice low and deep. "An answer for an answer. You tell me why that boy was here and where he received his magic, and I will answer your question about what happened earlier today."

"No bargain."

"You'll put me in an uncomfortable situation if you refuse to tell me why he was here."

"I don't see why I should tell you. You must have listened to our conversation."

Silence.

My eyes widen. He didn't listen to our conversation. He truly doesn't know why Kolb was here. So I'm not completely without leverage here. I draw in a deep breath and square my shoulders. My elbow is starting to sweat where he holds me, but I force myself not to move. Not even when his grip tightens, making my lungs squeeze in response.

"If you will not tell me, I will be forced to treat you as I treat those who betray me."

Something about the way he says those words takes me an extra minute to realize what he's saying. "You're threatening me," I say.

"Unfortunately, I am. And unlike some, I don't apologize when I kill."

My head goes light, my vision darkening, my knees buckling. The grip on my arm tightens again, but this time to keep me from falling. I hate myself, my weakness, my need to protect people who won't protect me. I'm small and weak and—

His hand has slipped beneath my shoulder blades, stabilizing me against him. His warmth becomes my shroud, the one thing that keeps me from blacking out entirely, this feeling that even though he's just threatened to kill me, there is *something* about him that I can trust. That I . . . *do* trust.

I hate him, I hate him, I hate him, I tell myself. But I don't. Not completely.

"I don't want to threaten you, Nadira," he whispers above my hairline, and if I didn't know better, I'd think there was a note of helplessness and earnestness in his voice. "Truly. But I cannot sacrifice everything I've spent my life protecting because you cannot decide if you should betray someone who I would bet my right hand has already betrayed you."

His words are like another blow to my gut. Because he's right. Kolb *did* betray me. Doing anything to help Jabir reinstate his hold on me is betrayal. I can't betray him if he betrayed me first. Even if I don't blame him for trying to save his sister.

Hadn't I decided that throwing my lot in with the Neverseen King was becoming more and more appealing?

Anger clears my vision and awareness enough to realize that my head has fallen against his chest, that he has one arm around me, holding me upright against him. I jerk away in revulsion, a sharp bolt of terror breaking through me. But the instant he lets me go, it's as though a tiny scrap of my composure fragments into dust. I'm unsteady.

I plant my feet wide, bracing myself firmly on the ground and trying not to let my body visibly shiver away the feeling of his touch. I'll *make* myself steady.

Maybe I can give the Neverseen King *just enough* information without hurting Kolb.

"He came to tell me to win," I spit, and somehow speaking the words makes me angrier. "He said to stop trying to escape."

"I'm flattered you're enjoying your stay with me so much."

I scowl.

"Why does he want you to win?"

"He wants me to become queen and fix all our kingdom's problems."

"Ah, yes. The tariffs and trade and all the rest. How human of you to worry about those things."

No wonder *those things* were crumbling to pieces. Apparently my sultan thinks they are beneath his notice. *How long have you been ruling?* I want to ask. Instead, my attention snags on that word *human,* and I realize he's never told me what he is.

He seems to realize it too, because he smiles again. "I owe you a small piece of information, do I not, Mourner?"

I open my mouth—but a large hand claps down on it immediately. My eyes widen, my blood spiking in my veins, my hand flying to the hilt of my knife. The Neverseen King grabs my forearm before I can unsheathe my weapon, and I have the impression that he's glancing over his shoulder. Then, with sudden force, he's dragging me off the flagstone courtyard, through the hibiscus bush where the vine disappeared, and into one of the recesses in the wall. He steps into the tight space, his form visible like a lump of blackness with a fluttering cloak.

His hand slips around my waist and pulls me backwards against him.

He is not made of shadow. He is undeniably physical.

He mutters something softly, and a sense of enclosure, of hiding, surrounds me—a spell. I suck in a few silent breaths, my heart racing in tandem with his. But I don't fight him, even when I become aware of his large hand splayed across my stomach, keeping my back flush against his chest. I don't fight him because even though I didn't hear the approach, I know exactly what he's doing. I've done it many times myself.

I wish I didn't now know that the top of my head fits perfectly beneath his chin.

We wait in silence, both breathing too hard but being careful not to make a sound. I'm not sure what his spell has done, only that he's done *something* to conceal us. All I know is that he is very, very warm, and there is a horrible, traitorous part of me that wants to know what he would do, think, or feel if I relaxed into him instead of standing so straight and tense.

He ducks his head close to mine, bringing his mouth near my ear. I stiffen.

"I am fae," he whispers. Then he straightens, and though we are much too close, I feel a measure of relief that at least his face is no longer so near mine. It's hard enough to think as it is without him whispering in my ear.

His words process belatedly. A fae? What's a fae? He must mean a djinn. Maybe that's just my people's term for a fae, and he doesn't identify with it. That would explain why he denied it.

Soft footfalls make me go rigid. The sultan's hand on my stomach presses me closer to him. I stop breathing.

A cloaked form darts between the closest archway, making straight for the gate. My awareness sharpens. It's definitely a woman, though which one is hard to tell. The color of her sirwal is impossible to distinguish in the darkness, and only her ankles are visible beneath the hem of her cloak. She keeps her hood low so even when she looks back to see if she's being followed, all I see is her mouth.

She's not tall enough to be Fathuna, and she's definitely not Eshe. Her bearing is different from Raha's, so I rule her out. But that hardly eliminates any.

A silent gasp steals from my lungs as the woman opens the gate, slips through it, and pulls it shut behind her. She disappears into the city beyond.

So we *can* leave.

But not without the Neverseen King knowing.

His chest expands against my back with a deep breath. He hasn't released me yet. I turn my head to the side. He obliges my unspoken request and tilts his ear down for me.

"Who was that? And why didn't the vine string her up too?"

"Dabria." His voice is a soft yet grim rumble.

Dabria. I bite the inside of my cheek. Either she's escaping, or she's communicating with someone. I find the second more likely; she's always spoken positively about the opportunity to become queen, and while appearances and words may be deceiving . . . my intuition tells me she's planning something.

I suppose I'll know tomorrow at breakfast.

"I imagine Bahd-a was afraid I was unaware that you were trying to leave, and thought to intervene."

Apparently Bahd-a's intervention was unnecessary and the Neverseen King was well informed of my attempt at stepping through the gates. "I wasn't leaving," I grumble.

He lets go of my waist. I scramble away from him as fast as I can and turn so I face him instead of having my back to him.

"I didn't know you named your plants," I say, compulsively smoothing down my clothes.

He leans against the corner of the recess, arms crossed. "It's just the name of their species with a vowel added to the end. They like that."

"There's *more* of them?"

Though I cannot see it, there's no mistaking the *feel* of the look he gives me. I've run out of clothes to smooth, so I rub my arm instead. Do I just leave now? Turn my back to him, return to my room, and curl up in my bed for another long, sleepless night? And try not to think about what it feels like to have his hand around my waist, holding me against him?

Hate it, hate it, hate it—hate him.

It's better than staying here with him, standing beneath the moonlight. What kind of wrong signal would that send? He needs to know that I do not trust him—*won't* trust him—and if he sees me putting my guard down, he'll believe that he has sway over me.

All I need from him is protection from Jabir. That is it. I'm not leaving here until I have it.

"Goodnight," I say abruptly.

"Wait."

My heart jumps. I stop, look back at him. He pushes off the wall and comes toward me. He seems so much realer, and though there's always an aura around him of *otherness,* I can see him. I cannot see his face or make out any of his features, but I can see the hood of his cloak, the broadness of his shoulders, the outline of his boots with each step he takes.

"Nadira . . ." He trails off when he stops, then sighs softly.

I stand still, not moving a muscle.

"I . . . I meant what I said about the man who enslaved you. So long as you live beneath my roof, you will have my protection from him. Should you survive this competition but not win, you will also have my protection. And if he should dare to lift a finger against you, I will make do on my threats."

My vision blurs. I blink quickly. "Why?" My voice shakes too much.

"Because the things he did to you are despicable."

Memories flash before my mind's eye, and each one is like a dagger straight through my lungs. The feeling of blood sliding down my neck as I stared at a crack in the wall of my cell room, the wretched helplessness of using my teeth to tear at each new knot Jabir would use to bind my wrists while he lashed my back, simultaneously punishing me and training me to escape my bindings. He never ran out of new knots to tie, and no matter how hard I tried, no matter how dangerous he made me, he always withheld just enough—enough for him to be more dangerous.

Despicable.

I shake my head, breathing hard. *No more memories. No more memories. No more. Can't—*

My vision clears. I'm staring at a stone wall, a thin *jurbah* rope hanging still as death in front of me. Where am I? Where is the Neverseen King? I glance over my shoulder, find a quiet fountain and the familiar layout of the courtyard beneath my window.

The Neverseen King is not here.

I press a hand to my chest, feel the raging beat of my heart like I've just sprinted for my life. I ran from him, didn't I? I fled . . . without a word.

"Nadira, is that you?" comes a hiss from above me. "What are you doing?"

I look up. Eshe leans out the window, gesturing for me to hurry up. My lungs are still heaving, and though my whole world feels off-balance, I wind the end of that rope around my hand and scale the wall as fast as I can.

CHAPTER 22

I STARE OUT my window, watching the sun rise as Eshe snores from my bed. I slept hardly a wink last night, but that's nothing new. During the scant bit of sleep I'd managed, there were dreams. When I try to remember them, it's like reaching out to touch morning mist.

They vaporize between my fingers.

But the Neverseen King was there, holding me like he'd held me last night. Jabir was there, and his voice echoed through my mind, telling me to give him a goodnight kiss as he bent, offering his cheek to me while my jaw throbbed and my scars tingled. They might have been separate dreams, or not. No matter how I try to recollect those images, they fade like the last note of a discordant song.

Protection.

Win the competition. Marry the Neverseen King.

I want the Neverseen King's protection. But if I try to win, if I actually try to prove I have what it takes to be the sultan's bride—his queen—am I playing right into Jabir's hand? Not to mention that if I try to win, I will make enemies of the other women.

Why did Dabria leave?

The sun crests the horizon, spilling golden warmth into my room and onto Eshe's face. I turn away from the empty courtyard, study instead the lashes fanning my friend's cheeks, the way her mouth gapes open and drool pools on the sheets. Her hair looks like a rat has started to make a nest in it and then exploded across the bed. Her wrist is bent, curling her fingers beneath her chin.

She's my first priority. No matter what happens.

Drawing the curtains closed so she can continue sleeping, I wait beside the door until I hear footsteps approaching outside. Quietly, I open the door, take the breakfast tray from the startled maid, nod my thanks, and shut the door again. I'll not have some overenthusiastic wench waking my friend from the few hours of sleep she has been able to get.

There's a folded note between the silver dishes. My ankle wobbles. I set the tray down quickly, careful to avoid rattling the dishes. Then I snatch the note and unfold it.

Stay away from the Neverseen King if you value your friend's life.

Oh wonderful. Death threats from one of the other women. Probably Gaya or Fathuna. Dabria and Safya seem the types with more important things to do than threaten others, and Raha doesn't need to write down threats; one glance from her is enough. Between Eshe's skills and mine, I'm not too concerned about this threat, though it certainly is good to know that at least one of the women is attached to the idea of being queen.

But wait—there's another note. It's not folded. Just a scrap of paper beneath the note from the other contestant.

Don't make me force-feed you. Eat breakfast. You're a grown woman, and you can't survive on air.

The corner of my mouth tips up. I set it back into a frown. "But what if the thought of food makes you feel sick?" I whisper into the air.

And yet, I eat. It's not exactly an enjoyable process, and I leave most of the food for Eshe, but I do try. When I'm done, I feel a little better. Not as shaky, a touch less anxious. My thoughts come clearer.

More footsteps sound outside my door, and I open it before anyone knocks and wakes Eshe. A tall guard in a turban greets me silently. I cast one last glance over my shoulder at my friend, still sleeping soundly on my bed. Then my fingers brush the hilt of the knife at my waist.

It's time for the third competition.

We take the hallway to the large spiral staircase. Hesitantly, I place my hand on the warm wood, not daring to pet the banister in front of a guard, and whisper in my mind to it: *Hello.*

Hello, it replies.

Do you know what the third competition is? I ask.

I won't let him sand you.

That's all I'm going to get, apparently. We reach the ground floor, then continue to the right down the hallway away from the courtyard. That's when a cold voice stops me in my footsteps.

"Mourner!"

I freeze. Ice stirs in my gut, running down my arms to my fingertips. Slowly, I turn.

A dozen paces away stands a woman in black, with a keen spark in her vicious gaze.

Raha.

Something about the way she looks at me makes my anger flare. I am *not* her prey, no matter if she's discovered my identity or not.

This strikes me as a trick—and I bet I'm not the only person she's called out to like this.

I lift my chin. "Are you calling for me?"

"Am I?" says Raha, and for the first time, the edge of her eyes crinkle as though she smiles beneath the scarf she covers half her face with. That smile is eager, hungry.

Unease ripples down my spine. *Has* she figured out who I am?

"My name is Nadira," I say coldly.

She takes two steps toward me, her nose wrinkling in a snarl. "And my name is Raha Shadid."

Shadid.

The ground goes unsteady beneath my feet. Seyyid Shadid—my first kill. A decade ago. I'd not been long past my first bleed when Jabir had forced me into that job. It was messy, terrifying, and I'd tried to run after it happened. After it had taken me *three slices* to finally kill him.

Jabir had found me and beaten me unconscious. I'd been unable to move for weeks.

"Good luck on the competition, Raha Shadid," I manage to croak. I have no idea what my face has revealed.

Then I'm forced to follow the guard, my steps mechanical, my back twitching with the expectation of a blade as sweat breaks out across my neck. But even though Raha can easily close the distance between us and cut me open, she doesn't. Maybe this guard deters her.

It seems like a hundred years before we reach the rest of the women, standing before a set of doors. What a strange thing it is to stand in this same line of women but a few days after we found ourselves in the Golden Hall, only this time almost half of us are already gone.

I stand next to Dabria, who greets me with a warm smile that I cannot quite muster in return. She must have come back some time in the night from wherever she went.

We actually can *leave.*

Maybe tonight I can help Eshe escape. *If* I survive this third competition.

Beyond Dabria is Safya, her shoulders still hunched slightly despite her bright eyes and the square, firm set of her resolute jaw. Then it's Fathuna, arms crossed and glaring at everything. Kanza wears more knives in her belt than I've seen on her so far. Gaya takes peeks at each of us—she's clearly the one who left the note on my tray, and I suspect I wasn't the only lucky recipient—and Raha takes her place at the far end.

"Where's Eshe?" asks Fathuna.

Gaya looks straight at me, suspicion drawn in thin lines across her face. Fathuna follows her gaze, and soon everyone except Safya and Raha is looking at me.

"Asleep," I say, not sure what else to answer.

"Asleep? Like, actually asleep, or is that your strange way of saying she's dead?" demands Fathuna.

"She is asleep. In bed. Mornings disagree with her."

Dabria laughs. Fathuna leans forward so she can scowl at me better. "What is *that* supposed to mean?"

"Perhaps I ought to go back to my room as well," says Dabria. "I'm quite fatigued."

"Of course you are," replies Safya quietly.

Safya knows. Knows that Dabria left the palace last night.

Dabria actually stiffens, glancing sidelong at the shorter girl. The girl who had no qualms killing Itr in cold blood yesterday. Does she know about the conversation I had with the Neverseen King? If she had, wouldn't he have noticed? But then again, he let Dabria sneak out without a word. Perhaps he let Safya spy on us without a word.

My insides churn. Maybe I shouldn't have eaten breakfast.

We wait outside a pair of double doors where our guards deposited us. These doors are beautiful, made of woven strips of acacia wood. Colorful jewels are inlaid into the design, like a girl might weave flowers into her braid.

Those doors open, revealing the steward waiting for us in a small foyer in front of two more doors.

"Welcome to the third competition," he says. "Find your way out of the maze. The first one to do so will take her noon meal with the Neverseen King. If he gave something to you this morning, you may use it during the competition. Begin."

And with a sweep of his hand, the doors behind the steward open . . . into pitch blackness.

If the Neverseen King gave us something? He didn't give me anything, did he? I rack my brain, trying to remember if I missed something on the breakfast tray. I don't think I did. Fathuna touches a pouch belted to her waist, and Gaya holds a cloudy, glass globe in the palm of one hand. Safya and Dabria, of course, don't reveal what he gave them, but neither of them glance around in surprise like I do. From here, I cannot see what Raha is doing.

My stomach sinks. He gave assistance to the others, but not to me? Am I supposed to take this as some compliment of my skill? I doubt it, considering that the Neverseen King explicitly said I'm not the most skilled of the group.

To think—I spent more time last night than I want to admit trying to forget how strong his chest felt at my back, the broadness of his hand across my waist, the sound of his voice in my ear.

Such a fool.

I'm not the only woman the sultan is courting. How do I know he's not giving the same attention to the others that he gives to me?

"We're supposed to just walk into that darkness?" asks Fathuna, scowling at it.

When I glance over at her, I discover that Raha is already gone. Safya steps out of our line and, within two steps, is swallowed by night. Kanza is right behind her.

"Yes," the steward responds blandly, leaning against the wall of the foyer and folding his arms across his chest. "And you're losing."

"I don't want to be the Neverseen King's bride," snaps Fathuna. "I just want to survive."

"Then you'd better move quickly."

"Didn't the Neverseen King give you a light?" asks Gaya, holding up her globe and giving a sly grin. She taps the side of it, and a greenish glow emanates from inside, like a candle behind a foggy window.

"He gave me some kind of a riddle," growls Fathuna, holding up a piece of paper. "What is a riddle supposed to do to help?"

"May I see it?" The words are out of my lips before I can stop them.

Gaya, Dabria, and Fathuna all turn to look at me. The steward arches a brow at us. "You have thirty seconds before the light of this foyer goes out and the door remains locked until you find your way out of the maze."

"Why would I show you?" says Fathuna, stuffing the paper into her pocket.

"What did the Neverseen King give you?" Dabria asks me.

I lick my lips. "I'll tell you, if you tell me what he gave you."

"He gave me a knife."

"Safya has rope. I saw it," says Fathuna.

"Ten seconds," says the steward.

The three of them look at me, waiting for me to say what he gave me. I'm not entirely sure why it feels like admitting a fault when I say, "He gave me nothing."

"Liar," Gaya and Fathuna say together.

But Dabria only shrugs one elegant shoulder. "The steward didn't say he gave each of us something. He only said *if* he gave us something."

The lights go out. We stand in complete darkness. Except Gaya's little light that bobs like an eerie eye in midair. That light floats there for a heartbeat, and then it's flying forward, swinging like Gaya is running, and abruptly goes out. My body tingles, my hands going clammy.

"Do you ever think one of these moments you'll open your eyes—and realize all of this has just been one long nightmare?" whispers Fathuna.

A soft sigh escapes my lips, and I find myself whispering back, "I'm still waiting to wake up."

But Dabria simply chuckles. "Have fun, girls." A draft rushes past me, and it's the only indication I have that she leaves us to brave the maze.

"Fathuna?" I whisper.

No answer.

It's so dark I cannot see my hand in front of my face. If I stuff myself in the corner of the foyer and wait it out, would the sultan come for me eventually? I run my fingers along the wall until I confirm that the steward is gone. For a heartbeat, I consider picking the lock. Is that cheating? But when I run my fingers down the carved wood of the door, there's no lock. No handle. Nothing for me to pick.

Keeping my hand on the wall, I turn and face the black-as-night maze.

There must be a way to go about this that doesn't take forever. I draw one of my knives with my right hand and follow my left until I'm out of the foyer. My fingertips buzz when I touch the wall of the maze. It's made of smooth limestone. I switch my good knife for my least favorite one—the one Eshe dented—and, kneeling, I carve a large X into the corner, an inch above the stone floor. The sound is loud, grating in the stillness.

If I'm blind, I need some way of marking my progress.

I move faster now, keeping my hand on the wall and following it until it turns. At each corner and turn, I bend and mark a smaller X into the stone. When I reach a fork, I pick a random direction, mark it, and follow it. Slowly, a map starts forming in my mind of the paths I've explored. I follow one down some ways, then frown when it brings me back the direction I just came. It isn't until I find my X that I can fit this misleading section properly into my mental map.

Soft light cuts through the darkness.

My heart quickens, my fingers readjusting their grip on my knife. I slow my pace, creeping up carefully on that light.

It's a tiny stone, the size of my fingernail, just lying there on the floor. It gives off the same muted green light as Gaya's globe. Did the Neverseen King give her this too? At the end of the path, there's another one, and another. It's a trail.

I don't follow the trail. Keeping my hand on the wall, I plunge back into the darkness.

That's when I stumble across the body.

I don't make a sound, but the sudden bolt of fright stabbing down my spine is so loud that I'm terrified everyone has heard it. My head goes light as I kneel beside the woman. Her robes are soft . . . and wet. I draw my hand back, wait until the dizziness passes, then feel in the dark until I find her wrist. She has the softest whisper of a pulse.

Who is it?

I long for Gaya's light and consider dragging this woman back to the soft glows of those pebbles I found. But alarm bells toll in my mind, my instinct insisting that I stay away from those lights. I don't know who put them there or *why*. At least in the darkness, I'm invisible.

My search of the woman reveals a belt full of knives. That eliminates Dabria. The softness of the material she wears eliminates Raha, and she's not wearing a cloak like Gaya was. She's not tall like Fathuna.

Kanza.

I unwind the scarf from my head and, fast as I can, bind it around what seems like a stab wound in her stomach. I work quickly, my awareness heightening with every second I have my back turned to the darkness.

Someone stabbed her.

Blood coats my hands, hot and viscous. My head swims, but I keep working. Sweat beads on my upper lip, trails down my back. I might have blacked out one or twice for a scant second—I cannot be sure. But I'm not leaving her here to bleed out in the dark, all alone. I don't want to imagine the shock, the betrayal, the pain she must've felt when that knife—

Dizziness assaults me. *I cannot think about it.*

Gritting my teeth, I unwind her sash and bind it around the wound on top of my scarf. Hopefully that will tide her over until I can get us out of this maze, and she can get proper treatment. If it's not already too late. Her heartbeat is so weak, so faint.

Curse you, Neverseen King. If not for him, none of us would be in this situation. If not for him—

A rush of air hits me in the face. I draw my knife, whirl. Blade meets blade in the darkness, the impact shocking down my arms. I dodge a strike, moving by instinct, and land a hard kick to the side of my attacker's knee.

The edge of a blade whistles through air as it comes for my side. I twist, snatch her wrist, yank her off-balance, and knee her hard in the neck. A slightly strangled noise cuts through the silence, but it's only a burst of sound that dies a mere second after its birth.

She uses her momentum to roll, yanking herself free of my grip. I draw my other knife, crouching in the dark by Kanza's limp form. Blood pounds in my ears, blocking out all rational thought.

Even though she was in front of me, the air shifts to my right, and I throw myself into a roll before the knife stabs into my back. Springing to my feet, I meet her attack. We thrust, parry, dancing in the dark to a song we've been trained in since birth.

It's Raha.

The deadly accuracy of her blows, the lightness of her feet, her ruthless attacks, her soundless movements—it's her. It's as though we are finally meeting each other, exchanging blows like pleasantries. One cannot truly know a person until they fight.

How one fights shows how they live.

Raha fights like she has no fear, like she is drunk on blood. She fights as though she wants something and will do anything to get it, even if she dies trying.

What is she learning about me?

Pain flares as she grazes my shoulder. But for once, it's not fear stabbing through my heart. It's anger, hot and heady, greedy for retribution. We women are victims of the Neverseen King's whims and games, and instead of banding together, instead of joining forces like we ought to, we fight each other. We make enemies of each other.

I sidestep her next attack, staying aware of Kanza's form. Raha probably believes that she is dead, but if I'm not careful I will give away that she's not, and Raha might dodge my blade only to drive hers into Kanza when I'm too busy defending myself.

Raha's weight hits me hard. I stumble back, barely block her knife, fall—and then we tumble across the floor, rolling as each of us tries to land on top. We're no longer quiet, no longer disguising our sounds as we fight in the dark.

I don't want to hurt her. But when she stabs her knife straight for my face, I stop holding back.

I dodge, pin one of her wrists with my foot, block her knee from slamming into my ribs with my other leg. Grabbing her other wrist, I yank—and then I twist and hit. Hard.

I break her arm.

Raha screams.

With the horrid crunch of bone ringing through the silence, rendering me lightheaded, I scramble away from her and swallow. My blood pulses with energy, but the rage has quieted enough for my hands to start shaking.

A whimper cuts through the darkness. There's no movement of air like she comes for me, giving me time to lean against the limestone wall and suck in deep breaths. My shoulder stings where she cut me, but I hardly feel it.

"I hate you," Raha spits between groans.

I hate myself too.

But there was something in her voice, something that makes me pause.

"Why?" I ask even though I know the answer, and I almost don't believe that the low, dark voice coming from my throat is mine.

"You don't know the years I've trained for this. The blood I've shed for an opportunity to fight you." There's desperation threading the blackness between us. Desperation, and deep, deep hatred.

"No," I say, because what else can I say? Dread plunges my stomach to the floor, and I squeeze my eyes shut as she keeps talking.

"You killed my father," says Raha. She sucks in a sharp gasp of pain. "And I *will* avenge him, Mourner. I will make you pay for the blood you've spilled. When you bleed, I'll make sure no one mourns for you, and I'll leave my own note by your corpse. *I'm not sorry, and I never will be,* it'll say."

Was she the one who found my note by her father's body? Did she believe the words of a young girl, written with a shaky hand? Did she know that when I killed her father, I killed myself?

I shouldn't ask, shouldn't reveal any weakness, but I need to know. "How do you know who I am?"

"Dabria confirmed it this morning. But I'd already had my suspicions."

Dabria knows I killed her uncle. How did she find out? Has she always known?

By the sands of the Great Desert . . .

"Why did you kill Kanza?" I ask, breaking the silence that has fallen.

"Because I thought she was you."

So she *does* think Kanza is dead. But every second I delay here is another second delaying the medical attention that could save her life. I could carry her out of here, but it might be too late by the time I'm through this maze. Were the glowing pebbles Raha's gift from the sultan? Did she leave them as a trap, knowing I'd choose to avoid their ghastly light?

What if Raha isn't the only one lying in wait to murder me? What if Dabria is also planning her revenge?

What if they're not the only ones with family that I've murdered?

Sickness hits me so suddenly I want to vomit. Raha trained to become an assassin for the sole purpose of killing me, but we cannot be more than a few years apart, and I have been committing assassinations for barely a decade. She couldn't have trained long, though clearly she didn't fight her trainer like I did.

Sometimes I can convince myself I'm just a girl. Just a girl with a horribly inconvenient habit of fainting at the worst moments, and who does what she must to survive. But moments like this, I'm confronted with my own reputation. I am the Mourner, ruthless assassin of Risya, who has never once missed a target, with a death count higher than the years she's been alive.

For the first time, I wonder if the notes I left cut like knives into the families of my victims. Were they read as a mockery, instead of a genuine apology? This darkness will swallow me whole. Light becomes a forgotten thing.

Kanza.

I'll never be able to get her out of here in time. Even though I've broken Raha's arm, I don't put it past her to attack again. Lifting Kanza will make me vulnerable to attack, and my shoulder hasn't stopped hurting. Did Raha cut me deeper than I realize?

I turn my face against the limestone wall and breathe out an almost silent, shuddering request: *"Please, sultan."*

And then, just like that, he's here.

The air is simply *different* when he's here. Fuller, warmer, and something *else*. I forget my earlier hatred. Relief is the one thing coursing through my body. I want—I want—

I want to be held.

Like Kolb would hold me after my jobs. Perhaps I convinced myself it was him that I wanted, and not the assurance that, despite my bloody hands, there was a fraction of me that was still desirable.

But when the Neverseen King kneels beside me and reaches out toward my wounded shoulder, I jerk away.

"Not me," I mouth. *"Kanza."*

He hesitates, as if he knows something else is wrong. But he moves, the sound of light shuffling breaking the silence punctuated by Raha's pained breaths.

"Who's there?" Raha growls when the Neverseen King lifts Kanza into his arms.

"Your king," he snarls back, rage simmering beneath his tone. "Shall I take you back too? Are your injuries too great to continue?"

"No," she spits.

Raha's sheer grit is intimidating. I don't want to fight her again. Getting to my feet, I place my hand back on the wall to continue working my way through the maze.

Air rushes past me. I set my face forward, purposefully ignoring the Neverseen King as he reaches my side.

"You're bleeding through your clothes," he whispers.

Perhaps if he didn't want injuries, he shouldn't have made us do this stupid blind maze. "Don't pretend to care."

"I care about the clothes," retorts the Neverseen King. "Blood stains are difficult to get out, and I'd rather not order new clothes for you. Arbasa's coffers are running low."

My words hurt him. "I'll suffer to wear blood stains."

Raha's breathing disappears into nothing. I reach the end of the wall, bend, mark an X, then stop. When a soft draft blows from one of the forks in the maze, I take that direction. He leaves, the air growing stagnant in but a moment. I give one last thought to Kanza, knowing that even if he can save her, I won't see her again. Then I continue.

My steps quicken as the breeze grows stronger. Drafts don't come from dead ends. I keep alert, waiting for a whiff of another woman, the rush of air, or hair prickling on my arms and neck for a sign I'm not alone.

Inside, my stomach roils. *I hate him. I don't hate him. I hate him. I don't hate him.*

It doesn't *matter* whether I hate him or not. All that matters is his promise of protection and surviving this wretched competition. I need to escape Jabir and keep Eshe safe. Nothing else matters.

The end happens upon me quite suddenly. One minute, I'm feeling along the wall, marking X's as I go, mapping this maze in my head, and the next, I'm running into a door. A door with a handle. My heart scrambles into my throat as I take that handle, turn it with a click, and light floods my startled gaze.

I wince, bringing up my hand to shield my eyes. For a moment, I'm still blind. Then my sight adjusts, and I'm standing at the apex of two converging hallways.

Dabria leans against the wall, wearing brilliant purple silk and a veil that sweeps away from her face. She smiles when she sees me.

"Are you the first out?" I ask, surprised and unsure why.

"Oh no," she says, laughing lightly. "Safya has been out for some time now. I do believe she might have cheated. I'm not sure where she went off to, though."

From the warm way she smiles, the friendly confidence with which she addresses me, I never would have guessed she knows my identity. But if she revealed this to Raha and possibly the others, then she clearly wants me to pay for my crimes.

"I'm right here," comes Safya's voice from down the hallway to Dabria's right.

Dabria's pinky twitches—the only sign she's caught off-guard. "There you are! What did you think of the maze? I've never experienced anything like it!"

Safya comes into view, expression serious and just shy of a glare. "You don't care what my thoughts are. You only care to know how I beat you through the maze when you went to all the effort to pilfer magic to use."

Dabria's smile freezes for one second. Then she's all tinkling laughter again. "Nadira, do you have any idea what she's speaking of?"

I don't respond. I'm not taking sides here.

"Is that blood?" asks Dabria, squinting at my dark robes.

"Yes."

Safya glances my way, brows lifting a fraction of an inch as though she is actually curious. When I offer no more information, Dabria casts me an arch look. "Whose blood, darling?"

"Kanza's. Raha's. My own."

Dabria's face pinches in concern that I would have believed real on anyone else. "Oh my. Did you three get in a tussle?"

I suppose one might call ambushing and attempting to murder unsuspecting women in the dark a *tussle.* I settle on, "Sure."

"And you won, I see."

For a moment, I consider saying nothing and letting her think I've killed them both. I decide against it. "Raha killed Kanza. The Neverseen King took her body away. Raha is still in the maze."

"Raha killed Kanza?" Now *that* is true surprise ringing Dabria's eyes.

Safya crosses her arms over her chest, keeping her weight evenly balanced between her two feet. "Wasn't part of your plan?"

Dabria tosses a smile Safya's way. "Don't make an enemy of me, sweetie."

"I will make an enemy of anyone who seeks to harm our King."

"Then you'd be wasting your time on me," says Dabria smoothly, casting me a knowing look, as though we share a secret understanding. As though she isn't disappointed that Raha didn't successfully kill me in the maze. "Have a lovely time, ladies. I'm off to prepare for this evening."

Safya glances at me. I meet her gaze. *Are you going to ask, or me?* she seems to want to know.

I draw in a deep breath, ignore the stinging of my shoulder. "What's this evening?"

"You two didn't hear?" Dabria's lips twist. "There will be a dance. We are to array ourselves like queens."

"I'll focus on that . . . *after* my meal with the Neverseen King," says Safya.

Dabria only smiles before she saunters off, all grace, beauty, and confidence. Safya looks at me once more, and I cannot read her expression. Then she turns and marches down the hallway after Dabria.

The two of them cut such different profiles in the hallway. I stay where I am as they leave. *Dabria used magic to get through the maze.* But how did Safya beat it so quickly?

While I watch, something snakes along the wall next to Safya, too subtle for Dabria to notice, but now that I've spotted it, I recognize it.

That wretched vine. *Badh-a.*

CHAPTER 23

WHEN I RETURN to our room, Eshe clucks over me like a hen over her brood of chicks. She washes and binds up my shoulder, scolding me soundly while I say nothing. Eventually, she stops, studying me.

I return her gaze. "What?"

"Do you have any idea how terrified I was when I woke up and realized you were gone? Or when I found the note on the breakfast tray threatening . . . one of us? I can't say I'm certain which of us it was for."

"It was for me."

"You don't seem concerned."

"I'm not."

Eshe huffs. "Well, I'm not concerned about you either."

I shoot her a look. "Gaya left that note, and unless I'm grossly mistaken, she's more bark than bite."

Eshe makes a noncommittal noise in the back of her throat. We eat together when another tray comes for us, and I try to keep my heart from leaping when there's another note for me. I tuck it into my sleeve and wait until Eshe leaves to get ready for the dance tonight. Once she's gone, I retrieve it.

She's recovered. I returned her home with no memory of what happened here.

The tension in my shoulders eases. I continue reading, and every line makes my heart beat faster and faster.

Do not presume to know what I do or don't care about. Have you considered that me bringing you here and making you undergo these competitions doesn't mean I want you to die or to suffer? Have you considered that there might be more at stake here, to force me to such drastic measures? You're smart, after all. You've figured some things out. Ask me your questions. Bargain with me, if that is the only way you will trust me. But do not accuse me of not caring. Every drop you bleed is a stain on my soul.

One might even remind you that I've given you a choice. Say you'll be my wife, and I will call this competition off. Say the word, and I will put an end to this.

I stare at those last words, written in that elegant, precise hand. I let it fall into my lap as I continue staring, my gaze now unseeing out the window.

Say you'll be my wife.

Say the word.

But those aren't the words that resound like a chord through my soul. It's what he said before them that hits me like a perfectly aimed arrow, past all my defenses, my distrust, my doubt.

Every drop you bleed is a stain on my soul.

He knows. He knows what it is to treasure guilt so deeply it becomes your new identity. He knows the agony of remorse, of regret. *He knows the burden I bear.* He knows, because he bears it too.

And in this moment, alone in my room with the sun shining on my face, I know for the first time what it is to see a soul as broken as mine . . . and find kinship there.

The tears come slowly at first. They well up until I can see nothing but light. Then they fall, and they keep falling, until the sobs shake my soul and I press the back of my hand to my mouth, biting my own skin so hard it leaves marks.

Every drop . . . a stain. Every drop . . .

I rock back and forth, then scoot off the settee onto the floor, wrapping my arms around my knees as I keep rocking and crying.

I'm sorry, I say in my mind to him. *I'm sorry for hating you. I'm sorry for not trusting you. I'm sorry—but also I still hate you. I still can't trust you.*

Then the words come out between sobs, shuddering and breathless: "I just want to know that I'm safe with you."

I want to know your name.

Paper flutters.

I swallow my tears, blink open my eyes. There, drifting through the air and landing beside my feet, is a parchment. I pick it up, looking for those words that pierced me so deeply.

Instead, when I read it, my eyes widen. It's a new note.

I can lavish you with jewels until you drown. I can serve you only the finest of feasts until you're lazy with satisfaction. I can shower you with gifts—whatever your heart desires. I will provide my protection from armies of enemies who may hunt you.

But safety is a promise I cannot give. You will never be safe with me.

My tears have stopped by the time I finish reading, and this time, they don't start again. After glancing around the room and not finding him, I set my jaw, gritting my teeth. *Right.* The Neverseen King has been clear with me that he wants an alliance, not a true marriage.

Well, I'm not ready to commit to anything yet.

I take both of the notes he left me, flip them over, and begin writing.

How many wives have you had? What happened to them? Why do you need another one? Why are there portals in this palace? Why am I not safe with you? What do I risk by allying with you? Is there anything I can do besides marry you that will make you let Eshe go? Why is there so much magic here? What is a fae? How long have you been sultan over my people? Why is the House alive?

I stop, catch myself breathing too hard. Quickly, I straighten my shoulders, lest I get too carried away. Glancing at the portrait of the blue-eyed woman on the wall, I force myself to write slower.

You said my people need me. Why? How? If I agree to be your wife, what would I be agreeing to? What would my life look like? Why don't you let us open our doors at night? What happened to Hulla? What situation is so dire that you will risk the lives of twelve women you claim to care about? Why didn't you tell us all of this before we started? What other questions should I be asking?

One question burns on the tip of my quill. One question that I can't bring myself to write. *How do you live with yourself? With the stains on your soul?* I move past that question to another that I haven't been able to let go.

Why was I one of the ones you chose to kidnap? And why do you act like you want me to be your bride? Do you give the same attention to the others? Do you tell them *that their people need them? In other words: am I special, or do you merely pretend I am? What is your relationship with Safya? How was your meal with her?*

And then, my last question:

What is your real name?

I know I'm forgetting important things, and it makes me rake my nails through my hair. But the longer I stare at the scraps of paper with my frantically scrawled questions, the more my vision blurs. My eyes ache after the tears, the sleepless night.

How are we supposed to get ready for this evening? It's not like I have a gown somewhere. There's khol, rouge, lip paint, and jewels in the drawers of the vanity, but it wouldn't take me hours to apply a little of this and that. Besides, I'm tempted just to go like I am—in my bloodstained, ripped garments with Eshe's sloppy bandage around my shoulder. I can't dance anyway, and food remains unappealing. What point would there be for me to make myself pretty? I'd only make worse enemies of the women who care.

My feet take me to the wardrobe anyway. Despite me telling myself it's stupid, my hands open the door. There, hanging right in front of my face, is a magnificent silk and brocade gown of a deep, rich magenta.

I shouldn't be this surprised, but I am. I gape at the shimmering, sparkling layers of fabric that are somehow both stunningly beautiful and yet subdued and subtle. It's a gown that wouldn't turn heads among a sea of gemstones, but if one stopped and peered closer, they would realize how it surpassed them all.

It's basically *pink.*

I'm definitely not wearing this.

But it takes more effort than it should to pull my hand away from the fabric and close the wardrobe door. I spin away from it, and find myself facing my bed.

Sands and stars, I'm exhausted. The dance isn't for hours. I could close my eyes for just a moment, and maybe—just maybe—sleep will find me.

When it's time for the dance, I forgo the beautiful gown. I barely take the time to comb through my long hair and cover it with a veil. With a rueful glance in my polished copper mirror at the bandage on my shoulder, I shrug, then regret the movement as I wince.

The Neverseen King wants an alliance, not a true wife. Beauty can't be a concern for him. So I won't bother.

If it was a concern, would you wear the gown? a voice inside me asks.

No, I reply immediately.

You're not sure, replies the voice. *You want him to think you're beautiful. You want him to want you. Isn't that what you desire, deep down? Someone to want you? Have you ever thought that maybe the reason you couldn't escape Jabir isn't because he was so good at keeping you captive, but because you didn't truly want to escape? Because he wanted you, and a deep part of you was afraid that if you escaped him, you'd be alone in the world . . . and unwanted by anyone.*

I don't respond to that nonsense. But when I reach for my doorknob to pull it open, to head toward the dance, my hand is shaking.

That's why you cannot stop thinking about last night, under the moon, when the Neverseen King held you. When he was so warm, and you wondered if he would kiss you. It isn't because you want him. It's because you want to believe that, despite what he says about only wanting an alliance . . . you want him to be unable to resist you. You want him to see you.

You want him to love you.

And that is why you're going against every rational instinct to run away from him. You want to believe that, despite the blood on your hands and the wickedness staining your soul, you are still loveable. Still desirable.

You think he will prove to you that—

I don't know where this voice is coming from, where these thoughts have been hiding, but this is *enough*. I'm going to this dance. I'll talk to Eshe.

That will get my mind off the guilt clawing up my throat, the unshed tears that have me in a chokehold.

I yank the door open.

And walk right into the Neverseen King's chest.

I gasp, try to scramble back just as his hands close like irons around my elbows.

"What are you doing here?" he demands, his voice threaded with something urgent.

"Release me. I'm going to your stupid dance." I can't look up at him, because then he might see something in my expression—something that reveals the thoughts that were just in my mind. But I already know he can hear the frantic pulse of my blood, the way my heart beats faster and faster, the way my lungs begin squeezing—

"What are you talking about? Nadira, something's wrong. Why are you here? How did you even get here?"

"You brought me here," I growl, but it comes out more like a gasp. I feel so *strange*. So unbelievably *cold*. It makes panic flare hotter, brighter until I can't breathe, can't *breathe, can't*—

Suddenly, he scoops me up into his arms. I fight, but I'm blind and weak. What is wrong with me? Why is he carrying me? What is happening?

With one hand he grabs my flailing wrists, pinning them to my knee as he holds me. Then he shifts me, presses a thumb to my throat, and commands, "*Breathe,* Nadira."

My airways open. I sag in his arms, panic flowing out of my limbs like blood from a gaping wound. He lets go of my wrists, and one of my hands catches hold of his tunic and clenches the fabric in a death grip. Then he's walking, holding me tightly to his chest.

"What is your name?" I whisper. "Why do you hide your face from me?"

"You're having a nightmare, Nadira. You need to wake up. I don't know how you're here—perhaps I was too close to you when you fell asleep. Whatever the case, you need to get out of here before you're hurt."

I *am* awake. A bit woozy, like I'm drunk, but I'm awake. I scowl against his chest, keeping my eyes closed as I breathe deeply the smell of worn leather and rich spice, and something that tingles in my nostrils.

Magic.

"You're my nightmare," I say drowsily.

His voice rumbles against my cheek. "I believe I told you that once, and you disagreed."

"Where are you taking me?"

"Right here."

I land on a soft bed—my bed. My eyes open, and I see *him*. He wears all black, with a heavy cloak. Gold embroiders the edges of his robes, with gold buttons down his double-breasted jacket. It's an unusual style; I've never seen anything like it. He's tall, his broad torso bending over me. But when I go to look up, he covers my face with one of his large hands so I see nothing but darkness.

"Wake up."

I shoot up in bed, drenched in sweat from head to toe. My mind spins so hard I might vomit. Stumbling out of bed, I trip over myself to the door, and yank it open.

There's nothing but empty hallway and the late afternoon shadow of my silhouette cast on the wall.

What just happened?

I close the door, lean against it, and slide to the floor. My clothes stick to my skin, and I reek of body odor and blood. My vision spins.

He was here. I felt him—heard him. I know he was here. But I was . . . asleep? I had to have been asleep; I just woke up. Hours have passed, judging by the angle of the sun.

A nightmare. It was only a nightmare. One that felt too real.

The wardrobe door is cracked open. Didn't I close it? Perhaps not all the way. Through that slit, silk shimmers. Soft, lovely, inviting.

With a growl, I lurch to my feet, grab the gown—careful not to muss it—and head to the washroom.

CHAPTER 24

WHEN ESHE FINDS me getting ready, she all but shrieks when I say I'm not going to use the makeup in my drawer. I protest that scraping the dried blood off my skin and wearing the gown was enough. But she will have none of it, and forces me to sit still while she works on my face, applying a variety of creams and lotions to "even my complexion." She dabs a thin brush in water, taps it off, and dips it into the powdery kohl before sweeping it across my eyelids. She follows that by rubbing rouge into my cheeks. Eventually, I stop tracking what she's doing and just stare at the painting on the wall of the golden-haired woman.

She has a story. A story with the Neverseen King. I will not make promises to him until I know what it is.

I cannot bring myself to look in the mirror when Eshe is finished. Instead, I pluck at the gold bangles on my wrist, the rings on my fingers. Though the dress is light and shimmering, it's a strange sensation to look down and see such a vibrant color. It's like I'm wearing the blossoms of desert roses spun into cloth.

"Where should I fasten my knives?" I ask, peering down my sheer sleeves and inspecting my bodice.

Eshe tosses me a saucy grin. "The idea behind a gown is that you *don't* wear knives."

"Out of the question."

She goes to my wardrobe, fishes around inside. "Ah ha!"

"What?" I turn. The swish of the gown's skirt around my legs makes me feel vulnerable. Maybe I should wear my sirwal underneath.

She holds up a gold belt, complete with decorative sheaths for two knives, that had fallen to the back of the wardrobe. "Apparently your Neverseen King anticipated your needs."

"He's not *my* Neverseen King," I grumble, taking the belt and inspecting the sheaths. Why am I surprised to find they'll fit my two biggest knives exactly? "You're bringing your knives, too, right?"

Eshe lifts an eyebrow, hikes up the skirt of her own turquoise gown to show sheaths belted to each of her tan thighs.

"That is a horrible place to keep knives." I clasp the belt around my waist. It slings low on my hips, a little looser than I prefer, but not too loose. "You can't access them quickly, and you'll expose yourself to attack while bending over and hunting through your skirts."

"Actually, it'll work in my favor. My enemy will be temporarily stunned by the sheer beauty of my leg, thus allowing me to finish him quickly."

I snort before I can help myself. But before I can comment, Eshe taps her bound up hair, then the neckline of her bodice. A flash crosses her face—of solemnity.

"They're small, but sharp. We both have our reputations to uphold, so I cannot just waltz in with a belt of knives like you. I'm just the silly friend who has somehow managed to stay alive this long."

I catch her eye, hold her gaze. *You're not just a silly friend,* I say to her in my mind. *You're everything to me.*

She smiles. As if she knew exactly what I was thinking. Then I cross the distance between us, grab my smallest knife from the table, and bend down next to her.

"What are you—"

I grab her skirt, part the bright folds, and make a clean slice along her hip. My bangles rattle together with my movements. I check her knife and sheath quickly.

"Hey! You can't just—"

"One more," I say, and slice again on her other side. I stand and find her glaring at me.

"This is the prettiest thing I've ever worn," said Eshe, crossing her arms over her chest. "You've just gone and ruined it."

"The folds of your skirts will hide the cuts. See? You can't even tell. And now you have a *pocket,* as it were, to access your knives faster."

Understanding dawns in her expression, and she rolls her eyes to the ceiling. "Sands and stars, Nadira, if you're not careful, you'll make me as paranoid as you one of these days."

I scowl at her. She grins. Whatever my thoughts on how effective her plan at stunning her enemy with her beauty, she *is* beautiful. The color of her gown, with its silver embroidered sash, brings out the sun-bleached highlights in her dark hair. She doesn't look at all like a thief; she could be a queen.

A knock sounds at the door.

We freeze for the span of a breath. And then Eshe bounds toward the door, a dazzling grin splitting her features.

"I've never been to a dance," she says, grasping the handle. "And certainly never in a *palace*."

"Enjoy it. Just don't let your guard down."

"Yes, Mother."

I glare at her. She opens the door, revealing one of the guards. When I don't move after her, she peers back at me.

"I'll follow in just a bit."

"If you don't come on your own, I'll be back to drag you there. I didn't spend an hour on your face just for giggles."

"I'll only be a minute."

The door closes behind her. I breathe deeply, only to take in a lungful of perfume. On the vanity, in the midst of the opened pots and jars of cosmetics, is the copper mirror. In its reflection, I see a pair of dark, painted lips. My own lips. They look much fuller than I remember, and even when I pull them into a thin line, they stay looking fresh and . . . dare I say . . . lovely?

"That thief is a magician with paint," I mumble to myself.

Then I strip my wrists of the bangles Eshe put on me, untie the tinkling decoration on my ankle, and cut the tiny gold bells off my slippers. I remove everything that makes noise except the dress. Nothing can be done for its soft swishing sound.

I fit two of my knives into the sheaths at my hips. But if the sultan thinks I'll leave the rest behind, he's sorely mistaken. My third long knife gets buckled to my thigh like Eshe's—a final resort. My skirts aren't as bountiful as hers, so I cannot get away with slicing open the fabric for better access. It hardly matters with the other ones at my waist. But I do stick my smallest knives in the caps of each sleeve, just behind my shoulders so the hilts are accessible enough but hidden by my hair that Eshe styled long and loose.

Soon, every one of my knives has a hiding spot. Except for Separator, which I leave behind. This is a dance, not an assassination.

I'm ready.

I draw a deep breath. Then I make my way to the door, almost giving into temptation to steal a glance at the rest of my face. But no matter how strong the pull, I cannot bring myself to look in that mirror.

A guard awaits me beyond the door. I let him lead me to the dance.

"Nadira al-Risya," cries the announcer.

My heart rams in my throat, an erratic beat that pulses against the tempo of swelling flute music. The oaken double doors open before me, and though the late afternoon sun is at my back, I take one step into the hall—and I'm plunged into night.

The only light comes from tiny sparkling candles suspended from the ceiling. They look eerily like stars, glittering over a ballroom of darkness and shadows. Little sparks alight throughout the hall, as though the figures spinning through the middle of the room dance among fireflies.

The music is different from any I've heard. It twirls around me, as if it wishes to catch hold of my fingers and draw me into its sweet embrace, twirling me through the dreams of midnight.

The Neverseen King dances in the heart of the hall, Safya in his arms. They move in a dance I've never seen before, gliding across the room together as one instead of two. It's dark, but not too dark to see the beautiful gown of deep crimson that Safya wears, its skirts flaring around her ankles. It's not too dark to notice Safya's smile, or the way she throws back her head and laughs.

Some of the other women dance too, with mysterious partners. The one dancing with Eshe, who has come aglow as though candles were lit inside her eyes, seems to be the steward.

"Enchanting, isn't it?" Dabria sidles up beside me, sipping from a golden goblet. "Fitting, too, that the Neverseen King should throw a midnight dance."

I say nothing. My eyes are locked on Safya, on the outline of the Neverseen King's shoulders.

Say the word.

Every drop you bleed is a stain on my soul.

"You look ravishing," continues Dabria, eyeing me sideways when I don't respond. "I wouldn't have put you in that color, but now that I see it on you it's quite stunning."

Her gown is golden, shining like a star in the shadow. The cut of it hugs her figure, though not so closely to be scandalous. In her typical fashion, it cuts away from her waist, revealing toned abdomen. Jewels practically drip from her neck, her ears, her wrists, her hair.

On anyone else, it would be overly gaudy. And yet, it suits her well.

"Thank you," I say, deciding I cannot get away with more silence. Gaya dances in the arms of a stranger, while Fathuna leans against the wall with a massive plate of food in her hands. That leaves . . . "Where is Raha?"

Dabria sips her drink daintily. "She never made it out of the maze, from what I hear."

Did she call for the Neverseen King to get her out? To remove her from the competition? The crack of her arm echoes through my mind. The room darkens.

"You're *finally* here!" cries Eshe, gasping as she stumbles to my side and grabs hold of my arm. "I was beginning to wonder if I'd have to come fetch you."

"I was a mere ten minutes behind you."

She waves her hand, still gasping. "You *need* to dance. They're completely different from the dances back home. They're so *exhilarating*."

Dabria chuckles. "You should convince Fathuna to join you. She could use some exhilaration."

Eshe chortles. "Why?"

"She's more disagreeable with each passing day. She says she wants to go home."

"Then I'm off to rescue the grump! Have no fear, I'll return her to you so agreeable that she'll even volunteer to make you baklava."

"I'll let you eat it. I fear baklava is not good for the physique." Dabria pats her flat stomach.

"Baklava is good for the heart, and what's good for the heart is what's good for the physique," chirps Eshe as she scampers off.

My lips twitch in a smile.

"I'm not angry with you, you know," Dabria says abruptly.

I look at her, startled. Her gaze is fixed on the dance before us as she sips from her goblet.

"You're different from what I always imagined the Mourner to be. Until Lord Kishon's death, I assumed you were a man in your thirties or forties. Lord Kishon and my father were close friends, you know. Sometimes it felt like our families were the only supporters of the Neverseen King in Arbasa, but I know that's not true. I've been waiting for my father to be killed, just like my uncle was."

I stand as stiff as a board. But I have questions, questions I need answers to. "Who told you I was the Mourner? And why did you tell Raha?"

"I don't know his name. We only share the mutual goal of desiring to save Arbasa before it collapses."

This man—this was who she visited last night.

"As for Raha . . . I thought she should have a chance at her justice. Perhaps I wanted a little of my own, too. But I cannot hate you now that I've met you."

Pity limns her words. I want to run away from that pity, to hide from it. I can't, so I keep my tone distant and detached, my spine straight when I ask: "Why are you telling me all of this?"

The look Dabria gives me is completely void of her usual smiles. "Because you need to decide whose side you're on."

What does that mean? What sides are there to take? I want protection from Jabir and Eshe's safety. That's it. I am not for or against the Neverseen King, and I am not for or against Dabria's family, Lord Kishon, the people of Arbasa.

The song ends. The Neverseen King bows over Safya's hand and escorts her off the dance floor. Toward Dabria and me. I force my hands to be still at my side and not fidget with my skirts or the knives at my waist.

His gaze is heavy on me. My breath goes shallow at the sight of his tall silhouette, at the warmth that seems to trail me from head to toe, as if he's giving me an assessing once-over.

Does he like what he sees? a small voice inside me asks. No matter that it's entirely irrelevant if he finds me pleasing to his eye. It's a strangely vulnerable thing to stand here, unmoving, having put effort into my appearance for the first time. If he hates me in bloodstained clothes, I can blame that on the clothes. But now, I am as beautiful as I can be. So if he finds me lacking, there is no recourse.

It is a challenge to meet his eye. Or, at least, where his eyes *should* be. But I finally do.

He stops. Lets go of Safya's hand. For just a hair of a moment, he doesn't move.

Then he bows.

My mouth has gone dry. Am I supposed to bow back? Or curtsy? I'm supposed to do *something,* right? My indecision paralyzes me.

He extends his hand. Mine twitches in response. But then he speaks. His voice is deep and rich, like the midnight ballroom around us.

"Dabria, would you do me the honor?"

A smile breaks across her face. She accepts his hand with a dainty twist of her wrist. "It is I who am honored, Majesty."

The music begins anew as the Neverseen King leads Dabria out to the floor. Eshe is gesturing to Fathuna, who pops a grape in her mouth and spits the pit nearly on Eshe's gown. Eshe laughs, grabs Fathuna's wrist, ignoring the plate in her other hand, and makes to drag her to the dance floor. Food spills off the plate onto the floor.

"Get off me, wench!" Fathuna shouts.

"If you're determined to be dull!" Eshe retorts, letting her go and instead running back to the floor, all but throwing herself in the arms of the steward. "Dance with me!" she cries.

"Is she drunk?" asks Safya, who has been standing very quietly at my side.

Nope. That's just Eshe. I shake my head, still trying to decipher Dabria's cryptic words and nursing my wounded pride that the Neverseen King chose her over me. Perhaps I should have forced myself to check that mirror back in my room. For all I know, Eshe could have played some fool joke on me and drawn black circles around my eyes or painted my cheeks blue instead of raspberry.

Safya and I watch the Neverseen King twirl Dabria around. She flirts coyly, with little laughs and batted eyelashes. She's lovely. Lovelier than either of us, with far more elegance and stately bearing.

Gaya, who has abandoned the dance floor, comes to join us. Her gown is a deep purple, and it's almost iridescent in the starlight, especially as the fireflies light up near her skirts.

"Has he kissed either of you yet?" she asks, standing next to me.

I can't help the jolt of surprise that goes through me, or the memory of last night in the courtyard. I blink away the feel of his hand around my waist, focusing my attention on the way Dabria beams in his arms.

Against my will, Kolb's voice resurfaces in my mind.

Win the competition. Become the Neverseen King's bride. Betray him.

Safya scoffs at Gaya. "I don't have time for your nonsense."

Gaya's eyes sharpen. "He kissed me. This afternoon. While you were getting ready for tonight. He—"

"I *said*"—Safya draws out the syllables in a firm tone—"I don't have time for your nonsense."

"You're only jealous because he hasn't kissed you."

Safya leans against the wall, making me realize that the wall is covered in flowering vines. After recent events, I won't go near vines voluntarily.

"If you knew the Neverseen King at all, you'd know that he wouldn't kiss any of us in these circumstances," said Safya.

If you knew the Neverseen King. The implication is unmistakable. Part of me falls a little lower at her words. I shouldn't keep watching the sultan dance with Dabria. I shouldn't be *like* this.

You will never be safe with me.

Truer words have never been spoken. If I don't find a way to free myself of him, he'll be my doom.

"Perhaps you don't know him as well as you think," Gaya says. With that, she turns and saunters toward the table at the far wall piled with food.

I stand by my earlier statement about Gaya being more bark than bite. Though I doubt many things regarding my standing before the Neverseen King, he didn't kiss Gaya.

If he asks me to dance, I can ask to confirm.

I catch myself. Of course, I can't ask. He'd think I was jealous.

The dance comes to an end.

The Neverseen King escorts Dabria to the food table—hopefully there's something there that is good for the *physique*—and then bows before Gaya. Safya and I stand there in silence through that dance, neither of us speaking, as the scene unfolds before us. The dance finishes. The sultan asks Eshe to be his next partner.

When he at last approaches us and I'm the last woman he hasn't danced with, I try to hide my dismay when he asks Safya again. He doesn't trade partners for two dances.

Is he punishing me? For . . . something? For my questions? He said to ask them, didn't he? Then was it a particular question that offended him? My questions about his previous wives, the portrait on my wall?

Something has made him angry with me, and now he intends to humiliate me at this ball.

"You look sour. Have some baklava."

I glance down at Eshe. She offers me a winsome grin and a half-eaten pastry. "I'm not hungry."

"You're jealous."

"Feeling snubbed."

"Jealous."

"Feeling *punished.*"

"Jealous." She pops the rest of the baklava into her mouth and chews loudly.

"Well, what if I am?" I demand. "It's not fair, and certainly even less polite, that he—"

He's suddenly here, right in front of me, a towering silhouette of night. I stop abruptly, but I don't turn toward him. After all, he's probably only here to ask Eshe. He bows. I keep my gaze on the floor, my shoulders stiff.

"Dance with me, Nadira?"

CHAPTER 25

IT HAPPENS AS though in a dream.

The Neverseen King holds out his hand to me. No remnants of the tattoo from our earlier bargain gleam on his wrist. For a moment, I want to snub him like he has snubbed me. I want to turn the embarrassment on him.

But instead, I place my hand in his. It is both a familiar and alarmingly new sensation to have his large fingers close around my slender ones. The hand that wields magic holding the one that bears a blade.

Then he draws me to his side, to the center of the starlit ballroom.

What if I don't want to be merely a weapon? What if I want . . . something more?

He guides me until I face him, my hand still in his. Though I cannot see his eyes, we hold each other's gaze as the music begins—soft, sweet, lilting. Like a gentle frolic through a garden of perfumed roses. His other hand comes to rest on my waist, making my breath hitch.

"I—I don't know this dance," I say quickly, my words stumbling over each other. "I've never danced with a man before."

"I will guide you," comes his oddly gentle response.

With that, he leads me into the dance. I nearly sputter, clutching his hand and his upper arm like I will drown without them. "I don't know what to do with my feet!"

He pulls me closer, so I'm face to face with his throat. That tingling scent of magic tickles my nostrils, yet beyond it is something richly spiced with a comforting musk. *His* smell. "Lean into me and relax. Your feet will find their place."

My hands don't relinquish their death grip on him, but when I look down, my feet move with his. I'm not tripping over myself or stomping on his toes.

In fact, it's almost as if I've danced this before.

Perhaps I *am* dreaming after all.

After a full turn around the room, I tear my gaze from my feet and look up.

He stares down at me.

I swallow, glancing to the side. "I'm not sure what I did to offend you, but I don't appreciate you attempting to punish me by making me wait this long before you asked me to dance."

He pulls me closer, ducking to bring his mouth near my ear. My breath catches. "How my heart beats faster, little assassin, knowing that being deprived of my attention is a punishment for you."

I jerk my head away from his, scowling. "I don't need your sarcasm. That is not what I meant and you know it."

"Do I?" He chuckles, a dark sound that spills down my spine. "I smell your jealousy, Mourner. But it is not nearly as potent as what I felt smelling that human boy's scent on you. If he had stayed longer in your room, I would have been obliged to rip him limb from limb."

"Simply for touching me?"

"You are one of mine."

"I think the *'one of'* is the problem here," I say dryly. "I'd prefer if you focused your jealousy on another one of yours and left me alone. I cannot say competing for a man suits my disposition."

He snorts, and if I didn't know better, I'd think he was grinning. "No, it certainly doesn't, because you hate sharing."

"Do I?" I fix a stern glare at him.

"Tell me, Nadira"—he draws close to me once again, and my heart leaps in response—"if we were the only ones in this ballroom, if there wasn't a single other soul in the world besides you and me . . . would you be glad I hold you in my arms?"

My lips part, the breath stolen from my lungs. Then I set my jaw firmly and look over his shoulder at a distant hanging star. "Have you asked all the women this?"

"So you *would* be glad."

"No!" I sputter, blinking rapidly as if that will bring my composure back under my control.

"Then why is your heart pounding? Why does your hand tremble in mine? Why is your skin flushed? Surely it isn't because you fear me, O assassin?"

"I do fear you," I say. It seems the only admission I can make that will redirect him from his alarming observations.

His grip tightens on my hand, his voice pitching lower. "How adept you are at saying truth while avoiding it altogether."

Why did I ever long for him to ask me to dance? I should have been grateful he spared me from this misery for as long as he did! "And how adept you are at—"

"Making you uncomfortable?"

"That is *not* what I was—"

He leans forward again, bringing his mouth to my ear and whispering, "Would you like to know why it took me so long to ask you to dance, Nadira al-Risya? Because I fear I am not so heartless as I should like to be, and I confess that the sight of you adorned like the queen sent my own heart racing. But brighter than any of these jewels"—His hand slips from mine to touch my dangling earrings, the back of his knuckles brushing my neck—"are your eyes. Though I live in shadow, I feel the weight of them, like a mountain upon my shoulders, a blade through my heart. You are lovely, Nadira, and I wish for . . ."

He stops. And does not continue.

My pulse thunders in my ears, my feet stumbling just enough to make my belly swoop low in my abdomen. I open my mouth, but my voice won't come. I try again. "Why do you live in the shadows?"

"Because I am a fae living in a human world."

The fact that he answered me catches me by surprise. Then, before I can respond, the Neverseen King sends me twirling under his arm. His arm extends, his hand still gripping mine. My eyes lock on a jewel-like glimmer where his eyes are. And then he's spinning me back, pulling me close once more.

This dance isn't exhilarating. It is heady, like centuries old wine. I will be drunk before it ends. And suddenly, I do not care that we aren't alone, that there are five other women watching us. We dance to a song of stars, twirling faster and faster through inky night. My feet move of their own accord, my gown like fluttering wings as I soar higher and higher.

"Lean back," comes the deep voice of the Neverseen King as he lets go of my hand to hold tightly to my waist. I obey, and he spins us in place together. Then he catches my hand and twirls me before bringing me back into his arms.

I don't mean to. I truly don't. But somehow, with the music threading through my blood and the magic of dance . . . a laugh bubbles up out of my throat, a bright golden laugh. When I meet his gaze, he's smiling. I cannot see it, but I *know* it deep in my soul, through the strange connection we've had since the first moment I heard the sound of his voice. I hear it again now.

"You, my lovely assassin, are the brightest star in all the world."

Is this . . . what *happiness* feels like? I give him a teasing grin. "A fitting bride, then, for the King of Night."

The dance slows, but his grip on my waist only tightens. Is it about to end? My entire being mourns the loss of the music, of his nearness, even while I still possess them.

"I meant what I wrote you," he says, and the words are nearly a rumble, emotion I cannot place lacing each syllable. "Say the word, and I will end this competition and take you for my wife."

The music resolves in one last, lingering note that continues in my heart long after the last strain has faded. We stand unmoving on the dance floor, one of his hands still gripping mine, the other wrapped almost possessively around my waist.

I open my mouth to speak, but no sound comes out. It's like we're locked up in a court of silence, without so much as an indrawn breath to anchor me to reality.

Be his wife. Be his queen.

"I . . ." Nothing else will leave my lips.

Win the competition. Marry the Neverseen King. Betray him.

You are never safe with me.

A moment ago, I was so weightless I could fly. Now, I am chained to the ground. I take one step backward, giving a tug on my hand. He releases it, but still his arm remains wrapped around my waist.

"Nadira . . ." he whispers.

"I—I . . ." Air knifes in and out of my lungs, squeezing my chest tight. The words come out in a gasp. "I . . . can't."

Then I'm twisting out of his arms, all but fleeing the ballroom in a flutter of shimmering silk. Even when Eshe rushes to my side, I shake off her grip on my arm. "I'm fine," I say, probably too sharply. "I will return shortly."

Why am I making promises to her I cannot keep?

I will not be returning.

The sun makes its rapid descent toward the horizon. Does the rule of not being out after dark still apply on nights when the Neverseen King holds a dance? Or is that rule suspended?

It might not matter.

I hurry down the long corridors, past strange doors, my feet silent on the cold tiles. A cool breeze chases after me, rustling my skirts and blowing my hair in my face. The setting sun casts the palace in a deep orange, the shadows of marble pillars thrown long against locked doors. One such door is overgrown with climbing roses slowly folding their blossoms closed, and the scent is nearly overwhelming when I pass it. It takes me back to the night the Neverseen King prevented me from leaving my room.

Maybe the Neverseen King will protect me from Jabir while I am here, but I know it as sure as I know my own name: the Neverseen King will be my death.

Now is the time to cut my losses, to give up on this world of magic, to return to my own world of blood and dust. More than ever, I'm glad I slipped that note into Eshe's knife sheath when I slit her skirts.

At your first chance, escape through the main entrance of the palace. If you're careful about it, I have reason to believe the sultan will not stop you. Stay safe.

When I reach the banister, my shoulders sag. I extend one hand, then let it drop. Goodbyes are the most bitter things in the world.

Why are you turning your back on him? part of me wants to know.

I clench my jaw, slipping out into the courtyard. The fountain still burbles, but only barely, the water bubbling at the top and languidly dripping to the lower level. Shadows lengthen around me, as though darkness wishes to wrap us all in her cold embrace. Ice fills my belly, reaching freezing tendrils into my limbs, building pressure inside me.

He wants you. No one else does.

I follow the path Kolb took only last night, making my way straight for the gate in a flurry of shimmering magenta silk. My mouth draws in a thin line as I hoist myself onto a window's ledge, then drop down into another covered portico. I wait, crouched in the shadows. When nothing pricks my senses, I continue moving.

Why do you run from him? the voice demands.

Don't you know? I say back in my mind. *It is better to be unwanted, than to be wanted by the Neverseen King.*

It is a terrifying thing to be wanted by a King of Night who has vowed never to love.

Or, if my intuition is correct: who has vowed never to love . . . *again.*

I reach the gate's courtyard. I stand in the darkness of the third archway, breathing in through my nose, out between my teeth. The sun's last rays shine into the courtyard, like liquid gold spilling across the flagstone and dripping into the shrubberies. My eyes snag on the recesses in the wall, and when I stare long enough, I can almost convince myself a tall shadow stands there, watching me.

Why do you go back to Jabir, like a dog to its vomit? The memory of his voice calls to me.

I'm not going back to Jabir. I never will. I will fight with tooth and claw against him if he tries to take me. I'm not the little girl whose family he murdered, the little girl who wept and screamed but could do nothing.

That girl is dead.

But the Mourner lives, and she will be free.

My heart nearly pounds out of my chest when I take the first step out of the shadows, into the light. The next step is easier and easier, until I'm running as fast as I can for that gate. It is open slightly, and a strong gust of wind blows it open further.

When my slipper lands on sand, I stop. I'm out of the gate.

I turn around.

Wind catches my hair, blowing sand into my eyes as I stare through the gate at the courtyard, the hibiscus bushes, the three arches that lead to the rest of the palace complex.

I tilt my head back, sucking in a deep breath and grinning.

Free.

"Not yet," I growl to myself, refusing to give in to the impulse to throw my arms wide and spin while laughing up at the sky. I'm not free until I've fully escaped Jabir. I need to get as far away as I can, as quickly as I can. If that means braving the Great Desert, then so be it. I'll need supplies; I might have to find a caravan to travel with. One that won't ask questions.

All this time. Everything that Eshe and I endured here at this palace—we could have left. We could have walked right out that gate unhindered.

My step halts suddenly.

Fathuna.

How many times has she said she only wants to go home? I have my overly cautious nature to thank for my delay in realizing that we were not truly prisoners here. Dabria has apparently been coming and going as she pleases. Gaya and Safya seem to have aims for the queenship and don't *want* to leave.

But Fathuna?

She isn't cautious like me. She's loud, bold, and demanding. She would have been the type to march out here in broad daylight and open the gates, just *testing* if anything stopped her.

Fathuna lied.

There is something here that she wants. Something she doesn't want the rest of us knowing.

Something is wrong.

Eshe.

I've gotten so caught up in my own struggles, my own thoughts and desires, that I abandoned Eshe in a pit of vipers. Giving her instructions to get out isn't enough. She is drawn to trouble like a moth to a flame, and there has been relatively little trouble with her while she's been here, which means she's overdue for a disaster.

The moment I slip back in through the gate, the wrongness hits me like a stone to the gut.

It's in the air, in the play of the shadows, in the angle of the sunbeams on flagstone. And it's been wrong ever since I left the ballroom; I had simply been too preoccupied to notice it before.

Drawing a knife in each hand, I slink close to the patches of darkness between pillars and arches, crouching in corners behind shrubbery. The count starts in my head by habit.

One, two, three.

I slip forward two more steps, dodging against a pillar and peeking out.

Nothing *looks* wrong. The palace complex is as it should be. But everything is wrong. Uneasiness simmers in my bones. Ought I to call out to the Neverseen King? Would he hear me like he heard me in the maze?

I don't *want* to need him.

Ten, eleven, twelve.

I reach the courtyard, and though the sun hasn't fully set, the fountain is completely silent. Restlessness drips down my spine. I enter the palace, every sense on high alert. The corridor has gone dark—darker than it should be.

The banister is stiff before me. Reaching out two of my fingers, I touch its surface.

It's ice-cold.

What is wrong? I send the words shooting into the wood through my touch.

No response.

Except . . . the very faintest shiver.

Lights spare me and the way my fist clenches as resolve hardens like rock around my heart. If someone scared my banister, I will make them pay.

But protecting Eshe is more important than avenging the palace furniture's fear.

Twenty, twenty-one, twenty-two.

I take three more steps. And abruptly stop.

There, not five paces from me, is a tall, unmoving shadow. One that is very much alive. Teeth flash in a visible grin. Then, a voice washes over me, from the top of my head to the tips of my toenails in pure horror. A voice made of laughter, drunkenness, and the spirits of the dead.

"Come play with me, little human."

CHAPTER 26

THE FIGURE BOLTS toward me like lightning.

Once upon a time, I would have screamed. Perhaps a scream would have saved me. But my voice is locked away, too deep in my chest to access. Not the smallest sound can leave my closed throat.

I stare at death. At my death.

And I don't even know its name.

"Dance with me!" cries the figure as he reaches me.

My feet won't move. But my arms do. I slice at the hands coming toward me. He dodges my knives, instead catching me around the waist and dragging me against his chest. One of his palms cups my cheek.

"How long it's been," he says, white teeth gleaming, "since I've played with a human."

I stab toward his chest and neck as I bring my knee up to kick him, and duck to dodge his grip on me. But he moves far too quickly, inhumanly fast, evading my killing blows. Then, something snatches hold of my knives—and wrenches them from my grip.

I gasp.

"Don't spoil my fun," he chides, laughing. "We will play *nicely*."

My elbow coming for his face shows just what I think of that. He catches it, pins it behind me, and drags me back to his chest.

"Naughty human," he tsks, patting my face just before I attempt to bash my head into his mouth. He dodges and pins my other arm. He's much, *much* too strong for me. I've never fought another man this fast or this strong.

Except one.

"Relax, sweet human. Don't be afraid. I play very nicely with my things."

Then he swings me around the hallway like we're dancing, a pitiful imitation of how the Neverseen King danced with me. He either doesn't notice how much I'm struggling against him, tears slipping out between my eyes, or he doesn't care. He moves so quickly that my feet stumble and trip over one another until I cannot catch my balance enough to attempt a kick. His grip on my arms is so tight it's like they're bound behind me.

My vision goes black.

Just for a moment. When my eyes come back into focus, the shadow is swinging me so violently my knotted stomach threatens to unwind and spill forth its meager contents on the floor.

I cannot fight him and win. Neither will my voice cooperate to scream for help.

I need to change the game.

The figure rips my hands between us, holding them like iron shackles, and then starts spinning with me down the hallway at a dizzying speed. I gasp for air, losing my balance and sense of direction, until all I see is darkness and a gleaming set of grinning teeth.

Then pain flares so shockingly bright, red-hot and burning, that my vision goes black again. When I open my eyes, the world spins like stars around my head, and when I draw in a breath, my body screams in agony.

"Whoops!" the figure is saying. "I wasn't watching where we were going! Silly me!"

He bashed my rib cage into the banister, I realize belatedly. If the pain of my swelling lungs is any indication, at least one of my ribs is broken.

He doesn't stop. He pulls on me so violently, so painfully, a cry wrenches from my throat. That one cry unlocks my voice, and desperately, I croak, "Want to play a different game?"

The eternal spinning stops. My brain rattles as pain throbs through my body. I almost stumble to my knees.

"What different game?" the figure asks, head cocked.

Each breath is sheer agony, but somehow I manage to say, "Kiss me."

His whole face lights up. "Kiss a human? I've never kissed a human before!"

"Kiss me," I gasp again.

He slips a hand around my waist, pulling me to him. I flinch at the pain shocking up my spine. Why is everything he does so rough? As if in answer, his fingers slide into my hair, digging into my scalp. "Human hair is so soft," he murmurs.

He's released my hands. I reach up slowly, wrapping my arms around his neck to draw him closer. He smells like sour wine.

"I've never kissed a human before," he says again, still grinning. "My first time."

"Your last time," I gasp against his lips.

Then I'm kissing him. His disgusting mouth molds to mine, tasting like rot, his hands tightening their grip on me—

I twist my fingers. And plunge the dagger I'd hidden in my sleeves into the back of his neck.

He yanks my hair back, wrenching my mouth from his as he gurgles. "That was *not nice*," he says quietly.

Then he roars, blood and spittle spraying my face. He grabs me by the throat, my knife still protruding from his, and slams me into the wall. Stars burst across my sight. My ribs scream in pain. I choke against his hold, tears streaming down my face.

Can't breathe. Can't breathe.

I'm going to die. I'm going to die. I'm *going* to *die.*

No, no, no, *please* no. I cannot die like this. I'm not ready. My life has been nothing but murder. Even if it's fitting that I die like this—*no,* please, no.

The darkness closes in.

Can't breathe. Can't—

The darkness flares a fiery crimson. The hand on my throat loosens, the silhouette of his leering face twisting to look to my right. It's enough for me to make out the hard-angled profile of my attacker, and to catch a glimpse of the sconces along the wall that burn with a strange kind of fire. A fire that makes me think of pure, unadulterated rage.

I try to breathe. Can't. Everything in my body is sheer agony. My eyes start to roll back in my head.

Then, a familiar voice thunders from down the corridor, "Unhand my *wife.*"

The sound that emerges from my throat is a rattle. The figure releases me. I fall to my knees gasping and pressing my hand to my throat as I desperately try to breathe. My broken rib screams when I cannot.

But somehow, I manage to look up.

The sconces lining the hallway flare a deeper, more vengeful red as a tall silhouette storms down the corridor. With the light at his back, I can see him. Not enough to make out the features of his face, but rather the furious set of his broad shoulders, the strength of the arms thrown wide as shadows swirl around his palms. His cloak billows behind him, and for once, he wears his crown. His knee-high boots seem to make the ground shake with every step. Or perhaps I'm the one who is shaking.

The Neverseen King is a mighty, terrifying sight.

Perhaps most terrifying of all, however, are the two severed heads that he holds in one hand by their hair.

Women's heads.

I vomit. The pain of the violent motion nearly makes me black out again.

"I wasn't going to hurt her!" says the other shadow, backing away and holding up his hands in a placating gesture. "I was just playing with her! It's been so long since I've had a human to play—"

The Neverseen King reaches him, thrusts out a hand, and grabs the shadow by the throat. He smashes him into the pillar across from me, knocking the sconce to the ground in a burst of crimson fire. The shadow's feet dangle above the ground as he scrabbles against the Neverseen King's hold on him.

"Do you want me to play with you?" the Neverseen King says, his voice deadly calm. "Get out of my House."

The shadow goes limp. The Neverseen King lets go—and the shadow falls to the ground in a crumpled heap.

A glint catches at his throat.

My knife.

The sultan throwing him against the wall must have plunged it deeper than I had been able to drive it. He pauses, staring down at the shadow, and then bends. In a swift motion, without releasing the heads he carries, he yanks my knife out of the creature's neck.

Then, he turns to me, holding the knife out to me, hilt first. "Your blade."

With my hand still pressed to my burning throat, I stare at him, at the heads he holds, at the blood dripping off my knife. A sob wracks my shoulders. I lower my gaze, burying my face in my hands. Every bone in my body quivers, each shudder eliciting pain.

Then warmth surrounds me. I peer through my fingers as the Neverseen King kneels in front of me. He shoves my knife into his belt, deposits the heads on the ground, and lays one giant hand on the back of my head.

"What has he done to you?" he demands, his voice low. "Tell me, and I will do the same to him."

"He's dead!" I burst out.

"So he is. And I will desecrate his remains for every injury he's caused."

I glance sidelong at the heads. The sparse light of the angry flickering torches and the last threads of dying sun illuminate the face of the one closest to me.

Fathuna.

And the other, I can tell from the jewels still woven into her hair. *Dabria.*

"Night is falling. We must hurry," says the Neverseen King. "Can you stand?"

I press a hand to my ribs, and even that slight pressure makes me moan. But for whatever reason, words form on my tongue, and then I'm speaking. "I'm not your wife."

"Too much nuance I didn't want to get into."

"Nuance? This isn't nuanced. I'm *not* your wife."

"Can you stand?" he asks, not bothering to answer me.

Squeezing my eyes shut against the pain, I mutter again, "I'm not your wife," and then I try to get my feet under me—

The Neverseen King's arm catches me beneath my waist and my knees, lifting me up against his chest. I suck in a sharp breath, blinking back tears at the movement.

"Lift your arm around my neck. I don't want to touch your injury."

I obey, wrapping my arm around his neck and holding tightly, leaving my other arm limp across my stomach. I press my forehead just beneath his jaw, and for the span of the breath I take of his smell, I don't feel pain. Then it's back with a vengeance, and I cling tighter to him with every step that sends pain radiating through my whole body.

"Eshe?" I croak.

His throat tightens. "Safe. In her room. Mostly unhurt."

"Mostly?"

"She split her lip taking a blow to the face from Fathuna. But I've told you before, your friend is more capable than you give her credit for. She held her own until I got there."

Relief sings down my spine. I relax against him. His jaw clenches and his arms tighten.

Safe, my soul breathes. *Safe with him.* My heart knows the truth, however, and it throbs a broken rhythm. There is no such thing as being safe with the Neverseen King.

His steps move faster and faster through the hallway. He keeps looking out the windows we pass at the setting sun, which is barely a sliver on the horizon.

With a growl, he redoubles his pace.

And then we've reached my room.

He shuts the door behind us quickly. Bolts it. Only then does he let out a great sigh of relief as the sun dips below the horizon, casting the world—and my room—in utter darkness.

A few more steps, and he reaches my bed. When he bends, about to lower me to the mattress, pain shoots up my side. A whimper slips between my lips, my grip tightening on his neck as I bury my face in the folds of his collar.

"Let go of me."

"I can't! It hurts."

Slowly, he lowers my legs to the mattress, keeping his hold on my torso. My skirts glitter in the darkness, like I wear a gown of stars. He takes his free hand and lays it gently against my rib cage, right against the break. I hiss, my nails digging into his shoulder.

"Two breaks," he growls. I'm not sure how he knows that without prodding. He's barely touching me. "I can heal it, but I'll need direct access to the skin."

"The skin?" I say stupidly, giving a short cough. I must have quite the collection of bruises ringing my neck.

"Yes. The skin."

We sit there in silence for the span of a few heartbeats, as though he's waiting for me to understand something I'm not. At last, he clears his throat and looks away.

"I can cut some of the gown away. Just enough—"

"You mean *my* skin?"

He gives me an arch look. "Whose skin did you think I was talking about?"

I only cough in response. He carefully unwinds my arm from his neck and lays me down flat on the bed. I try to focus on each painful breath, and *not* on the knife he takes out of his belt. *My knife.* Still stained with blood.

He could kill me. Take off my head like Fathuna's or Dabria's. He could—

I reach up, catch his sleeve as he starts reaching over me with my knife in hand. "I'll do it."

He hesitates, and even in the dark, there's a glitter where his eyes should be. They seem to study me. Then he pries my hand off his sleeve, places the hilt of the knife in my palm, and draws back.

Now begins the painful process of me attempting to cut off part of my own bodice.

I take a deep breath and hold it lodged between my teeth as I twist to angle the bloody knife. The bodice is tight against my skin, and I suddenly regret having to ruin the beautiful garment. The garment *he* selected—ordered made?—for me.

My hands tremble, but after fumbling, I make a clean slice down the side seam. More fumbling while the Neverseen King kneels by my bed, waiting as I manage another slice, this time parallel to the waistband of my skirt, creating a flap that can be pulled back. It bares just enough of my lower ribcage and part of my waist for him to heal it.

I set the knife down and lay back, finally releasing my held breath.

He bends over me, blocking out the sight of the moon rising through my window. His warm fingers land on my swollen and bruised skin. Then he turns toward me, holding out his free hand.

"What?" I demand through clenched teeth.

"Hold it."

"Why?"

"This will hurt. Probably."

I can handle pain, the stubborn part of me wants to shoot back at him. But instead, I take his hand. His fingers close around mine, a solid anchor. Giving into an unnameable impulse, I thread our fingers together. A jolt goes up his arm. Then he squeezes my hand.

"Just breathe." His voice is a low rumble.

And even though the pressure of his touch on my ribs is suddenly so intense that I arch my back, trying to twist away, his hand in mine doesn't falter. Not when I squeeze it so hard I'd possibly break a bone if it was someone else.

As the pain intensifies, his voice reaches out to me. Soft murmurs of encouragement. My foggy mind cannot decipher the words, but they comfort me nonetheless. It feels as though he's drawing the breakage out of me, out through my skin and into his own hand. Then the sensation loses the edge of its sharpness, dulling into something more manageable, like the ache of fresh stitches.

"Tell me what happened," I say between gritted teeth. "Who was that . . . thing?"

"Goken is—*was*—as worthless of a fae as they come. He cared for nothing but pleasure and thrill."

"You knew him?"

"I know many fae."

"Are you . . ." My voice cuts off with a flash of pain, a moan escaping my lips instead.

"Breathe, Nadira. Breathe."

I breathe, and if not for the pain, I think I could fall into the depth of his voice and drown in it.

No. I cannot think like that. I'm delirious from the pain; that's all. I'm not in my right mind. Making myself breathe, I force myself to finish asking my question. "Are you their sultan too?"

His bark of laughter sends a jolt through me. "Are you asking if I am High King of the Fae?"

I lick my lips. "I suppose I'm not sure what I'm asking."

He chuckles, shaking his head. "I am not the High King. I am one of his emissaries, as it were."

"There are *more* of you?"

"Not in my role, no. I serve in a unique position, so I have a prestigious rank at the High King's court." At this, his voice turns drier. "No one in their right mind covets my position. Unfortunately, there are more fools than not among my kind."

The Neverseen King answers to someone. *That* is certainly news. How can he be the sovereign of our kingdom if he is not sovereign over himself? I sort through the pieces I've puzzled together so far.

"You are sultan of Arbasa. But you are subject to the High King of the . . . *Fae.* Which means you . . .?"

His thumb sweeps over my rib, and for the first time, it's not agony. My lungs loosen. I draw in a deep breath, and then another. He glances sidelong at me.

"Better?"

I nod. "Better."

At last, he draws his hand away from my side, allowing me to smooth the fabric of my bodice back over my skin. I realize belatedly that our fingers are still clasped. I move to pull away, but he stops me.

"Your neck, now."

I touch the ring of bruises, swallowing hard against the scratchiness of my throat.

He looses a deep exhale, untangles our fingers, and slowly reaches for my neck. When my eyes widen and I flinch, he stops. His hands hover in midair between us. "I will not hurt you."

My jaw works as I stare up at him.

"Will you trust me?"

No. No. Never trust him. Never trust the Neverseen King. He will be your death.

"Let me hold my knife," I say, my hands fisting in the coverlet beneath me. The words seem to hang between us, a loud proclamation of my answer to his question. But he reaches into his belt again, produces my two large knives I lost in my fight with Goken. I take their hilts, squeezing the familiar leather-bound iron as the Neverseen King sits on the bed beside me. The mattress shifts beneath his weight, and I struggle to keep my mouth from going dry as he leans over me, reaching for my neck.

My eyelids shutter when he touches me. My hands shake with the need to jerk away, plunge my blades into his chest, and scream at him to take his hands off me. But he's promised not to hurt me. He's healing me with his magic, not choking the life out of me.

His fingers wrap around my neck, his thumbs pressed to the knot in my throat. His touch is light, gentle, but I gasp. At some point, I've lifted my blade, and it hovers in the air as though I'm about to stab him through the heart. He doesn't heed the knife, either because he trusts me not to murder him while he's healing me, or because he knows he can evade me.

"Are you almost done?" I gasp.

"Very close. Don't close your eyes."

I force my eyes open, discovering that his face hovers close above mine. There's a jewel-like flash in the shadow of his face. I meet that flash as his hands tighten just barely around my neck. Either the world is growing darker as night takes a deeper hold on the world, or I'm about to pass out again.

He's more than strong enough to kill me with his bare hands. Could I be in a more vulnerable position? I choke, even though his touch remains gentle.

"Breathe," he says gently, his eyes holding mine. "I won't hurt you."

"It's hard t-to . . . believe it."

"Why did you come back?"

"W-what?"

"You left. I felt it in my spells when you walked out that gate. But something made you come back."

I swallow against his fingers. "Eshe."

There's a low snort. "Of course."

"Did you think I came back for you?"

He draws his hands away from my neck, and my arm with the knife poised in the air falls to the bed, my entire body going liquid with relief. Then his knuckle brushes my chin, and I tense once more.

"No." He seems to give a dark smile. "But one could hope."

That simple statement shouldn't have affected me at all, yet warmth climbs up into my cheeks. I make to turn my head to one side, only for his knuckle on my chin to stop me. To my shock, his thumb brushes over my bottom lip. I freeze.

"I smell him on you," the Neverseen King says, his voice a deep rumble. "I smell him on your mouth."

I set my jaw in a firm line, knock away his hand, and drag myself into a sitting position. Part of me wants to marvel at the fact that my injuries are indeed completely gone, that he's truly healed them, and I am no longer in agony. Apparently that is simply what one does when one has magic—they *heal* every ailment.

Arbasa has a sultan with the power to heal. Where was he all those years ago, when I earned the scars I bear on my back, my hands, my jaw?

I fling my legs over the edge of the bed and stand up, leaving him there. "When your opponent is stronger than you, sometimes you have to get *creative*. If you'd gotten there faster, perhaps I wouldn't have had to resort to such *dire* measures." My tone is even drier than his.

"If I'd gotten there sooner, your thief would be dead."

My heart stutters. I force myself to take a seat on the settee, and gesture for him to take the seat across from me. "You said I could ask you anything. Sit, then, and let me interrogate you."

"I do not take orders from a commoner."

I scowl at where he remains on the edge of my bed.

"But," he says, and moonlight catches on grinning white teeth. "I'd heed a queen."

"You called me your wife to Goken. I think you can afford to extend the charade a little longer."

He chuckles. And curse me, I can barely keep myself from cracking a smile in return. With a heave, he shoves himself up to his feet with more force than seems necessary. He stands there, so tall, like a pillar of night. Each step that brings him closer makes me wonder if I should have made him stay there, far away from me.

There's something wrong with his steps. Something . . . *heavy.*

"Sultani—" I start to say.

He collapses to his knees.

I shoot to my feet, nearly falling in my own effort to get to him. He catches himself with his palms on the floor, breathing heavily. I crouch beside him, grabbing his arm without thinking. "Sultani? Sultani! What is wrong? Tell me what is wrong!"

His head swings toward me, and I catch another glimpse of a smile. This one is weaker than his last. "It seems I've overextended myself."

And then he drops to the ground.

"Sultani!" I kneel beside his fallen form, shaking his shoulder. "Sultani!"

No answer.

He's not injured, is he? Is it truly just overexertion, like he said? What if he was hurt during whatever happened at the ball? I must be certain. I give his shoulder a shove, trying to roll him onto his back. Stars and sands, he's heavy!

He is also out cold. No matter how many times I call to him or smack him, he doesn't respond. Finally, I manage to roll him onto his back. I check his pulse beneath his jaw, trying to ignore my own palpitating heart.

He's not dead, at least.

I hesitate, staring down at the enormous, shadowed body lying on my floor. Then I crouch beside him again and run my fingers over his torso, checking for injuries. I find buttons on another double-breasted coat of some sort. The unusual style of it strikes me yet again, and the material is thicker and coarser than anything I've felt before. This is probably the last thing I'd wear in a climate like ours.

He has no injuries that I can find. I withdraw my hands, get to my feet, and take a few steps back.

"The Neverseen King is passed out. On my floor," I mutter, cocking my head to one side. Then I frown, massaging the bridge of my nose. The absurdity of this entire day, these last few days, suddenly hits me so hard I take a seat back on the settee.

It seems either healing or using magic generally drains my sultan. Perhaps healing Kanza, me, and Raha was too much in one day.

What do I do now? Wait for him to come to? I shouldn't leave him on the floor, but considering how difficult it was for me to roll him over, I'd probably hurt myself trying to drag his deadweight to the bed.

My eyes run lazily over the room. Cosmetics are still strewn across the vanity's surface, but there, sitting precariously close to the edge, is a pitcher of water and wash basin.

The sultan wakes when I dump the contents of the pitcher on top of his head.

"Great Kings!" he cries, flailing his arms as though to swat the stream of water away. He rolls, gasping and spitting. "You heartless assassin."

I set the pitcher down and prop one fist against my hip. "Just be glad I didn't use my knives."

He shoots me a look as he shakes the water out of his hair. Then he's pulling himself up enough to lean against the bed. He doesn't try to stand.

"Are you going to faint again?" I ask.

He scowls at me. "Don't make me bribe you to keep this a secret."

I smirk. "I suppose fainting doesn't suit the reputation of the fearsome Neverseen King."

"You're one to talk," he growls back.

Now it's my turn to glare. He grins in response, and something about it strikes me as *different*. Like this is a true smile, one with threads of warmth in it. I look away, heat rising in my cheeks as I sit back down on the settee. Two litters could be carried between us with how far apart we were.

It's better this way.

"I want to know everything," I say, and my voice isn't cold or dark or dry. It's my own voice, earnest with a tinge of fear. "I need to know everything. The answers to all my questions."

He is silent. Then, at last, he sighs. When he speaks, his voice is like mine. Void of presumption and barriers. "Very well, Nadira. I will answer your questions. I warn you, though, you will not like the answers."

I steel my spine. "Go on."

CHAPTER 27

THE NEVERSEEN KING leans heavily against my bedpost, but with a flick of his fingers through the air, parchment from nowhere appears in his palm. My pulse quickens. It's my note. The last one I left for him.

"How many wives have you had? What happened to them? Why do you need another one?" he reads aloud.

You will not like the answers.

I believe him.

Dread pools like sludge in my stomach. Perhaps I don't want to know how many wives he's had. It'll only make me feel more foolish for the notions I've entertained recently of him and his offer of marriage.

When he speaks, his voice is emotionless. "I have had one wife."

I stare at him. Blink. Stare some more. "O-only one?"

"Are you disappointed?" he asks dryly. Is he smiling again? If he is, it's a much colder smile than before.

"But everyone says you've come for a bride every hundred years . . . for hundreds of years. How could . . .?"

"I thought you didn't believe the legends."

I don't bother answering that, and instead wait for him to continue.

He does continue, but not before torturing me with a few long, silent minutes. "I am called the Neverseen King because it is a title. While there has been a Neverseen King for a millennium now, I have been in possession of that title and responsibility for only the last hundred and ninety-nine years. The King before me often replenished his store of human brides. I, however, have taken only one bride. As much as I've tried to forgo taking a second, I can no longer avoid the necessity. Hence these competitions."

"Why have a competition? Why not simply pick your favorite? It's not as though we can resist your power. You could have forced any of us."

"My first bride . . . came to me willingly."

My eyes drift toward the portrait of the blonde, blue-eyed girl on the wall. His first wife—his only wife. *He loved her.* I gathered this much before, but somehow, it hits sharper now.

He tilts his head to see what I'm looking at.

He goes deathly still.

It's been a long, long time since he's seen her picture, hasn't it? He had it hidden—shortly after her death, perhaps? How raw is this wound of his?

"How long has she been dead?" I ask.

"Ninety-nine years."

I'm glad we sit so far apart. It helps me keep my emotions locked up tight so that we can have this necessary conversation. It makes this feel more transactional and impersonal, which is exactly what I want.

I don't want to feel things right now. This is about gathering facts. Nothing else.

"If I've surmised correctly, based on the number of doors I've seen," I say, breaking the silence, "you have some hundred or more portals in this palace. You can open and close them, but not without effort—and some break open by themselves. It's your job, as the Neverseen King, to keep them contained."

"And everyone thinks tariffs are the biggest problem Arbasa faces," he says darkly.

"Something about how your magic works requires a human bride."

"A human bride greatly reduces the strain of performing such magic, yes."

"But you've forgone a bride these last ninety-nine years?"

"I have."

"And you've struggled as a result?"

He shoots me a glare. "I think I've managed shockingly well, thank you very much."

"Then you don't need me?"

At that, he goes silent. My lips twist humorlessly.

"You've managed," I continue. "But you're reaching your limits, which is why you've *begged* me to be your bride."

"There has been no begging," he growls, clearly affronted.

"I *beg* to differ."

He vanishes from the floor. The next instant, he towers over where I sit on the settee, his silhouette taking up almost my entire range of vision. I jerk backward, startled. His hands plant on the carved wood edges of the upholstery on either side of my shoulders as he leans over me. His warmth floods my awareness. My throat goes dry.

"Do you want me to beg, Nadira?"

His proximity brings flashbacks that I don't want. I'm trying to keep my distance from him—not be reminded of what it was like to dance with him, to be held by him.

Would it be so horrible to be his wife? Now that I know he doesn't wear through wives like a pair of shoes, the idea isn't as repulsive to me as it ought to be.

His face is only a foot away, his gaze holding mine with the force of a windstorm. It's hard to imagine that he was unconscious only a few minutes ago. Right now, he's nothing but power and night, threaded with desperate intensity that makes me want things I have no business wanting.

Every drop is a stain on my soul.

We're alike—him and I. More alike than I'd ever imagined. What would happen if we joined forces? The Neverseen King, and the assassin?

Who would we be, together?

Kiss me, I want to whisper.

But then my gaze strays away from his, to the portrait of his dead wife on the wall. Finding my voice with difficulty, I say, "You can stand now, it seems. An achievement."

The sound that emerges from his throat is more growl than anything. He pushes off the back of the settee, marches to the chair opposite me, drags it out to fit his long legs, and drops into it. He stacks his boots on my table, sliding further down into the chair as he links his fingers behind his head. "Ask the rest of your questions. We don't have all night."

The cavalier sultan has returned.

"How did she die?"

He doesn't react. He has pulled away from me emotionally, hasn't he? This is the Neverseen King I saw in my dreams, the one that spun his crown on his finger and sent it hurling through the air. The one that slouches on his throne.

"Every hundred years, there is a celebration among the fae in their various worlds. Lulythinar, or as it translates to your tongue, *Moonshore*. This celebration creates a surge of magic, as it were, which makes the night of Lulythinar a rather . . ." He trails off.

"Too many portals broke open at once," I interpret. "You were overwhelmed."

"Most human wives don't survive the night."

Hence the legend. Numbness creeps over my body as I sink back against the settee. "Ninety-nine years. Lulythinar is almost here, isn't it? You need a bride to stand with you then. To die at Lulythinar."

The weight of his gaze pins me in place.

"The competitions," he says, "aren't because I love bloodshed. They serve two purposes. First, I need to know what my wife can handle, what her strengths and weaknesses are, and I must be certain the wife I choose can bear this burden with me. Second, I need *her* to know it too. That she can do this with me."

"But you said human wives don't survive the night."

His teeth flash, belying his devil-may-care pose. "I said *most* human wives. Do you think it's a wonder why I brought the city's most notorious assassin here, Mourner?" He sits up abruptly, planting his boots on the ground and leaning forward, elbows propped up on his knees and fingers steepled beneath his chin. "I have been forthright with you, but I will speak even plainer. Before you stepped foot in my House, I wanted you to be my bride. Not Eshe. Not Safya. Not anyone else. I wanted *you*. But if you fight me at every turn, you're of no use to me. I'd be better off marrying someone like Gaya. Because what I need—more than I need skills with a blade or cunning—is someone I can trust."

The air is stolen from my lungs. My body should be collapsing from exhaustion, but instead it hums with a heady thrill. He wants me—he *has* wanted me this entire time.

"When?" I ask softly.

"When, what?"

"When did you decide you wanted me as your bride?"

My whole world narrows to his next words, to the sound of his voice as each syllable hits me like a blow.

"I wanted you, Mourner, from the moment I heard there was an assassin in the city leaving apology notes."

I stare at him, dumbfounded. Something in my chest cracks open. I try to clamp it shut again, but part of me doesn't want it shut. Part of me wants to be ravaged by the pain of hope.

He saw me when I was a girl not yet sixteen, forced to do that which I loathed. He saw me during those lonely years of fighting, of killing, of failing to escape Jabir.

He sees me now.

And he hasn't run away. He has stayed here, with me. Despite who I am, despite my own wretched powerlessness, despite the blood on my hands, and the scourges of guilt weighing my soul down.

I look away before I say something stupid, swallowing heavily against the lump in my throat. He remains silent, studying me.

What would we be if we weren't the Neverseen King and the Mourner? What if we were just two people? A man and a woman? What would happen then?

It's ridiculous to entertain such notions. He *is* the Neverseen King. I *am* the Mourner. That cannot be changed. We are what we are.

We are two broken people who will only hurt each other if we get too close.

I find my voice with difficulty. "The rest of the questions?"

Paper rustles in the darkness. He reads from my note and then answers. "Why are there portals in this palace? It is because my House functions as the Bridge. The Bridge between worlds. It is not the *only* Bridge, as there are crossings between worlds throughout Faerieland and even some more in the human world. However, there are none like this one in scale and concentration. Some worlds can only be accessed through the Bridge, and it's by *far* the largest concentration of doors."

"It must be fought over, then," I say, glad for the distraction from my traitorous heart.

"It is, indeed. The High King of the Fae retains control over it through me, but that doesn't mean there aren't other fae, other peoples, and other . . . *things* that desire control."

"Was Goken someone who wanted control?"

"Goken liked toys. In his mind, humans made the best toys. There are many fae like him. If allowed through the Bridge into my House, they would love to go rogue in the human world. There are laws to prevent this, however, and no one is allowed through the Bridge without my censor."

"Unless they break out."

"Or someone breaks them *in.*"

My mind flashes back to the heads the Neverseen King had carried with him when he rescued me from Goken. My stomach pitches like it wants to be sick, but I ignore it. "Dabria and Fathuna . . .?"

"Were plotting behind my back, yes," growls the Neverseen King. "I intend to find out who with. They opened a portal and allowed in several fae, actually. That was why I took their heads."

He's threatened me before, of treating me like those who betray him should I do the same. Apparently it's true what he said: he doesn't apologize for those he kills. He has yet to speak a word of remorse over these deaths.

"Will you take my head without hesitation?" I ask. "If I don't prove myself trustworthy?"

His unseen gaze arrests me with sudden force. "Do you intend to betray me, Nadira?"

Kolb and Jabir want me to. Which is probably why I say, "No."

"Good."

"But if I did, you'd kill me like the rest."

"I would have to kill you, yes. I would be lying if I said I wouldn't hesitate, however."

I smile. "You would hesitate to kill me? How sweet of you."

"I *am* known for my sweetness," he says irritably. For one who enjoys doling out sarcasm, he sure doesn't seem to like it when I'm sarcastic back.

"It is good to know where we stand," I say. "That you will not hurt me unless I take a misstep."

Something in the air between us turns sharp, wrathful. "Do you think I take pleasure in death? Do you think I relish taking lives?"

"At least you take them of your own free will," I shoot back.

"Do I?" he demands, leaning forward. "How is being forced by circumstance any different from—"

"It's different because you have a *choice*."

"And what choice would that be?"

"To not kill! To erase their memories like the others, and give them back to their previous lives."

"And leave them for whoever conspired with them to find them and use them again? To give them an opportunity to betray me once more? To allow them to continue orchestrating the downfall of everything I've sacrificed to protect?"

"It may not be preferred, but it's still your own choice."

"I killed them, because if I hadn't I'd have put the Bridge at risk, and if the Bridge falls, do you know what will happen? The gates to all the worlds will be open, and it will be a war of such devastation that no one has ever before seen or will ever see again."

"What an unselfish soul you have, to devote yourself to preventing disaster." I hurl the angry words at him, wanting to hurt him. Wanting him to hurt me and show me that I should leave this place and never look back. "I don't think you care what happens to the Bridge. Why *would* you?"

"It's my duty!"

"But *why*? Why do you care a whit about your duty when it has only brought suffering to you? Why didn't you leave after your wife's death?"

"You think I have a choice in this? To leave my post here would be treason against the High King."

I shoot to my feet and stalk over to him. He remains seated, though there's no denying the power simmering beneath the surface, his muscles coiled to spring. For once, I look down on him, and I savor it. "You stay, not because you care about being a traitor, but because if you leave your wife's death will be in vain."

The rage that boils between us vanishes so completely, it's like the air has just been sucked from the room. He stares up at me, stunned into silence. I'm right, then.

Has he even realized this himself?

"You act like I'm the only one with problems between us," I growl, then fling a finger toward the painting on the wall. "But she has been dead for almost a hundred years, and you still aren't over her. Then you get frustrated that *I* am not ready to marry you."

His voice is deathly quiet. "I told you I am not seeking a true wife. I need an alliance."

I match the tone of my voice to his, coming closer to him like he's so often done to me. "Then tell me: were your words to me when we danced—were they a lie?"

He twists his neck to the side, breaking our gaze. He doesn't answer.

"Not a lie then." Which means that there is part of him—a part of him he wishes to bury—that cares about me. A part of him that finds me . . . *lovely*.

"I'm sorry I offended you," he says abruptly.

I freeze. Cold washes over me. "What do you mean?"

He brings his gaze back to mine, until our faces are much too close. "When I asked if you thought I relished death and killing. You hated being forced to kill, and what was done to you was horrible. Please do not take my statements about my situation to be any comparison to yours."

Now it's my turn to be stunned.

I stumble back a step, my fight and fury gone like a candle blown out. He catches my hand before I go too far, his fingers warm on mine, and that simple touch makes a sense of vulnerability wash over me.

"Let us not argue," he says softly, gently.

"What are we to do then, if not argue?" I reply, and my voice is equally quiet, but there's no hiding the hardness behind it.

"Do you want more answers?"

"At this rate, it'll take all night."

He chuckles. Then he gives my hand a tug—a request to come closer. Do I want to come closer? This constant warring in my soul is exhausting. I don't have the desire to pull away, but neither do I want to risk coming closer.

I stay where I am.

I don't let go of his hand.

I fight the urge to twine my fingers with his, to take comfort in his solid strength. Which is ridiculous, because only a moment ago he threatened to kill me.

He takes my hand, turns it over, and to my shock, begins tracing with his finger the lines of calluses on my palms.

My whole body goes stiff.

"You asked why you are not safe with me," he says quietly. "You are not safe as my wife because of Lulythinar. That is what I meant. Aside from that, nothing will harm you."

My words are breathless. "Unless I betray you."

His finger halts its movement. "You keep saying that. Perhaps I ought to ask you again: do you intend to betray me?"

"No."

"But . . .?" he asks, reading the uncertainty in my voice. His attention lifts from my hand.

"Someone has asked me to."

"Ah." He releases me. "So you have no plans to betray me. But you are keeping the option open. That is why you keep asking."

I walk around the table and sit back down on the settee, putting distance between us once again. "I won't betray you so long as I don't have a good reason to."

"Right. Because you have no true loyalty to me." He gives a wry smirk.

"Ought I?"

"Of course not. It would be foolish. And you, darling Nadira, are not foolish."

We sit in silence, staring at each other. I'm not sure what he sees. I see nothing but the shape of him, the outline of his tall, broad form. It strikes me as odd how well we've come to read each other in a few short days, despite him being mostly invisible, and me being . . . *me.*

What if, despite everything, I don't want to be afraid of him anymore? What if I don't want to do the smart thing and keep my distance? What if I want to be unraveled like a spool of thread—if I want that which will destroy me?

"Maybe I'm more foolish than you realize," I whisper. The fact that I even say the words proves that they're true.

The Neverseen King leans forward, his eyes flashing so brightly I catch a glimpse of them in the darkness. "Then marry me, Nadira."

Marry me.

Reason wars with desire, desperation with reservation, hope with fear.

"If I marry you, you'll let Eshe go." Once I say the words, their absurdity hits me. Eshe has been free to leave this entire time.

He only says, "Yes."

My hands clench the arm of the settee until my knuckles shine white in the glow of the moon. "Will you . . ." The words halt in my throat. I force them out. "Will you come closer?"

A wave of powerful emotion ripples out from him, something that is too tangled to discern. It hits me nonetheless, pinning me in place as I stare at the dark figure across from me.

He stands slowly, rising from his chair and unfolding to his massive height. My chin tilts up, dragged by the weight of his eyes upon me. My mouth goes horribly dry, my pulse thundering like a hundred horses loosened through the desert at midnight. He takes three steps toward me, skirting the table, until he's two feet from my knees.

"How close?" His voice has dropped in pitch, all but a rumbling in the shadows.

I swallow, barely able to maintain his gaze. He can sense my heartbeat—he cannot be oblivious to the effect he has on me. "Closer."

He hesitates.

It doesn't surprise me. He is as determined to protect himself as I am. But if I am to even *consider* pledging myself to him, if I am to risk it all for him, then I need the same from him. I need him to stop withholding himself from me.

I need him to care about me.

Because right now, I'm playing a deadly game with far too many odds stacked against me. I cannot be expendable. I cannot be a tool. If we are to marry, I need him for my husband as he needs me for his wife.

"Closer," I say again.

At last, he takes another step, then the final one, until he towers over where I sit, staring down at me. The air pounds between us, like the beat of wings. He is so still, so solemn. So determined.

I whisper, the sound nearly swallowed up in the depths of night, "Kiss me."

Shock throbs like a wound as the Neverseen King stumbles back a step. "No," he growls. "I won't kiss you."

My hand darts out, catches hold of a muscular forearm as he turns to abandon me. "Wait!"

He stops, his head tilted down and away from me, his chest rising and falling with rapid breaths. He could throw off my hold or vanish into nothing, yet he stays. I reach with my other hand, wrapping it around his wrist—disguising my checking of his pulse with the tightening of my fingers. His blood thunders through his veins.

"Stop that," he growls, flicking his wrist to dislodge my hold.

So perhaps I didn't hide it well enough.

"If you want to know if my heart quickens at your nearness, simply ask. It's not as though I can lie to you."

I don't ask. I already know the answer. If I wasn't sitting, it might have made my knees buckle. As it is, my hands tremble on his arm.

"I've told you I find you beautiful," he continues, a harsh and ragged edge to the words. "I've told you that I want you to be my wife—that I've wanted it for some time. Surely you know by now that I am . . . *fond* of you. What more do you want from me?"

My grip on him tightens until I'm almost clinging to him, my vision blurring with sudden tears as my chest constricts painfully.

Giving in to impulse, I lean forward and rest my forehead against the side of his elbow. He flinches in response while I draw in a deep breath of his scent. It soothes something deep inside me. Calms me enough that I can rifle through my mind for a cohesive answer.

I want all of you, I long to say. *All, or none.*

What I say, however, is, "I want you to kiss me."

His hand clenches into a fist, the cords of his muscles tightening in my hold. "I won't kiss you, Nadira."

His words are like twin knives through my heart. I press my face deeper into him, as if that will hide me from the sting of them. It doesn't work.

He is so determined to not care about me. Even though we are two lost souls adrift on an open sea, alone and forgotten, he doesn't want to care about me.

I take one more deep breath. "Then will you embrace me?"

A sound emerges from him—like a strangled version of something between a moan and a growl. Then he wrenches free of my grip, turns toward me abruptly. He falls to his knees, snatching hold of my wrist, and pulls me off the settee—

And into his arms.

My eyes fly wide, my body going taut with surprise as he crushes me to his chest. Then I melt into him, burying my face in his neck. He squeezes me tighter, almost desperately. He is everything that is warm, solid, and safe in this world. I can hardly breathe, but for once, I am happy to drown.

Maybe I *would* die for him. Maybe I would be glad for it, if only he would always hold me like this. My skirts flare across the floor, glittering with light from nowhere. His collar is wet with my tears as I wrap my arms around my sultan, wanting this moment never, ever, *ever* to end.

With each passing moment, the tension leaks from my body. Muscles I didn't know were tense unfurl, relaxing until I'm barely holding onto him. He shifts.

"Don't let me go," I whimper.

His arms tighten. "I won't. I'm just . . . readjusting."

He slides into a sitting position, and scoots so he can lean against the settee, keeping me against his chest. I shift too, sitting on the floor, drawing my knees to my chest, and curling against him with his legs on either side of me. He lets out a deep breath, letting his head fall back against the upholstery as one hand winds itself around the ends of my hair.

"I don't want to leave you," he whispers.

"Then don't. Please."

He tilts his head forward, his exhales stirring the top of my hair. "I'll stay longer."

"If you try to leave, I'll stab you."

He gives a low chuckle, and there's not even a hint of wryness to it. It makes me smile against his collar. He swallows, opens his mouth, as if he intends to speak. Then he shuts his mouth and snuggles me closer to him.

Though it's been ages since I could fall asleep at a decent hour, the sound of his heartbeat against my ear lulls me into dreariness. My wet eyelids are suddenly heavy. So, so heavy.

"Are you working magic on me?" I mumble.

There's a quiet snort as his heart skips a beat. It sounds like he's smiling. "No. What spell do you think I'm working?"

"One to make me tired."

"You are doing that on your own, I'm afraid, little assassin."

Those are the last words I hear before I fall into dreams of strong arms holding me above rising floodwaters, keeping me to a solid chest in a fracturing world.

CHAPTER 28

I WAKE TO a sunbathed face hovering above mine. Lips pull back from teeth in a wide smile as that face cocks to one side in my bleary vision.

"If it isn't the Mourner sleeping in on this fine day!"

I bolt upright so fast my head almost collides with Eshe's as I throw myself out of bed, only for my feet to give way. I wind up in a tangle of magenta skirts and bedclothes, twisted into such a constricting mess I very nearly draw a knife to cut my way out.

But I stop. Breathe.

It's only Eshe.

With a sigh, I fall back to the floor and stare at the ceiling arching above me. Flowers are carved into the scrolling woodwork, and I trace their petals with my eyes as memories flood from last night.

He held me.

That's my last memory. Did I dream it? I don't think so, but . . . maybe?

If I hadn't, then he *did* leave me at some point. He must have carried me to my bed and tucked me in. My eyes flutter closed. *Why* did I fall asleep? Why couldn't I have stayed awake?

When I open my eyes again, Eshe's face hovers just above mine. She's grinning, cross-eyed, while using her fingers to pull down the skin under her eyes to make *quite* the expression.

I would have groaned if I didn't give a quiet snort instead. "The cats dragged in a thief, it would seem. I was worried about you, idiot."

Eshe's clown-face rotates, her eyes unblinking, as though she is a very creepy doll.

I move to whack her stupid face with my elbow, and *that* finally makes her yank away.

"Worried about *me*?" she asks, lifting an eyebrow before flipping into a cartwheel. "I've told you—I have nine lives, like the apparent cats that dragged me in. I always have more to spare."

I smile, scooting up into a sitting position. It takes me some time to unwind myself from my blankets, but during that time, I slowly become aware of how oddly . . . *rested* I am. What's even stranger—

I'm starving.

There is a breakfast tray on the table. Steam wafts from a half-drunk cup of tea. Cinnamon curls into my nostrils, suddenly evoking an almost frantic hunger. I get to my feet, all but stagger to the settee—my face heating at last night's memories—and stuff my face with thin bread slathered in hummus and piled with olives and tomatoes, a handful of dates with salt and goat milk butter, hunks of cheese, and spicy sausages.

I pay no mind to Eshe's bugged eyes or raised eyebrows as she slinks to the seat across from me. The one the Neverseen King sat in last night.

"What happened?" Eshe demands when I lean back and lick my fingers.

Akhh, I don't know the last time I was this full. It's amazing. I almost want to lie down and go back to sleep.

"Who did this to you?"

I look up. "Pardon?"

"*Who* did *this*"—Eshe waves vaguely at the empty breakfast tray before me—"to you."

I shoot her a narrow look. "What's wrong with me eating breakfast?"

"It's not *wrong*!" cries Eshe in exasperation, throwing up her hands. "It's simply not like you! And for the record, I don't think I've ever seen you sleep. Something's up. My guess is that it has something to do with a certain hunky shadow whose name starts with an N and rhymes with *everbean sing*."

"What happened last night?" I ask as I pour myself a cup of qahwa. This brew is golden, and it tastes of saffron when I sip it.

"I smell evasion on you."

"Does evasion smell like qahwa?"

"Did he kiss you?"

I blink. Set down my cup. Heat climbs up my neck. "No."

A dark expression wars to overcome Eshe's chipper mask. Does she believe I'm lying to her? Is it fear that flexes her jaw? Or hurt?

No matter what convoluted mess of feelings for the Neverseen King have tangled themselves inside me, Eshe comes first. She will always be first. Which means I need to be brutally honest with her, even if neither of us wants the truth.

"He has asked me to marry him," I say.

There is no mirth in Eshe's gaze. "And you're considering it."

Her tone sends my gut plummeting to the floor. My full stomach turns heavy and leaden. I don't want her disapproval. I don't want a rift in our friendship.

She is the only true friend I've ever had. I'm *not* losing her.

But what if she walks away from me? What if I cannot convince her to stay?

I get to my feet, stalk to the wardrobe, and rip open the door. Fresh clothes are folded inside. They're dark brown and black—my usual colors. I peel off my ruined bodice and try to ignore the ache in my heart when I step out of the shimmering skirt. It's as though removing the clothes I wore when the Neverseen King held me in his arms means that I'm letting go of those memories. Shortly, I'm dressed in fresh sirwal and tunic, with my knives in their proper places and a scarf over my hair.

"I am considering it, yes," I say when I can delay no longer. "But I have made no promises."

Eshe folds her arms across her chest. "Well, if he's going to marry you, do you think he'd be open to the prospect of a second bride? I like the food here. We can be our own mini harem and take turns wearing the crown."

She feels betrayed. It's threaded into her tone, into the things she's not saying. The temptation to bury my face in my arms—or resort to begging—is almost overwhelming. My shoulders sag, and I say quietly, "I'm sorry I didn't tell you."

"What do you want?" Eshe asks, leaning forward in her chair. Gone is the flippant ridiculousness that she wears like a second skin. "Do you *want* to marry him? Or is he coercing you?"

What can I answer her? I don't for some time, as I attempt to unravel all the things I don't want to admit to myself, much less her.

"Your heart is involved, then," says Eshe, after the silence persists.

She knows me too well. I lift helpless eyes to her. "I don't know what to do." My head falls into my hands as my nails dig into my scalp. "If I leave, Jabir will find me. I know he will. I'm not going back, Eshe. I'm not going back to him!"

"No. You're not. And if the Neverseen King doesn't make sure of it, then I will."

I almost snort. Eshe is no match for Jabir. Still, her sentiment calms me. *She isn't going anywhere.* I let go of my head, rake my hair out of my face, and sit up.

She regards me seriously. "Nadira. This situation is very complex. Don't be angry with yourself for being confused and frustrated."

Another knot in my chest unwinds. Why didn't I tell her everything as it happened? Why didn't I seek her counsel before now? Why did I fear that she would abandon me if she knew everything?

Eshe is a better person than that.

"It is not a situation to be making rash decisions. Much less life-altering decisions, such as whether you will marry the man who kidnapped you or not."

"Why do you think I've struggled so much?" I mumble, and almost give into the temptation to drop my face into my hands again. "It makes me want to run away. To *prove* I can leave, and then return of my own accord. To prove I'm not here because he forces me to be."

I suppose I *did* run last night. I did leave. And I came back.

But that was for Eshe.

"Despite the kidnapping," continues my friend, "I know you, and I know you don't thoughtlessly trust people. In fact, it's the opposite. But there's something different here. Something in your face. Something in the fact that you *slept* and *ate*."

Nervousness crawls down my spine at where this is going.

"There is part of you that finds the Neverseen King trustworthy. Despite everything. There is part of you that, dare I say, even . . . *likes* him."

Now I definitely cannot meet her gaze. Heat roars into my cheeks.

"I'm right, then," says Eshe.

"And if you are?" I growl, shooting a glare at her.

"Why do you trust him?"

My fingers twitch, aching for the solidity of a knife in my grip. My gut rolls into a knot, and I don't want to voice the thought that immediately pops into my mind at her question.

Because he is like me.

"He promises to protect me from Jabir," I begin slowly. "Even if I don't agree to be his wife. He said he would protect me. If there was nothing good or trustworthy in him, wouldn't he have promised it only if I agreed to be his wife? It would be his bargaining chip over me. He has been patient with me. Kind to me."

He's also threatened to kill me.

This is, indeed, quite the ugly situation. Now that Eshe has pointed it out, it's hard to unsee.

"You're not answering my question," says Eshe.

"I wasn't done."

"You are trying to convince me to trust him. I'm asking why *you* trust him."

I glare at her. She smirks back. I sigh. My hand has found its way to the back of my neck, where it scratches much too vigorously. When I try to speak, I squeeze my eyes closed. "Because . . . he has lost like I have."

"Wicked people can lose things."

"Don't forget that you're speaking to one," I mutter.

"I'll say it again. Stop trying to convince me to trust him. Tell me *why* you trust him."

"I did!"

"No, you didn't."

"You're insufferable."

"And you're arrogant, cold, standoffish, untrusting, and a myriad of other things! Do you think I care?"

We glare at each other for a long moment. Something hot bubbles up inside me, something molten, but something undeniably true. And then, before I can stop them, the words are spilling from my lips.

"I trust him because he makes me feel seen and safe. He makes me want to believe I'm not a lost cause. He makes me hope for good. He makes me want *more* for my life. And with him, I have a purpose—a purpose that isn't murdering for wicked men. A purpose of *saving* instead of killing."

Eshe studies me. The silence between us echoes after my outburst, and I long for her to say something. To tell me I'm an idiot for feeling these things for the man who kidnapped me. She'll tell me that it's dangerous—insane, really—that I've *almost* begun thinking of him less as our kidnapper, and more as . . . a *rescuer*.

She ought to be concerned about me. *I'm* concerned about me.

But Eshe doesn't look concerned. Her face is drawn in lines of consideration, not alarm. At last, her eyes lift to mine. "Then perhaps it isn't your worst idea to marry him."

"What?" I burst out. "You give terrible counsel!"

"Trying to escape with Kolb that one time topped this, almost certainly."

"*That* was not my idea. That was Kolb's, and believe me when I say, I learned my lesson!"

She chuckles. Then we're staring at each other, as if there's a million things we need to say to one another but it's too much, so only silence has the weight to communicate the things on our minds.

"How are you?" I ask.

"Never better!" she chirps, leaning over the table to pour herself more qahwa. "I'm telling you, I'd consent to being chained in a dungeon the rest of my life if it meant I could keep eating like a queen."

I give a small smile, lifting my own cup to my lips. After a sip, I ask again. "But how are you? Truly?"

Now it's her turn to swallow several mouthfuls of qahwa before answering. The cup gives a little rattle when she sets it back down on the tray. "A little off-balance, I confess."

I listen, waiting.

"I'm not an assassin," she continues. "I am not accustomed to so much death and brutality in such a short span of time. There's always violence on the streets, and I'm used to that. I have learned to avoid most of it. But that violence is done out of desperation, starvation. This is different. I was surprised last night when I caught Fathuna and Dabria giving each other a look. A look that told me something bad was about to happen. I was *not* expecting Fathuna to prick her finger right then and flick the blood onto the floor. It happened so fast none of us could react. Not even the Neverseen King. Not until several more shadow-beings like him spilled through another portal in the ballroom."

If only I hadn't run away, I could have helped. Maybe I would have seen it sooner, been able to act faster.

Unlikely. I was too confused after my dance with the Neverseen King last night to notice anything.

"How many?" I ask.

"Six. I think."

"And they wreaked havoc on the ballroom?"

"It wasn't so simple as that. Only a couple went crazy, going to grab me or the other women. Except Dabria and Fathuna. No one touched them. The Neverseen King took those shadow-people out quickly enough, but the others he didn't touch."

"What do you mean?"

"He told them to leave. One of them said something about being sent to take over the Bridge, and things escalated. There was a woman among them, and she kept saying something like, *'Can you truly be intending to marry a human?'* It was a little challenging to keep up with what was happening since the argument got heated, and a lot of it sounded like gibberish."

Another language, perhaps?

"That was when utter *chaos* ensued."

"What? What happened?" I demand, gripping the hilt of my knife subconsciously.

"The shadow-things attacked the Neverseen King. And then Dabria flicked her wrist, and—believe me when I say chaos ensued—she had some ball of light in her hand. Like she had magic? From somewhere? Fathuna had her weapons out, and the two of them herded Gaya, Safya, and I into a corner. Dabria was saying things like, *'Don't worry. No one will get hurt if you cooperate.'* Which, obviously, I didn't believe for an instant."

Despite my pounding heart, I cannot help my slight smile. The Neverseen King is right. I don't give Eshe enough credit.

If not for her, I probably wouldn't still be alive today.

At the same time, Dabria's voice drifts across my memory.

You need to know whose side you're on.

I had assumed she was on the side of the Neverseen King. I couldn't have been more wrong.

"Then one of the shadow-folks told the Neverseen King if he didn't stop fighting them, he'd kill his humans. Which, I don't appreciate being called *his*, but the fight did stop. He looked over at us, at Dabria and Fathuna. I was ready to throw myself at one of them, but Safya whispered, '*Wait,*' to us, and at this point, I'm pretty terrified of Safya. So I listened. One of the shadows said something about being the new Bridge King—I didn't know what in the Great Desert he was talking about—and how the Neverseen King had better not hurt his betrothed. Which seemed to be either Dabria or Fathuna, but I was too confused at this point."

To think, all this was happening while I was contemplating my escape. A sudden burst of nausea hits me. I lean back against the settee. Maybe I shouldn't have eaten all that food for breakfast. "And after that?"

"Honestly? I'm not quite sure. Safya attacked Dabria, so Gaya and I went for Fathuna. Everything seemed to happen at once. Lots of yelling. Fighting. And then it was over. The shadow-people were gone, the portal was closed, and the Neverseen King had killed Dabria and Fathuna. Just in time, too. Fathuna was about to take off my head, and Dabria was choking Gaya while fending Safya off with her glowing magic thing. There might have been a magical vine in there, too. I was slightly preoccupied with surviving to note the particulars."

Yes, I definitely should not have eaten. I am rather inclined to vomit the contents of my stomach out the window.

"He was kind to the three of us, helping us and asking if we were alright. Then he told us to get back to our rooms as quickly as we could and bolt the door before the sun set. After that, he broke into a run, flinging open the ballroom door and racing into the hallway. He shouted your name. I started to go after him, to make sure you were alright, but he told me to get to my room and that he would make sure you were safe."

My belly turns warm, flipping in a way that should make the need to vomit more urgent. Instead, it's pleasant. Almost heady.

"Well," says Eshe after a few minutes. "*This* is when you tell me your side of the story. Where you went. Why your gown was ripped. I need every juicy detail."

"Did you find my note?" I ask. "The one I left in your knife sheath?"

"Was that what that paper was? I was a little busy when I drew my knife. I think it fell to the floor or something."

I should have had the guts to just tell her about the opportunity to escape instead of writing it down. I just hadn't wanted to commit to anything before I knew what I wanted. After drawing a deep breath, I explain everything that happened last night, from the moment I left—that I'd left because he'd asked me to marry him—to the moment I fell asleep in his arms. As much as I long to keep that particular detail to myself, I ignore the heat climbing into my cheeks and say the words.

Eshe deserves to know.

I tell her about Lulythinar. About the sultan's first wife, who even now stares down at us from her mounted spot on the wall. I tell her everything he told me. It's while I'm speaking, while my eyes roam everywhere in the room except her face, that my gaze snags on a slip of parchment sticking out from beneath the empty pitcher on my vanity.

A jolt ripples down my spine.

A note. From him.

Could I feign interest in the mess of cosmetics on the vanity to read it? Or perhaps pretend I'm cleaning? So Eshe doesn't notice?

I stop myself. I am done hiding things from her.

"I think he left me another note," I say as I stand and make my way to the vanity. My hands give a slight quiver as I slip the paper from beneath the mirror. Eshe leans precariously over the back of her chair, trying to catch a glimpse of the note I hold.

I fight every instinct and read the note aloud. "Nadira. I didn't answer the rest of your questions last night. You want to know what happened to Hulla." I draw in a shaky breath before continuing. "She is dead. The House is not the same at night. A precaution against things that might escape portals. I wasn't fast enough to save her."

Eshe says nothing. She sinks an inch lower into her chair, her skin going fractionally paler than before.

"You want to know why I didn't tell you all of this at the beginning. My reasons were twofold. First, because I did not regulate the activities of those who chose to come and go, I did not want too many secrets to be spilled."

It still angers me that we were free this entire time, and it was my own cautious nature that kept me from discovering the truth.

"The second reason," I continue reading, "is simply that you were not ready to hear the truth. I know my palace is difficult for some. I wanted to allow you to adjust to the House first. Once you proved you could handle that, I've been trying to show you things without overwhelming you too severely."

"I have not been overwhelmed for a single moment since I arrived," proclaims Eshe with an irritable huff.

I almost smile . . . until I see the next line, and my mouth goes dry. I almost forget to read it aloud. After clearing my throat, I begin. "You also wish to know the details of my relationship with Safya."

Eshe's hand shoots up, her finger pointing at me. "I *told* you that you were jealous!"

"I don't have to read my private correspondence aloud."

She grins and pops back on her heels in the chair, holding onto the armrests. "Please, do continue."

I give her an arch look. Then I continue. "You want to know how our private meal was. Which is, I daresay, a rather personal question. But because . . ." I trail off, my face turning hot.

"Because *what*?" Eshe demands.

Akhh, why did I decide to not keep secrets from her anymore? My face must be the color of a tomato when I manage to finish the sentence. "But because you were so beautiful last night and—"

Eshe chortles.

"—and . . ." Now my face burns brighter than a furnace. Sands and stars, *why* did he write this? He must have known I was going to read it aloud and meant to torture me. Perhaps to get back at me for asking him to kiss me.

"What? What, what, *what*? You can't just choke and turn crimson and *not* read what he wrote! I'm much too invested!"

I glare at her. "I'm skipping this part."

"Oh no, you don't! If you skip it, I'll come grab it from you!"

"How? You can't reach it," I say, grinning despite myself as I hold it high above my head.

It happens so fast I cannot react—and Eshe's knife has flown straight through the air, through the note, and pinned it to the wall behind me. I whirl, but Eshe has already vaulted over the back of her chair, climbed onto my vanity and sent pots of rouge and khol rolling off the counter.

"Don't you dare!" I shout as she leans over, reaching for the knife and the note embedded in the wall. When she only laughs, I launch myself at her. Not fast enough, apparently, for when I tackle her to the ground, she has the knife in one hand. We roll on impact, and I end up banging my back into the bed frame. Then I'm reaching for the knife, struggling to reclaim my note.

But it continues to be one of my greatest flaws that I underestimate Eshe, and she knows very well that I couldn't hurt her. I certainly am not expecting it when she flips me over her back, then gives my shoulder a hefty shove with her foot, knocking me down just as I'm getting to my feet.

That gives her just enough time to start reading, "Because you were so beautiful last night and you—" She cuts off, shrieking and guffawing as I regain my balance and clip her feet out from beneath her. She rolls away from me, almost terrifyingly heedless of the knife she holds, then scrambles to her feet and runs behind the settee. That's when she barely stops cackling long enough to finish the sentence on the page. "—smelled like the blooms of desert roses, rare vanilla bean, mingled with the most exquisite heartbreak."

I can't keep myself from flushing hotter. "He meant it to be mocking, for heaven's sakes! That's just what he does!"

That doesn't stop her from letting out another peal of laughter. "The smell of heartbreak! Can you even imagine? Maybe it smells like rotten muskmelon, because my heart certainly breaks to have such deliciousness go to waste!"

"Give it back," I growl from the other side of the table.

"I'm not done yet," she manages between cackles. "Does he say anything else? Oh! Oh, what's this?"

"Eshe."

"Whoa, he calls you out here!"

I might actually die from mortification. "*Eshe*."

Nothing will stop her from reading aloud: "*My darling Nadira*—sands, either he really likes you or he *is* mocking you—*it touches me that you are so envious of the attentions I've given Safya*. Now this is a little mean on his part. I think he likes it when you're jealous."

"Both of you take great sport in tormenting me," I say sourly, dropping into Eshe's chair and folding my arms across my chest.

She peers over the top of the Neverseen King's note and waggles an eyebrow. "It's what friends are for, *darling* Nadira."

It is confirmed: this is the absolute worst decision I have ever made in my life. I hold my hand out to Eshe, glaring at her. "May I have it back, *please*?"

"Let me make sure he doesn't say anything else about how you smell." Her tongue slips between her lips as her brows furrow in concentration and her eyes skim the rest of the note. "Nope. Nothing more about your smells. It's safe for you to read."

She tosses it to me. It barely makes it over the back of the settee. I'm forced to get up to retrieve it. I make sure to shoot her my darkest glares. She only mutters, "Vanilla bean and heartbreak," under her breath and giggles.

When I finally have the note in hand, I read the rest of it to myself.

My darling Nadira. It touches me that you are so envious of the attentions I've given Safya. While I must admit our dinner was pleasant enough, she is not the one I have asked to wed. She is not the one I write notes to every day. She is not the one who fills my thoughts.

I've told you before, and I will tell you again. You, Nadira al-Risya, are the one I want. I cannot begrudge you your hesitation to trust me, but it does put me in a precarious situation. If you will not wed me, I must find another.

If you find it any consolation, Safya is not ignorant of my need for an alliance instead of a true wife. She is aware that sentiment is not part of the agreement.

As for your final question, the one regarding my name, I must inform you that I could never give such a powerful thing to a human. I find your lot to be rather careless with names, and I cannot risk mine falling into the wrong hands.

I will, however, entrust my name to my bride. Such is her right.

With that, I must be off. There are enemies to vanquish and human kingdoms to neglect. I bid you good day, Mourner.

There's no signature. I fold it in half and drop it onto the table. Eshe leans against the windowsill, streaming sunlight giving her dark hair a fiery red sheen. She smirks at me.

"So. You've successfully seduced the Neverseen King. How does it feel?"

"There has been no seducing!"

"I didn't say it was *purposeful* seducing."

She cocks one wicked eyebrow.

"He only wants an alliance. He refuses to care about me. Or anyone."

"And your point is?"

"That . . . he doesn't want me like *that*."

"Nadira."

"What?" It comes out more defensively than I intend, but the way she says my name makes my hackles rise in defense. It's even more alarming that her face has softened, and that smirk has disappeared.

"Do you want to marry him?"

"No," I say immediately, and it tastes like a lie. "If I marry him, I'll die."

"Will you?"

"It's very *likely* that I will."

"Is that the only reason you don't want to marry him?"

"It's certainly a significant deterrent."

"What if—just for this one moment—you didn't think about life and death. What if you set aside your fear and your self-preservation—"

"A brilliant idea," I say.

"—and what if you asked yourself what you *want*. You're not a slave anymore. You're not bound to anyone. You're not bound to this palace, to the Neverseen King, and you're not bound to Jabir anymore."

"I might find myself bound to him if I'm not careful."

"But right now, you're free. You're your own woman."

Those words sink into my mind like a stone into the courtyard fountain. She's right. I *am* free. If I wanted to leave this all, if I wanted to walk away forever, the Neverseen King would help me. I'm sure of it. He promised as much. He promised to protect me from Jabir.

I can choose my future.

So why don't I want to leave?

"What do you want, Nadira?" Eshe asks. "It's your decision."

My decision.

It seems impossible that I could make my own decisions. I could live a normal life—far away, most likely. But a normal life nonetheless.

I wouldn't have to kill. I could bury my knives in the desert sand and never look back.

What if I never had to clean blood from beneath my fingernails? What if I never had to scrub it out of my clothes? What if I could forget these last two decades of my life as Jabir's slave?

What do I want?

The truth is that I don't know. I've known for so long what I *don't* want that I've neglected to consider what it is that I actually *do* want.

As if reading my mind, Eshe says, "You should think about it."

"What do *you* want?" I ask.

She gives a soft snort, scooting onto the window ledge and extending her short legs. "Not much, in truth. A full belly, a comfortable place to sleep, at least one friend. And I want to do things that make me feel alive."

"Things like almost dying?"

Her eyes sparkle when she grins. "There's nothing quite as intoxicating as almost dying."

"I beg to disagree."

She chuckles, and we stay like that for some time in companionable silence. Truly, I do not know how I wound up with a friend like her. Eshe is the only good outcome of Jabir forcing me to do these jobs. If not for them, I'd never have met her.

Perhaps, very rarely, good could come from bad.

"I also want to help the street orphans," Eshe says softly. She doesn't look at me when she says it, instead staring out at the courtyard below us, the birds flying through the sky. "I want them to be fed . . . and protected."

Memory of our first meeting washes over me. The only blood I wasn't forced to shed. The only blood I will never regret shedding. The lashes Jabir gave me for that city guard's life were ones I relished. I would have taken a hundred more. No girl of fourteen should ever have to endure what that guard was doing to her when I found them on my way back from my third assassination.

I still remember when my eyes locked with Eshe's for the first time. The gold-flecked brown eyes that slowly shift from the courtyard to mine now are different—and yet still the same.

"I'm going to take a walk and clear my mind," I say.

"Have fun! If you need me, I'll be in search of near-death experiences."

I roll my eyes, but cannot help my somber smile as I open the door to my room and slip out.

CHAPTER 29

I WANDER FOR several hours. Up and down hallways, peering at the different doors I dare not open, distracting myself with their strange designs from the whirl of thoughts crowding my brain. I visit the banister and waste far too much time stroking it and delighting in its creaking moans of happiness.

There is no sign of Gaya or Safya. I'm not nearly as unsettled by the quiet fullness of the palace air as I was when I first arrived. Granted, it is early afternoon by now and there is something far less menacing about a place when the sun reigns at its zenith than during the depths of midnight.

At some point, I blink, and the door I'm facing comes into focus. It's a pair of towering oak doors, carved with motifs of dancing creatures with wings. Most of them seem human, but others resemble butterflies or dragonflies.

I haven't opened any doors I've come across today.

But I open this one.

Darkness greets me. This darkness is warm, inviting—like an embrace in the dead of night. There are no stars hung from the ceiling today, no fireflies illuminating the ballroom. No sweeping strains of music.

The door gives a creak, then a thud as it shuts behind me.

Night becomes my shroud. It echoes with each of my steps across the polished floor to the center of the room. And for once, I'm not afraid of it. I'm not waiting for the shock of a blade in my back. Perhaps I ought to, considering what happened here last night.

But I'm simply not afraid.

It's a feeling I long to bottle up, to save and savor for those long hours between dusk and dawn when I inevitably try and fail to fall asleep.

What would life be if I wasn't afraid all the time?

When I'm standing in the midst of the ballroom, I close my eyes and lift my arms. It's not difficult to imagine him here with me, holding me again as we spin through dreams and starlight. I move my feet in an awkward attempt at last night's dance. Without him to guide me through the unfamiliar steps, I stumble more than glide. As I go, however, I fumble less. My muscle memory takes over, carrying me back through one of the few moments of my life when I was truly happy.

Even though I'm alone, I smile. There will always be happiness here, in these steps, these movements. I want to remember them forever, no matter where I go. I lock them deep inside myself where no one can take them from me.

A hand catches hold of mine.

Another slips around my waist, drawing me to a solid chest.

My eyes open. I stop dancing.

The Neverseen King stares down at me, our fingers intertwined and our hearts pounding the same erratic rhythm. He says nothing, and neither do I.

Then, in silence, he draws me back into the dance. We start slow, keeping to the basic steps. He sends me spinning under his arm, then twirls me until my back is flush to his chest for the span of two steps.

It is enough for his heart to pound against my shoulder, enough for me to breathe in that scent of his that my body cannot help but associate with safety as his hand splays across my middle.

He spins me out again. When he brings me back to face him, this time I'm the one to step closer to him, to tighten my grip on his upper arm. His head dips forward toward mine, his mouth coming near my ear as his breath tickles my neck. But he says nothing, and we continue dancing. When I close my eyes, I can almost imagine threads of music wrapping around us, entangling our souls with every step, every spin.

We inch closer, until there's hardly a whisper of air between us as we dance. His lips hover at my hairline, warming my scalp with each exhale. Instead of having a chaste hand on my waist, at some point his grip shifts, until his arm is completely wrapped around me. Holding me to him.

We slow our dance until we stand still in the center of the ballroom. His arm keeps me close as we stare at each other—king and assassin. Shadow and woman. I wait for something I cannot name as my heart thuds painfully in my chest, so hard he certainly must feel it.

He bends forward again with agonizing slowness, until he leans his forehead against mine. My breath catches in my throat. He seems to hesitate. Then his nose gives mine a little nuzzle, almost as if he cannot help it. Somehow it's that scrap of contact, not his hand in mine or his arm around me, that makes me tilt my chin up to his.

Please kiss me, I want to beg. I want to know if this is real, that I'm not imagining this connection between us.

But the moment I lean forward, to span the distance between our mouths, he turns his face away. Such a slight movement—yet it hits me like a blow. A blow that leaves behind a cavernous aching in my chest. That ache is quickly replaced by coldness, hardness. I tighten my grip on his hand and shoulder.

"Why?" I whisper.

"You know why." The words are a ragged growl. And yet—he doesn't let go of me.

He wants to be close to me. Just not *too* close.

I won't have it.

"Because you don't want to be heartbroken when I die," I say, and though I try to keep the coldness out of them, the edge of dark ruthlessness lingers. "How much faith do you have in me, Neverseen King? In my survival of Lulythinar?"

His jaw works, and he still doesn't turn his face back to me. "I have great faith in you."

But greater faith in the overpowering strength of Lulythinar, it seems. I chew on my cheek as I consider this.

He wants an assassin for his bride, does he? He wants a woman of strength—a woman who will fight for him, for all the worlds. A woman who will kiss death.

Very well.

I will show him what it is to have a killer for a wife.

"Bargain with me," I say, lifting my chin.

Those words almost seem to rip his arms from me. He steps back, and one of his great hands lifts to scratch his neck. An oddly uncertain gesture for one so powerful, so *other*.

"What bargain?" His deep voice is a mere rumbling in the shadows.

"A kiss—"

"No," he answers immediately, turning away.

"—for an answer," I finish.

He stops. Glances back at me. "What?"

"If you kiss me, I will give you my answer to your offer of marriage."

His throat bobs. "If you make me kiss you only for you to say no—"

"Then you can focus your attentions on Safya," I say, and then add dryly, "or Gaya."

He is quiet. Considering. The air we breathe turns thick, and it coats my lungs like syrup.

"Deal."

My wrist burns, and this time when I look down, the glowing tattoo on my skin is of a knife, its hilt a crosshatch over my pulse, its blade pointing toward my elbow. The Neverseen King glances down at the matching, glowing tattoo on his wrist.

And then he looks up at me.

My heart pounds. Until I can think of nothing else—nothing but that first step he takes toward me, then the second, and the third. He stands before me, staring down at me, his eyes flashing.

He makes no move for a long moment.

Perhaps both of us are waiting for the other. Perhaps he is as terrified as I am.

Then, slowly, one of his great hands reaches toward me—pauses in midair—before continuing until his fingers land lightly beneath my jaw. He tilts my face up toward his. I swallow as his thumb brushes over my bottom lip.

This is a horrible idea.

A horrible idea I do not regret. Not as he bends toward me, not as his hand slides from my jaw to tangle in my hair as he pulls me against him. My breath shudders out of my lungs as my eyes flutter closed—and his exhale is warm across my face.

His lips brush mine, and that single contact sends sparks straight to my gut.

Then his mouth is on mine, his hands in my hair, around my waist, pulling me against him with sudden urgency. I kiss him back, searching for the answer I need from him as I reach up and wrap my arms around his neck.

Time stops. I'm hardly aware of anything except his lips moving with mine, his arms crushing me to him. Suddenly my back hits a wall. I open my eyes to realize we've moved across the room, and he pins me while he kisses me.

He wants this. He wants me. He wants us. Not just a sacrificial bride. He can pretend all he wants, but the truth is plain. My heart soars into the stars, with hope and dreams of a future of belonging.

He truly isn't as heartless as he pretends to be.

Unfortunately, the same is true for me.

The ache that starts in my chest is so subtle I don't notice it until it builds and sharpens into something like a dagger. The longer he kisses me, the deeper he kisses me, the more I break into tiny, fracturing shards.

It's too much. *Too much,* and I am drowning. I'm going to pass out. If there was ever a moment I didn't want to pass out—sands and stars!

He pulls back abruptly, catching my head as it lolls backward.

"Nadira?"

I breathe hard, my chest heaving. His hand is still around my waist, holding me so close his belt digs into my stomach. His other hand, wrapped around the back of my head and tangled into my hair, slides to my throat and presses two fingers to the hollow of it.

"Breathe," he urges, sounding strained. "Breathe, Nadira."

My airways open, and I tilt my head to the side, staring into pitch darkness while I pant. The Neverseen King remains where he is, letting go of me and placing his forearms against the wall, encasing me as he leans his forehead against mine.

"There," he gasps. "I kissed you. Now tell me your answer."

My head spins and spins, until the world tilts away from me. I want to reach up, wrap my arms around him, and cling to him. I want him to say sweet things to me. *I want him to kiss me again.*

But even the thought of those things causes a surge of vertigo and sends my gut roiling.

He will be the death of me.

I'm not ready to die.

"What is your answer?" he asks again, and the strain still hasn't left his voice. Neither has he pulled away from me. Does he long to kiss me again, as I long to kiss him?

I drag my gaze through darkness, until I find the faint glow of the tattoo pulsing at my wrist. It's been sliced clean down the middle—half of it gone, fulfilled. The other half remains. But when I continue turning my head toward him, when I find his face hovering not even a hand's breath from mine, when I realize I'm encased by his powerful arms and shoulders, I . . . *can't.*

I'm not ready. I thought I was, but I'm not.

I meet his gaze anyway.

The air changes in that instant when he realizes his mistake. He curses under his breath and pushes away from me.

"I'm a fool," he growls.

I straighten as cold air blankets me from head to toe. The world stops shifting around me, and my stomach settles now that he's not so close anymore. My mental clarity returns, and with it, a stabbing guilt.

I shove that guilt away. I'll deal with it later.

"I will give you an answer," I say, drawing up to my full height. "But the terms of our bargain do not dictate when. I will tell you when I have an answer."

He rakes a hand through his hair, clenching it into a fist. His low voice scrapes down my spine. "I didn't think you this cruel, Nadira."

"Neither of us is as heartless as we pretend," I growl back. "But if we stop pretending, we lose everything. You ask for me to lay my very life down at your feet without you promising anything in return. Allow me my cruelties, Sultani. They are the only things keeping me alive."

He should know that cruelty is nothing but a mask to make weak people feel strong.

"Then was my kiss supposed to be my promise of . . . what, Nadira? What do you want from me in exchange for your life?" Anger threads his voice, but it cannot completely conceal the rawness underscoring each word. The desperation.

I lower my voice. "If I am to give you my life, then you must give me yours. I will take nothing less."

"My life isn't mine to give," he shoots back. "It never has been, and it never will be."

"Then you shouldn't dare ask for mine!"

"If this was about me, you know I never would have!"

"If this was about you, you'd have left me to suffer under Jabir's hand until the day I—"

"Stop!" he growls, catching my clenched fist out of the air, gripping my wrist tightly. "I beg you to understand—"

I pull on my wrist, but he doesn't release it. "Let go of me," I demand, and the moment the words are out of my mouth, realization hits me. Suddenly, there is something I desperately need to know. "Why, Sultani? *Why*?"

"Why, what?" A note of . . . *something* enters his voice. Is it fear?

I meet his gaze, that jewel glimmer in the darkness surrounding us. "*Why* won't you let me go?"

Silence slices through the air.

Counting starts in my mind.

One, two, three, four.

Five, six, seven.

Eight, nine, ten.

My chest rises, falls.

Eleven, twelve, thirteen, fourteen.

Fifteen.

Sixteen.

Seventeen.

Does he even know the answer?

Whatever he says—it might be enough for me. It might make me throw everything else to the wind and promise myself to him. It might be enough for me to risk it all, to take my stand at his side.

Or it might make me walk away forever.

Twenty, twenty-one, twenty-two.

I stand barely a full pace from him, his grip on my wrist the only thing linking us in this shroud of night. Despite our proximity, it is like we stand on two ragged cliff edges, a chasm between us. Neither of us wanting the distance, but both of us terrified to take that first step.

What would it be like to never be afraid?

What would it be like to take that step, to risk it all?

But for *what*?

What benefit could outweigh the cost set before us?

"Because," he says at last, and his voice is like a cracked clay pot—threatening to break at any moment. His fingers tighten on my wrist. Is that the slightest tug, trying to pull me closer?

I wait, breathless.

"Because something changed inside me that moment you walked into the Golden Hall on that first day and looked straight at me. Because, *you*, Nadira"—His voice drops, its edges painted in anguish—"for the first time, in ninety-nine years . . . You have given me hope."

I stare at him, struck dumb.

"These many years have been a torture for me. Unending, spent in the dark, *alone*, with nothing but a ceaseless battle to fight. There was no reprieve from sorrow, from the constant ache of emptiness."

My vision blurs, making the gleam of his eyes refract like diamonds on welling pools of unshed tears.

Torture.

Unending.

Spent in the dark.

Alone.

No reprieve from the sorrow, the emptiness.

Something pulses between us—our broken hearts beating in tandem. It aches, aches so sharply I want to bend over, to wrap my arms around my knees and rock myself into oblivion. To encase myself in ice, in nothingness. But the Neverseen King's ragged inhales, his vice-like grip on my wrist, keep me anchored. They bind me to this sea of pain, holding me while the tempest rages around us.

"But *you*, Nadira, *you*—" He chokes.

I close my eyes and bow my head, letting silent sobs wrack my body, rattle my shoulders.

"For the first time, I have *hope*. Hope for a new beginning, a new meaning. Hope for a different end. Hope that there might be goodness in the future." His voice has dropped to a whisper, but then, his grip tightens on my wrist.

Almost painfully.

And to my shock—his hand starts glowing. Golden light bursts from his fingers, striking my eyes, illuminating his powerful forearm and each sinew that threads beneath his skin. I look up in shock, wet trails of tears carved into my cheeks, and find his eyes glowing with that same golden light. They ring sapphire blue irises, shooting golden light into my face, my agape mouth.

When he speaks again, his voice isn't broken. It is whole, undergirded by a soul-deep strength that hits me like a tidal wave, almost knocking me back a step.

"I will *never* let go again, Nadira. Whether you choose to fight by my side or not, I refuse to lose this hope. With you or without you . . ." The golden glow subsides as his voice lowers, dropping as his hand loosens on my wrist, shifting to thread his fingers through mine. "Dawn will come again."

Dawn will come again.

Can I believe that? My own dawn was so short—it ended so suddenly with Jabir's blade. My parents' blood. That look in Baba's eyes when he fixed his gaze on me for the last time as that sword came for his neck.

The light vanished from my life the moment it vanished from his eyes.

Dawn isn't coming back, the voice inside me cries. *It is swallowed up in night.*

Is night so bad? Is hopelessness so bad?

I look up at the Neverseen King, at the glow fading from his eyes.

Perhaps dawn will come for him.

But me?

I am a murderer. I have the blood of dozens on my hands. If dawn never came, I would deserve it. All those names flood my mind, each one etched into my very soul. I remember their faces, their families. I remember every detail of the plots I devised to kill each one.

I never missed a target.

Every name that Jabir gave me—*dead.*

If I refuse to hope, to believe, then I will never be disappointed.

If I give up on this, on *him*, he cannot hurt me. He cannot betray me, or take my life, or let me die. But if I *do* hope, then he will have the power to utterly and completely destroy me.

"Nadira," the Neverseen King growls, tightening his grip on my hand. "Don't give into the despair."

"Don't give in?" I repeat as ice wraps around my heart, as hollowness swallows my soul. "You're mistaken, Sultani. I *am* despair."

And then, I throw myself into that ice deep inside me, the ice that has always been there. I let it close over my head. I let it drown me—I don't fight the panic. Ice coats my lungs, chokes out my air. It surrounds me, fills me, blocking out the distant sound of the Neverseen King screaming my name.

I focus on the core of my gut, that place where that voice lives, speaks.

Yes, it rasps, delighted. *Give in. Stop fighting. Let me make you stronger. Let me make you never afraid again.*

I will never be afraid again, I say back, wrapping myself in that ice. Burying myself. *I will never be afraid again. No one will ever hurt me.*

Because I won't care.

I will be death.

I will be the Mourner, and my blade will strike true. It will cut, slice, carve—and I will forget every name. I will stop trying to wash the blood off my hands. I will embrace its stains, its stench.

The first life I will take is Jabir's. I'll savor it. I'll show him the face of the monster he created. Everything he did to me, I'll do to him. His pleas and cries of pain will be my anthem.

I'll show them all why they feared the Mourner.

I will be the one thing I refused to be. Until now.

I will be ruthless.

And I will enjoy every second of it.

Something dark and ugly chuckles deep inside me.

Then I explode.

CHAPTER 30

THE WORLD SHATTERS.

Into

tiny

pieces.

I am the refracting glass of an enormous chandelier. I am every cut, every facet, every knife-sharp edge of each suspended crystal. I fall—

And I break.

My voice is swallowed whole by the earsplitting scream of ice and glass. I am nowhere, everywhere. I am everything, nothing. Wind sweeps each of my pieces into a tornado, a billowing column of shards to tear into flesh, ripping, rending.

I open my mouth, but no sound comes out. I cannot cry for help, cannot fling out a hand to catch hold of something. There is nothing to be done but *be* the ice, be the coldness seeping into my skin.

Death. Destruction. Despair.

Then, the screams stop. The winds stop. The breaking stops.

My ears ring.

Everything is *so cold.* I shiver, clutching my arms around my torso. My hands meet with the bloodstained garments I wore in captivity and the braces around my bare arms.

I open my eyes.

I blink. Close my eyes again—and open. But no, the scene before me doesn't change.

There is no night-filled ballroom. I lie open and exposed in the middle of . . . a frozen lake? As far as I can see: *ice.* Ice like glass, a window into the world below where I lay, shivering. An overcast sky stretches to the ends of the world in either direction.

Where am I?

Where is the Neverseen King?

Something sharp and hot burns through me at the thought of him. He's not here, not anywhere near me.

He's gone.

The air turns colder around me. My teeth chatter, my breath puffing like a cloud in the air before me. It's so, so, *so cold.* I've never known cold like this. When I glance down, my fingers are blue.

I'm going to die.

It won't be a blade through my heart after all.

But *where* am I?

I need to get up. I need to start walking.

There's no strength left in my body. Whatever just happened drained me dry. Frozen teardrops stud my lashes, and I blink, hoping beyond hope with each blink that this nightmare will end.

Did I fall through some portal? Did I accidentally open one? If I did, how in the world do I get back? Will the Neverseen King come for me?

I will never let go again, Nadira.

That voice inside me promised I wouldn't be afraid anymore. But I'm afraid now—more afraid than I've been in a very long time. Afraid

I will die out here alone, afraid no one will ever find me. Afraid that I could vanish, and no one would notice or care.

Afraid that the world would be better if I was gone.

I will never let go again. I refuse to lose this hope.

The Neverseen King would care. Eshe would care.

I may have given up on myself, but they never did. They have seen the worst in me, and yet Eshe stayed by my side. Defended me, fought for our friendship. The Neverseen King held me, kissed me, and no matter his own burdens and scars, there is one truth I can anchor my soul on.

He cares about me.

He *cares*. Enough to keep extending his hand. Enough to fight with me, to fight *for* me.

Perhaps all this time I wanted him to give himself to me, he actually was. The times he didn't leave, the times he held me, left me notes. Each scrawl of ink, each tray of food, each time he fought me—

All tokens of *him*. Of his heart.

Laid before me.

Perhaps it's time I got to my feet and fought for him.

Each movement is agony. My bones are so brittle with cold that they threaten to break beneath my weight. But I pull a knife from my belt, slam it into the ice, and use it to get to my unsteady feet.

I turn around.

That is when I freeze. When the whole world freezes, and my heart stops beating.

Standing not five paces from me is a form I know better than the weight of a knife in my hand. Small, beady eyes cut straight through me, and a wide, dark smirk splits a bearded face.

"There you are," says Jabir.

I must be dreaming. This must be some strange nightmare—some *something*. Whatever it is, it's not real. I move to take a step back, and nearly slip on the ice.

"You'll freeze to death standing there." He holds out a garment to me. A cloak? "Come, I'll get you some place warm."

My jaw aches with the memory of his spiked gloves. My back throbs with the pounding of phantom lashes. Every instinct in me shouts to run, to hide, to flee. I tamp down on each of them. I learned the hard way that running and fighting only made it worse.

"Come, come child. You'll catch your death." He smiles at me, holding out that cloak that will do almost nothing against this bone-penetrating cold.

"Wh-wh-where are w-w-w-we?" I stutter.

His smile widens into a grin. "You don't know?"

I only stare at him in mute response. If I knew, I wouldn't have asked, now would I?

"Come. I'll tell you once you're not freezing to death."

"Where are we?" I demand, louder this time.

Jabir's eyes glitter like crystals of ice. "Inside you."

The cold bites into every inch of my skin, leaking into my marrow. I'll freeze solid soon. I probably only have minutes left to live. It turns my mind sluggish, making it nearly impossible to think. I'm not sure I could make sense of this even if my body wasn't slowly shutting down.

I still hold my knife in my hand.

There's only one thing that makes sense to do.

My hand shakes with each movement, but I manage to turn my left hand up—

And with my right, I use my knife to slice my wrist open. Blood wells, freezing solid as it drips onto the ice. I look up at Jabir, my blood the one stark color in this frozen wasteland of gray. He tries to say something, but the sound is lost. His eyes go wide—

I blink.

I'm still cold. Still lying on ice.

But this time, I'm not alone. Something warm wraps around me, holding me. There's a voice above me. Not Jabir's. It's deep and rich, but frantic.

"Nadira, wake up, girl! Wake up!"

"I'm awake," I croak, shivering.

"Oh, Great Kings!" comes the gasp, and then a forehead presses against mine.

I close my eyes, reveling in that touch, that scrap of warmth. "Why is it so c-cold? What happened?"

Silence is my answer. I try to sit up, only to discover I'm arranged in the Neverseen King's lap. There's no time to blush because a strange light is cast over the previously dark ballroom. The whole room is reflective, catching shreds of light and multiplying them until I can clearly see the entire room.

It's covered in . . . *ice*?

Sharp crystals jut out of the wall, the ground. Lethal points ready to impale anything that steps too close.

A shiver slides down my spine. My voice grows frantic. I grab the Neverseen King's shirt—find it torn and wet in my grip. "What happened?"

His answer is pained. "You did this."

I'm already shaking my head. "No—no. I didn't do this. I don't . . ."

The panic starts to close in again, that cold seeking to devour me. It builds in my stomach. *Oh sands.* It's like the floodgates have opened, and now I cannot shut them.

"It's coming again!" I gasp, fighting the panic, but with that cold running like icy water to my fingertips, the panic only redoubles. "What is happening? What is happening to me?"

"Breathe!"

Pressure builds in my gut, my chest, my hands. I fight it, trying to shove it down with every scrap of strength in me. The effort wrenches a scream from me, my back arching. "Get away from me! I'm going to hurt you!"

"Nadira!"

"I *can't*!" I scream. I'm about to explode again—about to break into tiny shards of ice. About to tear him apart. Oh stars, I'm going to kill him. I'm going to kill him, and I cannot stop it. "Get *away*! Let me go!"

A growl bursts from him, and he flips me onto my back, out of his lap. I can barely think about anything except the fragmented control I have over the avalanche about to break free—but I have enough awareness to be relieved. Maybe now we'll finally let go of each other, once and for all. He will continue his fight, and I will destroy myself as I was always destined to do.

Then an enormous, solid body flings itself over mine, two powerful hands grabbing my wrists and pinning them wide so my palms face either wall.

"Sultani!" I gasp, and then I scream again as my body arches with the strain.

"Release it," he growls in my ear. "Stop fighting it."

"I *can't*!" It comes out as a sob. "I'll kill you!"

"Release it!"

"I can't!" The tears leaking out of my eyes freeze solid against my cheek, my fingers turning to ice, buzzing. My ribs will break open if I keep fighting this. I'm sobbing. I don't want to go back to that lake, to Jabir. To *myself*. "Help me, Sultani! Help me!"

His hands squeeze my wrists, his body the only warmth in this freezing world. His low voice anchors me in the midst of the storm as he brings his mouth to my ear and snarls, "Let *go*, Nadira."

I clench my teeth, gripping my restrained hands into fists, my spine arching off the ground. The storm churns harder, faster, darker inside me. My awareness narrows to the ice, to my gut.

But this time it isn't Jabir's voice speaking to me.

It's low and deep and steady. *Let go, Nadira. Let go.*

With a sob, I loosen my fists.

The world explodes into shadow black and ice blue.

My lashes flutter. My mind is fogged, my body limp. But there is one thing I am very aware of, and that is the heavy weight on my torso, the hands pinning mine, long hair tangling with my own dark strands.

Weakness runs like water through my limbs.

"Sultani?" I croak.

"I'm here."

"You're not dead?"

"Don't think so."

We stay there for a moment longer, breathing heavily. I'm not sure either of us know what is happening, but there's no denying the sheer relief pouring down my spine, flowing down to my toes and fingertips.

"What was that?" I ask, terrified of the answer.

"That was magic, Nadira."

"I . . . I don't know what you mean."

"That was *your* magic."

It's like that sentence hits my brain—and my brain immediately rejects it. That's not possible. I'm not a spellcaster. I'm not a djinn. Wherever this ice came from, whatever I just experienced—it's not real.

Abruptly, I shove up on my elbow. "Why are you wet? Are you bleeding?"

He grunts as he pushes himself up on his hands, the weight of his gaze almost pinning me in place. *Almost.* But then his silence twines between us, echoing off the blasted sheets of ice on either side of us.

I scramble up gracelessly, grip his shoulders, and push him back so he sits against the wall.

"I hurt you," I say, the pitch of my voice rising with panic. I run my hands over his tunic, his arms, feeling for injury, following the telltale wetness. "You're bleeding. I—"

He grabs my wrist. His voice is low, urgent. "You need to listen carefully to me."

"I'll listen while I bind your wounds. Tell me where it hurts!"

"Nadira—"

"Is this it?" I'm searching just beneath his ribs. "Did I cut you with ice—"

"Nadira!" He grabs my face with both hands. I freeze, my eyes shooting to his. "We don't have time. I'm cut, but not badly. Nothing serious, so forget it. What *is* serious is that your blasts decimated my wards on the palace. Including a few wards binding portals."

"Some portals opened?" I breathe, my hair falling in my face. My gut sinks.

"Yes, and there are more that might break soon. Listen closely to me because I don't have time to repeat myself."

I nod, and his hands don't move from holding my head.

"I can feel that three portals are open. If one more opens, the House's defenses will activate, as they do at night. I need you to find Eshe, Safya, and Gaya, and get them into your room as quickly as you can. Bolt the door. Whatever you do, *do not step foot outside your room*. Understand?"

A thousand questions burst across my mind. I nod again, my gut sinking further and further toward the floor as I rein in those questions. Now isn't the time for a meticulous plan.

"If you encounter anything, *run*. Don't fight unless it's the only option."

He's going to attempt to fight all of tonight's battles and close every portal by himself. I don't like it—not one bit. But what is there for me to do when I've suddenly become so volatile, and I know nothing about the enemies we face?

I'll do what he asks. I give a quick nod to show him my agreement.

He pulls me toward him, resting our foreheads together as the breath mingles from our open mouths. "Nadira."

He says my name like it's a goodbye.

It isn't. I won't *let* this be goodbye.

"Neverseen King," I growl in return. A fiery challenge.

He gives one dry, half-hearted chuckle. "My little assassin bride." It's an answer to my challenge—a promise that he will return to me whole.

If we survive this, I'll marry you. The words are on the tip of my tongue.

But then his touch melts away as a warm wind rustles my hair.

He's gone.

CHAPTER 31

MAKING MY WAY across the ice is tricky business. Every sliding step of the way, my mind reels. *I did this. I did this. I did . . . this? No, definitely not.*

Maybe it's all one big misunderstanding.

I stumble against the doors, catch myself on a knob, and force them open. A rush of warm air blankets me from head to toe—a desperate relief from the cold. But even though I'm no longer frigid, something cold sits in my gut. A heavy, slumbering thing ready to burst forth at the least provocation.

I shove the sensation aside, because the second thing I notice once I'm through the ballroom doors is the shift in the atmosphere.

Something is very, very wrong.

It's midafternoon, but shadows fall in a way that sends a shiver up my spine. A preternatural stillness cloaks each pillar, each hallway.

ANASTASIS BLYTHE

The fountain has gone silent.

Where is Eshe? She was in my room last I saw her, but she said if I needed her she'd be in search of near-death experiences. A facetious line, certainly, though probably terrifyingly accurate.

I slip down the hallway, moving as quickly as I can while still being silent and keeping my eye on my surroundings. I'm not *that* far from my room, but with the strange silence blanketing the palace, my skin crawls with every step.

Will I ever make it back?

A sudden melancholy washes over me. What if I never make it back to my rooms, or find Eshe? What if I never have a chance to marry the Neverseen King?

Where did *that* thought come from?

And why can't I shake this dreadful hopelessness seeping into every pore of my body?

I'm going to die tonight, aren't I? That's what this feeling is. It's my intuition, telling me that I'm in my last hours, my last *moments* . . .

Why is the hallway suddenly so dark?

Something slicks down my spine, cold as ice and wet as a tongue. Something that stabs like a paralyzing fear through me. I know this sensation.

I'm being watched.

Breathing in a deep, fortifying breath, I keep walking. Though every cell in my body begs me to turn around, to see what stalks me, I cannot let it know that I sense it. Is the sagging of my soul, the wet blanket of hopelessness, coming from whatever follows me?

I force my feet to keep the same pace.

My awareness tingles as I sense something coming closer, faster, *closer*.

Grab your knives, the tips of my fingers plead, aching for that solid familiarity against my palms. That comfort of knowing I am not truly helpless.

I restrain myself.

Grabbing my knives, even letting my hands drift closer to those hilts, would betray my awareness of the creature following me.

The darkness deepens, slowly reducing my vision of the rest of the hallway. Thoughts fill my head, thoughts that don't even seem to be mine, but reach into every pocket of hope and strength inside me, tearing holes like the roots of a parasitic vine.

I should stop fighting—I should give up. There's no point. I always knew I'd lose. I've spent my life awaiting the moment of my death. There is nothing to do now but lie down, and just . . . let . . . it . . . happen.

I can almost feel the breath of an open, gaping mouth behind my neck. There's no helping my stiff spine, even if I chant silently to keep myself from running or whirling around with knives raised.

Keep walking. Keep walking. Keep . . . walking.

Those vines stretch deeper into my mind, a sensation that is real enough I almost reach up to touch the back of my head. I fight them, shoving against them, willing them away—

It would be easier just to give up.

Give in.

All of this suffering will be over in a moment.

You will never feel pain again.

I blink against blindness. What if I *did* stop resisting? What if I let those roots dig deep . . . deeper . . . all the way—

They flood my body, so sudden and so painful I nearly cry out. And then—

They reach my gut, where that icy wasteland lies in wait. Those tentacled, prying fingers dive straight into the ice. And immediately freeze. The darkness shifts, and there's something like an unexpected *blip* in the air between me and the creature hunting me. The ice inside me reaches up, up, up, following those roots, overcoming their silent struggles. Another silent *blip*. A rippling wave bursts from behind me, and the darkness gives way to flickering light.

That's right.

A slow smile spreads across my face.

I whirl, knives flashing in each hand, and pin the creature against a locked door. The world brightens quite suddenly, enough for the creature to be visible to my sight. It's humanoid, and I have it by its neck, my arm pressing its windpipe into wood. It's . . . *not* a shadow, as I'm so used to, but a physical, featureless body. If I took a blob of black paint and drew a proportional stick man, with no depth or characteristic, that's what I have pinned against the wall. Perhaps the greater surprise, however, is that it doesn't move. As though its entire body is . . .

Frozen.

"Get out of my House," I snarl at it, my voice low. "Go back to where you belong. And close the door behind you."

I step back, prepared for it to launch itself at me.

It doesn't move.

The darkness vanishes in a second, coalescing back into the creature, as though it's nothing but a statue of the deepest, densest ink that spread itself too thin a moment ago. I stare at it as the sun slices into my eyes, as that feeling of depression and hopelessness sinks away from me.

Then the body's legs start shortening, its ankles vanishing into its feet, and its feet spreading wider and wider—

It's *melting*.

My jaw sags. In the span of a minute, the entire creature is nothing but a puddle of melted darkness on the ground.

I turn and run. As fast as I've ever run before. My breath saws in and out of my lungs, and if I was any less afraid, I could gasp, *"Oh sands, oh sands, oh sands!"* I have no idea what just happened, but I suspect I shouldn't still be alive, and that can change in an instant if I don't move very quickly.

When I round the corner, there's the banister—and something huddled beneath it, toes peeking out. Another . . . *thing*? Or one of the women?

"Gaya?" I breathe.

Her head pops around the corner, and her eyes are as wide as moons. "Nadira?"

"Get to my room! Now!"

With a whimper, she scrambles to her feet and we race up the stairs together. I grab hold of the banister, and there's not a scrap of warmth to be found. Instead, it shudders.

I wish I could comfort it.

Gaya and I reach the second floor and I lead the way, both of us sprinting for our lives. I fling open the door, and she blows past me into the room. Her skin is white as starched linen.

"What is happening?" she breathes.

Eshe isn't here. I curse under my breath as I slam the door behind us, then run to the window and fling aside the curtains. The courtyard is empty, the fountain lifeless.

"Stay here," I say, ignoring several more questions from Gaya. There's no time for answers. I hardly even know what is happening.

I pull the door shut, whirling to a stop outside my room. Where could she possibly be? I look up and down the hallway—and desperately hate the unending illusion of it. I hate the sunlight streaming through the window ceilings, as if it doesn't care that my life is crumbling to pieces.

Then a scream pierces the air.

Without another thought, I barrel down the hallway toward the scream. I draw my knives, one in each hand. *Please don't be too late. Please don't be too late.* My legs pound, my heart pumping, until—

A roar rips through the corridor.

My feet stumble, and I almost fall flat on my face when I reach the source.

Ahead of me, two bodies throw themselves against a great carved wood door, inlaid with gleaming pearlescent stones. *Eshe and Safya.* Eshe screams again from the effort of shoving against the door. Something's trying to get out.

I don't have to wonder for long what it is.

Safya stumbles back, letting out a growling grunt, and a long reptilian head shoves past her guard, through the doorway. Two enormous nostrils flare, scales gleaming a luminescent crimson.

"No, you don't!" Eshe shouts, shoving against the door with all her might.

They cannot keep the creature contained. They need to run. I know this, and yet I hurl myself forward until it's three of us pushing, shoving, giving cries of effort and pain. I throw my weight into it, grimacing. For one moment, the door closes a few inches, and a burst of hope flares like a bright flower in my gut.

Then the reptilian head gives a large shove, and all three of us stumble back. Eshe screams again. Safya and I don't, but sweat streams down our foreheads. My limbs quake from the effort.

We're not going to—

A fourth pair of hands slam into the door, above mine. Familiar warmth floods my back. *He's here,* my whole body sings, weeps. *He's here.*

The door slams shut.

Without shifting my weight, I turn. My eyes meet shadow. But he's more than shadow, and his irises gleam back at me as he looks down, his arms braced against the door over my head.

"Neverseen King!" Safya breathes beside me.

There's something in that tone . . . something I definitely don't like.

"What muscles you must have!" chirps Eshe between gulps of air. If my face wasn't already so flushed from exertion, I might have blushed on behalf of her.

The door at our backs gives a sudden shove, and I'm almost thrown to the ground. The Neverseen King braces himself, leaning harder, *closer* to me.

"Get to Nadira's room," he growls. "All three of you. Now!"

"We're going to help you." Safya's face is set in determination, her dark brows lowered over her eyes. "Tell us what to do."

Another powerful shove on the door sends Eshe sprawling. She stumbles to her feet, sweat dripping off her nose as her gaze swings between the door and the rest of us.

"Get to Nadira's room," the Neverseen King repeats, strain lining every syllable. "That's how you can help."

Safya's jaw tightens. *Stubbornness.* But also . . . something more? My gut sinks despite myself. It's hard to imagine that someone who *voluntarily* murdered another woman in cold blood could harbor any sort of warm regard.

The Neverseen King looks down at me, his gaze intense and desperate. *Take them,* he seems to say, even as the door gives another lurch, and his powerful shoulders strain harder.

"Listen to him," I growl, ducking under his arms and grabbing Eshe. I make to grab Safya, but she jerks away from me, her nostrils flaring. "If he needs us, he'll come get us."

We both know it's a lie.

She doesn't move.

"Safya," the sultan groans, holding back the door against an onslaught of hits. "*Please.*"

That's what makes her lips tighten, and she shoves off the door. Together, the three of us break into a sprint, making for my room. It's not long before we reach the familiar door. Eshe flings it open, and we barrel into the supposedly safe space.

I pause in the doorway, glancing back.

I'm just in time to watch the Neverseen King's shadow vanish—and the door burst open. That reptilian head emerges, wide slitted eyes unblinking as it surveys the hallway. Then, like a bat climbing out of a cramped space, claws reach through the doorway, pulling a slender, gleaming body through the small opening. Its wings come with it, folded tightly against its scales. Once it's free in the hallway with nothing but its long sinuous tail flicking back and forth in the doorway, those wings expand, then tuck back in.

One eye catches mine.

That great head swings my way, extending its neck and raising that head toward the crystal skies. Its jaws open, and light sparks in a cage of teeth.

A dragon.

I slam the door shut and bolt it firmly.

Then I turn around, half daring to breathe as I face the three women staring at me with various shades of shock and fear. Safya stands alert by the vanity. Gaya is curled up in the corner by my bed. And Eshe has collapsed onto the settee.

A roar splits the air.

Gaya pulls her knees up tighter to her chest, hiding her face against them.

"What happened?" Safya demands, eyes fixed on me.

"We don't know!" cries Eshe, flinging up her hands. "One minute, everything was normal. The next, something changed in the air, like a wind. Then . . . chaos!"

"You know." Safya prowls a step closer to me. "You were with him when it happened, weren't you?"

My tongue cleaves to the roof of my mouth as another roar shakes the palace, as a sudden smallness takes over me. I didn't think much of Safya's quiet, hunched shoulders at that first meal. Not until she stabbed Itr, and the realization of her ruthlessness washed through my core.

Now? This isn't a healthy respect that flows through my veins.

It's terror. Terror, like I knew at Jabir's hand. It's the terror that comes when you face someone that has embraced the stains of blood.

With a shudder, I realize I haven't. Not truly. I *thought* I had, back in that ballroom. I'd given into that despair, the freezing ice inside me.

In one flashing movement, I can throw one of my knives and hit Safya right in the heart. Or I could go for her head. I can do it this very instant. I could end this terror right now. The fear mounting with each of her purposeful steps toward me could be completely gone with one move. My competition for the Neverseen King could also be gone with that same flick of the wrist.

But I *can't*.

The realization sends helplessness washing down my spine. I'm not the villain I thought I could be. I'm not the ruthless killer, the coldhearted murderer.

That's not who I am.

I *cannot* be that.

And it makes me deeply vulnerable.

I want to fold my arms around myself, curl into a ball like Gaya. I feel like a small child, the same girl who waited that moment after Jabir killed Baba. Who *waited,* as Jabir's beady eyes met mine, knowing that the next minute, my blood would run hot and sticky to join my parents'.

Safya's knife flashes. It presses into the vulnerable flesh of my neck. I freeze. My vision tunnels. Eshe shouts something.

"What did you do?" Safya growls.

Even though my mind insists I'm helpless, my muscle memory takes over. I catch her wrist, block her second knife, twist and duck under her guard. My knives are out, twin scythes of light between us. She blocks my blow, and then we're circling one another in the cramped space. Like caged animals.

"Enough!" Eshe yells. "There is a *dragon* out there! We need each other! Stop trying to kill each other!"

I puff a strand of hair out of my eyes, not once letting my gaze leave Safya's. She ignores Eshe. "Tell me what you did, Mourner."

The title grates against my spine. I flash my teeth. "Ask the Neverseen King."

"I don't understand why someone as good as him took an interest in *you*," Safya snarls back. "He is powerful and fearless. You are nothing *but* fear. And you're pathetic."

She's right. We both know she's right. Fear has governed my life for far too long. But she's also wrong.

The Neverseen King isn't fearless. If she thinks he is, then she doesn't know him.

I straighten and sheath my knives. "If I'm pathetic, then you wouldn't waste your time on me. Eshe's right. It would be stupid to kill each other now."

Safya doesn't have time to answer before an ear-splitting shriek tears through the air outside of my room. The door's bolt seems an extremely thin protection against the dragon and whatever else roams the palace halls. The Neverseen King likely has some spell of protection on this room, but I don't know what its limits are—or if I broke that spell too, along with the others. I march to the window, flinging aside the curtains and looking down. We ought to plan an escape route should something break down the door.

But what I see sends my body turning to ice.

Everything is *almost* as normal. Except for a creeping fog that rolls through the courtyard. As I watch, it reaches the shrubberies by the fountain. They immediately shrivel and turn black—nothing but husks. My eyes widen as the fog drifts through the courtyard, turning every living plant black and sucking the fountain dry of water until the basin is empty and cracked.

It's a matter of minutes before the courtyard is bare.

The fog turns away, coming back toward the palace. My gut sinks as it sends white, curling fingers climbing up the walls, sneaking into windows.

Searching.

"Get back!" I cry, scrambling away from the window.

"What?" demand Eshe and Safya at the same time. Gaya remains curled on the floor against the wall in a fetal position.

"There is . . . it looks like a poisonous fog. It's coming for the window!"

"What can we use to block the window?" Eshe asks, casting around the room desperately. She yanks the covers off my bed. "These?"

"We cannot secure it on all sides," Safya says, but she darts across the room, flinging open the wardrobe.

Eshe watches her. Then her eyes brighten. "The wardrobe! We can hang the blankets, rip up the baseboards so the wardrobe covers the window. The blankets will create more of a seal!"

Safya and I look at each other, as if expecting the other to voice a protest. Neither of us do. A second later, I've run to the wardrobe. With loud huffs and puffs, Eshe shoves aside the furniture, clearing a path for Safya and me to bring the wardrobe.

"Sands, that looks heavy!" She frowns as we grunt and struggle for a grip on the enormous piece of furniture.

It *is* heavy. In the end, it takes all three of us to move it. Eshe climbs on top, draping the blanket over the back of it and securing the top by closing the wardrobe door over the fabric. Then we shove it against the window.

We stand back.

Gaya peeks up from between her fingers. It seems my assessment of her was accurate. She's more bark than bite. For the first time, I wish she had a little more bite.

A loud *crunch* echoes from outside our room. The three of us whip our heads toward the sound, and glance uneasily among ourselves. I close my eyes, hoping against hope that the Neverseen King is alright.

What if my . . . so-called *blasts* broke more portals than he said? What if he cannot close them all in time? What if something happens to him, or to Eshe?

And it's *my* fault?

I shudder, rubbing my arm and gritting my teeth. It's Eshe's nervous voice that breaks through the thoughts swarming in my head.

"Um, Nadira? Safya? It's not working."

"What?"

I spin around, and deep horror pulses through my whole body.

Thin threads of mist wriggle through the cracks, coalescing into a long arm that reaches, *reaches*—

"Gaya!" Eshe screams.

CHAPTER 32

GAYA'S HEAD WHIPS up just as the longest finger of mist reaches toward her leg. She screams, scrambling backward, trying to get away. But she's against the wall, and there's nowhere for her to go.

Eshe dives for her as the mist latches hold of her ankle.

I grab Eshe around the waist, swing her off her feet, and hurl her onto my bed. She rolls, pops up to scream at me.

It is already too late.

Gaya's skin turns white within seconds. She slumps, her eyes rolling back as the mist crawls over her body. I stumble back a step, my stomach convulsing with such horror that I dry heave.

Mahja died like this.

It was one of the few times I witnessed the Neverseen King's fear, when she stumbled to her knees before him, deathly pale.

"You couldn't have saved her," growls Safya to Eshe as she whirls toward the door. "We've got to get out of here. Now."

The room is silent as I watch, frozen, as every bit of color leeches from Gaya's body. Every bit of *life*. It's like this mist is a parasite, sucking everything dry.

My mind flashes back to Lord Kishon's assassination, just hours before the Neverseen King captured me. His body slumped over his desk, blood everywhere. *So much blood.* It had been so fast it was practically painless, and he hadn't had time to be afraid. I had never wanted to kill him—or any of the others. I'd done what I could to make it swift.

But he is still dead. As dead as Gaya is now, killed by some mindless mist.

The images of her body and his flash back and forth in my mind.

For all that I tried, all that I fought, am I still no better than this formless leech?

"Get over here, Mourner, before you're next!"

Safya's voice snaps me out of it. The mist starts crawling away from Gaya's body. Coming for the rest of us. I leap into motion, running to the door even as Eshe cries, "But he said not to open the door! There's a dragon out there!"

"Better a dragon than this," is Safya's snarling reply as she throws back the bolt and wrenches the door open.

Darkness floods the doorway. Water splashes into the room, and Eshe stumbles back, screaming. Safya leaps out of the way of what seems to be a long tentacle flailing into the room, grasping for limbs. It catches hold of a small table leg and yanks the piece of furniture into the darkness. The crunch of splintering wood and splashing water—and a stomach-curdling bellow—slice through the air.

Eshe dodges around another tentacle and shoves the door shut.

The three of us stare at each other, wide-eyed. Stunned.

"There is a *river* in the hallway," she gasps.

If one more portal opens, the House's defenses will activate. As they do at night.

This is why the Neverseen King told us never to leave our rooms after dark. This is what killed Hulla that first night. The House has . . . *defenses*. Safeguards against creatures that might escape. This was why he was so specific in telling us to not open our doors, when it was perfectly fine to escape out our windows across the palace grounds.

I glance behind us, at the mist crawling over the settee, sending shooting tendrils up the walls. Searching. For *us*.

Terror pumps blood through my veins at an electrifying pace. We're surrounded. Surrounded by death with nowhere to go. There's a ravenous mist behind us. A river—with a monster, no less—in the hallway.

A river.

An idea flashes through my mind. Bright—and a little insane. That's alright. We need insane. The only other option is to die.

"Whatever idea you just came up with, we need it immediately," says Eshe, recognizing my sudden expression. Her back and hands splay against the door, her chest heaving.

I touch the hilt of my knives, but don't withdraw them. "Get your weapons. Both of you. Safya, I saw a crossbow on the bottom of the wardrobe. I need you to use it." I pause, then add quickly, "Don't shoot me. This is only going to work if I'm alive."

She tosses me a glower, either because she's insulted I would feel the need to say that, or perhaps she doesn't like me insisting that she needs me. Whatever the case, she leaps into motion, and before Eshe has gotten her knives out and moved aside from the door, Safya is back with the crossbow. Loaded and aimed at the door.

"I'm going to open this door," I say quietly, heart pounding as I glance back at the mist coming closer, closer. "You two need to keep the tentacles occupied. Kill it if you can. I think it's part of the House's defenses, so it might not die, but we have to try. I'm going to . . ." I swallow, my vision suddenly tunneling. I force the darkness away with a blink. "I'm going to freeze the river."

"You're going to *what*?" demands Eshe.

This will probably go very poorly. For the first time, I'm pushing past my denial and really hoping the Neverseen King was right when he said I had magic.

I throw open the door. This close, it's not as dark. Rushing water splashes on the threshold, spilling into my room loud and fast. Two tentacles shoot for me. I dodge to the side and duck, letting Safya's arrows whiz dangerously close.

A bellow tears into the hallway. *A hit.*

The tentacles don't stop flailing. If anything, they whip faster, their suction cups grabbing hold of plaster and wood, ripping so hard that cracks form along the walls. *Desperate to stop us.* Pulling my least favorite knife from my sheath and sparing half a thought in apology toward it, I slam it into the wall. My anchor.

Then I lean out into the doorway, ducking under the tentacles that Eshe and Safya try to keep occupied by slicing pieces off, and plunge my free hand into the river.

It's so cold. *So cold.*

I squeeze my eyes shut.

And panic.

How am I supposed to do this? I don't know how this works! I'm mostly still in disbelief that I would even *have* magic. How can I throw myself into a situation like this where I have no chance to learn, no chance to practice? I'm going to get myself killed and others with me. This is stupid—idiotic! And I *can't*—

No.

I *can*. I can, and I will. Back in the ballroom, I did this. When that strange creature attacked me—I did this. I did it then, and I will do it now.

The only other option is to die.

To let Eshe die.

I *won't* let Eshe die. Even if it kills me.

I focus on that determination, on that ironclad will. I focus on that ice deep inside my gut. It greets me with a cold, wicked smile.

I think of the Neverseen King. Of how much I . . .

The scream rips from my very soul as that strange well of power bursts forth. It flows from my fingertips, flickering like fire, but solid. Rock solid. I sink deeper into that frozen lake, sending every cold part of me pouring out into the river. I send it further, wider, gritting my teeth and shoving when met with resistance until I hit a firm wall on all sides.

"Nadira!"

Eshe's voice yanks my awareness back to my surroundings. I open my eyes.

My hand is buried in ice. Ice that stretches the length of the hall, ice that rolls in waves and pins the giant tentacled monster. Two of its arms are free, the upper half of its mouth chomping uselessly at the ice.

I glance back.

Eshe stares at me with a slackened jaw. Safya stares me down through the sights of the crossbow, her brow cut in a grim line.

The mist has reached my bed.

"We've got to get out of here," I gasp, yanking on my arm and finding it locked beneath the ice. "Away from the mist!"

"You're stuck!" Eshe cries, dodging one of the two tentacles and falling to her knees beside me.

Safya, her mouth tight, slips past both of us into the icy hallway. I glance back at the mist, only a few feet away now. And my hand is still stuck. Eshe pulls out a knife and begins chipping away at the ice. A precarious plan.

"Can't you just unfreeze it?" she gasps, eyes wide as she keeps looking over my shoulder.

Unfreeze it? I close my eyes, trying to think of heat, of warmth, of hot qahwa. All that I find inside me is ice-cold. "I don't think I can!" I yank on my arm, squeeze my numb fist to make it smaller, to wriggle. *Anything.*

The mist is getting so close. It only has to touch one of us before it's too late.

My vision blackens at the edges, but I fight it.

I'm not dying like this.

The ice suddenly gives, a mix of Eshe's efforts and mine. We scramble to our feet and slide into the hallway. Eshe nearly falls on her back trying to dodge the last two tentacles reaching for us. I grab her collar and drag her out of the way.

We cling to each other and slip down the hallway, almost tripping and falling every few seconds on the slick, uneven surface. Where did Safya go? Where can *we* go?

A scream echoes from deeper down the hallway. "Get down!"

I drag Eshe to the ground with me in a tangled mess of limbs as something whizzes overhead. Something that sounds like an arrow, but whirs past in a blur of crimson fletching—nothing like what's on Safya's arrows. A second, then a third follow. Eshe and I huddle against the ice, breathing hard. Can we not stand anymore without fear of being shot?

I hate the House's defenses.

"Here's the stairwell!" Eshe pants in the darkness. She scoots toward it, pulling me with her. "We need to get *out* of here!"

"Careful!" I whisper under my breath. "It's so hard to see and we don't know what other—"

Eshe pitches forward. And screams.

Panic sears my brain.

I grab her arm, twisting in a flash and anchoring my feet against the wall. With her free hand, she scrabbles at the floorboards, trying for purchase. Her entire body hangs from my grip, her legs kicking in midair.

Because the stairs aren't *there*.

It's just an empty drop.

My mind catches up to my hyperventilating body, to the words that are being muttered over and over again between gasps. *My* words. "I've got you. I've got you. I've got you."

"We've got this," Eshe says back, her nails digging into my arm. Sweat slickens her grip, but a moment later she manages to throw her other arm toward me. I catch her.

Shoving on my legs, I pull her back up to the slippery ice until she's on all fours. We grip each other's forearm, breathing in tandem, and when she looks up, our gazes snag together.

"We're going to get out of this," I say.

Her face mirrors my own determination. "We're going to make it."

I squeeze her arm. *Together*.

Then with a look cast toward the darkness where Safya disappeared, I pull my *jurbah* rope from my belt and scoot closer to that drop. My stomach pitches when I slip on the ice. I grab for the wall and cling tightly, breathing rapidly through my nose. I pry my fingers loose and loop my rope around the top post of the banister. Unraveling the rest of it, I estimate the length to the next level, tie a fat knot several feet above that, and hold tightly to it as I lean closer to the edge. Peering over into the darkness.

Running, slipping footsteps make me pause. I whip my knife out by instinct as I turn toward the sound. Yet somehow, I know who it is even before Safya's lithe frame emerges from the shadows.

"The other staircase is missing its stairs too," she growls. "But we can't stay on this level while the mist is searching. We need to get to the bottom level, where the mist has already been."

So she didn't abandon us.

The grudging respect I've had for her grows. Perhaps it's not as grudging, despite the fact that I will always be on edge around her. Just as she'll kill me if it'll serve her, she'll help me if it helps her.

I may not like her, but I know where I stand with her.

"I have rope." I test my knot, then glance back at Safya. "We don't know what's waiting for us on the ground floor."

"I can go first," says Eshe, reaching for the rope.

"I'll go." Safya snatches it before Eshe can, and despite how I feel like I should protest, I don't. Instead, I scoot back as Safya throws it over the drop. She doesn't hesitate as she grips it, climbs over the edges, and lowers beyond our view.

How is she so unafraid? Or does she just hide it better than I do?

The rope goes slack, as though she's dropped off it. Swallowing to keep my stomach from leaping out my throat, I ease myself to my belly and peer out over the edge. It's so dark that it's almost impossible to see, but I manage to make out a crouched Safya on the floor below. Slowly, she rises to her feet, looking around her.

Nothing bursts from the shadows.

The ground seems solid. She isn't swallowed up by a monster.

She looks up, eyes flashing as they meet mine, and waves me to follow.

"I'm next," chirps Eshe. "That way if I fall, I fall on top of her. *Or* you can catch and pull me up. If I went last and you fell, I'd just fall too trying to catch you. And I don't think Safya could handle two falling bodies."

"Your logic is impeccable."

She flashes me a grin as she grabs the rope. "*I'm* impeccable."

"Of course." It takes everything to keep my voice somewhat light as she lowers herself over the edge. She's going to fall. Or if she doesn't, something is going to hurt her.

She winks, and then her head disappears.

I step forward, gripping the banister with a white-knuckled grip as I lean over the drop while Eshe shimmies down the rope and lands on her feet.

A roar splits through the quiet, shaking the foundation of the palace. The banister shudders in my grip, ice cracking beneath me, wood and stone groaning. Dust falls from the ceiling. I tighten my grip, waiting for the movements to stop.

The sound came from the lower level of the palace.

"Eshe?" I call, keeping my voice quiet.

"Sands!" she breathes. "Stay there, Nadira!"

"What's going on? Eshe!"

"The dragon is coming this way," Safya growls, right before the palace shudders again. "Stay there. We'll hide until it's past."

"Wait!" I hiss. "We need to stay together!"

They're already gone, scrambling away into the darkness. I curse under my breath. Glancing back toward the door of my room, I find tiny trails of mist starting to leak from under the door. If I stay on this level, I'm going to die.

I'm in no mood for a dragon, but at least I have a chance.

I grab the rope, swallow against the plunge of my stomach as I brace my arms and legs, then start to lower myself.

A door swings open down the hallway. I freeze, my head still above the ledge.

Two creatures barrel out of the door. I barely get a good look at their humanoid frames, their sagging skin, hunched backs, and boney limbs before their bald heads swivel straight toward me. Huge, moonlike eyes set in craggy faces snag on mine.

They launch themselves at me.

I prepare to drop to the ground and roll, but when I look down, a long shadow casts over the floor. Smoke fills my lungs. Oh stars.

I'm bait. Just hanging here. Spots flash across my vision.

One of the creatures grabs the rope and pulls, trying to haul me up. I twist my ankles tighter, then let go with one hand and swing toward the banister, catching hold just as the other creature rushes forward with a cackle, and slices one long, razor-sharp talon through the rope. It falls with a quiet thud to the ground. I gasp, swinging from my one slippery hand. The stench of smoke becomes almost unbearable. A red ember glow shines in my periphery.

With a grunt, I swing one leg up, hooking around the banister. If my grip slips, my leg will snap clean in half. I dismiss the thought and use that leverage to pull myself up further, my core clenching. I get a grip with my other hand, hauling myself up so I cling to the banister like a monkey to a tree.

That's when I look up.

And find a terrifying, sharp-toothed grin only a foot away from my face. I freeze.

A series of clicks emerge from its throat as it tilts its head at me. It balances precariously on the banister, its long fingers holding itself steady as it stares down at me. Then it lunges.

Teeth come straight for my neck.

I dodge. My grip loosens, and one arm flails in midair as I swing to the side, hanging upside down. The clicks continue as the creature pounces, hovering on the banister above where I hang. I scramble to keep my grip, my hair swaying like a beacon to the dragon below. My core contracts sharply as I swing further up, catching hold of a higher support beam and pulling myself up.

The creature whirls, pounces again.

I let go with one hand, holding on with my left hand and whipping out my knife with my right. Hair falls across my eyes, sweat pouring in rivulets down my face, my back, making my clothes stick to my skin. I hook my ankle around another beam as the creature perches on the smooth handrail above me. Grinning at me and leaning down, teeth flashing.

A cry rips from my throat as I fling myself upward.

My knife hits true, slicing straight through flesh and bone. For a moment, everything stops, and my face is inches from the creature's moon eyes, the crags of its nose. It gives one last mournful click.

Then I rip my knife free and pull myself higher—out of the way—as the creature falls.

Below me, heat bursts in a sweltering wave. I dare to glance down just as a pair of great reptilian jaws snap around the creature's body.

I barely manage to keep from vomiting and betraying my spot. I cling to the railing, breathing hot air in and out of my gaping mouth, my entire body taut and tense with the effort to hold myself here. When I twist and look over my shoulder, there's no second pair of moon eyes. Did it run away? Hide? Is it lying in wait for me?

A strong sense hits me. One I know so *achingly* well.

The Neverseen King is here.

CHAPTER 33

MY BODY FLOODS with such desperate relief that I almost release my grip and fall to my death. Catching myself, I haul myself higher and higher up the banister until I finally reach the top. My arms and legs shake as I pull myself back onto the slippery ice.

Part of me just wants to die from exhaustion.

An enormous, strong hand grabs me by the throat.

A wave of shock pounds into me as I'm lifted right off my feet, gasping for air. My back hits the wall hard, my feet dangling as instinct makes me claw at the Neverseen King's grip with my fingernails.

I can't even gasp as my vision starts to go black.

Then, just as fast as it came, the hand opens. I fall to my feet, then my knees. The uneven ice bruises hard against my tender skin—until it's not ice anymore. It shifts, melting away into a soft rug. The normal rug that lines this hallway. Did he manage to close a portal, and thus deactivate the House's defenses?

"Nadira?" the Neverseen King hisses, his voice almost frantic as he drops next to me. He curses—a sharp, angry sound. "What are you doing? Great Kings, I almost killed you! Where did the other—" He whips his head around, his shoulders rising and falling with panting breaths.

"I killed it," I gasp, leaning against the wall.

My vision is suddenly blocked by his shadow looming over me, bending down close to my face. Eyes widening and throat going dry, I can almost forget the ragged pain of each swallow as the Neverseen King's fingers—now so gentle—brush against my neck. The callused thumb he runs across the fresh bruises scrapes against tender flesh, but not unpleasantly. I shiver, whether from the constant pounding of adrenaline or the rush of blood from his proximity. From his severe mouth hovering so close.

"Does this hurt?" he asks.

Another roar from below us sends dust crumbling from the ceiling and my bones rattling. The Neverseen King throws his arms against the wall, bowing his head over mine, his body a shield against raining debris. I keep one hand on the wall, while the other has somehow found its way to his tunic and clenched hard in the fabric. I can almost feel the pounding of his heart beneath my fingers once the rumbling stops.

He tilts his head so we're looking at each other. Only separated by a hand's breadth. It's strange to stare into a face lost to shadows, and yet . . . it's like I can see him anyway. The part of him that matters.

One of his hands lets go of the wall, lands gently on my neck. My instinct is to stiffen, my breath coming faster, but I try to not react.

"It'll just take a second," he says. The strain hasn't left his voice.

Eshe. Safya.

Are they alright? Did they hide—or did the dragon find them and crush them in his jaws like he did to that other creature? And what about the mist? Is it reaching for us even now?

I grab his wrist. It's so wide my hand can't wrap around it. His gaze sharpens, and I look away. "Don't." The word is a little raspy, but I clear my throat and continue. "You need your strength."

"What?" He frowns.

As much as I want to stay here, sheltered in his arms, I'm desperately aware of the danger around every corner. Now that I can breathe, I push his wrist away, shooting him an arch look. "I don't want you fainting again."

"I knew I wasn't going to live that down," he growls, but makes no move to fight me. Instead, he pushes up to his feet, then offers me his hand while glancing over his shoulder down the hallway. I grasp his forearm, and he hauls me up. "Where are the others? Why aren't you in your room?" He sniffs, and almost stumbles back a step, cursing sharply. "Do I smell *Crenfyre* up here?"

"There's a mist," I say. I haven't let go of his arm yet. "It came in through the window."

He hasn't let go of mine either. But he does curse again. "Then you *did* freeze my poor octalthi. Where are the rest of the women?"

"Downstairs. And . . ." My stomach turns.

"And *what*?"

"Gaya's dead."

Silence falls. A silence in which I think he closes his eyes, flexes his jaw. Then he's in motion, dragging me toward the stairwell. The stairs are back. *Such* a relief.

"The dragon!" I gasp, stumbling down the steps after him.

Right then, an alarmingly close screech echoes down the hallway from below. The Neverseen King ducks below the rail, plants a square hand on my head, and shoves me to my knees beside him. With each quiet pant, his shoulders brush mine, his cloak half falling over me as we hide.

"I closed two of the portals so far," whispers the Neverseen King. "There's two more left. The dragon's, and Crenfyre."

I shoot a look at him. "Already?"

Teeth glimmer back at me—a grin. "I told you I've managed quite well on my own."

Before I can help myself, a small smile twitches the edge of my lips. I have the almost overwhelming urge to tuck in closer against his side. The brush of his shoulder against mine is nearly torture. I want to lean into him.

But we're trying not to die.

I need to keep my stupid brain clear.

"What do we do?" I whisper, getting my knees up into a crouch and planting my hand squarely on the floor. My other hand rests on the hilt of a knife in my belt.

"I need to close those portals. Especially Crenfyre. Then it's just taking down the dragon . . ."

Just taking down the dragon. Of course. He says it as if he's done it a hundred times before.

"The sun will set soon," he continues, his deep voice nothing but a rumble, "and the House's defenses will activate again. If you and the others can stay safe until then, the House might manage to kill the dragon while I'm . . . busy."

"If the House doesn't kill it?"

"Then I'll have to hunt it down when I'm free."

"Can it leave the palace? Escape into the city?"

The shadow of his jaw flexes. "Yes."

"Then we can't wait until you're done closing the portals to deal with the dragon." I glance back over my shoulders up the staircase, just checking to be sure the mist hasn't started creeping down the stairs after us.

So far, so good.

The Neverseen King is silent. He knows I'm right but doesn't want to admit it.

A harsh roar makes both of us flinch and duck lower. It sounds like the dragon is pacing the hallway. Looking for a way out of the palace? Or more people to eat?

"Let Safya, Eshe, and I take care of the dragon," I whisper, almost not believing the words escaping my mouth. A week ago, I wouldn't have dreamed of voluntarily going after a monster.

A week ago, things were very different.

"And let you three be killed?" he hisses. "No."

"Seems slightly hypocritical, coming from the man who forced us into lethal competitions in the first place," I hiss back.

"Do you take sport in purposefully misunderstanding me?"

"Do you take sport in coddling me? I'm an *assassin*, Sultani."

"You remind me of that so constantly I'm beginning to think you believe me incapable of remembering. If I intended to *coddle* you, I'd tie you up and lock you in a vault until this was all over."

I shoot him a glare. "We are clearly operating on two different definitions of *coddle*."

He wipes a hand down his face, sighing. "We're acting like idiots. Listen, Mourner, you can go after that Kings-cursed dragon if you are thus determined. But if Eshe dies because you three are *humans* facing a *dragon*, then don't blame me."

As if on cue, a scream bursts into my awareness.

Panic floods my body. The Neverseen King curses. I'm in motion before I can even think, flying down the stairs. He runs at my heels, already abandoning his portals.

Orange glows at the end of the hallway, like embers between the cracks of dragon scales. But the scream came . . . from the other direction? The dragon's head swivels toward us at the same time I swivel mine toward the other end of the hallway.

"Get out of the way, idiot!" Eshe hisses. "I'm *distracting* it!"

I sag in relief.

"I'm going to close the portals," says the Neverseen King—and vanishes.

But not before one of his hands finds mine and squeezes.

It's so discombobulating that I barely remember to duck beneath the railing before a volley of fire shoots through the hallway, straight toward Eshe. She scrambles out of the way, slipping into some hiding spot I cannot see.

My heart pounds as heat waves blast my face. Kill a dragon? What do I know—what do *any* of us know about killing a dragon? The creature marches down the hallway on its four legs, making the foundation shudder with each step as it swings its head from side to side.

An arrow whizzes through the air from the opposite end of the hallway, where the dragon just was. *Safya.* It bounces harmlessly off scales, clattering to the floor. The dragon doesn't even turn.

I stay in my hiding spot, not daring to breathe as the dragon lumbers past me. Smoke clogs my nostrils anyway, until my eyes burn and I can barely keep from choking.

Get out of the way, Eshe! I want to scream.

If arrows cannot pierce its scales, then knives will be equally useless. Unless I can somehow get close enough without it sensing me to slide my knife between them? Or maybe we ought to focus our efforts on its eyes, nose, mouth?

Both sound like expedient ways to die.

My eyes snag on something in front of me.

My rope.

I snatch it up quickly, winding it around my hand, feeling the frayed edge where the moon-eyed creature had cut it. Can we choke the dragon? Is such a thing even possible? Are we strong enough? Perhaps if we had leverage . . .

It hits me just as Safya screeches and releases a volley of arrows at the dragon, making its head swing back toward her. Dangerously close to me.

I know exactly how to kill it.

It's so obvious, I feel stupid.

But how can I do this without killing myself? That remains the question.

Working furiously, I pull my small, pronged anchor from my belt and securely knot the rope to it. I tie new knots along the rope, a foot or so apart. I rip my askew headscarf from around my neck and dodge the whipping dragon tail that smashes into the banister, breaking wood into kindling.

Then I release my own shout.

The dragon's golden eyes swivel toward me, angry fire puffing from its nostrils. Two slit pupils narrow at the sight of me, then dilate.

Oh sands.

I turn on my heel and race up the stairs, abandoning the headscarf to flutter to the ground. Apparently I didn't need to coax it into chasing me as much as I expected. It's riled up and furious after the games Safya and Eshe had played with it.

Tucking its wings in close, its claws catch hold of the stairs and banister railing, wood breaking and moaning as the enormous creature launches itself at me. I run as fast as I can, cursing with each pounding beat of my frantic heart.

Sorry, banister, I think as I lead the dragon around the curve of the stairs. It gives me just the slight advantage I need, slowing down the dragon so I can reach the top before its jaws snap me in half.

The moment I'm at the top, however, my skin almost burning from the heat close behind me, I have a new danger. My eyes don't have time to adjust to the darkness after seeing fire, so I don't know *where* the mist—Crenfyre—is exactly.

This could go so wrong, so quickly.

Gritting my teeth, I launch myself at one of the wall sconces. It immediately shifts under my weight, but doesn't give out as I pull myself, panting, up the wall and balance one foot precariously on the sconce, the other on the slight lip of the door frame's lintel. Crenfyre seemed to generally stick to the floor.

But being this high puts me almost at eye-level for the dragon that has torn its way to the top of the stairs. Perfect for being roasted to a crisp.

"Why is this my life?" I mutter under my breath as I yank out my rope and squint up at the chandeliers hanging in between the expansive glass panes on the ceiling. These chandeliers aren't the multifaceted crystal wonders that hang from the ceilings of other rooms in the palace. They're much simpler, made of polished brass, and hanging from a chain.

The dragon roars.

Everything shakes. I fall into a crouch, gripping the underside of the door lintel with my fingernails in one hand, and the curved underside of the sconce in the other hand. The sconce gives, pulling away from the wall a fraction more. I curse again, bracing myself as I stare wide-eyed at those furious, slitted pupils as they burst onto the second floor.

Crimson scales glow orange with the fire ready to burst from the dragon's throat.

No time to catch my balance, I shove up on my feet and throw the rope and anchor up toward the chandelier. *Please, please, please, please—*

It catches.

I leap. *Please hold. Please hold. Please hold!*

The chandelier swings wildly. I fly through the air, away from the dragon, trying to pull myself up the knots I tied. Then the trajectory of my swing changes, heading right toward the dragon's gaping jaw that extends to me.

There's no time to think, breathe, curse.

I desperately pull myself up one more knot, grab hold of the chandelier, and *barely* manage to swing my legs up just as teeth snap empty air beneath me.

"Oh sands," I whimper, clinging to the underbelly of the chandelier like a fly. If I wasn't so terrified, I'd be throwing up from this gyrating motion.

"Nadira!" screams Eshe from the staircase.

"Go away!" I scream back. "Don't distract it! I've got a plan!"

The dragon moves directly beneath me. I try to pull myself up on top of the chandelier, but my fingers grow slicker with sweat by the second. My muscles quiver with strain. Maybe my sweat will drip into its eyes and sting them.

I'm going to die.

This is it.

And in such a stupid way.

The dragon lifts itself up on its hind legs, its elongated neck bringing its head closer to me. Closer, closer, *closer.* Apparently it doesn't want to roast me—but eat me raw.

"Oh sands," I breathe again.

The dragon freezes.

I try to peer over my shoulder without losing my grip. Something white swirls around the dragon's feet, leeching the color from its glistening red scales, crawling over its magnificent body. The sight is almost . . . *sad.*

I look away, clinging to the chandelier and staring my unfocused eyes at the sunset stained sky, visible through the glass ceiling. Blood rushes to my head. I almost died. Now is not the time to be mourning the loss of a beautiful creature that would have snapped me in half with its powerful jaws.

Now is time to figure out how to get down without facing the same fate as the dragon.

The palace shakes when the enormous body hits the ground. The chandelier shakes too, and another whimper escapes my lips as I fight to keep my grip. If only I was certain enough of my hands that I could swing my legs free, find the rope, and balance my feet on a knot. Alas, if I move one inch, I'm going to fall. Right into the swirling mist.

"Nadira?" calls Eshe.

"Don't come any closer," I call, my voice trembling with my limbs as I cling to the chandelier. "The mist is below me!"

"Nadira!" She must be at the top of the stairs, craning her neck to look up at me. "How did you get up there?"

"Go away!" I shout again, and I barely restrain a whimper as my grip starts to slip. "The mist will kill you!"

"It's still occupied with the dragon," she says flippantly, then whistles low under her breath.

"*Eshe*. Please."

"You should worry more about yourself than me."

"I *am* worried about myself," I grit out.

There's silence for a long moment. I breathe in and out through my teeth, sweat dripping into my eyes as I stare up at the window ceiling. At the last light of day leaking away into night. What if the Neverseen King cannot close Crenfyre's portal before night falls and the House's defenses activate again? I assume this hallway will turn back into a river, and it seems too much to hope it would still be frozen.

My nails scrape polished brass as they slowly slide, losing their grip. I curse, tightening my fingers. The strain brings tears to my eyes.

"Safya!" calls Eshe. "I need a second opinion here!"

"Don't call her!" I cry. "She'll shoot me down!"

Eshe doesn't respond. Perhaps she glares at me for my *jaded* opinion of people. But Safya has already threatened to kill me, and now is the perfect opportunity.

When Safya comes up the stairs, she's so quiet I don't know she's come until Eshe says sweetly, "Don't kill her, or I'll bite off your big toe. And *eat* it. Now, how do we get her down?"

"Watch the mist," Safya growls, and it sounds like she's retreating.

"Yes, thank you, I am. Now how do we get her down that does *not* involve shooting or bodily harm—*and* gets her out of the way of the mist? It's still directly below her."

"Not my problem."

"Stop where you are," Eshe snaps. "Don't you dare take another step down."

A deliberate step sounds through the air. Followed by a second. Then a third.

"We are your only option," snarls Eshe, and I think it might be the darkest I've ever heard her voice. "You may think the Neverseen King is your ally, but he'll sacrifice any of us for his purpose, and he won't hesitate to kill us if we cross a line. You can walk away now, but if you do, you'll lose your only allies. If you're in trouble, we won't help. Not if you leave now."

"There's no such thing as an ally," Safya replies, her tone cool. "The sooner you learn that everyone has their own agenda, and that you're either a tool or an obstacle, the better off you'll be. It's a miracle you've survived as long as you have."

When I try to twist my ankles into the chandelier for a better grip, it starts swinging. Even though the motion is subtle, it sends my stomach pitching. I count my breaths, waiting for it to *stop*. During the span of those breaths, there's no sound coming from below.

Then a quiet hiss: "You assassins and your cynicism. Doesn't it ever get old?"

"Not really thinking about cynicism right now," I gasp. "Just stay away from the mist. I'll . . . think of something."

A lie. Thinking is impossible right now.

"Hang on, Nadira. I'm going to find the Neverseen King."

"Don't! Don't distract him! He needs to—"

"Wait! The mist . . ."

"What?" I gasp, jerking my head up as blood rushes to my brain. The chandelier starts swinging again. "Is it reaching higher?"

"It's . . . it's . . ."

"It's *what*?"

"It's melting. Into the floor."

"It is?" Hope surges so heady that I nearly forget to maintain my grip. "It's going away?"

"Yes! It's half gone already!"

He did it. He must have closed the portal. Bless him! I could weep from relief.

"Keep holding on! Once the mist is gone, I'll grab your mattress and pull it out beneath you. In case you fall."

I *should* be able to fall and not get hurt, but I don't trust myself with something as simple as rolling when I hit the ground. My muscles shake too much, adrenaline clouding my vision, panic muddling my thoughts.

Then his voice cuts through the panic. Sharp, authoritative, but also . . . *afraid*. "Nadira! Where—"

"We're up here!" calls Eshe.

He's back.

His heavy footsteps thump against wood as he hurries up the staircase. He curses sharply.

"The mist is almost gone!" Eshe calls up to me. "I'm going to—"

There's a muted sound, like the Neverseen King has snatched Eshe's shoulder before she dove into action. "Don't move until it's gone. The edge of its fingers are invisible, and even in this form it's deadly. Don't step into the hallway until it's gone."

"But she might fall!"

"Mourner?" he calls. "Can you hold on for another minute?"

I ignore the cramping in my hands. "Yes!"

"When the mist is gone, I'm going to stand below you. When I tell you to, let go. I will catch you."

No chance. I'll flatten him. I say nothing, however, because I don't have the strength to argue.

"Nadira?"

"Yes?" I grit out.

"Will you do that?"

"No."

The Neverseen King lets out a short sigh. His voice is darker, firmer. "You can trust me. I won't let you be hurt."

That's easy for him to say—he won't be the one falling through empty air.

"It's gone now!"

"Hold still, thief."

Another moment passes. The sky is almost dark through the window, one star shining in the twilight.

I'm going to fall. I can't keep—

Footsteps.

"I will catch you, Mourner."

I cling tighter, my fingernails almost prying off their nail beds. I shake my head. To just . . . *let go*. It feels impossible. I'll just have to hang here until my grip breaks, and I fall, fall, *fall*. But I cannot make myself let go.

"I'm right here."

I squeeze my eyes shut. Shake my head. Whimper. "I can't."

"You *can*."

"Can't."

His voice turns to iron. "Let go. Now."

"No."

"Give me your knife," he says to Eshe.

My heart nearly explodes in panic. "Wh-what—"

"Either you trust me, and you let go, or I will cut the chandelier down."

"A knife can't cut brass!" I cry, tears leaking out of the corners of my eyes.

"A spelled one can," he replies darkly. "Last chance, Nadira. Trust me. *Let go*."

I can't. I can't. I can't. I can't. I can't—

"You. Can. Let. Go. *Trust me*."

I close my eyes. My limbs quake like a leaf in the wind. It's too much. The storm of emotion, the need to survive, rushes like water through every inch of my body. *Survive, survive, survive.*

Everything up until this moment has been about fighting for every breath in my lungs, for every beat of my heart. Even if my rational brain knows the best thing to do is let go, my body screams at the thought. It's suicide. To fall with my back to the ground, to fall with no strength to even land properly.

But maybe life is more than survival.

If I can just . . .

I let go.

Just as the sharp slice of metal on metal cuts through my awareness. Suddenly, I'm weightless, I'm—

Falling.

I let go of the chandelier, blood rushing like a torrent through my veins as I wildly wheel my arms. As though that can stop me from breaking my spine on the ground beneath me. All survival instinct abandons me in an instant, and I'm left with nothing but the expectation of death.

Fall.

Fall.

Fall—

Suddenly, it stops.

Something catches me. Spins me around. My back hits the wall—not the floor—at the same time a large forearm also hits the wall above my head. An arm is around my waist, holding me to a solid chest as I gasp for air.

My eyes open.

A pair of gleaming eyes stare back at me. *So close.*

Neither of us say anything for a long moment. We just breathe the same hot air, staring at each other, while our chests heave and I fight to remember what just happened.

Then, softly, I say, "You caught me."

His voice isn't amused when he replies, "You're surprised."

I . . . I am. And I'm not. I'm both, and I don't know how to explain it. So I say nothing, lean my head back against the wall, and close my eyes. I'm not sure my body will ever stop shaking. My feet won't be steady again.

"You killed the dragon," he says.

I open my eyes and somehow manage to arch a single eyebrow. "You're surprised."

"Well," Eshe chirps from somewhere behind the Neverseen King, "if we're done surprising one another, should we . . . find some place to stay? Until morning? Just so we don't . . . you know, *die*?"

The Neverseen King's gaze holds mine. Something sparks in his pupils.

Then a loud voice thunders from outside: "Come out of your palace, Neverseen King! We have you surrounded!"

Suddenly I'm not pinned by the Neverseen King's weight against a wall. I'm curled in a ball on a frozen lake. I'm kneeling on the floor of my former cell-room, forced to look up into the face of my captor, my jaw caught and held with the spikes on his gloves.

That was Jabir's voice.

CHAPTER 34

"COME OUT AND we won't attack!" Jabir shouts from outside. "There's no need for anyone to get hurt."

He's here. He has come for me. He will take me back.

But Jabir isn't more powerful than the Neverseen King. How could he threaten his sovereign? I want to dismiss this as stupidity, but every time I underestimated Jabir, I paid for it dearly. My slaver is many things, but *stupid*, he is not.

Several horrible realizations hit me, one after the other.

The artifact. Kolb said it broke down djinn magic. Could it cripple the Neverseen King's power?

The floor plans. Jabir wanted me to plan a break in for the palace. Something he didn't want me knowing.

The vision of him in the icy wasteland of my magic. The way he always knew where I was, always found me when I ran. The way his voice has haunted me.

Jabir is trying to overthrow the Neverseen King—and has been working toward this for possibly *years*. And he's not just some peasant who has cobbled together more peasants for a rebellion.

The Neverseen King's gaze shoots to me. When he speaks, his voice is measured and calm, but so dark. "How did they know the palace wards were down, Nadira?"

Suddenly his closeness doesn't feel safe and intimate. He is a cage around me, pinning me to the wall, cutting off my escape.

The implied accusation catches me so off-guard, my body goes rigid and my tongue can't form words. I stand there, fully aware of his charge, of his sudden desperation that I assuage his fears, but I can't think.

He's going to kill me.

He said he would. This is his hesitation. I don't know how long it will last, only that it will eventually end, and there will be nothing I can do to keep him from killing me. I always knew, from the moment he showed up in my room, that he would kill me. It was only a matter of time, and now—

Stop it.

Stop it, Nadira.

I close my eyes, grit my teeth, and reach down into that well of power sitting in my gut. *I'm not helpless.* Even against the Neverseen King.

"No," I growl. "I didn't betray you."

"Then *how* did they *know*?" he growls back, leaning closer to me. So close, that I'm almost swallowed up in his shadow, dwarfed by his sheer size. "The wards haven't been down a full hour—and there's an *army* outside of my House? It's almost as if they were prepared."

"I didn't do it."

"How long have you known about your magic?"

"I didn't know before today!"

Suddenly, he flicks his wrist, and then it's one of my own knives that he brings to my throat, pinning me to the wall with his forearm against my shoulders and chest. I suck in a fast breath, my awareness focusing on the tip of my blade grazing over my pulse.

His voice drops so low it's a rumble. "Are you lying to me?"

He's going to kill me. He's going to kill me. He's—

"Don't take another step, Eshe," the Neverseen King growls before I can answer. His gaze hasn't left mine. "Put away your knife, and stay back. Don't make me kill your friend."

"She's not lying, you brute," Eshe snaps. "Put away *your* knife and step back. I don't want to have to kill you."

"I am waiting for *her* to answer me." The Neverseen King brings his mouth toward my ear and the skin of my neck pebbles from his warm breath. He whispers softly, so only I can hear. "You know what I've sacrificed for this Bridge. You know what I've already given up, and if you think I'm not willing to give you up too, then you're mistaken. So answer me, Mourner. Tell me why I shouldn't separate your pretty head from your pretty shoulders. Convince me." With those words, he twists his head just slightly, and I can almost feel his dark grin spreading across his face. The grin he wore in that dream I had of him, of him in his throne room.

I clench my fists. "I'm not lying. I don't know how Jabir knows, or what his plans are, but I didn't betray you."

"And you expect me to believe you?"

"I told you the truth."

"*What* is the truth, Nadira? You tricked me into that kiss. You manipulated me. What proof can you give me that you haven't been manipulating me this entire time?" His grin is gone, utterly gone, replaced by a calm, but deadly rage. "Has everything been a lie?"

His mention of our kiss almost makes me go dizzy. I can hardly think with that knife at my throat. Am I even breathing? I shut my eyes, barely restraining a whimper behind my teeth. What can I do? What can I say to prove myself?

Somehow, I grit out a vicious, “Don’t be a fool.”

“Oh, I’ve been a fool alright,” he snarls. Then, louder, “Eshe, I don’t want to hurt you. Stay. *Back*.”

“Get out of here, Eshe,” I rasp.

“I’m not leaving you,” she shoots back.

A boom from outside: “This is your last chance, Neverseen King! We have you surrounded!”

The Neverseen King growls wordlessly, but he doesn’t move. He keeps me pinned to the wall, his eyes never leaving mine. The knife still rests against my throat. It bobs when I swallow.

“If I wanted to betray you, I could have done it ages ago,” I grit out, my voice low and calmer than I feel. “Don’t insult me with your flimsy accusations. We both know this hasn’t been a lie. You are just angry that you came to care for me after swearing never to care again after your wife died. It would be easier for you if all of this *had* been a lie, wouldn’t it?”

Then, despite my trembling hands, I reach up, wrap my hand around his wrist, and push the knife away from my throat. He lets me do it, even though his eyes burn with an inner war.

“Nadira?” a new voice calls from the floor below.

A young man’s voice.

My blood runs cold. What in the Great Desert is *Kolb* doing here?

But I shouldn’t be surprised. It’s my own fault he’s here. He still believes Jabir is saving his little sister.

Footsteps pound up the stairs. “Nadira? Where are you?”

Like the wind, the Neverseen King pulls back from me, and cool air washes over my body. He vanishes into the shadows—invisible, but oh so present—as Kolb reaches the top of the stairs. His curly hair is a mop of chaos, and his lip is split, his clothes covered in dirt. “There you are!” he cries. “We’ve got to get out of here. Jabir sent me to find you. Come on!”

“What is going *on*?” Eshe demands, storming toward him.

He whirls, throwing up his hands and eyebrows raising in surprise. “Eshe! You’re here too? Come on, we’ve got to hurry! Jabir’s about to attack this place!" His gaze darts to where I stand against the wall, my chest heaving and my hands shaking. In a few steps, he crosses the distance between us, reaching toward me. He catches the back of my head. I'm so dazed, so frozen, that I barely process his intention to kiss me as his words rattle around my head.

"I'm so glad you're alright," he says gently. And lowers his mouth to mine.

Suddenly, he's ripped away from me. He hits the far wall by the staircase, grunting on impact. Black cloak swirls in the rush of air between us as the Neverseen King snarls.

"Don't you *dare* touch her. She's *mine*."

"Neverseen King!" Kolb whimpers, falling to his knees and bowing his head.

The Neverseen King stands over him, the powerful outline of his tall form a shocking contrast to the lanky boy at his feet. My senses return to me with a flash of panic.

"Don't kill him!" I burst, rushing forward and grabbing the sultan's arm. He flinches at my touch, his head whipping toward me. "Please."

He yanks away from me with a sweep of his cloak and storms down the stairs. "Come with me, Mourner. Go hide in your room, thief, if you don't want my House to eat you alive in a few minutes."

He didn't kill Kolb. Relief floods me, and I barely have time to consider before my feet are in motion, following the Neverseen King by instinct.

But then I stop. Turn around. Kolb is slowly pulling his bracing hands away from his face. His large eyes meet mine in worry, fear. Emotion thickens my throat.

"Your sister is dead," I choke. "Jabir lied to you. Get out of here before you're dead too."

His face pales. Then it twists into an ugly snarl—an expression I've never seen on his sweet face. "No, she is *not*. Do not lie to me! Jabir is getting her medicine. She will be *fine*!"

"She's been dead for days! You need to get out of here!"

"You're a *liar*! A filthy liar!"

I swallow bile and flee. I lay my hand on the banister, which took some serious damage from the dragon. Nevertheless, there's a faint warmth, a subtle hum in the splintered wood that slips past my skin into my awareness. *Stay safe,* I tell it in my mind.

Stay safe, it replies.

The outline of the Neverseen King grows harder to distinguish from the darkness of the palace. It's almost night. Only the faintest glow of sunlight is visible when we reach the bottom of the staircase and face the open doors into the courtyard.

The courtyard that is now gray and lifeless, the stone fountain cracked and silent.

Does he believe me? Does he believe I didn't betray him? Or is he about to test me further—or return me to Jabir as punishment?

I draw a knife in each hand as we step into the empty courtyard. My senses go on high alert, my eyes straining for anything out of the ordinary. Any sign of movement.

The first movement is that of a slight form slipping to the Neverseen King's side.

"Go hide," the sultan growls at Safya. "The House is about to turn. I don't want you getting hurt."

"I will stay by your side," she replies, her voice threaded with iron.

"Those at my side have a death wish."

I steal a sidelong glance at him. He moves swiftly, with determination, but there is something ice-cold about the way his rage burns. Wounds as deep as his cannot heal, can they?

The three of us move swiftly toward the gate, and I become aware of two sets of footsteps following us at a distance. Eshe and Kolb. Why can't Eshe do what she's told for once and stay out of danger?

And why won't Kolb *leave*? He has no ties to Jabir now.

Finally, we reach the arches leading into the courtyard before the gate to the palace. Me, at the Neverseen King's right, Safya at his left. Before us, barely visible in the light of the dying sun, is a mass of dark silhouettes beyond the gate. And one painfully familiar silhouette standing just inside the gate.

The Neverseen King stops.

A glint of teeth catches the rays of the rising moon as Jabir smiles. "There you are. Out from hiding, at last."

I tighten my grip on my knives, my heart nearly pounding out of my chest. The scars on my jaw and back throb in agonized memory.

The Neverseen King's voice is cold and controlled. "Go home."

"We are calling for your abdication, Neverseen King," Jabir calls. A cheer goes up in the men behind him, and he smiles. "We've suffered under your negligent hand for too long. We want our throne back. Step down peacefully and no one will be hurt."

The Neverseen King is quiet for so long that I steal a sideways glance at him. An army stands before him, and yet he doesn't flinch. He does not retreat one step. And if I wasn't so terrified of why he intended for me to come with him, I'd be honored to stand at his side.

As though sensing my gaze, he turns slightly, the flash of his bright eyes burning into me.

Then he faces Jabir once more. "Are you Jabir?"

"A pleasure to make your acquaintance, Neverseen King."

"Then tell me"—his rumbling tone turns into a snarl—"why did you enslave Nadira?"

A gasp lodges in my throat. My attention whips to him, to the furious set of his shoulders. *What?* Why in the Great Desert would he be—

"I can smell your fae blood," continues the Neverseen King. "Did you sense her magic?"

"What?" I blurt, unable to swallow back the word.

"Did you enslave her for her magic?" he demands, ignoring me. "You did, didn't you?"

Even from across the courtyard, the clenching of Jabir's jaw is still visible. I know that look. That look always meant I was about to be punished. My feet root to the spot, black spots dancing across my sight.

The Neverseen King believes me. He believes I didn't betray him.

"The girl has nothing to do with—" Jabir starts.

"This has *everything* to do with her," snaps the Neverseen King, drawing himself up taller. "Now answer me like a man, or retreat like a dog with your tail between your legs."

It happens too fast.

Too *fast.*

There are arrows.

There is blood.

I can't think.

Not as the Neverseen King falls to his knees, a gasp wringing from him. Not as three arrow shafts protrude from his chest. Blackness overcomes my vision as Safya falls. Silent as a dead bird.

Only I remain on my feet. Unharmed. Untouched. Immobile.

He's not dead. He presses a hand to his chest, but I recognize the agony of his quiet, shuddering breaths.

He could have dodged those with his unnatural speed. Could have vanished. Could have—

But he *couldn't*. Because Jabir has that artifact. And when I keep expecting the Neverseen King to *do* something, to rise up and show the tremendous power I know he has, he doesn't.

His shadowy head whips toward me, and his invisible gaze sears me from the inside out.

Panic.

And then there's Jabir, walking toward me. His hand out. A falsely sympathetic look on his features. "Come home, my girl. I've missed you."

It's not just Jabir walking toward me. His army filters through the gates, running to surround the three of us. The gasping Neverseen King, the dead Safya. And me. The Mourner.

There's a growing puddle of blood.

"You've done your job well," continues Jabir. "I commend you. Now come. If you—"

Blood reaches my boots.

Jabir keeps talking. I don't hear him.

But I come.

One step after the other, leaving bloody footprints in my wake. Echoes of the Neverseen King's earlier words wash over me as ice grips my heart in its tight fist.

For the first time, I have hope. Hope for a new beginning.

My knife hits true. The soldier next to Jabir crumples to the ground. My first nameless kill. Jabir's eyes go wide, and he shouts something. The soldiers surrounding us respond at once.

But I'm moving in another dimension. One made of silence and measured exhales.

One, two, three, four, five.

Soldiers run toward me. Weapons drawn.

I will never let go again, Nadira.

Six, seven, eight.

I dodge a falling scimitar. Shove a knife up into the soldier's ribs. Blood drenches my hand. Hot, sticky, thick. I wrench the knife free, fling my arm in an arc and release the knife so it hits another soldier about to attack the sultan.

Twelve, thirteen, fourteen, fifteen.

Dawn will come again.

My eyes lock on Jabir's. Even as he retreats, slipping into the mass of his soldiers for protection, I don't lose sight of him.

He shot the Neverseen King. *My* Neverseen King.

Twenty, twenty-one, twenty-two.

My body moves in the dance I've practiced since childhood. I steal another scimitar until I'm cutting through soldiers left and right, so fast I cannot keep count. The hairs on the back of my neck alert me to dodge, to duck, to sidestep.

Nadira, don't give in to the despair.

At some point while I fight, pushing forward through Jabir's army, stepping over dead bodies, a distant realization finds me.

There are too many.

Forty-five, forty-six, forty-seven.

By the time I get to Jabir and force him to call his men back, the Neverseen King could have been killed. Could have *died*. And Eshe—she could die too, if she hasn't hidden herself.

There's also my own strength to consider. I cannot fight forever. I cannot take down an entire army by myself.

At least, not with a blade . . .

With or without you, dawn will come again.

The moon rises overhead.

Fifty-eight. Fifty-nine. Sixty.

I stop. Throw my scimitars into the chests of oncoming soldiers.

Dawn isn't coming back. It's swallowed up by night.

I close my eyes. Reach deep, deep down inside myself where the cold burns in my gut. "You wanted a monster, Jabir?" I whisper, the pounding of approaching feet vibrating beneath my boots. "Fine. I'll be your monster."

Something inside me shivers.

A scream bursts from my throat. Ice surges through me, blasting from my hands like a tidal wave. It takes all my strength, all my fury, and swallows it whole. I fall to one knee, my hands outstretched, my lungs heaving as I gasp for air.

I lift my head.

Dead bodies surround me in almost every direction. Impaled by great spikes of ice. Only a few soldiers remain—the soldiers who'd been sheltered from the blast by their fellows.

So . . . *many*.

My shoulders sag, my jaw dropping.

What—what have I done?

I look down at my shaking hands. They're smeared with blood.

I just . . . I just . . .

Motion catches the tail of my eye. I whip around in time to see Jabir turn on his heel and run. Straight for the gate. His remaining men rush to follow as I wipe blood from my mouth and get to my feet.

I'm not about to let him get away.

But first—

I spin, almost stumbling on my wobbly legs.

There is the Neverseen King, dragging himself to his feet, despite the arrows still protruding from his chest. Eshe is at his side, and he shoves away her reaching hands.

"I'm fine," he growls. "I just need . . . a minute." Then he looks up, and our gazes meet. He says nothing, surrounded by all those dead bodies and ice. Despite his obvious lie—he is *not* fine, nowhere *near* fine—a broken part of me knits back together.

Then I'm sprinting. I don't care that the ice blast zapped my strength. The night wind blows my wild hair behind me as I leap, catch the iron spikes at the top of the gate, and vault straight over to the other side. I land lightly, rolling up to my feet and ripping out my knives.

Of the fleeing men, there's only one I care about.

I latch onto that familiar tall form, the one I always ran from. The one I never would have chased.

I chase him now.

He sprints across the sandy, paved street leading into Risya and dodges into a dirty alleyway. I follow, skidding on stone and leaping over fallen crates, dodging small lumps of sleeping orphans. Ahead, Jabir leaps, grabs hold of a low roof edge, and swings himself up. His turban comes loose and comes flying back toward me. I dodge it as I swing onto the roof behind him.

I've never seen him move so fast.

But I'm fast too.

Starlight bathes the rooftops of Risya, catches Jabir's free-flying hair and illuminates unusual streaks of blue as he leaps from one rooftop to the next. The jump is too far for me, but there is a fat clothesline stretched between the windows below us. If I wasn't so set on my quarry, I would have been afraid of falling. Now, I run across it as if I've been an acrobat my entire life.

Because I'm *not* letting Jabir get away.

I pump my legs harder, my focus never wavering. The further I chase him, the more certain I am about where he's going. I alter my course slightly, angling my pursuit to keep him in my line of vision while cornering him to the right.

He drops back into the streets. I jump toward an overhang, grab the wood, and swing myself to the ground after him. He goes straight, but I duck into an alleyway to the left, scattering feral cats as I go.

For once, I feel as though I could chase Jabir for days and never slow down.

He is *not* getting away.

Not this time.

Never again.

It is time for him to pay.

When I race down a familiar narrow street, a single rickety lantern glows at the dead end like always. And there is Jabir, his shoulders heaving as he fumbles with a key to unlock the door.

I raise my knife, breathe an apology to it, and throw it.

It hits exactly where I wanted it to: through Jabir's sleeve and into the door, pinning him to the frame.

He stops. Turns.

I throw my second-to-last knife. He lets out a cry as it pierces straight through his hand, pinning it to the door so he can't rip the first knife out of the wood. Blood wells around the wound and drips down his wrist, falling to the dusty ground.

His key clatters to the ground.

"Your magic won't work here." Jabir's grating, pain-filled voice rises above the huffing of our combined pants for air. "I have the artifact. It nullifies magic."

His beady eyes study me. We face each other as we never have before, lantern light washing us in a dance of flame and shadow.

Now *he* is the one who is trapped.

Nowhere to run.

Nowhere to hide.

Slowly, I approach him. His eyes travel up and down me, as though seeing me for the first time. Seeing me as the monster he created me to be, not the little girl who was always so terrified of him.

"Those assassinations weren't for *clients*, were they?" I say. "They weren't other people's enemies. They were *your* enemies. They were people who supported the Neverseen King. You had to get them out of the way so they didn't try to stop you when you led a rebellion. I had to kill Lord Kishon so he wouldn't set the city guard on you. Were those mostly city guards in your army tonight? Did you buy them out with the money from Eshe's thievery? Don't even bother denying it."

He only gives me a little, crooked-mouthed smile.

"My entire *life*," I spit, "was spent killing people *for you*."

"Well, not *all* of them," Jabir corrects with a shrug. It's an awkward shrug, given that his hands are pinned. "There were some clients. You created quite a reputation for yourself with those quiet, untraceable assassinations and those apology notes."

"*You* created that reputation for me."

"Did I?" he challenges.

I don't respond for a minute, hating that his implication is more right than I want to admit. He is only responsible for my being an assassin. I did the rest.

"Why do you hate the Neverseen King so much?" I demand, stalking another step closer.

Cold steel enters his gaze, and the temper I've dreaded for so many years flares to life as he spits a volley of words. "My grandmother was a courtier in the High King's palace. She was wealthy, respected, and had everything she ever could have wanted. But she was in the wrong place at the wrong time when the High King got angry, so he banished her to the human world. And the Neverseen King placed her here in Arbasa, where he could *keep an eye on her*. What he really meant was so he could humiliate her, strip her of every dignity. Fae can live for millennia, but not here. She *died*. My mother *died*—as a beggar. And when I tried to plead with the Neverseen King to let me take my mother back to Faerieland so she could recover, he refused to let me into his gate. My mother wasn't the one who was banished. And yet because *he* controls the Bridge, none of us can return home."

He flexes his fingers and winces, even as he glares at me with barely contained rage. Blood slides down the door in a steady stream. But I'm not done with him yet.

My voice carries on the night wind. "Why did you kill my parents?"

"Because I wanted you," he snarls.

"Why me?"

He inclines his head toward the palace, grimaces at the pain the movement causes. "It was as he said. I could smell your magic. I saw you in the bazaar and suddenly, I had a chance. I knew Lulythinar was swiftly approaching, and that the Neverseen King hadn't gotten a new human bride and would soon be desperate for one. With your magic, I knew you'd be a good candidate. So I waited until your family went back home and then . . . I took you."

I took you.

Three benign words to describe the worst moment of my entire life.

"I taught you the skills he would find valuable. I made you as attractive of an option as I could."

His voice rings in my ears. I can hardly believe it. My being kidnapped by the Neverseen King had been the *plan*. Had been the sole reason for my capture in the first place.

"And I thought that if he didn't take you for his bride, when your magic manifested you could still break into the palace. Perhaps even assassinate the Neverseen King himself. His overthrow has been long overdue." He chuckles, his incisors glinting. "So I bought a tracking spell from a spellcaster and put it on you—and another on your magic."

My glare darkens. "That's how you knew I was there in the first place. And that's how you knew the palace wards were down."

He smiles.

"If you know so much about magic—if you have this *fae* blood—then why did you try to take down the Neverseen King? If you knew anything about this palace, you'd know that this throne is bondage."

"Not if there was someone else who wanted the Neverseen King's position."

I blink slowly, turning this over in my mind. "You . . . made a deal. With a fae. This fae couldn't send you back to Faerieland, but he *could* give you Arbasa. And this fae would have the Bridge. *You* were the one Dabria left the palace to meet."

His smile widens, despite the *drip, drip, drip* of his blood. That smile grates down my spine like the edge of a dull blade.

"Why are you answering my questions?"

"Because I know you're going to kill me."

"Then why aren't you fighting?"

His smile almost . . . *softens*. "You're so different from the child you were that first day."

The child that screamed for her mama and baba. "Are you proud of your work?" I spit.

"Very much so. Now come. If you're going to kill me, girl, then kill me. It's not as if I relish the idea of ripping my hand through this knife to get away. Will you make it quick and painless, like all your other assassinations? Or will you prolong it, to make me pay for what I've done to you? Will you torture me, I wonder?"

There's a trick.

I tighten my grip on my knives and take one step closer.

His fingers flinch so subtly I almost miss it.

He's afraid of me.

The realization almost makes me sick. At the same time, a cold assurance fills my core. It's not a trick—it's *bluff.*

The red silk turban he's worn for years is gone, and for the first time, I realize that the very tips of his ears are pointed. The wind catches the edges of his tunic, his sash, his hair. It tugs gently for several long, silent minutes.

"This kingdom needs a ruler. A *true* ruler, Nadira," Jabir says. I hate listening to his voice. I hate how it always sounds like he needs to clear his throat, like his vocal cords are made of gravel. "Perhaps we lost tonight, but this kingdom isn't going to submit forever under neglect. The people will rise up, Nadira. Whose side will you be on? The side of your king, who tramples us underfoot, who has stolen this kingship as a façade for his own purposes? Or will you serve your people? Will you fight for those who die in the streets every day?"

"I will be no one's slave any longer."

"And yet, you so violently defended your kidnapper. Are you so enthralled by him that you will become *his* slave—his *wife*? To be disposed of like all the rest?"

He still believes he has power over me. Even now.

I take another step closer.

Jabir's breath comes faster. Still, his smile widens. "Kill me, little girl. You'll find you're not rid of me so easily. I will stay with you long after—"

He freezes. His eyes bulge.

That expression of pained shock sears like a brand across my brain.

Then his body falls, his blood leaking into the sand as his eyes stare unseeing at me. I cross the distance between us and use numb fingers to rip the blade from his neck, my second from his hand, and my third from the door. My vision goes black. It clears a second later, just enough for me to clean my blades on his sleeve before I sheathe them again.

I stand.

My feet won't move. My eyes won't look away.

He's gone. Just like that. I killed him. The man who made my life a living hell.

"I killed your men for hurting the Neverseen King," I whisper. "I killed you for murdering my parents."

Jabir's life for my parents'. The most unfair trade under the sun.

I stare at his body, slumped against the door that was my prison for the last ten years. When I draw in a deep breath, copper coats the inside of my nostrils. I let it out in a sigh.

I'm still not the monster I always wanted to be.

If I was truly a monster, I'd savor the sight of Jabir's blood. I'd laugh over his corpse. I'd desecrate his remains. His death wouldn't have been fast. I would have dragged it on for hours—for *days*.

But I didn't.

Because deep down, I'm nothing but a frightened little girl.

No amount of magic, power, violence, or skill can change who I am. Nothing can make me strong when it is my soul that's weak.

I curse bitterly under my breath and march back to the palace.

CHAPTER 35

ESHE AND THE Neverseen King are fighting when I return.

"I'm just going to break the shaft!" she snaps at him. "Stop being so ornery!"

"Get your hands off the arrow! I am perfectly capable of getting it out myself!"

I try to avoid looking at the bodies I'm stepping over. But one body, one with an unruly mass of curls atop his head, sends my gut churning. I'm not sure what I should think or feel, so I tear my eyes away and walk past him. The numbness of my limbs has spread to my mind and heart.

"You have three arrows in your chest. How are you not dead, you giant shadow freak? You are in *no* position to be tending your own wounds."

"Stop projecting your mortal limitations upon me! I am a fae with healing magic, you *thief*."

"Well, it clearly isn't working as fast as it needs to!"

"Because you won't give me any room to breathe!"

They stop when I approach. Eshe pulls back from where the Neverseen King leans against the courtyard's middle arch. His eyes shoot to me. I ignore their scrutiny, despite how it burns into my skin. Instead, I drop to my knees beside him.

"Nadira—" Eshe starts.

"Jabir's dead. The rest of the men are gone," I say. "We can't tend these wounds here. It's too dark. Eshe, I'll need you to find me—"

Something crackles to my right. I look up just as light flares in the Neverseen King's palm. I wince at the sudden brightness, but my eyes adjust quickly as he holds it up. Enough that I can see the dark blue tunic he wears. A tunic stained with blood.

Part of me dies a little to see those arrows still there, rising and falling with each of his labored breaths. How *did* he not die? Are his internal organs made of iron?

"Don't worry about me," he says, and despite the pain roughening his voice, there's something soft in his tones. "I can deal with this."

My vision goes suddenly blurry. "And I suppose you were going to *deal* with that army too? You're the Neverseen King! You can't die in a stupid way like this!" I choke on a sob, and it's a helpless anger and hurt that floods me. "What was I supposed to do if these arrows had killed you? Were you just going to *let* them keep shooting you? Why did you even let them shoot you in the first place? What is *wrong* with you? If you'd died, I would never have forgiven you!"

The Neverseen King stares at me.

Eshe stares at me.

I twist my face away, grinding my teeth together and trying to swallow my tears. I go to wipe my eyes with my hands, only to realize they're covered in blood. The tears fight harder against my resolve.

"I'll . . . go find some water," says Eshe, getting to her feet and hurrying away.

"Be careful of the House's defenses," calls the Neverseen King after her.

Just like that, we're alone. The Mourner and the Neverseen King.

I swallow my tears and lock them away. There is only the barest quaver in my voice when I speak. "I know you can do this on your own. But please, let me help you."

His lack of protest is answer enough.

He holds his glowing ball of light in one hand, illuminating his chest but doing nothing to penetrate the shadows around his face. Maybe another day, I'll have space to be hurt that he still hides his face from me. For now, I'm just thankful he's alive.

I lean forward and use one of my knives to slice open the collar of his tunic. Between my shaking hands and my care to avoid jostling the arrows, it takes me several minutes to cut the fabric away.

He says nothing, only breathes harder when I peel the fabric away to reveal his bloodied flesh. Another time I might have ogled the muscular definition of his torso or wondered over the strangely golden cast of his skin in the light. As it stands, all I see is blood. Blood, and those wretched arrows.

He could have died.

If they'd succeeded . . .

I shudder. Then I grab the first arrow shaft, the one that seems to be the shallowest. "I'm going to break this. It'll hurt."

He grabs my wrist, stopping me. "Nadira . . . I'm sorry."

My eyes flick up to his, to the darkness wreathing his face.

"I'm sorry I doubted you. I'm sorry I frightened you with these arrows. I wasn't expecting them to shoot when they did, And then I couldn't . . . my magic—it was *blocked*. And I'm sorry—"

"Shh, don't talk. Let me get this—"

"—for bringing you here at all."

I stop. "What?"

His breaths become ragged, the hand holding the light shuddering. He's in so much pain. Why won't he just sit still and let me deal with these arrows?

Then he can heal himself if he's able.

Nevertheless, his free hand lifts. Two rounded knuckles brush my cheek, skate under my jaw, until he catches my chin. My lungs freeze. My heart, however, gallops away like a horse freed of its rider.

"Nadira," he murmurs. "This world is so broken. I want nothing but for you to find someone you can be safe with. Truly safe. Someone who can be everything you need while you wrestle with the darkness of your past. Someone who doesn't have their own demons."

"Are you telling me to leave?"

His gaze holds mine.

"I'm fine," I growl. "I survive. That's what I do. That's what I'll keep doing."

"But life is so much more than surviving, Nadira. I want you to experience how good and beautiful it can be. You won't find that with me."

I take hold of the arrow shaft and, before he can stop me, break it. He grunts, his light flickering as he draws in a long, agonized inhale.

His hand doesn't leave my face, however. Slowly, while I use his tunic to staunch the fresh flow of blood, he tucks my hair behind my ear.

"I want you to be happy."

"I don't care about being happy."

"That's because you don't know what it's like."

I blink back more blurriness. "That's probably good. It makes me more pragmatic than you."

His shirt isn't enough. I unwind my sash and turn it to the inside layers where strangers' blood hasn't soaked through. I press it against the wound.

"Actually, there was a moment I was happy," I whisper.

His attention is hard on my face. Waiting.

I snap the shaft of the second arrow. His head tilts back, a low groan escaping his clenched teeth. I break off the third before he has a chance to expect it. The sound he makes is sharper, louder, and I grit my own teeth as I stuff fabric against the wounds.

"I was happy when we danced. The first time," I say briskly, then add: "After you ignored me all night."

"You cannot still be angry about that. I told you exactly why. And it isn't ignoring if my awareness and attention was on you all night, no matter who I danced with."

"Your definition of *ignoring* is wrong. You cannot purposefully ignore something you're unaware of."

"Nadira."

"What?" I demand, scowling at him.

He reaches up again, cupping my face with his hand. "It's alright to cry."

I last an entire second before I crumple into pieces, folding over myself and bursting into rivers of tears. It's miserable—he can't even hold me. Not until those arrowheads are extracted from him. So I lean my head on his stomach as I weep, as my shoulders shudder.

He lays his hand on the back of my head and strokes my hair.

I killed so many people. Dozens—in one fell swoop. Jabir is dead, but there's no relief. No relief from the constant hollowness inside me. Killing him could never bring back my parents. It fixes *nothing*. Nothing, except buying my freedom.

And Kolb. *Kolb.* He was *stupid*, so stupid. Even so, he was one of the only friends I've ever had. I didn't mean to kill him. To think, I could have killed Eshe too.

Safya is dead. Gaya, Dabria, Itr, Hulla, Fathuna, Mahja.

Death follows me everywhere I go. No matter where I run, it hounds my steps.

What do I do?

There's no escape.

I'm not sure how long we stay like that. Eventually, my tears dry up. Still, I don't move. I stay leaning against him, letting him stroke my hair. And I believe my favorite delusion, that somehow I belong with him. That our stained souls deserve the torment of each other's nearness.

"You're free to go," he says at long last. "Jabir is gone. He won't touch you again. You're a free woman. I want you to leave and find happiness."

I push myself upright. When I speak, my voice is soft but hard. "Do you want to marry me, Sultani?"

He seems to stop breathing for a moment. Then growls, "I've told you a thousand times. What I want doesn't matter. It never has, and it never will."

"Do you want to marry me, Sultani?"

"Nadira, for all that's—"

"*Do* you want to marry me, Sultani? Stop evading me and answer the question."

He glares at me, a look no less potent for being unseen. He curses under his breath, sharp and low. Then he extinguishes the light in his hand, shoves up, and catches me by the back of the head.

And pulls me into a kiss.

His lips capture mine with force, with a wretched determination that shatters me to my core. I fall into his kiss, a whimper dying in my throat as tears I didn't think I had left find their way down my cheek and over his knuckles.

Just when I think he's about to pull away, his hand fists in my hair and he lets out a growl, kissing me harder. Fiercer.

Then he lets go.

I sit there, stunned. My lips buzz. My whole *being* buzzes, like lightning cutting across the desert sky.

"There's your answer," he says darkly, raking a hand through his hair. "Since you were so determined to have it. Now please, if you would just *leave*, it'll be easier for me to think through my options here. Take your freedom, Mourner, and do with it whatever you will. Find a good man—if you want—and forget we ever met."

"I'm not leaving."

"Then you are a fool."

"Well, so are you!" I snap back, glaring at him. "You could have just answered *yes* to my question instead of kissing me!"

"Are you angry I kissed you?"

"I'm angry that you won't stop telling me to leave long enough for me to tell you that I've decided to marry you. Stars and sands!"

"Wh-what?"

"I agree to marry you."

He goes deathly still. "You—no, you will regret it. There's nothing here for you. You need to leave. You and Eshe both. See what happened to the rest? Safya is dead. Gaya is dead. If you stay, *you will die*."

And somehow, this is the last piece of assurance that I needed. Before, I was afraid he would use me up, spend me like coppers in the market. I was a tool to him. All this time, I've been desperate to know that he would fight for me. For my life. I wanted assurance that I was worth more to him.

Now I have it.

Because he would rather give me up if it meant I would have a greater chance at living.

I close my eyes. Perhaps I am a fool. But I've made my decision. Live or die, I want to do it by his side.

My eyes flash open just as I hear Eshe's pattering footsteps coming toward us, punctuated by the familiar splash of water in a bowl. Once we sterilize my knife and I've washed the blood off my hands, I'll cut these arrowheads out of him, and then he can use his magic.

My gaze latches onto his, and there is hope, desperation, and utter dread swimming in the shadows facing me. "I will marry you, Neverseen King. That is my final decision."

He's silent for a very, very long time.

Finally, at last: "Then tomorrow at dusk, I will take you as my bride, Nadira al-Risya."

EPILOGUE

The Neverseen King

THIS IS THE longest it has ever taken me to walk through the city.

Normally, I slip into the dream realm to loosen the bonds of physicality and time to cross large distances quickly. But despite my House's abundant magic, healing always drains me dry. It was especially difficult because of how much energy I expended trying to keep my body *from* healing around the arrows before Nadira removed them.

So I walk like a human, clinging to shadows and using what little glamour ability I have left to disguise my heavy steps and wreathe my form in darkness.

Nadira and Eshe are safely back at the palace in Nadira's room. I hope they are resting, just like I made them believe I would. But as much as I long to rest, I cannot.

That has been the summary of my life these past ninety-nine years.

Not that I can sleep well anyway.

At last, I make it to the narrow street where Jabir and Nadira lived. Even if I didn't know where it was, the stench alone is enough to tell me *exactly* where I'm going.

The lone lantern hangs by a blood-streaked door. It burns dangerously low, illuminating the corpse collapsed on the ground.

I remember him now. His real name—his *fae* name, given to him despite the human blood mingling with the fae in his veins—was Shalfol.

Red light pulses from his robes in an ugly, angry aura. Each step toward the body makes me grimace, and eventually I'm forced to let every last shred of glamour fall away. I step into the light, feel the firelight across my face. Then I brace myself against the door, fighting my unsteady legs, as I lean down and pluck the source of that red glow out of Shalfol's belt.

A golden egg, encrusted with gemstones and pounding with a wicked spell, sits in my palm. The stench is almost unbearable at this proximity. I know this stench, this magic.

The Wolf made this.

I let it fall to the ground. Summoning my last reserves of strength, I crush it beneath my heel. The gold, paper thin and made brittle from the spell, cracks open. A ghost of a scream tears free from the remnants as red bursts forth in a cloud. Then the spell dissolves, leaving behind nothing but broken gold and jewels.

My magic comes back to me in a wave, like the comforting embrace of a lover. I reassert my glamours with ease.

Now that the spell stench is gone, Shalfol's blood is the strongest smell in the narrow street. Beyond it, however, if I lean closer to the door . . .

I can smell the distinct tinge of Nadira's blood coming from inside the abode. I smelled it the night I came for her. Remnants of it coated the walls, the floors, the thin blanket and lumpy cot in her room.

She bled so much here.

The fury that climbs like a clawed animal up my spine nearly overwhelms me. I don't know the entirety of her story, but I know enough.

Enough to feel the pressing weight of guilt that she will marry me tomorrow.

I never should have brought her here. Never should have involved her in this. Never should have let myself . . . let myself . . .

And left her in Shalfol's hands? a quiet part of me asks.

I wish I hadn't given into my foolish whims. I never should have met her. Those apology notes of hers—I knew my very soul called to hers from that first moment. I knew she was broken like I was. And I stupidly gave into the desire to experience, for the first time in almost a hundred years, what it is like to not be alone.

It was my own wretched desire to feel seen and understood that made me bring her here.

I never should have been so selfish.

"I can't save everyone," I growl under my breath.

I can't save everyone.

I let go of a few shadow glamours to draw lines around the building. I mutter the spell under my breath, and a blue glow appears beneath my finger as I drag it around the walls, the shared roof, until I've outlined exactly the bounds where Nadira's blood lies.

Then I take the dying lantern and throw it against the wooden door.

Fire catches, eager and starving. I back away, staying in the darkness as light burns brighter, as flames lick up Shalfol's clothes. The fire doesn't cross the lines I drew, but soon the entire building is engulfed.

My business here is done.

I clench my fists and turn my back on Nadira's former prison. I will not take out my rage on the corpse, no matter how much I long to. He was her kill. His body was hers to desecrate.

The return journey to the House takes even longer than the first. I walk through the broken spells on my gate. And there before me, in the light of the moon, are dozens of dead bodies littering the courtyard.

She killed for me.

Nadira, the woman who hates killing so much she'd do almost anything to avoid it. Nadira, who broke Raha's arm instead of her neck. Pure wrath had burned in her gaze. Those tortured eyes of hers that always sent my thoughts scattering—it was like every restraint ripped away.

There had to be over a hundred dead bodies. And she killed them all.

She *slaughtered* them.

For *me.* After I'd accused her of being a traitor and a liar.

I'm still not sure if I'm shocked, horrified, or in awe. Am I touched or terrified?

I pick my way through skewered bodies, willing the last dregs of my strength not to give out just yet.

No, I'm not terrified. Not of her, not of the sheer power of her magic, not of her capacity for brutality. I knew there was magic buried deep inside her the moment I first laid eyes on her. Its strength, its brand of power, nor its manner of awakening were things I predicted, however. I'd assumed she'd come down with blood sickness if her magic ever manifested. But no—she's one of the few. One of the lucky ones, if I dare suggest it.

I'm not scared of her.

But I hate that I couldn't dodge those arrows. I hate that anything drove her to that massive slaughter. Because now it haunts her. Her own hatred of herself was in every step she took when she'd returned to the House.

I make it back to the courtyard Crenfyre has utterly ravaged.

And there, sitting in the window, bathed in starlight, is Nadira.

She doesn't see me. She just sits there, one long leg hanging out of the window as she stares up at the sky. I let my eyes travel over her beautiful face, memorizing the cut of her cheekbones, the long lashes, the elegantly arched brows, the thick dark hair blowing in her face, the set of her lovely mouth. A mouth I never should have allowed myself to kiss, not in a thousand years.

"Nadira," I breathe, and her name feels like a goodbye.

Tomorrow, she will become my wife.

Dread as I have known few times in my life sinks into my gut. There is nothing I can do to save her.

She will die.

And it will be my fault.

THANK YOU FOR READING THIS BOOK! IF YOU ENJOYED IT, PLEASE CONSIDER LEAVING A REVIEW ON AMAZON.

COMING SOON:

the NEVERSEEN KING

Only one fate awaits the bride of the Neverseen King.
But I will not die.

MORE FROM ANASTASIS BLYTHE

THE ZHENINGHAI CHRONICLES

Maiden of Candlelight and Lotuses
Guardian of Talons and Snares
Warrior of Blade and Dusk
Princess of Shadows and Starlight
Captive of Twilight and Treachery
Daughter of Darkness and Dreams

THE KING AND THE ASSASSIN

The Assassin Bride
The Neverseen King (Coming Soon)

ABOUT THE AUTHOR

Anastasis Blythe makes her home in central Texas with her husband. When she's not writing, she gardens, accompanies local bands and choirs on piano, rescues feral cats, and tries to keep up with the laundry. She loves exploring the world through reading, walks in nature, and thoughtful conversations.

To stay connected with her, be sure to sign up for her newsletter at AnastasisBlythe.com/Nadira.

Connect with Anastasis online at:

Website - AnastasisBlythe.com

Instagram - @AnastasisBlythe

Facebook - Anastasis Blythe

Goodreads - Anastasis Blythe

www.ingramcontent.com/pod-product-compliance
Lightning Source LLC
Chambersburg PA
CBHW020341310726
48979CB00015B/2450/J

* 9 7 8 1 9 6 0 6 0 6 0 6 8 *